# LEGACY OF ATLANTIS

# LEGACY OF ATLANTIS

# JOHN TOPPING

The Story Plant
1270 Caroline Street
Suite D120-381
Atlanta, GA 30307

Copyright © 2023 by John Topping

Story Plant Hardcover ISBN-13: 978-1-61188-348-0
Story Plant Special Hardcover Edition ISBN-13: 978-1-61188-389-3
Story Plant E-book ISBN: 978-1-945839-71-9

Visit our website at www.TheStoryPlant.com

First Story Plant Printing: March 2024

Printed in the United States of America
0 9 8 7 6 5 4 3 2 1

Also by John Topping:

Runaway

# CHAPTER 1
## THE MOON IS A HARSH MISTRESS

I toed the rubber in the bottom of the seventh, about to throw what I hoped and prayed would be the last pitch of a no hitter. My heart pounded. My fingers tingled as they gripped the seams of the baseball. I looked over at my dad. He gave me an almost imperceptible nod and his "you've got this" look. I took a deep breath and started my windup.

A buzzing noise sounded.

The mound faded away as I woke up and hit the snooze button on my alarm. I still had a few minutes before I had to get up. The lights brightened slowly in my room. My uncle's doing. He doesn't like me oversleeping. I glanced at the picture of me and my dad. It's a few years old, taken after I pitched my first shutout in the Little League AAA playoffs. I suppressed a sniffle and glanced at my mitt and ball sitting on the bedside table next to the picture. I slipped my legs off the side of the bed, picked up the ball and gently lobbed it against the far wall. I had plenty of time to slip on the glove as the ball floated toward the wall, hit and slowly drifted back. Hard to play catch on the Moon, with one-sixth gravity and all.

You'd think that living in Clarksville would be fun. That's what I thought when I'd moved here. The problem was, being the new kid's never easy, even when you're living on the Moon. I moved up here a few months ago to live with my uncle. I was glad to move, to get out of my old house. Now that I'm here, I wish I could go home. I was always a better than average student, but up here everyone's smart. Made me feel like an idiot.

The alarm went off again. I slipped on my iLet, got up, brushed my teeth and went to our living room/dining room. As usual, I found breakfast waiting with a note from my uncle.

"Special treat today, Charlie, in celebration of your field trip. Have fun, but remember, this is the Moon: one wrong move and . . ." He'd drawn a poor picture of a skull and crossbones. Sometimes my uncle's a bit weird.

The oven popped open and the smell of bacon and eggs wafted through the air. My mouth watered. This must have cost my uncle a bunch of food coupons because the farm dome had just recently added hogs. While eggs were rare, pigs were even rarer. I began to wolf down the eggs and bacon when my uncle's cat, Nim, jumped up on the table. How my uncle convinced anyone to let him bring a cat to the Moon was beyond me, but he did. Nim rubbed up against me, purring.

"Here you go." I slid my plate over and rubbed between her ears.

Nim seemed satisfied as she licked at the yolk. She licked her paw and gave me an "is that it?" look. When I picked up the plate, she leapt off the table and floated through the air into my uncle's bedroom. It still amazed me the way Nim had adapted to the Moon's gravity. Better than me.

Somebody began to bang on the door, startling the heck out of me.

"Just a minute." I jumped up and opened the door. Jamie stood there grinning like the Cheshire Cat. "Let's go. Don't want to be late for the field trip."

I followed him to the Tube station, struggling to keep pace with Jamie's loping stride. For some reason they called the maglev subway a Tube station here. Maybe some British influence in the design of Clarksville. A couple of the kids that lived on the outskirts of town were already on the train as Jamie and I got on. School was located near the middle of town, in the center of the small crater where they'd started building Clarksville. We had about a ten minute commute on the train.

"So, what d'you think? Whose group will we be in?" Jamie glanced my way.

"Don't know. Hope we're not with Richard." Richard was one of the cool kids and had given Jamie his nickname—the bear. I was curious as to why until I saw Jamie in the showers after gym. He had the thickest matt of brown hair across his back that I'd ever seen. It rivaled the hair on the back of one of my baseball coaches who we'd also called the bear.

Jamie rolled his eyes up. "Acts like he owns the place. But don't let him get to you. That's what he wants."

I nodded. "After weeks of sims, I'm ready to get outside."

"It's not that different from the Gym Dome or the Hangar." Jamie'd been outside before. In fact, he was scheduled to get his moonwalk permit after this field trip.

"Think they'll throw a test at us?" The first time I'd been in a vacuum in a suit was in the main hangar. Half the class ended up with one malfunction or another. I got lucky, but Jamie's suit had a doozy. His legs swelled up when the pressure seal reacted as if he'd developed a leak in both legs. He collapsed to the ground, grunting in pain. I went to help, but Trolga made him crawl to the airlock on his own.

Jamie shook his head. "Doubt it. This is for real. But you never know with Trolga."

I scowled at the thought. "Hope we don't have her leading our team." Olga Larsen was our history teacher. She was Swedish. Sounds good, right? Blond, *Sports Illustrated* swimsuit edition? No way. There was a reason she was called Trolga—short, fat, jet black hair and skin that looked as tough as leather. She must've looked like a crow amongst a flock of snow geese in school in Sweden. Her favorite hobby seemed to be lecturing us.

Jamie grunted in response.

"So, how goes your memorization of pi?" Jamie was convinced that memorizing pi to five hundred decimal places would help him get a scholarship to MIT or Cal Tech.

He shook his head. "Saw on line that a fifteen-year-old just got a scholarship to Cal Tech after memorizing pi to 750 significant figures. Don't think it'll work twice."

"Go figure." I smiled, but Jamie just scowled at my lame joke.

I tapped my fist against his arm. "No biggie. You're the brainiest kid here, and that's saying a lot. You'll get in wherever you want." Jamie's parents worked for Dahak mining, and, while everyone up here made good money, it was not enough to pay for a top-notch college without a scholarship. He did great in all of the sciences and math, but had trouble in Trolga's history class. While he memorized all the facts, he couldn't put them together in an essay—and Trolga loved essays.

"Maybe your ridiculous knowledge of baseball stats will get you in. You could easily be on ESPN." I'd first met Jamie shortly after arriving when he'd found out that I was a baseball player. He quizzed me on my favorite teams, players and stats. We'd get together to watch as many MLB games a week as we could. He'd know the stats of every player on every team as they came up to bat. If he didn't become a scientist he knew enough to become an MLB manager.

Jamie's eyes widened. "You really think . . ." But then he shook his head. "Hey, have you asked Rhea out yet?"

I looked down at the floor of the train, at the wrapper of gum lying next to the seat, and kicked it.

Jamie chuckled. "I didn't think so."

When we arrived at the school's station, we went straight to the assembly hall. There weren't many seats left, but, then again, calling it an assembly hall was a joke. My ninth-grade homeroom class back in Seattle had more seats than this auditorium. The only seats available were next to Richard's clique. Richard smiled at us.

"Come on, Oso, have a seat." He tilted his head toward the end of the row.

Richard stuck his leg out as Jamie tried to squeeze past him. If Jamie hadn't expected the move, he might have tripped and fallen onto Richard's girlfriend, Imee. That would have caused a real row.

Jamie tentatively stepped over Richard's legs, half expecting Richard to raise his knee up and goose him. He probably would have if half the faculty wasn't up on the stage in front of him and if Imee hadn't hit him in the arm.

"You too, Rook." I guess Richard hadn't come up with anything worse than rookie for me—yet. I was the newest kid in school and a baseball player, so it made sense.

Richard pulled his legs back and smiled. I squeezed past Richard, then Imee. Jamie'd left a space between himself and Rhea, forcing me to sit next to her.

Rhea smiled at me as I attempted to slide past her. I glanced down at her, but tripped over one of her feet, falling toward her. I whirled my arms around, trying to regain my balance. I must have looked like an idiot, as I heard a few chuckles. Rhea reached up and stabilized me, enabling me to grab the chair in front of her.

"Sorry." My face flushed. I looked into Rhea's ruby-red eyes. Little flecks of gold seemed to glitter in them.

Rhea smiled. "No problem. Is that what your windup looks like?"

I gave a half-hearted laugh and took the seat next to her. I glanced over at Jamie. He gave me a thumbs up as if I'd orchestrated the whole thing. I turned to say something to Rhea, but she'd leaned toward Imee and whispered something in her ear. Imee giggled and then leaned over and whispered into Richard's ear. He glanced over at me and laughed. My face flushed.

Fortunately, Principal Blaubecker walked up to the podium. "Ladies and gentlemen . . ." He cleared his throat as if to signal that he didn't really think we were ladies and gentlemen. "You will be divided up into three groups of nine students and one of ten."

I swear he looked at me when he said that. There had been a perfect even number of thirty-six sophomores and juniors in the school until my arrival. I had thrown a monkey wrench in the entire buddy or, as my uncle would say—he's British—bloody system. My uncle did point out to our pin-headed administrator, Dr. Valerie Jackson, that I increased the numbers in the two classes to a prime number, thirty-seven. Dr. Jackson didn't find that at all amusing. Did I say that my uncle's the math and science teacher at the high school and the college? In fact, he was sitting in one of the chairs behind Principal Blaubecker. I hoped he wasn't going to lead my team. If he did, he'd never let me out of his sight.

"I know all of you are looking forward to the trip outside Clarksville. It's a rite of passage for all of our students here. After this, most of you will be certified to moonwalk on your own."

I looked around. Kids were shifting in their seats. Principal Blaubecker's "most of you" did not include me. This would be my first trip outside.

"Dr. Merl Ambrose will outline the science project for the trip and then read off the list of mentors and their teams. Doctor?"

My uncle slid his feet along, taking little pee pee steps as if he was worried that he'd float away if he walked normally. As he got up to the rostrum, I hunched down in my seat. He wore the typical jumpsuit that most residents of Clarksville wore, but, somehow, his always looked crumpled. He pushed his round, wire-rimmed spectacles up on his nose—and no, don't ask me why he wears glasses this day and age or why he calls them spectacles—and cleared his throat.

"This year we have two science projects for each team. In addition to the traditional geological sampling for helium-3, we will be looking for magnetic anomalies. As usual, the team that comes up with the highest concentration of helium-3 will be exempt from my next test and will be allowed to spend the class period in the Gym Dome. In addition, I have arranged with Dr. Larsen that the team that maps out the most magnetic anomalies will be exempt from her next history test as well. Good luck!"

My uncle looked my way as I tried to shrink further down in my seat. One time he actually waved at me. I didn't hear the end of that for weeks. Principal Blaubecker came to the rescue.

He edged up to my uncle and cleared his throat. "The list, Professor."

Startled, my uncle turned back to the podium. "Ah, yes, the teams."

My uncle pulled a wrinkled list out of his wrinkled jumper and laid it out on the podium. He straightened his glasses again and squinted at the list.

"This year we will have four teams, three groups of nine and one of ten. With Dr. . . . ."

I tuned my uncle out and started to think about the quest. My uncle had always been fascinated by the small magnetic anomalies that surrounded the city. He told me about them all the time. Every time someone discovered a new one, he couldn't wait to get to the site. When the anomaly turned out to be ferrous rocks, he'd go into a funk. It was as if he expected to find the remains of some alien technology out there. There'd been some excitement, years ago, when I'd still lived in Seattle with my parents. They'd found a magnetic anomaly close to one of the old lunar bases buried a couple of feet underground. Turned out to be an old Russian lunar probe from the sixties that had never been documented. The Soviets had hidden the failure and it took some digging to track down the launch. After that, the talk shifted from aliens to uncovering the bodies of dead cosmonauts on the Moon.

Jamie elbowed me and rolled his eyes. I mouthed, "Trolga?" He nodded. He keyed a message into his tablet. I opened mine and read: "Rhea's in our group."

"Richard too?" I glanced down the row. Richard's glare answered the question.

I looked up at the podium. Fortunately, my uncle was engaged in conversation with one of the other teachers. The screen behind the stage indicated that Dr. Larsen's group was to meet in ready room four. Trolga had already headed for the door.

"Move it, Charlie. I'd like to be the first team out." Richard reached past Rhea and shoved me as I stood up. Due to the low gravity, I lost my balance again and stumbled into the aisle. Rhea glared at Richard.

She looked down at me and smiled. "You ok?"

I couldn't help but smile until I saw the look on Richard's face. I nodded, grabbed Jamie's hand and stood quickly, too quickly. I bumped into Imee, but Rhea grabbed me before I stumbled. She chuckled as my face reddened.

"Takes some getting used to. Took me six months."

I'd been there almost four months.

Now Richard looked ready to yank my head off. I smiled meekly at Rhea. "Thanks. My uncle's cat's doing much better than me." We funneled toward the ready room.

"He's got a cat? You've got to be kidding. I didn't know anyone had pets up here." Imee looked back at us.

I nodded dumbly.

Rhea chimed in, "I used to have a cat before we moved up here."

Jamie elbowed me.

"Why don't you come by some time and see her. I'm sure she'd love the attention." I smiled lamely.

Rhea smiled back. "Ok, it's a date."

Before I could react, Richard banged into my shoulder as he hustled past me.

# CHAPTER 2
## FIELD TRIP

I had planned to be one of the first to get to the ready room since it still took me longer to put a suit on but walking with Rhea made me forget. Everyone was in their suit standing by the hatch to the hangar where the rovers were parked. I worked the final glove on, leaned over to pick up my helmet and stood. My shoulder bounced off what felt like a wall.

Although I was much taller than her, Trolga seemed to loom over me.

"Since you're last, Mr. Thomas, you will be my buddy."

Fortunately, I didn't have my helmet on. Otherwise I'd have had to listen to the laughter of the others. I was sure that Richard was gleeful. He looped his arm over Rhea's shoulder, but she pushed it off as Imee gave him a glare. Richard and Rhea had broken up just after I arrived at Clarksville.

"Here, hand me your helmet." Trolga extended her meaty hand. Despite being a head shorter than me, her hands were huge.

I waited for her to put the helmet over my head, but she just stood there.

"Well?" She held one hand on her hip.

I glanced around. The girls were pulling their hair back into ponytails. The only other guys that had hair as long as mine had their hair pulled back in man buns. My jaw dropped open.

"While we're still young, Rook." Richard slapped the arm of one of his friends as Trolga gave me the evil eye.

I hesitated. I'd kept my hair long for a reason. I'd been born with a congenital defect—pointed ears. My parents had them bobbed by a plastic surgeon, but they kept growing back. At first they thought it was a tumor, but the doctors said that it was merely some strange genetic quirk. I was teased so badly in grammar school that my parents finally moved. That summer, I grew my hair out enough to cover my ears. I'd kept my hair long ever since.

"Mr. Thomas . . ." Trolga glared at me. "I'd like to get on with the field trip."

"I, I, I . . ."

"What!"

"Need a ponytail holder?" Rhea walked toward me with one in her hand.

I didn't know what to do, but Richard did. He'd walked up behind me, yanked my hair back with one hand and reached for the ponytail holder with the other.

Rhea gasped as everyone went silent. Even Trolga remained speechless. My ears aren't that pointed—not like Spock or anything—but they do come to a small point.

Not knowing what to do, I did the only thing I could. I grabbed the ponytail holder, pulled my hair back and fixed the ponytail. "What?" I raised my hands.

Richard came up and put his arm around my shoulder. "Well, Rook, guess you've earned yourself a new moniker—Dobby."

Everyone in the room other than Jamie and Rhea started to laugh until Trolga's voice boomed out. "ENOUGH! Mr. Thomas's 'condition' has cost us enough time. Now, helmets on and let's get to our rover." She slid the fishbowl-like helmet over my head and, with a quick twist, latched it into place with a force that could have broken my neck if she'd been holding my head.

"Follow me." Trolga strutted toward the airlock. She looked down at the computer screen built into the fabric of the left arm of her suit. Nine green lights flashed next to a list of names. She pressed the code on the sleeve of her suit and the door opened. Trolga herded us into the airlock and then followed us in. When she pushed a button against the wall, I felt the vibration of the pump in my feet. The skin of my suit began to pull away from me as the pressure dropped. When the pump finished, Trolga hit another button, opening the outer door.

We walked into the hangar. One of the rovers was already heading out the door, its six large wheels kicking up some lunar dust. I followed our group to the closest rover. It was much larger than the dozen single-seat lunar cycles resting against the wall or the half dozen four-person rovers parked in the rear of the hangar. I walked around it like my father used to do when he'd taken us for a flight in his single-engine plane. The wheels came up to my chest. The clear glass bubble at the front contained two seats. As I walked by, Richard sat down in one and began to strap himself in. He grabbed a handle, and the robotic arm shot out just to my right. I almost stumbled as I jumped back. I could see him laughing through his helmet. I glanced at the robotic arm. The metal claws were aligned so it looked like Richard was robotically shooting the bird at me.

I finished my walk around the rover as the last of my team climbed on board. Trolga waited for me to climb aboard before she got in and sealed the door. She flipped on her radio and cleared her throat.

"While the rover's being pressurized, everyone WILL leave their helmets on. Take your seats and strap in."

I sat down on the bench seat next to Jamie. The seats were large to accommodate the spacesuits. I strapped in. Once Trolga had made sure we were all strapped in, she took off.

"The trip will be about thirty minutes. I've picked a location close to the hills to the southeast of Clarksville that holds good prospects for high concentrations of helium-3. My team has won four out of the past five years. We will win again this year. If you want to talk, switch to channel three so I don't have to listen to your puerile blather." She cut off the mic and hit the accelerator.

I looked around. Nobody seemed to be looking at me. I replayed in my mind Rhea's gasp. I guess that was the end of her coming over to see Nim. Dobby . . . I liked Rook a lot better. I'd read *Harry Potter* in middle school just like practically everyone else and I liked the character of Dobby, but being called Dobby was something totally different. Unlike at home, I couldn't change schools here.

A beep interrupted my brooding.

"Call from Jamie," a computer-generated woman's voice announced.

"Accept."

Jamie's face appeared in the heads-up display instead of the camera. "How come you never showed me . . . you know, your ears?"

Jamie was my best friend on the Moon, but I hadn't told him. Even Uncle Merl didn't know. I shook my head, but that didn't mean anything in my helmet. "I don't know. Didn't know you that well at first and then, well, I didn't think about it. Been hiding my ears for most of my life."

"You're talking to the bear, man. I've been the butt of hirsute jokes since I hit puberty and the hair on my back started growing. My mom tried waxing it, but that hurt like shit and it just grew back."

"Sorry, should've told you. But hair's normal, pointed ears aren't."

"Look, this is a small community. Everyone's smart, Richard notwithstanding, and everyone's a bit nerdy. Once they get used to it, they'll get over it—Dobby."

I gave a weak chuckle as I remembered the laughing and Rhea's expression. "I hope so."

"Well, I know so. Rhea won't care. When she was dating Richard, he never called me bear or oso."

Jamie must've been reading my mind. I hoped he was right.

After a brief pause, Jamie added, "Listen, everyone else is playing *Invasion Force V*. Want to join in?"

I'd played the game a few times at home on Earth, but never got into it. When not playing baseball and football, I'd spent the time hiking. My parents loved it, and they used to drag me along. Once in a while I'd take a friend along, but my parents would always embarrass me by telling the story of the time they'd seen a sasquatch off in the distance. They'd whip out the fuzzy photo as proof and I wouldn't hear the end of it for weeks. Pretty soon, I stopped inviting friends. Lesson learned.

Never got into video games, but up here there wasn't much else to do. The Dome was a must. The big, open holographic blue sky and clouds made me feel like I was outside in a park, but there was no baseball diamond or even a place to throw a ball. You couldn't even run on the grass. While the Gym Dome was fun, particularly the sky-ball games, I was so new that I got crushed every time I tried it. Besides, most of the kids were either total bookworms (most of their parents were scientists, after all) or really into video games.

"Charlie, you in or not?"

"Sorry, I was thinking. Don't really feel like it right now."

Jamie's eyes were sliding to the left. "Damn, she got one of my androids. Okay. Maybe on the way back. May need your help."

"Deal." Jamie's face faded away giving me a clear look through the hyperplast faceplate of my helmet. From the gold sheen on all the helmets, it looked like everyone was doing something other than just sitting around. I couldn't lean forward due to the shoulder straps, so I couldn't see through the hyperplast bubble at the front of the rover.

"Rear camera display."

The heads-up display shifted to the rear camera. I could see the Dome, the Spire and a few of the other larger buildings peeking up over the lip of the crater behind us. The rover kicked up a bit of dust, but not enough to mess up the view of the camera mounted on the rear of the rover. Trolga was making good time because the Dome and the Spire were smaller than I would have thought.

"Location of other rovers?"

A map replaced the camera's view and green dots appeared on the map. It looked like the view from a satellite above Clarksville and probably was.

"My location in red, please."

A red dot appeared to the southeast of Clarksville. The dots were all spreading out, away from the city.

"What's the distance from Clarksville?"

"Twenty-four point eight six kilometers."

"In miles please and switch the default to miles."

"Acknowledged. 15.45 miles."

"Distance to destination?"

"Seven point two three miles."

"Front camera display."

The scene shifted from the map to the front camera. Still relatively flat terrain, but I could see a few boulders in our path. Trolga began a series of turns around them. When we got past a large one, the hills began to slope in front of us. Helium-3 was more abundant in shadowy areas, but most shaded areas were also less accessible. Trolga must be heading for one of those. As if on cue, my display cut off and Trolga's siren-sweet voice interrupted my thoughts.

"Ladies and gentlemen, please stop your incessant jejune prattling and pay attention. For some of you"—she glared at me—"this will be your first time on the lunar surface. While these suits are practically indestructible, you will be walking in an extremely inhospitable environment. Temperatures will vary from 100 C to -181 C at night. Your suits will protect you, but they are day suits. They are not rated for overnight exposure. In order to find rich concentrations of helium-3, we will be in an area with lots of shadows. Temperatures will be much cooler there. Keep watch on your temperature gauges. Your suit will warn you well before you can get into any trouble. Keep with your buddy. While we've never had a suit failure, there's always a first time."

With that cheery note, she shut off her radio.

I was never very good at metric, but everyone up here used it. Fortunately, computer conversions were simple. Even I knew that 100 C was the same as 212 F, but the surface reaching the boiling point of water? That was hot!

"What is -181 centigrade in Fahrenheit?"

"It's -293.8 Fahrenheit."

I let out a whistle. I knew these suits were good, but that was like going from a pot of boiling water into a bath of liquid nitrogen. I hadn't really thought about this as anything more than a typical school field trip, but now Trolga had given me second thoughts. I looked around. No one else seemed too concerned. But, then again, my last field trip had been to the Seattle Zoo. The rover pulled to a stop. Trolga had stopped just outside the shadow of a large boulder.

"You ready?" I recognized Jamie's voice.

"Sure. Been looking forward to this. Just like in the Gym Dome, right?"

"Right." Jamie patted me on the back.

A suited figure ambled down the center row of the rover toward the door. I didn't need to see the name on the suit. Richard was the only kid I knew that owned his own suit. Despite having plenty of room, he made sure to lean his shoulder into me as he walked past. Reminded me of my days playing first base when some jerk would intentionally bang into me at the bag, even though the ball beat him there by a mile. One time, I did drop the ball and the umpire actually called the guy safe. Couldn't believe it.

"I'm at the hatch, Dr. Larsen. Permission to open?" Richard sounded smug, as usual.

I checked my suit again. All lights were green.

"Granted," was all that Trolga said.

Richard opened the door and jumped down to the lunar surface. One by one the others followed with their buddies. A different color hovered over each helmet to make it easy to know who your buddy was. My color, picked by my buddy, Trolga, was puce, an ugly purple that she wore all the time. I had to wait until Trolga finished in the cockpit before exiting. She walked down the aisle with a gadget in her hand.

"Here." She handed it to me.

"What is it?"

"Your uncle asked me to give it to you. It's some kind of magnetometer."

I looked at the device. Seemed simple enough. My suit's display linked into it the minute I touched it.

Trolga walked down the stairs. The rest of the group was waiting for us. I walked forward and bumped my helmet against an overhead cabinet. I didn't think anybody saw me do it.

"Coming, Charlemagne?" Trolga was just trying to get my goat. At least she didn't call me Dobby. From the chuckles in the background, I knew that she'd used the open radio channel.

"It's Charlie, Dr. Larsen." I jumped out the door and floated gently to the surface. At least I did that gracefully.

"Whatever." She ushered me into line with my classmates. "Now, each of you has a sniffer, and you've been trained on how to use it. I want you to spread out in groups of two and cover the quadrants that I've assigned to you." A display of the area appeared in our helmets. Each quadrant was assigned a color that matched the color for each team of two. "I have it on good authority that this area should be rich with mineable helium-3. Charlie will be with me and, since he lacks training with the sniffer, I've assigned him the task of tracking magnetic anomalies."

Despite knowing how to use the sniffers I knew better than to interrupt Trolga.

"Ok. Fan out. I've programmed one of the rover's nanosatellites to hover over us so communication shouldn't be interrupted by any topography."

I looked up but couldn't see the nanosatellite. Richard and his teammate took off toward their assigned area. The others followed suit. I waited for Trolga to make a move.

I knew that she was staring at me through the mirror-like sheen on her faceplate. I could feel her eyes boring into me.

"Well, what are you waiting for? You can go play with your uncle's toy." She turned, not waiting for a reply. Technically, she was my "buddy" and we were supposed to stay together, but I didn't dare say anything to her. She followed the group fanning out in front of her. From the chatter on the radio, I knew that Richard had already located a thread of helium-3. They began to follow it. I looked down at the device that Trolga had given me. It looked like something my uncle had cobbled together—makeshift and homemade. I flipped the button at one end. It didn't seem to do anything. I turned toward the rover. The device began to beep loudly. Lots of magnetic alloys there. I turned away and began to follow the group. The magnetometer would beep every time I pointed it in the direction of Trolga or one of my classmates. The clutter from the rover and from my classmates' suits blocked any other readings. As we approached a large boulder, my classmates and Trolga stayed along the shady side. Since the boulder didn't look that large, I decided to cut around the sunward side to see if I could pick anything up while the boulder blocked the clutter from the suits and the rover.

As I stepped away from the shade of the boulder, my visor immediately darkened. With no air to cut its brilliance, the sun bore down on me. I began to sweat, but the reading on my suit said that the coolant was working and that, while the outside of my suit was heating up rapidly, my suit's temperature remained a pleasant seventy-two degrees. I began waving the magnetometer around as I walked. At first it didn't beep, but when I passed in front of another, smaller boulder to my right, it gave off a faint beep. A small arrow appeared in my visor, pointing in the direction of a giant boulder. I was over halfway around it. Nobody had missed me yet. I headed in the direction of the next boulder. As I bounced toward the other boulder, the beeping grew louder and the arrow kept pointing deeper into the boulder field. Something magnetic was out there and I was getting closer. I glanced over my shoulder. A few of my classmates had rounded the giant boulder. The magnetometer began to point me back toward them. I hurried to get behind the next boulder.

Once I did, the magnetometer pointed me further into the boulder field. I hurried, loping forward in long, ten-foot strides. I almost fell once, when my stride brought me down on a small rock. Fortunately, I caught my balance before falling. Had I fallen, my suit would have sent a warning beep out to Trolga. That was the last thing I wanted.

The beeping got louder. The device almost pulled me forward. I rounded another mid-sized boulder and the arrow pointed downward. I stopped but didn't see anything. I bent down and began to brush the dust away. A glint of metal shone through. I pulled it, but it wouldn't come loose. I took the multi-tool from the side of my suit and pushed the button on the picture of a shovel. It popped out just like in practice. The multi-tool was cooler than anything I'd had as a scout, but, then again, it probably cost more than my dad's car back home.

I dug around the object. The first few inches of dust were easy to get through, but then the ground became solid rock. I pushed the pickaxe button and began to chip away at the hardened ground around the metal object. It didn't look like a piece of space junk. From the way it was stuck in the ground it must've been there a long time. Involuntarily, I lifted my arm to wipe the sweat from my face. My arm banged against the faceplate of the helmet. It reminded me how easy it was to forget where you were. I stopped for a minute to catch my breath before redoubling my effort with the pickaxe. I worried about damaging the object, but I was getting frustrated. Besides, it was almost impossible to swing hard in the spacesuit. I felt a crack on my final swing. I bent down to see what I'd done, but my faceplate had fogged up. I'd been working so hard that the air conditioner of the suit couldn't keep up. I stepped into the shadow of the rock, agonizing as I waited for my suit to clear.

After what seemed like forever, I could see again. I bent down and brushed the loose dirt off the object with my glove. I picked it up and held it out in front of me. The way it glinted in the light, it had to be metal, but what? Given the size it seemed lighter than aluminum. Hexagonal in shape, it was about the size of the silver-dollar pancakes my mom used to make. I flipped it over. A thin layer of dust adhered to it. I brushed it with my glove and gasped. A black symbol stared at me—a symbol that I'd seen before.

"You're in deep trouble, butt-wipe."

I knew that voice. Richard. I glanced to my left. Richard and Eric stood there.

"We'd found a heavy concentration of helium-3 when Trolga noticed you were missing. Didn't you hear us calling you?"

I shook my head. "No. But . . ."

"No buts. Head back to the transport—now! Dr. Larsen, we've found Dobby. Dr. Larsen?" Richard faced in the direction of the rover.

Nobody answered. "Now you understand why I couldn't hear you. Something in the rocks must be blocking the radio signals."

"Doesn't matter. Head back—NOW."

Something inside me told me to palm the artifact. I returned the tool to my suit and slipped the artifact into my collection pouch.

"Okay, let's go." I didn't wait. Instead, I headed back along the trail that we'd left in the lunar dust. When we turned around the second large boulder the radio began to crackle and then burst into life.

Before I could respond, Richard did. "We found him in the boulder field, Dr. Larsen. Too—"

Larsen's voice interrupted on her override channel. "Mr. Thomas, you've wasted half our field trip. You'll be missing the next one. Now get back here, immediately!"

"You heard the lady!" Richard shoved me from behind. I stumbled forward, just catching myself against the edge of the boulder.

"Yeah, you heard her." Eric shoved me too. They both loped back toward the rover.

I followed quickly after them but couldn't keep up. I was stewing as I came around the last boulder, not paying attention. Richard stuck out his leg and tripped me. I stumbled forward. I instinctively tucked, but that only made things worse in the low lunar gravity. I did two flips before my helmet bounced off a boulder. Laughter filled my ears. Enough. I grabbed a rock lying next to me and pushed myself up. Everyone had turned away, heading toward the rover. I gripped the rock. Even though it was the size of a softball, it felt like a whiffle ball. I stood up, did a wind up and threw the best fastball that I could in a space suit. It looked like a perfect strike. Rhea's shout brought me back to my senses.

"Charlie!"

I suddenly realized that the rock could kill Richard. "Richard, look out!" I extended my arm as if to grab the rock before it hit Richard. I willed the rock to slow down. Unbelievably, it did. Others had heard Rhea. They turned toward us as Richard began to turn around. The rock decelerated and arced to the surface, landing at Richard's boots, kicking up a small amount of dust.

Richard laughed. "I thought you said you were a ball player." He glanced around. "Dobby can't even throw a rock!"

I was too stunned to react. The rock should have hit Richard. Instead it had slowed down, as if I'd willed it to slow. Rhea stared at me in horror.

"I didn't mean . . ." But Rhea loped toward me in what constituted a run on the Moon. Then I heard Trolga's voice.

"Walk slowly toward the rover, Mr. Thomas."

Her voice sounded different, almost panicked. That was when I noticed the red light—and the hissing noise too. I began to walk.

"Computer, what's the red light mean?"

In its usual calm voice, the computer answered, "You have a leak in your suit. You have seven minutes and thirty-six seconds to repair the leak before your air supply is depleted."

I began walking quickly toward the rover. Even Richard looked worried as I passed him. I took a deep breath. It didn't help.

"Seal the leak!"

"Not possible. Please make your way to a pressurized location."

Where was the leak? If Rhea could see it, then it must be pretty bad. My feet felt colder. Was it my imagination or was there a leak in my boots?

I glanced down but could see nothing. Trolga grabbed my arm and walked with me back toward the rover. It seemed farther away with each step, but I knew that was my imagination. I glanced up. I saw it. A crack in my facemask. That wasn't supposed to be possible. I tried to run, but Trolga held me back.

She stopped in front of me. "Walk, don't run. We have plenty of time." I looked up. While I couldn't see her face through the gold coating of her visor, I could see myself in its mirror-like sheen. A star-shaped crater glared at me from the upper right-hand corner of my visor. Cracks shot out from it. While I was looking, one of them began to inch its way down in front of my eyes!

"I'm having trouble breathing." I gasped.

"That's just your imagination." Trolga turned and pulled me toward the rover. It was over a hundred yards away.

My classmates gaped at me. Trolga put an end to that.

"Everyone, in the rover. Now!"

The kids started loading up, but the crack continued its creep across my visor. One suit ran toward us. He had something in his hand.

"I've got the tape, Ms. Larsen."

It was Jamie. Tape?

"Stop, Mr. Thomas."

"But..."

"Stop!"

Every muscle in my body wanted to run for the door of the rover, but somehow I managed to stand still. My mom used to keep a roll of duct tape in her desk drawer in the kitchen. She said she could fix anything with it. I hoped she was right. Trolga took the tape from Jamie and quickly pulled it over my visor. The crack had almost reached the other side when she pulled the tape across it. She kept applying more tape until I couldn't see.

"Good. That'll slow the leak. We have time to get you to the rover."

"But I can't see and it's hard to breathe!"

"Don't worry, we'll guide you." I felt an arm on either side of me. I began to walk with them. I didn't know whether it was my imagination, but I began to feel dizzy. I tripped, but they held me up. My head throbbed.

"I don't think..." I began to go limp.

"Quickly, lift him into the rover! Now!"

Arms grabbed me. I blacked out.

# CHAPTER 3
## FOUND AND LOST

I awoke in a darkened room.

Uncle Merl looked down at me, concern creasing his brow. "So, kiddo, how do you feel?"

I lifted my head. It throbbed. My uncle fluffed a pillow and slid it under my head.

"Take it easy. You're suffering from hypoxia."

I looked perplexed.

"Your suit suffered rapid depressurization. It's like you climbed Mount Everest without any oxygen."

I nodded, but my head throbbed more. "What happened?"

My uncle got up and paced for a minute. "Somehow your faceplate developed a crack. Almost all of your air leaked out. If your friend, Jamie, hadn't thought about the emergency tape in the rover, you may not have made it."

"I tripped and fell. Took a few tumbles, but I thought those faceplates were practically unbreakable."

"They're supposed to be. Your helmet's getting tested. Dr. Larsen was white as a ghost when I met her at the rover hangar. Never seen her like that."

"She's white as a ghost all the time."

My uncle chucked. "You're right. Seems to have an aversion to sunlamp therapy. Must be due to the way she'd look in a bikini."

I laughed weakly. "Please, my head hurts. Picturing Trol—Dr. Larsen—in a bikini isn't doing me any good. What'd the doc say? How long do I have to stay in bed?"

"As soon as your headache goes away, you should be good as new. No long-term issues at all. Here, have some tea." My uncle handed me a cup. He was big on tea. I shook my head.

"You need it." He pushed the cup toward my lips.

I took a sip. It tasted surprisingly sweet, not like the bitter stuff he sometimes drank.

"Tastes good. What's different?"

"I added a bit of honey and agave nectar."

I took another sip and handed the cup back to him. I looked up at him and pulled my hair back. "So, what do you think of the ears?"

Uncle Merl laughed and patted my arm. "It's a genetic trait in your family. Your ears are just a bit more pointed than normal." He pulled back his grey hair, revealing slightly pointed ears.

My jaw dropped. "Is that why you wear your hair long?"

Uncle Merl shook his head. "Not really. I just like it this way." He gave me a wry smile. "The ladies seem to like it."

I didn't know how to reply to that so an awkward silence enveloped the room.

"You know your mother had slightly pointed ears. It runs way back in her family, all the way to Scotland."

I shook my head. "I never noticed."

"That's because she got her ears bobbed as a child." Uncle Merl looked deeply into my eyes as if trying to find something. "For some reason yours seem to grow back."

He patted my arm again and stood. "Enough for now. While I don't like adulterating my tea, I needed something to hide the taste of the sleep compound that I added."

I yawned. "Why?"

"I know you too well—take after your parents. You'd never sit still long enough. Now you'll get a good night's sleep." My uncle padded toward the door as Nim jumped up onto my bed, curled up next to me and began to purr. By the time he shut off the lights, I was already drifting into dreamland.

I awoke to Nim licking my face with her sandpaper tongue.

"Nim, stop it." She didn't usually do that since she knew I didn't like it. Nim jumped down, gave a meow and scratched at the door.

"Ok, ok." I sat up. Fortunately, my head no longer throbbed. I got up and opened the door so Nim could get to her food, water or whatever else she was after. I was heading back to bed when I saw the light flashing on my iLet. I hit answer and a hologram of Jamie popped up.

"How's it going?"

"I feel fine, other than my uncle drugged me to make me sleep."

"Must have been strong because it's Saturday. You slept for over a day."

"What!" I glanced at the clock.

"Nobody's told us what was going on. Even Richard's shown some backhanded concern." Jamie smiled.

"Yeah, right." I shook my head.

"Well, he did make a big deal about the spastic Earther that screwed up the field trip."

"Uh, thanks for getting the tape. My uncle tells me that you may have saved my life."

Jamie looked down and kicked one foot against the other. "You'd have done the same." He looked up at me. "We were all freaked out when we saw that crack growing across your faceplate. That's not supposed to happen. They're going over all the helmets now. I heard them say that they think a micrometeorite may have creased it, weakening it just enough for your fall to crack it."

I nodded. "What are the odds?"

Jamie responded quickly. "Oh, about one million four hundred and ..."

I interrupted. "Only you would actually know the odds. You should have the pointed ears. You've got a brain like Spock's."

Jamie grinned. "Rather have them. The hair's a throwback. Makes me look like a knuckle-dragger. Just glad I'm up here rather than a high school in Peoria."

My stomach growled. "How about heading to Space Waffles? I'm starved." They served powdered eggs and veggie bacon that almost tasted real, but the hash browns and pancakes were out of this world.

"Already ate, but I'll meet you there." Jamie hung up.

I reached for the baseball on my bedside table but spotted the 1964 Kennedy half dollar that my father'd given me years ago. His father had given it to him, and— "Oh my God!" I ran for the door as I activated my iLet to call Jamie back.

"What?" Jamie said.

"Meet me at the Tube station."

"No breakfast?"

"No time. I'll explain on the way." I didn't wait for an answer. I sprinted down the hall toward the Tube station, banging my shoulder against the wall when I forgot about the low gravity. Out of breath, I got there just before Jamie rounded the corner from his apartment block.

"Jeez, you must be in a hurry. What's up?"

The doors popped open and we got on. I looked around and signaled Jamie to walk to the front of the car, away from the two men in the back.

"So, what's so important for you to miss breakfast?" Jamie sat down.

I sat down next to him and spoke quietly. "What did they do with the pouches?"

"What?"

"The pouches from the field trip." I tapped my side.

"Don't know. With everything that happened, man, that was scary. That crack kept growing."

"The pouches!" I implored.

"Well . . ." Jamie scratched his head. "The medics were in the hangar waiting for you. They put you in some contraption, a hyperbaric something or other, and took you away. Trolga got us through the airlock, told us all to go home and then took off. For all I know your collection pouch is still on the rover."

"Is the rover in the hangar?"

"Don't know. I'll check." Jamie typed something on his wristband screen. He nodded. "Yep."

"Good. That's where we're heading." I looked out the window down the tunnel.

"But why? What's the big deal?" Jamie crossed his arms.

"Because, idiot, I found something."

"What!" Jamie's eyes widened.

I smiled like the cat that ate the canary and folded my arms.

"You've got to be kidding! An artifact?" Jamie almost shouted. Heads at the back of the car turned toward us.

"Shhh." I nodded.

"Holy shit! Russian or Chinese?" Jamie lowered his voice.

I shook my head. "A metal hexagon about the size of a silver dollar. I pocketed it when Richard found me. After I tripped and my faceplate cracked, I forgot about it."

"Doesn't sound Russian. Chinese?" The train slowed.

I shook my head again. "It had a raised head of a ram on the body of a serpent."

Jamie scratched his head. "Never heard of anything like that."

I nodded. "That's my point."

We got out and walked through the first of the airlocks on the way to the hangar. A few adults were around. None of them paid any attention to us. We got to the ready room and hit the key pad to cycle through the airlock. A red light flashed: *Access Denied.*

"What?" I looked at Jamie and then through the small window at the suits hanging there, tantalizingly close.

"Just give me a minute." Jamie had his holographic keyboard up. "Done."

The red light switched to green and I heard the lock pop open. We turned the handle and walked in.

"Guess I should be paying more attention in computer class."

"No need, bro, not when you've got me around."

I chuckled.

The suits hung against one wall with helmets in a shelf above them. The other wall contained lockers. There were no locks on the lockers, but, then again, who would steal anything on the Moon?

My suit was easy to pick out because there was no helmet above it. I walked over to it. The collection pouch was on the side. I slipped my hand into the pouch. Nothing! Where was it? My pulse began to race.

"What's wrong?"

"It's not in there. Maybe it fell out when Richard tripped me!" I looked around.

"Let me take a look." Jamie used the flashlight app on his iLet and peered into the pouch. "Nothing. Maybe it's the wrong suit." Jamie glanced around the corner. "There's another suit without a helmet." He headed around the corner.

I lifted the pouch again, checking for a crease that might be hiding the artifact. Nothing. I was in such a panic that I didn't even hear the airlock door swing open.

"Looking for this?" Trolga was standing there holding up the hexagonal artifact. She smiled and tossed it in the air like a coin. In the low gravity it spun end over end until it stopped just short of the ceiling and then drifted back down to her hand. As it slowly turned, I could see the shadow of the ram's head/coiled serpent flipping over and over.

"Give that to me!" I launched myself toward her, but, in my anger, I forgot about the lower gravity.

Trolga easily side-stepped me as I flew past her, banging my shoulder into the wall. "Now, now, Mr. Thomas, remember who you're talking to.

"I was wondering what you were doing off on your own so I searched your suit after they carted you away. Now, as to this piece of junk, I'm keeping it for the time being. If you know what's good for you, you'll keep your mouth shut." She glanced up at the empty shelf above my space suit. "Freak accidents do happen, and your uncle's an old man."

I glanced around, catching Jamie out of the corner of my eye. He shook his head and I quickly shifted my gaze up at the camera. I didn't think that Trolga could see Jamie from her vantage point. She followed my glance.

She laughed. "How stupid do you think I am? The cameras are down for routine maintenance." She pocketed the artifact and walked out the airlock.

# CHAPTER 4
## DOME PARK

After Trolga left, Jamie walked around the corner.

"I wouldn't have believed it if I hadn't heard it myself. What's she got against you?" Jamie's eyes darted from me to the airlock.

I shook my head. "No clue. I knew she didn't like my uncle, but she threatened to do something to him."

"Dude, that's nothing. I think she sabotaged your helmet."

"What! No way." I glanced at the empty shelf above my suit.

He shrugged. "You tell me. We've got to get back out there."

"Let's get out of here before the cameras come back on. You don't want her to know you were here."

Jamie glanced up and then at the door. "You're right." He opened the door. "See if anyone's there."

I stepped out. Nobody in the hall. I shook my head.

"Good. Let's split up. You head for your apartment and I'll head for the other station. Meet me at the fountain in Dome Park in an hour."

Jamie was walking away before I could say anything. I headed for the train station. I didn't have long to wait. I got on the train and headed back toward my apartment. The trip was a blur. I didn't know what to think about Trolga's revelation that she'd taken the artifact and that she might kill me or my uncle. Why? It made no sense. Why would she hide the discovery that someone or something had been to the Moon way before men? And I was convinced of that. In fact, I had just realized where I'd seen the symbol before. When I got home, I went to the closet where my uncle had stored some of the personal effects belonging to my mother and father. I pulled out the small box that he'd packed for me when he'd come to collect me.

Opening the box, I lifted the Yankees sweatshirt from the top. I remembered my father wearing it to little league practice. A family picture was wrapped inside it. It showed my mother and father with me after I'd pitched my perfect game. Choking back a few tears, I put it to the side and dug through the box: more pictures, the needle-point pillow that my mother had made of my family tree, the family photo album. Finally, in the corner, I saw it—my mother's Atlantis journal. It was a hobby of both my mother and my father. They were amateur archaeologists and were convinced that Atlantis had really existed. Most of our summer vacations had something to do with searching for Atlantis. I remember taking a diving trip to Bimini with them one summer. We had a great time fishing and snorkeling, but my parents had been disappointed by the underwater "Bimini Road."

I flipped the journal open. My mother's clear, flowing handwriting greeted me. I choked back the flood of memories and the tears as I thumbed through the journal. About halfway through I found the drawing of the ram's head on a serpent's body. It looked exactly like the mark on the artifact. My mother's notes indicated that they'd found the drawing on several potsherds in a pre-Minoan tomb in Crete. They'd also found similar symbols on trips to Patagonia and Australia. She'd written that the wide disbursement and age led her to believe that the symbols were Atlantean.

What was an Atlantean symbol doing on a piece of metal on the Moon? I scratched my head.

Nim gave a meow as I passed the kitchen. Her bowl was empty. That reminded me that I hadn't eaten either. I got her food out and poured some into her bowl. I then grabbed a bottle of water and a nutrition bar. They actually weren't bad and I could eat it on the run.

I headed out the door and finished half the bar before I got to the train. I took a seat. My mind must have been somewhere else because I was totally zoned out when a wad of paper hit me in the head. I looked up. Rhea was standing there with her best friend, Imee.

"Hey, Rhea, how's it going?" I smiled weakly.

"I was starting to worry. I said hello and then texted you, but you just sat there. Maybe that shortage of air addled your brain."

My face flushed.

"What's wrong, cat got your tongue?" Imee chuckled.

"If I hadn't fed her before I left, she probably would've." I knew that sounded lame as it came out of my mouth. "You should come by and see her." I remembered Rhea's shocked look at my ears and held my breath.

Rhea smiled. "We will. Where you headed?"

I breathed a sigh of relief. "Dome Park. Thought I could use some fresh air." Dome Park was located in the exact center of the massive hyperplast pressure dome that sat on top of one of the newest sections of Clarksville. In the Dome you could walk around "outside." The holographic technology was amazing. In addition to the blue sky and clouds, they even had the occasional holo bird flying by. It made life in the tunnels of Clarksville a bit more tolerable. While Dome Park had actual grass areas, you couldn't walk on them. The park also had a handful of trees, a pond with a fountain with koi swimming in it, and a field of Astro Turf.

"We're heading that way too. There's a super typhoon in the Pacific heading for the Philippines. We'll be able to see it in about half an hour." Rhea glanced at Imee.

"What about the hologram?" I was looking forward to some blue sky.

"Their doing a recycle on the hologram. They timed it so everyone could get a view of the typhoon."

"Great. I'll look out for it. I've seen satellite pictures, but never seen one from up here. Should be cool." I smiled.

Rhea scowled.

"What did I say?"

"Imee's from the Philippines." Rhea had her hands on her hips.

"Sorry." I glanced over at Imee.

Imee smiled. "She's just yanking your chain. My parents are in London and my grandparents moved to Australia years ago."

Rhea began to laugh. "Easy pickings, Charlemagne, or should I say Dobby!"

I glared at her, but inside I didn't really mind her ribbing. She had the prettiest red eyes. They sparkled like rubies.

"Mind if I take a look at those ears?" Rhea didn't wait for an answer and leaned forward.

I drew back slightly, but then thought better of it. "I don't mind."

As she leaned in she softly brushed my hair to one side. At her touch, I shut my eyes. I smelled the slight scent of flowers mixed with something I couldn't quite place. I inhaled deeply and opened my eyes. Her chest rested just in front of me with the top few buttons opened on her blouse. I stared at the beautiful round curves of her breasts, watching them rise and fall with her every breath. I hadn't been that close to a girl's boobs since my girlfriend in Seattle had let me touch hers.

"Mind if I touch them?" Rhea asked.

I nodded. Exactly what I'd been thinking as Rhea's fingertips gently touched the tip of my left ear, sending a tingle down my spine.

"They're really not that bad. Kind of cute." She pulled back.

"Uh huh." I didn't pull my eyes off her chest until Imee hit me in the arm.

"We're up here, Dobby!" Imee glared at me but Rhea hadn't seemed to notice my stare.

I cleared my throat. "My uncle told me that the trait runs in my family, kind of like your red eyes."

Rhea smiled. "My grandmother does have red eyes."

I nodded. "And my uncle's ears are slightly pointed."

"Really? Is that why his hair's so long?"

I shook my head. "Don't know, but he did tell me that the pointed ears has something to do with Scottish nobility."

"So, you're telling us your family's royalty?" Rhea asked and glanced over at Imee as Imee crossed her arms and tapped her toe on the ground.

"Really more of a clan thing than royalty," I backtracked, looking down.

Fortunately, the train began to slow to a stop. I let the girls get off first. Rhea's hips swayed seductively from side to side, drawing my eyes. Her tight blue jeans inflamed my imagination as I pictured the curves hidden beneath them.

I stumbled as the floor sloped up toward the escalator. Fortunately, I grabbed the handrail. It could have been embarrassing if I'd stumbled into the girls. We took the escalator up to the surface. The girls stood side by side, talking about something that I couldn't make out. As they got off the escalator, Imee glanced back at me. Rhea nodded her head.

Just before entering the large airlock at the edge of the station, the girls moved toward the wall and grabbed an emergency air mask each. My uncle always made me take one, but, when he wasn't around, I didn't.

"Has anyone ever had to use one of those things?" I pointed at the masks.

Imee shook her head. "Don't think so. Rhea, you've been here the longest."

"Not since I've been here." She slipped the mask into the bag at her side. "But my mother told me that someone almost died when an air seal jammed right after they finished building the Dome. Ever since then, they've required that people get an air mask before entering Dome Park." Rhea looked me in the eye. "I guess it's about as rare as a faceplate cracking on a space suit."

I nodded, took a mask off the wall and followed the girls down the airlock corridor.

Rhea looked over at me. "Be ready when we come out into the open. Dome Park's very different with the hologram off."

Rhea hadn't been kidding. Stars twinkled even though the Sun was up. It felt like I was on the surface without a spacesuit. I took a couple of deep breaths and looked up at the Earth. It was night and the city lights of Europe and Africa sparkled.

I looked over at Rhea. She and Imee were looking skyward. "You meeting anyone?" I kept my head up as if I were looking at the Earth, but was really glancing their way out of the corner of my eye.

Rhea smiled as if she was reading my mind. "Just a few weather buffs like me." She paused. "We're going to Richard's house to watch from his deck, then go for a swim."

While relieved that I wouldn't have to figure out a way to get away from her, I wasn't happy about her going to Richard's. Then it dawned on me. I knew Richard's family had money—he had his own personal space suit after all—but a pool? On the Moon? "Next you'll tell me he'll be barbecuing real burgers and dogs."

Imee looked down at her feet, but Rhea laughed. "Hope so. I'm hungry and could use a good burger. Veggie burgers just aren't the same. I'm sure he wouldn't mind if you came along. You could borrow a bathing suit."

Despite everything, a smile creased my lips. "I'm sure that would go over well." I thought about Rhea in a bikini and wanted to blow off my meeting with Jamie. I just couldn't.

She laughed and smiled at me. "You're right. Too bad. I'd like you to be there. Here, hold my bag." She handed her bag to Imee and started to take her top off. She looked up. "May as well get some sun."

I did well to keep my mouth closed. Under what I'd thought was a blouse, but was really a beach coverup, she wore a bikini top. Never thought I'd see a bikini or a beach coverup on the Moon. I couldn't keep my eyes off the iridescent bikini flashing in hues of red, green, yellow and turquoise, let alone what it covered. I didn't even notice when Imee took off her cover up, revealing an even skimpier top.

"Like it?" Imee turned back and forth as if modeling for me, causing the colors to shift and sparkle as she moved. "Richard had it flown in on the last shuttle from Earth. Too bad you can't come to the party with us. You should see the bottoms!" Imee blew me a kiss as they turned and walked off, laughing together.

As they bounded away in those long, floating lunar lopes, I wondered whether they were just teasing me or whether Rhea actually liked me. I shook my head, wishing I could go with them. I hadn't seen girls in bikinis anywhere other than in the holos since I'd gotten to the Moon. Reluctantly, I turned and headed for the fountain in the center of the park.

Jamie waited there, staring at the koi swimming in the pond. The low gravity didn't seem to affect the fish. I guess they were used to feeling no weight anyway. I walked up to him.

"Beautiful day, huh? Not a cloud in the sky." I looked up.

Jamie gave me a glare. "Cut the crap. I may have figured out what Trolga's up to."

"You're kidding. What?" I glanced over my shoulder, but Rhea and Imee were out of sight.

"While you were off finding your artifact, we were taking samples for helium-3. Turns out, we hit the mother lode. But Trolga didn't report it right away. I thought it was because of your accident, but after seeing her threaten you, I did a little digging. Looks like Trolga made a huge bet on Dahak Mining right before turning in the results. The company's stock went through the roof when they announced the helium-3 find. She's made millions, enough to retire anywhere she might want. If an artifact's found in the area, it'll shut down production and she'll lose everything."

I nodded. "Makes sense, but she threatened to kill me and my uncle! That's a bit much."

"Not when millions are at stake. And guess who owns most of the stock in Dahak Mining—Richard's father!"

"No way!" I shook my head.

Jamie nodded. "He's rich enough without it, but he's a prick. He doesn't like that Rhea's paying so much attention to you."

"What? That's ridiculous. Besides, I thought he and Imee were an item. Why would he care about Rhea?"

"They are, but Rhea was Richard's flavor of the month before you arrived."

I breathed a sigh of relief, but then shook my head. "Rhea doesn't like me."

"Dude, what planet are you from? She's eyed you since the day you got off the shuttle."

I shrugged. "Why? I'm a lanky six foot two with pointed ears. What could she possibly see in me?"

It was Jamie's turn to shrug. "Who knows when it comes to girls. But I tell you this, she used to lead Richard around by the nose. Can you say 'whipped?' Richard claims that he dumped Rhea for Imee, but I think Rhea's the one that did the dumping."

"Not that I'm gay or anything, but Richard's handsome and rich. Why would Rhea be interested in me after having dated him? She's the most beautiful girl on the Moon. She has her pick of anyone." I looked down as a gold and white koi swam an infinity loop in front of me. Neither the mathematical fish nor Rhea liking me made any sense.

"Like I said, who knows when it comes to girls. Maybe it's the ears."

I was just about to shove Jamie when he held his hands out in front of him. "Just kidding, dude." He noticed the backpack on my shoulder. "What've you got in there?"

I pulled my mother's journal out of my backpack, remembering why we were here. "We can't let Trolga stop us." I showed Jamie the ram's head serpent.

"This symbol was on the artifact. My parents were convinced that it was a symbol for Atlantis. Searching for Atlantis was their big hobby."

Jamie laughed. "You're kidding, right?"

I put the journal away and turned to walk away.

Jamie grabbed my shoulder. "Sorry, but that's kind of hard to believe." He looked at my backpack. "Can I see that drawing again?"

I nodded, pulled it out and opened it to the page with the drawing.

Jamie nodded. "So you found a symbol of Atlantis buried on the Moon. That's wild. We've—"

Jamie's voice faded out. My vision clouded over and I felt like I was shooting down a foggy tunnel. As I approached the end, there was Trolga. She glared at me, laughing. Her face had distorted and her nose shot forward, changing color. Her nose and mouth were morphing into a beak. Her eyes intensified and narrowed behind her beak. Her hair became feathered. She looked like a harpy. She let out a high-pitched screech. I began to drift toward her. I flailed my arms to stop, but only picked up speed. There was nothing I could do to stop. She grew in size and snapped her beak. She was going to tear me to shreds. I tried to scream. Nothing came out. I felt heat on my right cheek. I managed to turn my head in that direction. A bright light seemed to be boring a hole through the mist. Trolga let out another screech. A figure was walking through the tunnel cut through the mist by the light. It was Uncle Merl. He wore a long grey robe. As he approached he lifted a staff and pointed it at Trolga. A golden ram's head topped the staff. The eyes of the ram began to glow. A ruby-red light shot out of them straight at Trolga. The mist engulfed me and I began to fall. I heard a splash and came around with Jamie grabbing me out of the fountain.

"You all right? I was talking and your face went blank. Then you dropped your parent's journal and turned white as a ghost. I said your name, but you didn't reply. I even snapped my fingers in front of your face, but you continued to stare." Jamie held my arm, steadying me.

I was soaking wet. I looked back down in the fountain. A handful of koi swam a complex dance where I'd fallen in. Orange, black, red and white rapidly swirled under the water. They were mesmerizing. Something about the way they were swimming . . . They seemed to be forming a pattern in the water, only I couldn't quite figure it out.

Jamie grabbed me. "You ok?"

I nodded.

"Looked like you were drifting off again."

"I don't know. I feel a little dizzy. Must be something to do with hypoxia."

People were starting to come over. Jamie grabbed me. "Let's get you back home. We can figure out what to do later."

I nodded. Jamie picked up the journal, shoved it in the backpack and hung it on his shoulder. We headed for the Tube station.

# CHAPTER 5
## ROVER RESCUE

Ibarely remembered coming home with Jamie. By the time I got to the Tube, my head felt as if someone were pounding it with a sledgehammer. It hurt so bad that Jamie wanted to take me to the doctor, but I shook my head and mumbled "home."

When we got there, we found a note on the kitchen table propped up against a glass filled with a cloudy, yellowish liquid. It said: "Drink me." I recognized Uncle Merl's handwriting. I gave Jamie an "I told you so look," drank the bitter-tasting elixir, and hit the sofa. I closed my eyes and didn't even hear Jamie leave.

Pounding on the door woke me up. Thank goodness my headache was gone because the pounding would have really hurt.

"Just a minute." I looked around for Nim. When I didn't see her lurking near the door, I told the computer to open the door.

Rhea stormed in and stood in front of me, hands on her hips, her face flushed. "What happened to you? I've been calling and texting."

I smiled. She looked good even when she was angry. I glanced down at my iLet, but the holographic list didn't come up. "Damn, Jamie must've shut it off. Came back from Dome Park with a horrible headache. I was taking a nap."

Rhea shook her head. "Nap! I ran into you at Dome Park yesterday!" Rhea's arms dropped to her side and her voice mellowed. "Jamie asked me to check on you."

"Why?" Still a bit foggy from my drug-induced nap, it took me a minute to realize what Jamie was up to. When I did, I flipped on my iLet's holographic text list. Jamie's text appeared halfway down the list.

"Dahak Mining's shutting down the area later this week. Today's the last chance we've got to get out there. I'll wait until ten. If you're not in the hangar by then, I'm going by myself." It was time stamped first thing in the morning.

I noticed Rhea reading over my shoulder. "What, he's gone outside? Why?"

I sucked in a deep breath, trying to decide what to say.

Rhea slapped my shoulder. "You're hiding something. Jamie's been my friend since we were little kids. Tell me!" Her cheeks flushed as I felt a slight tingle at the back of my head. A thought popped into my head that I should tell Rhea. I shrugged. Weird, but I'd already decided to tell her.

She glared at me, her ruby-red eyes almost glowing. "Well?"

I felt that little shove again, but ignored it. Perhaps a lingering effect of my uncle's concoction. Rhea's cheeks had flushed with anger, so I told her. "I told him about the artifact that I found."

"Artifact?" Rhea raised an eyebrow.

"On the field trip, before my faceplate cracked, I found a piece of metal." Rhea's expression didn't change. "It was buried."

"He risked getting suspended for a piece of junk!" She tapped her foot on the ground.

I shook my head. "It wasn't junk. It was smooth, with a picture of a ram's head serpent on it. It wasn't space junk."

"Where is it? Show me!"

I looked behind me. It felt as if someone had just given me a shove between the shoulder blades. Weird. "I can't. Trolga's got it."

"Trolga? Why?"

"Good question. Jamie and I went to look for it after I'd recovered from my hypoxia. Trolga confronted me in the ready room. Fortunately, she didn't see Jamie since he was around the corner when she came in. She's got it. She threatened me to keep me quiet."

"Why? That makes no sense."

"Jamie thinks it has to do with the huge helium-3 discovery that you guys made while I was digging up the artifact. Trolga bought a bunch of stock in Dahak Mining. If the artifact came out, they'd shut mining down and she'd lose a fortune."

"Either way, Jamie's out there. We've got to find him and get him back." She grabbed my arm, pulling me toward the door.

"Hold on. Jamie's been gone for hours. He's got plenty of air. Besides, if Trolga's watching, she might do something."

"What? Hurt you? That's ridiculous. Besides, we've got to get Jamie." Panic strained her voice.

"Why?"

"There's a meteor shower coming. We've got to get him."

I hit my iLet. "Call Jamie . . ."

"I tried that already. I can't reach him. We've got to go. Something's wrong."

"How much time before the meteor shower?"

"Three to four hours."

"That barely gives us time to get out there and back. Let's go."

We rushed to the Tube station, caught the first train and went straight to the hangar. When we got to the airlock to the ready room, I stopped and stared at the keypad.

"I don't have the code."

"Step aside. I do." Rhea hit her iLet and then punched a few of the keys. The door swung open.

"How?" I followed her through the door.

"You should pay more attention in computer class. Just kidding about computer class. After that last field trip, I earned my right to sign out on my own. A code comes with that right." Once the door opened fully, she didn't waste any time and went straight for a suit. I did the same. She was in her suit way before me. I was fumbling at it.

"Let me help." She gave the seams and clasps a quick look and gave the one that had been giving me trouble a quick turn. "You're clearly no Paul Muad'Dib."

I smiled. "And this is no stillsuit."

She smiled back and then grabbed my helmet and raised it over my head. She paused when she saw my expression. A brief wave of panic washed over me, but I suppressed it.

I pulled my hair back and nodded. "Go ahead."

She popped the helmet into place. All green lights flicked on the display.

She flipped her shoulder-length auburn hair back, put it in a pony tail and had her helmet on before I could offer to help.

"I set our radios to short range channel three so we can talk."

I nodded, and then realized that nodding in a helmet is ridiculous. We peered through the window. She keyed in her code again and the door to the airlock swung open.

"What about the meteor shower? Won't they stop us?"

"I already submitted a travel plan that has us back well before the shower starts."

I eyed the single-person moon cycles, but Rhea patted my shoulder. "Not today, hot shot. You don't have your licenses, and I'm not rated for the cycles yet." She headed for a four-person rover. I followed. She climbed in the driver's seat and grabbed what looked like the steering wheel from a car. I sat in the passenger seat, surprised at the simplicity of the controls. I'd expected it to look like the cockpit of an airplane and to steer with some kind of joystick. Instead another steering wheel sat in front of me.

I looked out the bubble-like hyperplast windshield. The hangar doors stood open as usual. Rhea pushed a button, grabbed the wheel and the rover lurched forward.

The area around Clarksville had smoothed out over the years, but once we turned off the road to the helium-3 mines and headed toward the hills where I'd found the artifact, it got a bit bumpy. Despite the bumps, Rhea kept the speed up.

I just sat there, useless. "Computer, display the amount of time left before the meteor shower begins in countdown mode."

The generic female voice said: "Acknowledged," and a green countdown clock appeared on the top right side of my faceplate. We had three hours and twenty-eight minutes remaining. I recalled that the drive out to the site took just over twenty minutes.

"How're we going to find Jamie?"

Rhea shook her head. "This is the Moon, dummy. We'll follow the tracks of his rover and then his footprints."

Being a greenhorn got old. One of these days, I'd stop acting like an Earther and learn the ropes on the Moon.

I glanced over at Rhea. She'd released the wheel in front of her. I shrugged and grabbed the wheel. Nothing happened. I glanced at the panel in front of me. Between us was a switch that said left and right. It was toggled to the left. I reached down to flip it.

Rhea grabbed my arm. "No!"

I pulled back, not expecting her reaction. "Why? I thought I'd give it a whirl."

She flipped off the tint on her visor and looked over at me. I flipped mine off.

"Because you're not trained on rovers. I am." She tried to sound calm, but her voice got shaky.

"Come on. I had my license on Earth and drove to school every day. It looks simpler than my old pickup." I reached for the wheel again.

"No!" She grabbed my arm hard enough to feel her grip through the suit, but I didn't let go of the wheel. I felt that tingle up my neck again. I glanced over at Rhea. The flecks of gold in her eyes seemed to spark in anger, then they mellowed. "Charlie, please."

I toggled the switch back to left. "Ok. But why? I'm a good driver." I looked at her through the helmet and could have sworn that tears were running from her eyes.

She blinked and looked away.

"You ok?" I heard a suppressed sniffle.

"Yeah. Look, it's just . . ."

I touched her shoulder—all I could do in a spacesuit. "What?"

She glanced over at me. Her tears had stopped.

"It's just— I grabbed the wheel away from my brother, Rob." A sob escaped her lips.

I released the wheel and looked forward. Autopilot had us following Jamie's tracks. "What happened?"

She gave me a furtive glance and then looked forward. I had just about given up on her telling me, when she started to speak. "I was fifteen. I'd talked my brother into driving me down to the liquor store to get beer for me and a couple of my friends. He'd just gotten a '38 Camaro and was ready to take it for a spin. He took a back road with lots of turns and took manual control of the car. I laughed as he whipped around the turns. He glanced over at me when a deer darted across the road in front of him. I grabbed the wheel and yanked it."

Rhea sniffled a couple of times. "I yanked too hard and the car went off the road before the autopilot could take over." She paused.

"Did he . . .?" I asked softly.

She shook her head in the helmet. "No. But he got thrown from the car and broke his back. He's a paraplegic. And it was MY FAULT." She broke down and started crying again.

I patted her shoulder through the spacesuit. I looked ahead. The autopilot on the rover guided us forward.

Rhea regained control. "Sorry, but when you grabbed the wheel, you kind of reminded me of my brother. He was a baseball player too."

I nodded. "And your brother's still on Earth?"

She nodded. "Yep. He stayed with my father after the divorce. My mother and I moved up here when she took a promotion with Dahak Mining."

I had no clue what to say, so I took my mother's advice and said nothing. Unfortunately, when I thought about Rhea's mother, I thought about where Rhea got her ample cleavage from. Her mother liked wearing tops that pushed her boobs together. Richard joked in the locker room that Rhea's mother was a MILF. I glanced over at Rhea, glad she wasn't a mind reader. She stared out the windshield. "So, your mother works for Dahak?"

"Yep. She worked for Dahak in their Bedminster office. After the accident, she and my father would get into arguments all the time. She caught my father having an affair with one of Rob's physical therapists. That was that."

"Divorced?"

"Yep. My fault again."

"No. It wasn't your fault. It was just an accident."

Rhea faced forward, remaining silent. I thought I heard a sniffle but kept quiet. Rhea glanced at the screen. "We'll be there in ten minutes. That should give us well over an hour to track down Jamie and get back to the rover."

I nodded, glad for the change of subject. "It shouldn't take more than ten minutes to get to where I found the artifact. If Jamie's there, we'll get back quickly and beat the meteor shower by a mile." I glanced at the internal thermometer of my suit. It read seventy-two degrees. It felt hotter. "Computer, drop my suit temperature by two degrees."

"Acknowledged."

I took a deep breath and sat back.

"So you're hot?"

I glanced sideways. "Didn't know you could hear that."

"You just need to move your eyes to the right twice to shut off exterior communication."

"Thanks. Didn't know that."

"Sorry for lashing out at you and dumping all my shit on you."

I chuckled. "No problem. I'm used to catching shit from people."

Rhea gave a little chuckle.

"Can I ask you something?" I glanced over.

"Sure. Shoot."

"Jamie told me that you broke up with Richard before I arrived. Now Imee's dating him, but you and Imee seem like best friends."

Rhea laughed. "That's it?"

"When one of my buddies started dating my ex, I didn't talk to him for a month."

"Imee and I hit it off from day one. She's the type that you can just talk to, you know."

I didn't really, but I nodded.

"I liked Richard, and he was/is the alpha dog here, so when he asked me out, I was flattered. After a couple of dates, my mother asked me what I was doing. Rather than lying about meeting Imee and a couple of the girls, I told her I had a date with Richard. She flipped out. Said that was great and that I should make sure to keep him happy.

"I gave her a funny look. But she just rambled on, sipping on her bourbon, and telling me that Richard's father was one of the richest men in the world. Everyone knew Richard was rich. He liked to show off the newest gadget, his private spacesuit and throw parties at his house under the Dome, but I had no clue he was that rich."

"Was she right? Is Richard that rich?"

"Well, his father is and he's got quite a trust fund. Anyway, my mother just droned on and on about Richard and how lucky I was to be dating him. Just about made me want to throw up. Anyway, despite his arrogance, I liked Richard and could deal with his bragging in the locker room about us doing it."

"Did you?"

Rhea turned and gave me a glare. "Have you done it?"

I blushed so hard that I was sure Rhea could see it through my facemask.

"I thought not. But I'll bet you second base that you've bragged about doing it with your baseball buddies."

I was tempted to lie, picturing going to second base with Rhea, but my delay answered the question for me.

"I thought not. Most kids our age haven't done it and those that have typically don't brag about it." Rhea laughed. "Cat got your tongue?"

"I guess so. Nim's quite a cat." Trying to change the subject.

Rhea laughed. "Anyway, I'd considered 'doing it' with Richard, but when my mother started trying to pimp me to Richard, I'd had enough. Richard pushed me pretty hard, but I managed to hold him back. That's when he really started talking up our sexual exploits in the locker room.

"Imee'd arrived about a month before and we hit it off really well. She actually knew how to make my favorite sushi. Sure, she had to substitute local tilapia for tuna, but that was way cool. She invited Richard and me over to have dinner with her and Steve. Richard shocked all of us by bringing tuna. He knew it was my favorite and it was delicious. We split up into separate rooms after dinner. Richard and I . . . We got to making out pretty heavy. He started trying to get my pants down, but I stopped him. He got so pissed that he said maybe he should try it with my mother. After all, everyone knew she was a MILF and a slut."

I gasped. "He actually said that?"

Rhea nodded. "THAT was the straw that broke the camel's back. I ran out of the room and the house. When I saw Imee the next day, I broke down and told her about it. That's when she told me she knew how to take care of Richard if it was ok with me.

"I was taken aback. I asked if she was going to kill him or something. She laughed and shook her head, explaining that she knew many more pleasant ways to shut a man up. After all, Richard was cute and rich. She grew up on the streets of Manila and had learned how to fend for herself. That's how she got her scholarship to go to school on the Moon. She asked if I would mind if she took him off my hands. I squeezed her hands and said that I'd be grateful, but to be careful.

"She laughed and said not to worry, she knew how to take care of herself. The next day, I dumped Richard. Of course, he told his buddies it was his idea. Several girls immediately fawned on him to console him, but Imee stayed aloof. Something about her got to him, and within the week, he asked her out. When she said no for the second time, he came up to me and told me not to throw a goat down the well when it came to Imee. I laughed and said that I'd said nothing to Imee, but would be happy to. Richard scowled and left. The next day, Imee and Richard had their first date. Since then, Richard's tolerated me, Imee's been on his arm almost constantly, and he's stopped telling lies about me. Imee's happy, I'm happy and, evidently, Richard's happy. I don't know what she's doing, but I'm happy for both of them."

It would take me a while to process what Rhea had just told me, but I knew she wanted me to say something. Fortunately, the auto-pilot chimed, and the rover slowed.

"To be continued, ok?"

Rhea nodded. I flicked my eyes twice to the right before letting out a sigh of relief as Rhea pulled up alongside Jamie's rover and began to shut the rover down.

"Before you do that, let's try the radio. The rover's got more range than our suit radios."

"You're right. I'll modulate channels since we don't know what channel he's got turned on. Jamie, come in, Jamie."

Nothing but static answered.

"Jamie, it's Rhea and Charlie. Come in."

Nothing.

"If you hear us, head back to your rover. There's a meteor shower heading this way."

Still nothing. "I guess it's time we hoofed it." I popped the magnetic seat lock and walked back to the door. Before opening the hatch, I looked back.

"Go ahead. Just launching a portable nanosatellite to keep us in touch with the rover."

# CHAPTER 6
## METEOR SHOWER

I opened the hatch, skipped the steps and jumped down to the surface. Dust kicked up as my feet hit. I loped forward a few more steps to give Rhea room to jump down. She did and we headed around to Jamie's rover. His footprints followed several sets coming back from the other direction. I recognized the large boulder at the edge of the boulder field where I'd found the artifact.

"Damn."

"What?"

"I forgot to grab magnetometer." Someone must've put it in the ready room after my accident, but I hadn't seen it.

"We're here to look for Jamie, not artifacts." We rounded the boulder and the trail of footprints reduced to two sets going out and one coming back.

I caught a glint out of the corner of my eye. It looked like something shooting through the sky.

"Was that a meteor?" I pointed up toward where I'd seen the glint.

"Sorry. Should've warned you. I programmed the nanosatellite to follow Jamie's footprints. You probably saw the sun reflected off it as it accelerated."

We continued in silence. I glanced around, but kept my main focus on the footprints.

"I think I found the artifact around the next bend." I tried the radio. "Jamie, do you read me? Jamie?" I used both voice and text since text requires far less bandwidth. I listened. Nothing but static.

Rhea kept following the two sets of prints around the corner.

"Must be something in the rocks. I didn't get any messages or radio chatter when I was here before."

"Strange. Never heard about the nanosatellites not working." Rhea was a few steps ahead of me. She stopped as she rounded the corner and flipped the high beams on her helmet lights to get a better look.

"Looks like he's been here, digging."

The hole I'd dug was now much larger. "Must've given up and gone further into the boulder field." I glanced at the countdown clock. We still had well over two hours to find Jamie, get back in the rover, and make it back to the hangar.

Rhea turned her light back down to normal. "Let's go."

She didn't wait for an answer. I followed. I saw a flicker of movement out of the corner of my eye. I swung my head around. Nothing. Probably just a shadow. Nevertheless, a tingle ran up my spine. I loped on after Rhea who was now a few steps ahead of me.

We continued on for about ten minutes. Jamie's footprints trailed off into the distance.

"Charlie, think you can pick up the pace?"

"Of course," I blurted out a bit too quickly.

"I didn't mean anything by it, but you don't have the practice I do. Watch ahead for rocks and try to pick your landing spots. If I get too far ahead, just let me know."

"I'll keep up."

"Just don't get reckless." With that, Rhea began to bound down the trail. I pushed off and followed. With each stride, we floated over two of Jamie's less hurried steps. The trail passed through a narrow gap. I thought Rhea would slow, but instead she pushed off, leaping upwards. She floated up and up and up, landing on the top of a boulder. Must have been thirty feet up if it was an inch.

"What was—"

"Shhh!" She waved with her hand for me to stay down.

"There!" She pointed off into the distance. She jumped down onto the next boulder and then down again to the surface. I loped forward to catch up. "I thought I heard whistling. Wanted to check and see. The signal was stronger on top of the boulder. Definitely a whistle. Sounded like 'Take me out to the Ball Game.' We're close."

I chuckled. That'd be Jamie.

Rhea took off again at a faster pace. It pained my ego, but when I had to use my arms to push off a boulder, I slowed down. I lost

Rhea turning around a corner, but wasn't worried. You didn't have to be an Indian to be a tracker on the Moon. The dust would hold our footprints for ages. I slowed and followed, listening to the radio. I could hear Rhea breathing heavily as she ran, but static grew. I ran as best I could but didn't catch her. I turned a corner and stopped. In front of me floated the image of a tall blond woman. She hovered about a foot off the ground, looking right at me. Her almond-shaped turquoise eyes sparkled with flecks of gold. She wore a diaphanous turquoise gown that matched her eyes. She raised her right index finger and signaled me to move forward. Despite myself, I began inching forward. She radiated warmth and comfort. She turned. I followed. I'm not certain how long I followed her, but the next thing I knew, Rhea was shouting my name. I blinked. The lady vanished.

"Charlie, come in. Charlie, do you read?"

I shook my head and looked down. No footprints. I must've been hallucinating. What else would explain the lady? An air leak? My heart skipped a beat, but all readings were normal.

As I rounded the next boulder, I spotted Jamie and Rhea standing in the shadow of a boulder, bending over.

"What is it?" I loped forward.

They said in unison, "You've got to see this."

I loped over and looked into the shadow where they'd been staring. Jamie leaned against his shovel. He'd dug down into the regolith. I focused my light. It reflected off a . . . helmet!

"Oh-my-God!"

Jamie had cleared the dust and chunks of regolith from the top half of the spacesuit, but the balance remained buried. It looked as if it had fallen and been covered with dust and soil. A faded emblem on the shoulder showed a ram-headed serpent like the one on the artifact I'd found.

"Definitely not Chinese or Russian," Jamie said. "This'll put a halt to the mining operation and to Trolga's windfall."

"What's it look like?" I tried shining my light through the visor, but it reflected the light right back.

"No way to tell until we get it back to Clarksville and open it up."

I looked up at Rhea. "You mean you want to take it back?"

"What else can we do?"

I glanced at the countdown clock glowing in the upper right-hand corner of my helmet. "We don't have a ton of time. Have you tried pulling it out yet?"

Rhea and Jamie looked at each other. "I didn't want to damage it. It seems like the dust hardened around it."

"Well, let's try. If we go back without it, they'll never believe us and we won't be allowed back out."

I walked behind the suit and slipped my arms under its arms. I lifted. Stuck.

I bent down and brushed the loose dust off the legs. I then picked up Jamie's shovel and started scraping along the right leg of the suit. Jamie used the small pick in his multi-tool and started chipping on the other side. Rhea walked around to the head of the suit. She flipped on her lights to bright mode.

"What're you doing?" I asked.

"Taking pictures. We've got to document what we're doing." She looked at Jamie. "Did you take any pictures?"

Jamie's head drooped. "No. The magnetometer started going nuts. I just started brushing the dust away until the top of the helmet appeared. Totally forgot about pics."

"Doesn't matter. This'll have to do. Keep trying to free the legs." Rhea walked around, snapping pics with her suit camera.

The dust had hardened around the legs. As I scraped it with the shovel, it broke into pieces which I then brushed away with my hand. "I wonder how long it's been here?"

Jamie looked up. "It was totally buried under the dust when I found it. The first layer came off easy, but the rest is like cement. That must've taken a long time."

I was breathing heavily as I chipped away around the edges of the leg. "A real long time. Maybe those stories of ancient aliens were true?"

"It could be human," Rhea chimed in.

"You ever seen a suit like this?" Jamie asked.

"No, but who thought that the Russians had lost cosmonauts on the Moon until they found the remains of that crashed Soyuz? Who knows what the Soviets were up to back in the sixties and seventies?" It wasn't what I was thinking, but it was possible.

"Maybe, but from the way you're working at the legs, Jamie's probably right. It's been here a long, long time." Rhea backed up and took a picture of us working on the body.

"What about that ram's head serpent symbol?" I thought about the old Bond movie, Moonraker. "This guy could be from some private group that nobody's ever heard of."

"We'd've heard about it by now," Jamie said.

"Not if this guy died up here. They may have given up and tried to hide their failure." My shovel suddenly slipped. A big chunk broke loose behind the leg. I grabbed it and pulled it away.

"I think I've freed it." I lifted the leg and, sure enough, it came free. Jamie redoubled his effort. After a few minutes he had his side freed as well.

I walked behind the suit and bent to lift it.

"Give me a second. Let me get in a good spot for the picture." Rhea walked about four paces behind the feet. "Ok, go ahead."

I slipped my arms under the arms of the suit and lifted slowly. It came out easily. I was about to pull it to its feet when I saw a puff of dust behind Rhea. I paused.

"What's wrong?" Rhea asked as Jamie walked over to help me. "Stuck?"

"No, but . . ." I saw another puff of dust about a hundred yards behind Rhea. I dropped the body and backed against the boulder. "Get against the boulder, quick!"

"Why?" Jamie was beginning to bend over to pick up the suit himself until a puff of dust rose up next to him. "Meteor shower!" He backed up against the boulder.

Rhea bounded toward us. "Must've started early."

I looked at the countdown clock. We had over two hours until the shower was supposed to start. "What do we do?" Puffs began to land more frequently.

"No way we can get back to the rover." Rhea scanned the area. She pointed. "It looks like there's an outcropping about half a klick in that direction. If we can get under there, we should be fine."

I was about to suggest staying where we were when something pinged off my helmet. "I've been hit!"

"Let me see." Rhea looked at me quickly. "Just a scrape in the paint. Looks like a micro meteor hit the boulder behind you and a flake of rock bounced off the helmet."

"How do you know?"

"Because if the meteorite had hit you, you'd be lying next to our friend. We need to head for the overhang. Let's go."

Rhea took off quickly. Jamie looked over at me. "Let's go, buddy. I hope you've got your lucky half dollar with you. We need it."

We both took off. Jamie and Rhea quickly outdistanced me. I still didn't have the Lunar lope down. I kept my head down and said a quick prayer. We'd only be in the open for a few minutes, but I remembered what the crack in the faceplate had been like. A meteor shower was not like a rainstorm, and there were nowhere near as many meteors as raindrops in a rainstorm, but still. I looked up. Only a few paces to go. Rhea and Jamie were already under the overhang. I tripped on a rock and stumbled forward, bumping my head against the side of the helmet. Jamie and Rhea caught me.

"You ok?"

"As long as I didn't crack my faceplate again."

They both laughed.

"How long do you think we need to wait?" I checked my oxygen supply. I'd only burned through about a quarter of the tank.

Rhea answered. "If the report's right, only about thirty minutes, but, then again, the time was off by over an hour. Jamie, how's your oxygen looking?"

After a brief pause, he answered, "Just under half a tank. That should be good for more than enough time."

"So now what?" I picked up a rock from the ground and flung it out as far as I could. It flew and flew until it almost reached where we'd left the suit.

"Impressive. I guess you were a pitcher. After that lame throw on the field trip, I was starting to think you were full of it." Jamie picked up a rock, wound up and threw it as hard as he could. He angled it up higher so it would carry farther. I watched as it went farther than my throw, hitting the boulder where we'd left the spacesuit.

I began looking for another rock.

"Boys!" Rhea huffed. "Have you thought that you might hit the suit or even cause some of those loose rocks on top of the boulder to fall down on our find? If you need to show off, throw at something else."

I already had another rock in my gloved hand and would have looked stupid dropping it. I spotted an outcropping of rock about thirty-five degrees to the right of where we'd found the body. "Bet you can't hit that outcropping, Jamie." I threw the rock up in the air. It felt about as heavy as a ping pong ball, but was as large as a baseball. I stood by the edge, went into as much of a windup as I could in the spacesuit, and heaved the rock at the outcropping. It flew straight and true, just like my throw at Richard had, but this time it didn't slow. It nailed the outcropping squarely.

"There you go, your turn." I slapped my hands together and began looking around for the next rock. I walked back farther into the overhang. I was about to reach for a rock sitting up on a ledge when it began to glow. I pulled my hand back. The glow extended up from the ledge and outlined the shape of a door.

"Guys" I grabbed Rhea's arm. "See that?"

"What, my great throw? It went right over the top of the rocks you hit."

"No, behind us?" I pointed.

They both turned quickly, their lights overpowering the glow.

"What?" Rhea said.

"I don't see anything."

"Turn your lights down. I saw a glow back there." I pointed toward the ledge. Their lights both dimmed. I expected to see the glowing doorframe, but there was nothing there. I reached forward, but felt only solid rock. "It's gone."

"Right. Didn't think you were the type to make up scary stories."

I wish I could have seen Rhea's face since I couldn't tell whether she was mad or amused.

"Don't you have stories of ghosts on the Moon? I kind of feel like Gandalf and Bilbo hiding in the cave in the Misty Mountains during a storm. What if a door opened in the wall and goblins grabbed us?" I grabbed Jamie.

"Cut it out, Charlie. Isn't the body out there enough?" Rhea sounded upset.

I'd guessed wrong. I picked up a flat rock at my feet and tried skipping it through the dust. It just buried itself instead of skipping. "Sorry. Just trying to kill time. Always loved the *Lord of the Rings*."

"More of a *Harry Potter* fan, but we're on the Moon stuck under an overhang with meteors falling all around us." I always thought that Rhea was tough, but she sounded like she was about to cry. I would have given her a hug but for the space suits. No way was I going to tell them about the glowing doorway or the ghost of the turquoise-eyed woman hovering by it, signaling me to come with her.

# CHAPTER 7
## MOON DANCE

We hadn't seen a puff of dust in over ten minutes. Unlike on Earth, you don't see a streak in the sky since there's no atmosphere for meteors to burn up in. Since Jamie's oxygen was dropping and we still had to get the space-suited body we'd found back to the rover, we decided to risk going out into the open.

Jamie and Rhea bounded out across the plain. I took a couple of steps and then looked back under the overhang. Sure enough, a slight glow again outlined the doorframe. The ghost of the lady glided out of the overhang and beckoned me back toward her. I should have been scared to death, but something kept me from panicking. In fact, I wanted to turn back. Was I going crazy? Neither Jamie nor Rhea had seen a thing. I shook my head, resisted the temptation to turn back and loped after Jamie and Rhea at my top speed. They expected me to fall behind, but I was learning so I arrived just as Jamie began lifting the body.

"Piece of cake." Jamie held the suit out in one hand. "Now, how do I carry it?"

"You don't," Rhea answered.

"Why not? It's light as a feather." Jamie lifted the body over his head with one hand. It began to slip and he just managed to grab it and lower it with both hands. I laughed.

"We've got about two klicks to walk and you're low on oxygen. Even if the suit and body only weighs about fifty-five pounds on the Moon, it still has a mass of over three hundred pounds. Go ahead, throw it over your shoulder and take a few steps."

Jamie took a few tentative steps and then began the lunar lope. After the second lope he began to lose his balance. He struggled and managed to steady himself.

Out of breath, he said, "So, what d'you have in mind?" He didn't sound happy.

Rhea pulled a couple of Velcro straps out of her pouch. "Lay the body down."

She lifted the legs and slipped one strip of Velcro around the ankles, made a loop and then left a three-foot strip on either side. She then did the same thing under the arms and around the chest of the astronaut.

"Hand me your multi-tools."

She attached the Velcro to each one. I figured out what she was doing, so I picked the multi-tool up on the helmet end.

"Not so fast, Charlie."

I lowered the astronaut. "This side's heavier, so I thought I'd carry it."

"Yep, but it's also awkward with the helmet sticking out. Since I'm better at walking on the Moon, you take the feet."

"But I can hold the helmet out." I picked up my end and showed her.

"Yes, but that could throw your balance off. Can you dance?"

I was taken aback by the out-of-the-blue question. "Why?"

Jamie chuckled. "I can guarantee she's not asking you out on a date!"

I was sure that Rhea had her "really" face on, but one of the problems with the reflective faceplates was not being able to see anyone's face.

"If we're going to move at anything faster than a slow walk, we'll need to coordinate. I'm going to play a song over the radio. We need to take steps in time with the music. Think you can do that?" All I saw was the reflection of my spacesuit in Rhea's mirrored faceplate.

"Sure. But if the helmet gets heavy, let me know and we can switch off."

Rhea ignored the comment. "Jamie, stay behind us. Something might fall off the body."

"Astronaut," I said. "He, she or it deserves that. Body sounds so weird."

"Ok, astronaut."

We both picked up our multi-tools and started back along the trail of footprints, with Jamie picking up the rear. Rhea chose a recent hit by a group from Athens, Georgia.

"Ready? We'll start with short lopes."

"Ok, you lead."

She pushed off the surface and I followed. Her idea worked as we picked up speed. We got to the rovers in no time. Just before leaving the boulder field, the radio started working again. We picked up the radio beacon indicating that the class-4 meteor shower was over. A few texts popped up for me, but nothing major. I'd deal with them when I got back.

I wondered if Rhea or Jamie had gotten anything. Their parents probably kept far closer tabs on them than Uncle Merl did on me.

"Anybody looking for us?" I was hoping we'd be able to go back quietly without attracting attention.

"Just my mother," Jamie answered. "I've already let her know that I'm fine and that I'm hanging with a few friends."

Rhea ignored the question and continued on toward the door to Jamie's rover. "Let's get the body . . . astronaut, into Jamie's rover and head back."

She opened the door and stepped in. I lifted the astronaut up over my head as she stepped in and then carefully followed.

Rhea got out, but I stayed, looking at the space-suited figure on the floor. The reflective material persisted in keeping me from seeing what was inside. While the suit would fit a human, it could contain anything.

"Coming?" Rhea turned and looked at me.

I considered it. Were this Earth with the chance to ride in a car with her, I'd have said yes, but here it didn't matter. I looked down at the ancient suit. "I'd like to ride with the astronaut and look over the suit."

"Thought you might. Let's talk about what to do on the ride back. Keep the suits on the short-range channel so nobody picks up what we're talking about."

Jamie climbed in and stepped around the astronaut to get to the front of the rover. "Why not just send pictures ahead? That way, Trolga and her gang can't stop us." I strapped in and Jamie did the same.

"Don't be too sure of that," Rhea replied. "They could intercept us and claim it was all a prank."

Or worse, I thought. I looked out the front of the rover and saw Rhea's rover swing out in front. "I think Rhea's right. It sounds Hollywood, but helium-3's the lifeblood of Clarksville. A bunch of people're going to be pissed about stopping the mining in an area this rich."

I stared down at the astronaut as we drove, trying to think. Most of Clarksville's population was comprised of scientists and their families and people working for Dahak Mining. The scientists would be ecstatic about our find; the Dahak people would hate it. It reminded me of the story in ecology class of the huge dam being stopped by an endangered fish. They'd found a couple of the small darters in a stream that would be flooded by the dam. The huge power company building the dam had sued and lost, but that wasn't the end of the story. One employee of the company that lost his job due to the project's cancellation got drunk one night and dumped poison in the stream, killing off all of the endangered fish. He went to jail, but the dam ended up getting built.

If our astronaut turned out to be an alien, it would be like the rare fish; somebody would be willing to do almost anything to make it disappear. Before causing such a huge brouhaha, we needed to find out more. I didn't know many people in Clarksville, but I did know my uncle. While eccentric, he was very smart and was one of the senior scientists in Clarksville. He'd know what to do.

"So, any thoughts on what to do?" I didn't want to just suggest going to my uncle. The rover jostled as Jamie hit a rock.

"Let's flood the web with those pictures that Rhea took and make sure that we're greeted by a huge crowd." While brilliant, sometimes Jamie lacked imagination.

"Unless we have a convenient accident before we get back. Besides, we're only thirty minutes out and they control the hangar area. They could stop us, quarantine us and take the body, then claim the whole thing was a hoax." Rhea again voiced one of my fears. I shuddered as I recalled the dream of the harpy-like Trolga trying to devour me. An accident seemed like a very real possibility to me.

"But you signed out the rovers. There'll be a record."

"Yeah, and how easy would it be for them to change that?"

"I guess Rhea's right. Besides, I kind of fudged on signing out." Jamie's voice lowered as he made the admission.

"So what did you do, hack the system?" I knew the answer before I asked it.

"Well, I tried to sign out, but somebody'd already signed out the rover. So I kind of changed the reservation list. What? I had to get out here. They were about to make the area off limits!"

Jamie hit a rock and we bounced.

"Watch it." I looked down at the astronaut. His head had bounced, but he didn't seem to mind. His faceplate wasn't too different from ours with its frustratingly reflective gold coating. The rest of the helmet was a faded red, made of some hard material. The suit was a flexible, dirty off-white material. A faded ram's head serpent patch covered the left side of the chest. I popped my seatbelt off and touched the suit with my gloved hand. It appeared to be made of some high-tech fabric that was less bulky than what we used. The suit had no backpacks or other external devices. They must have used some highly efficient internal recycling system for life support. No way this was some lost Soviet cosmonaut.

I strapped myself in. "I think we should call my uncle. After all, but for him giving me the magnetometer, we wouldn't have found the artifact or the astronaut. He'll know what to do."

"My mother works for Dahak, so she's out," Rhea said. "Your uncle does seem to be a reasonable sort." She paused. "Ok, do it."

"I'll shoot him a voice-text so we can stay off the radio."

I used the voice activated system in the suit to compose the text to my uncle. "Uncle Merl, I'm on the way back from a trip in a rover. You around?"

I only had to wait a few seconds.

"Yes, Charlie, what's up? I thought you were at our apartment recuperating."

"I went out with Jamie and Rhea for a quick trip. We got stuck in the meteor shower. Fortunately, we found a ledge to duck under."

"Glad to hear u r ok." His text looked normal, distracted and impatient.

I had to get his attention. "Jamie found some very interesting samples with your magnetometer."

"Really?"

"Yes, sir. We'd like you to take a look at them. One rock was in the shape of a ram's head." This time it took my uncle a few minutes to respond.

"I'm at my office. Can you find your way over to the university hangar?"

I paused the text feature. "Rhea, he wants us to head to the university hangar. Know how to get there?"

"No. Didn't know there was a university hangar, but the nav computer'll know. Follow me."

"I've already got it programmed in. You follow me for a change." Jamie accelerated the rover to get in front of Rhea. He probably expected Rhea to gun it and keep in front of him, but, having heard about her brother's wreck, I knew she'd stay back.

"How long for us to get there?" I asked.

"The way Jamie's driving, we may never get there." Rhea sounded a bit put out.

"We're fine. This is a well-traveled area. No boulders around here. Should be there in twenty." Jamie kept pushing the rover hard.

I went back to my texts. "We're on the way. Some of the samples are fairly large. I'm sure you'll be interested."

"Ok. See you soon, Charlie."

I went back to the radio. "My uncle's going to meet us there."

"Good. Enough said. We're about in radio range. Time to go radio silent."

I leaned back against the bulkhead and closed my eyes. The next thing I knew, I was looking up at the Earth. It looked normal, but . . . different. I didn't recognize the continent directly above me. Despite that, it seemed familiar—like home. I recognized Tierra del Fuego and the Cape of Good Hope, but the land below them looked different. A burst of radio chatter interrupted me and I began to run in the familiar lunar lope. I was running through a boulder field that seemed very familiar. I stopped, looked up, and saw several brilliant flashes erupt over the unknown land, my home. I cursed under my breath. Radio chatter began again. Light began to sparkle above my head. My personal shield had activated. I started running harder. I turned a corner and looked toward the overhang and the entrance to our base. Safety. I might just make it. Alarms began sounding in my suit. I glanced up. The twinkling lights above me had stopped. I felt a pang of panic mixed with regret.

Jamie's voice yanked me back to reality. "There. The hangar lights." I banged my helmeted head against the back of the rover at the sound. Must have dozed off. I shook my head and glanced down at the astronaut. My dream had seemed so real.

The terrain abruptly changed as we drove onto the smooth floor of the university's hangar. Jamie's voice chimed in. "We've got company."

I walked forward and looked over Jamie's shoulder. "Probably my uncle."

"There are two of them." Jamie pointed.

"He probably brought somebody along." I squinted at the figures as Jamie slowly drove closer to them. I recognized the older type of suit and the glint of blue from the small Scottish dragon patch my uncle had added to his suit. "Looks like my uncle, but I've got no clue who's with him."

Jamie pulled into an open parking spot and Rhea pulled in next to him. We popped the hatch and jumped down onto the floor of the hangar. We walked around the back of Rhea's rover as she joined us and then toward the two suited figures.

"Uncle Merl?" I waved.

"It's me, Charlie." The suit I'd recognized raised its hand and waved.

"Who'd you bring with you?"

"Professor Betrys. When you mentioned the samples had set off the magnetometer I knew she'd be interested."

I stopped just short of the two figures. Both had their faceplates set to clear. My silence registered my concern with my uncle. A smile formed on my uncle's lips as he gave me a slight nod.

"Don't worry, Charlie, Glenda can keep a secret." He gave me a wink.

I headed back toward the rover. "Uncle Merl, please have the airlock ready."

"Will do, Charlie, but what's the . . ." He whistled loudly as we carried the body off the rover.

"Now just one minute, Merl, I didn't sign up for anything like this." Professor Betrys had her hands on her hips.

Uncle Merl gently grabbed Professor Betrys's arm. "Take a harder look at that suit, Glenda. It's old."

Professor Betrys looked and whistled. "What have y'all found?"

"That's what we hope you can tell us." Rhea and I carried the ancient astronaut into the airlock.

# CHAPTER 8
## LOTHLORIEN OR VULCAN

As usual, I was the last out of the suit. Jamie and Rhea stood at a window. Rhea was leaning over Jamie's shoulder, but when I walked over she smiled and gave me a hug.

"Quite the adventure, huh? Bet you didn't expect this when you got up this morning."

"What, you didn't?" I smiled.

Rhea hit my arm.

"Quit it and look." Jamie pointed through the window. My uncle and Professor Betrys stood over the astronaut lying on a metal table. All sorts of equipment encircled the table. My uncle and Dr. Betrys wore their spacesuits.

I made the mistake of voicing a question. "Why're they working in a vacuum? It'd be easier without suits on."

Jamie gave me a glare. "And watch the body inside turn to dust?"

Rhea nudged me. "Looks like they found a hole in the helmet. Probably killed by a micrometeorite."

"Just like we might've been if we hadn't gotten under that out-cropping." I watched as my uncle picked up a drill while Professor Betrys pointed a sensor just above the hole. The drill bit entered the helmet.

"Wonder what they're doing?" I was anxious for them to get the helmet off so we could see what the alien looked like.

"Just flip the switch to your left, Charlie." I looked up. My uncle was looking at me through his spacesuit. I flipped the switch. We could now hear them.

"Just about through. There." My uncle pulled the drill back.

"Looks like the helmet resealed itself after it was punctured. Atmospheric reading coming through. Nitrogen, oxygen with minor components. An Earthlike atmosphere." Professor Betrys scanned the computer readouts. I looked over at Jamie and Rhea. Could the astronaut really be Chinese? My shoulders slouched. Rhea, as if reading my mind, smiled and squeezed my hand. I smiled back.

"Readings coming in. The atmosphere doesn't match the current or recent Earth atmosphere."

"Is it alien?" my uncle asked.

Professor Betrys hesitated. "Nooo. Computer says this is an Earth atmosphere, but from about a million years ago!"

"Holy shit " Jamie blurted out. He glanced at both suited professors. "I hope the radio's only one way."

Either it was or they ignored his expletive.

"Let's get the helmet off." Professor Betrys put the atmosphere sensor down and picked up a small circular saw.

"Let me try something first. I hate to damage the suit if we don't have to." My uncle bent down and peered at the helmet from one side and then walked around to the other side.

"Merl, the suit's old. There's no way the latches'll still work, even if you figure them out. I'll set the saw to cut at a depth of one centimeter so we don't damage the body."

My uncle ignored her and walked behind the helmet. He pushed a button and the table lowered. "I think I've figured it out."

"My homemade shrimp and grits says you didn't."

"Deal. Now, hold the torso up so I can lift the helmet."

Professor Betrys bent over the torso as my uncle placed his gloved hands under the helmet.

Jamie's iLet emitted a foghorn sound, making Rhea and I jump.

"Sorry guys. Parents." Jamie stepped back as my uncle began to pull the helmet off. He slowly lifted it—too slowly for us. We could first see something red. I thought it was a strange color for alien flesh until the helmet moved high enough to reveal a ghastly grey, wrinkled neck. Next the chin cleared. My uncle paused as Dr. Betrys placed a pad under the neck to support it. She slid it back as my uncle slowly pulled the helmet back. The face appeared pale and desiccated.

"Looks like a mummy, doesn't it?" I turned to Rhea.

She nodded. "What do you expect? If the atmospheric readings are right, it's a million years old." She glanced over at me, but, instead of a glare, she smiled and reached out her hand for mine.

"What's that snake-looking thing around its neck?" It reminded me of the vampire-like assistant to Jabba the Hutt from *Star Wars*.

Rhea pushed a button on the window. Our view zoomed in on a spot on the astronaut's neck.

The tentacle became long, braided hair that looped around the astronaut's neck.

"Can't believe I thought it was a tentacle."

Rhea squeezed my hand. "I did too. Kind of looked like it."

The helmet came off quickly once they got passed the ears.

"Damn, it's Spock." Jamie glanced over at me and then back at the astronaut.

I glared at Jamie.

"What? I'm a Trekkie, and those pointed ears do look like a Vulcan." Jamie crossed his arms. "But, come to think of it, maybe a long-lost relative of yours. While your ears aren't quite so pointy . . ."

Rhea glanced at me as I pulled my hair over my ears. "That's ridiculous. How do you know it's not Elrond? At least Middle Earth has a pre-industrial Earth atmosphere!"

"Sorry, guys, I'd love to stay and argue, Vulcan, elf, or some long-lost relative of Charlie's, but I've got to go. Parents are pissed." Jamie paused and looked at the astronaut. He then lifted his hands in the split-fingered Vulcan symbol of goodbye. "Live long and prosper." He turned to leave. "And take some pics, Charlie. I'll swing by your place tonight."

Jamie took off as Rhea refocused her attention on Elrond. I kept my eyes on Rhea, thinking how much she looked like Elrond's daughter, Arwen. I smiled and looked back at our astronaut.

"What about the suit, Merl? Give it a try or use my drill?" Dr. Betrys looked down at the face of the astronaut.

My uncle reached over and grabbed a syringe. "Don't think we have time right now. Let's get a DNA sample." Without waiting, he stuck the syringe deep into the astronaut's temple. Rhea gasped and looked away. I couldn't pull my eyes off what my uncle was doing.

He withdrew the syringe. "Got it. Now let's see what we've got." He walked over to the wall, pressed a button, and a drawer slid open. He dropped the syringe in the drawer. It closed.

His voice came over the radio. "Computer, analyze the genetic structure of the sample. Include a phylogenetic tree to compare the sample to the nearest species on Earth. Now we wait."

Rhea turned to me. "What do you think?"

I held up my fingers in the Vulcan salute. "Live long and prosper." Despite my joking, I was thinking back to my vision of walking on the Moon. It seemed so real.

Rhea smiled, but looked back over at the astronaut's body lying on the table and then back up at me. "Given all the stories of elves that have existed for years, I think that perhaps he's from an ancient race that lived millions of years ago. Maybe the elves from fiction have a basis in fact?" Her ruby-red eyes locked onto mine. I couldn't look away.

She took my look the wrong way. "I know, sounds crazy, right?"

"No. Not at all! I was thinking the same thing."

She hit my arm. "Now you're kidding me."

I shook my head. "No. Look, the air came from the Earth of over a million years ago. The astronaut has ears like an elf. Why not?"

She smiled at me. "You're sweet." She leaned over and kissed my cheek.

I just stood there like an idiot, not knowing what to do as my cheeks flushed. Fortunately, my uncle saved the day.

"Here come the readings. Damn, these new computers are fast."

Both of us looked up as a screen on the wall of the lab lit up. A chart appeared on it. Lots of colored lines crisscrossed each other. Greek to me.

Professor Betrys whistled. "Damn. Hard to believe. Amazing. We're going to rewrite the history books."

"You're right, but let's be certain, make sure there's no contamination. We need another sample." My uncle began to look around. He picked up another large syringe. Rhea turned a bit pale.

"I'd better go. My mother'll be wondering where I am." She turned to leave.

"Rhea."

She turned back. "I'll come by tonight to meet you and Jamie."

I smiled and watched as she walked away.

"Charlemagne!" My uncle's voice jolted me. I looked back through the window.

"Yes?"

"Pay attention! This is historic, and you discovered it."

My eyes dropped to the floor briefly. "Yes, sir."

"Let him be, Merl. Open your eyes." Professor Betrys smiled at me through her visor.

"Oh, all right. Charlie, if you're just going to sit there, make yourself useful. I've got a bag sitting by my chair in my office at home. Bring it to me."

"Yes, sir." I turned to leave.

"Oh, and while you're there, feed Nim and make me a PBJ. And a Coke."

"Yes, sir."

"Betrys, you want anything while Charlie's going?"

I paused and looked back.

"Make that two PBJs, grape jelly if you've got it. And a Diet Coke."

"Yes, ma'am." I left for our quarters.

# CHAPTER 9
## PEANUT BUTTER AND JELLY

Nim greeted me with her usual disdain as I entered our quarters. I grabbed an apple from the marlin-shaped crystal bowl my uncle kept on the breakfast table and took a bite. I puckered my lips. Much tarter than the ones I'd gotten used to in Seattle, but then I was happy to have apples on the Moon. The hydroponics guys were good, real good. I took another bite and grabbed Nim's food. She came running over at the sound of the cabinet opening and began rubbing against my legs, purring. I bent over and scratched behind her ears.

"Yes, girl, I know. We've been gone a long time." I put her bowl down.

I pulled out the peanut butter, a large jar of Jif, straight from Earth, and a jar of locally made grape jelly. I was glad that one of my uncle's few extravagances was importing peanut butter from Earth.

"TV—on." The computer recognized my voice and the screen embedded in the wall came on. Flats fishing in the Bahamas popped up. Back in Seattle, I'd watched a few hunting and fishing shows, but now that I was stuck on the Moon, they'd become a staple for me.

After spreading the peanut butter, I couldn't resist. I made three PBJs instead of two. I picked one up and took a bite as I walked into my uncle's office. Sure enough, the backpack was where he said it would be. Strangely, mine sat right next to it. I hadn't left it there. I picked them up and set them down by the kitchen table as I wolfed down my PBJ. I wrapped up the other two, stuck them in my backpack and sealed it. My iLet vibrated. I walked over to the fridge and pulled out a water and two Cokes.

"Yes?" I popped open the Coke and took a swig.

"Charlie?" Rhea sounded different, edgy.

"What's up? Didn't expect to hear—"

"Just shut up and listen."

"What?"

"Jamie's in the hospital."

"What!"

There was a knock at the door.

"They're claiming that you did it."

"That's ridiculous." I yelled at the door: "Just a minute."

"I know, but— Is that the—" The connection dropped off and the door swung open. Two uniformed men strutted in. Nim lunged out the door behind them. I started to go after her, but they grabbed my arms.

"Mr. Thomas, please come with us."

"Why? My cat. She's loose." I tried to pull away, to grab the backpack, but their grips tightened on my arms.

"Just come with us and don't give us any trouble." One pulled me toward the door, but the other stopped him.

"Hold up, Evan." The man eyed my half-eaten sandwich. He let go of my arm, grabbed it and took a bite. "Damn, it's real peanut butter." He spotted the jar of Jif, unsealed my backpack, stuffed the Jif inside and pulled out the other sandwiches. "Our lucky day. Two more sandwiches."

"Hey, that's my uncle's stuff."

"You'll shut up if you know what's good for you."

Evan's grip on my arm loosened slightly. "Hand me that other sandwich, Doug." Doug reached for the sandwich and handed it to Evan. Evan's grip loosened more. I kicked him in the shin, pulled away and made a dash for the door. Before I got there my legs collapsed under me. I fell, bouncing off the door.

"Damn, kid, that wasn't smart." Evan walked over and kicked me in the stomach. I grunted in pain. "That happened when you fell after we hit you with the neural neutralizer. Now, if you do it again, I think your next fall will break your nose, maybe even cause you to lose a few teeth." Evan grabbed me and yanked me up, but I couldn't stand. My legs tingled like they were asleep. I tried to talk, but couldn't.

"Wish you hadn't used the neutralizer. Now we've got to drag 'im."

"I didn't use a full charge. He'll be able to walk in a few."

"But she told us to bring him ASAP. Let's go." Evan slung my backpack over one shoulder as they each grabbed under my arms and pulled me up, dragging my legs and feet along the ground.

"Good thing we're close to the Tube station or I'd really be pissed at you. That's going to cost you that jar of Jif."

"No way! It's mine."

"Arm wrestle for it?"

"Screw that. How about hoops in the Dome?"

"You're on."

My legs began to feel less rubbery and I could move my jaw. "Where are you taking me?"

"So the neutralizer's wearing off. Good. Now shut the hell up. You'll find out when we get there." Doug turned toward Evan. "These neutralizers are cool, but I still like the old Tasers. They really hurt." He smiled, showing a gap in his teeth.

"Watch out for him, kid. He's a real sadist. If I were you, I wouldn't give him an excuse." Evan laughed.

I nodded, but then Doug slapped me hard on the back. I let myself go limp, almost falling out of their grasp.

"Watch it, I almost dropped him."

"Next time I'll hit him harder, so you do drop him. He deserves a busted lip."

"We were told to bring him in in good shape." Evan looked concerned.

"And why do you care what that witch says? She's not our boss." Doug pulled on me harder, forcing Evan to move more quickly.

We were getting close to the Tube station. I didn't know what to do. I hadn't hurt Jamie, so why would he blame me for putting him in the hospital. It must have been Trolga. She must have found out about our discovery and conspired to shut us up. I had to warn my uncle. I tried to wiggle my toes. They moved! The tingling in my legs had faded to almost nothing, but I continued to let them drag limply below me.

We approached the last corner to the Tube station when something launched itself through the air at Evan. He never stood a chance. Nim's claws dug into his face. Before he could grab at her, Nim leapt at Doug. He was reaching for the neural neutralizer at his waist, but Nim was too fast. He dropped it as Nim's claws raked his cheek.

I picked up the revolver-shaped neutralizer, turned the cylinder to the highest setting and pointed it at Evan. He was reaching for his own weapon. I squeezed the trigger. He dropped like a rock.

"Nim, back." Nim jumped away from Doug as I squeezed the trigger again. Doug dropped to the ground as well. I grabbed my backpack and slid the neutralizer into it. I didn't know how long they'd be out.

"Nim, go home." Nim sat there licking the blood off her left paw as if nothing had happened. She glanced up at me, then turned and sauntered back toward our apartment. I ran for the Tube and jumped on. I had to get to my uncle before they did.

# CHAPTER 10
## ESCAPE

I got off the Tube at the university stop. I spotted a few uniforms, so I ducked my head and walked behind a couple of university students. Fortunately, the students headed toward the science wing. When we reached the corner, I turned off toward the bio forensics lab where I'd left my uncle working on the body. As I turned the last corner, I stopped in my tracks. Several security guards had my uncle by the arms. He saw me, but quickly turned his head. I ducked back around the corner. As I did, my vision clouded. The walls disappeared around me and I seemed to float upwards. I saw my uncle being led away in handcuffs, but I drifted in the other direction, toward the university hangar. I saw myself get in a rover and drive off, away from Clarksville. My eyes clouded again and I got a strong sense of vertigo. I reached my arm out and was back in the corridor. I rubbed my temples. The vision had left me with a slight headache. I didn't believe in premonitions or telepathy or anything like that, but the rover sounded like a good idea. I headed for the university hangar.

The locker room was empty. I quickly slipped into my suit, grabbed my backpack and stepped into the airlock. A couple of people lolled at the far end of the hangar, but they paid no attention to me. I went straight to a rover, climbed aboard and headed out. I didn't have any idea where to go, so I headed away from the university and hit the autopilot to take me back along our prior track. I sat thinking until the rover jarred to a halt.

I looked around. The spot where we'd left the rover before was still about a half a mile away. I glanced around. A red light flashed on the control board.

"Computer, what's the red light?"

"A recall order has been issued to all rovers."

"Override!"

"You are not authorized to override the recall command." The rover began to make a wide turn. I tried grabbing the wheel Nothing. I was heading back to Clarksville. I knew what would happen when I got there. I couldn't go back. I walked back to the airlock.

"Computer, open the hatch."

"You are not authorized . . ."

"Shut up!" I grabbed the handle. It didn't budge. I kicked the door. "Damn." I'd end up in custody with my uncle. Something red caught my eye—the emergency evacuation switch. It would blow the door off the rover. I was already in so much trouble, what would a bit more matter? I opened the cover and pressed the button down for five seconds.

The computer's voice kicked in. "Emergency decompression in five, four, three . . ."

I backed away from the hatch.

". . . Two, One." The hatch blew out, sucking me right out with it. I flew several yards out the hatch and landed hard, bouncing. After the third bounce I managed to steady myself.

"Computer, any suit damage?"

"Negative."

I watched as the rover continued on toward Clarksville. A small debris field surrounded me. Everything that hadn't been locked in place had flown out of the rover. I spied my backpack. I was glad it was sealed against vacuum. Next to it lay an emergency oxygen tank. The gauge read full. With the efficient air scrubbers in the suit, I had plenty of air to walk back to Clarksville if I wanted, but a little extra wouldn't hurt. I bent down to pick it up and an alarm sounded in my helmet.

"What's that alarm?"

"It's the automated recall from Clarksville. It will sound every sixty seconds until you return to Clarksville."

I tied the tank to my backpack, slipped it over my shoulder and began to follow the old rover tracks. Sure enough, in exactly sixty seconds the damn alarm sounded again.

"Can't you shut that thing off?"

"Not authorized."

I continued on, turning back once to watch the rover trail off into the distance. If they wanted to find me, all they'd have to do was bring the rover back out and then follow my footprints. I picked up the pace and began to lope across the moonscape, taking giant strides as if I were wearing seven-league boots.

The damn alarm sounded again.

"Turn the volume down!"

"Done."

"All the way."

"Acknowledged."

I mumbled to myself, "Dumb computer." I made it to the hills in no time. I started following the path among the boulders that we'd followed before. There was a mess of prints at the start of the path. I quickly got to the spot where I saw three sets of prints heading in and three heading back. The footprints coming back had sunk deeper into the layer of dust. Rhea's prints were next to mine and Jamie's alongside them.

That gave me an idea. I looked up at the massive boulder resting along our path. The top appeared to be about thirty feet above my head, but there was a ledge only fifteen feet up. I should be able to make that. I bent down, pulled my arms back and jumped as high as I could. I sailed over the ledge and kept going until I was just above the top of the boulder. I stuck my arms out and started spinning them for balance, but the backpack clipped to my right side made my weight distribution uneven. I landed on my right foot, but my momentum carried me on. After a couple of hops I banged hard against the side of the boulder and then bounced to just shy of the edge before regaining my balance. I looked back. My slipping had disturbed a few pebbles, but the boulder didn't have dust on it. It would be hard to track me up here.

I looked down at where our trail led off. A series of large rocks dotted the path. If I could jump across a few and then climb down, I could get to where we'd found the astronaut. I took my time with every leap, taking care to compensate for the backpack. After the first few hops, I started thinking about an old cult film that I'd watched once with my dad. Giant worms under the sand hunted a group of people, and the only place they were safe was on boulders and rocks. Not *Dune*. The moon was not Arrakis. This was a cheesy movie with terrible special effects, but, as a young kid, it had given me night-mares. My mother had scolded my father for letting me watch. Now, as I looked down, I didn't see any worm sign, but I could see the spot where we'd dug out the ancient astronaut. The rocks jutted out over the trail in one place, so I carefully climbed down and lowered myself off the ledge. There were so many footprints in the area that I doubted they'd be able to distinguish the new ones if they came looking for me.

I walked over to the prints that headed toward the cave where we'd taken refuge during the meteor shower. I lowered my boot into one and then carefully stepped in the next print. I tried my best to land in each set of footprints.

I made it to the cave and looked around. There was no glowing light and no ghost hovering there to greet me. Now that I was out here, what was I going to do? Solving the mystery of the glowing light and the ghost had driven me here, but now that I was here, staring at a barren moonscape, reality settled in. I had plenty of ox-ygen, but I was a fugitive. I couldn't stay out here forever. Once I returned they'd probably throw me in jail. They had my uncle and I was wanted for putting Jamie in the hospital, running from those guards and damaging a rover. I sat down, leaning my back against the rear of the cave.

I held my helmet in my hands and bent down. "You've really gotten yourself into a pickle this time, haven't you, Charlie?" I said out loud.

*No, Charlie, you did the right thing.*

I lifted my head and looked around. Nobody was there.

"Now you're going nuts," I said to myself out loud.

*No, Charlie, you're not.* I looked around again. Something glowed in front of me. It looked like a cloud of gas with little lights shim-mering in it. The cloud began to get denser, finally taking the shape of—my uncle. Instead of his usual disheveled demeanor, he looked more like the Uncle Merl from my dream, the one that drove the harpy-like Trolga away. He wore a long grey cape and no glasses.

I took a step back.

*You have nothing to fear, Charlie.*

I shook my head. "Uncle Merl?"

*That's right, Charlie. Your talents are finally starting to appear.*

"Talents?"

*Surely you remember the telepathy back at the lab?*

I shook my head. "What?"

The apparition laughed. *Charlie, you and I share the same heritage, the heritage that led you to find the medallion and then the astronaut.*

"What do you mean?"

My uncle's image shimmered. *I don't have enough time to explain. Hopefully later, after the danger passes, you can return and I can explain. Take refuge . . .* Uncle Merl's image blurred and his voice trailed off . . . *in the base.* The apparition faded.

"Uncle Merl, wait! What base?" I was alone again in the cave. I leaned my head back against the rear wall of the cave and thought, "Now what?" I looked up. The roof of the cave seemed to form a perfect arch. There was something there, at the top. Why hadn't we seen it before?

"Zoom 3X." The helmet zoomed in on the roof. While worn down, there was a carving at the top: a ram's head with the serpent body, just like on the medallion! This was no cave! I remembered my dream of the astronaut running along on the Moon and looking up. Was this where he was trying to get to, the base? I stood and looked at the back wall. Just like the last time, the outline of a door began to glow faintly, but this time the light grew stronger, washing the cave with a cobalt-blue glow. A handprint began to glow halfway up the door. I extended my gloved hand into the glowing print. At the touch of my hand, a door slid open.

It was dark. I should have hesitated, but I didn't. I stepped over the threshold. Nothing happened. I took a couple of small pee pee steps. A sudden vibration crept up my legs. I turned. The door had shut behind me. I turned and placed my hand against the door. No glowing handprint. Nothing.

I tried to swallow, but had a bad case of cottonmouth. I took a sip of water from the helmet's straw. It didn't really help. I did the only thing I could do: turned and walked on. From the light of my helmet, it appeared that I was in some sort of tunnel. I looked down. An inch or so of dust covered the floor. On Earth that could have meant centuries; here, millennia? I kept going. I couldn't get lost. All I'd need to do was follow my footprints back to the door. I counted my steps anyway. After seventy-seven paces, the tunnel ended in a huge round opening, like the opening of a giant's bank vault. I stepped past the door and flipped my helmet lights to their highest setting. The light barely touched the other side of the room. It seemed to be larger than the basketball gym back home. Large machinery lined one wall, with a few pieces of spartan furniture in its center. I took a step forward and felt that vibration again. I looked back. A massive door had sealed the entrance to the tunnel.

# CHAPTER 11
## MOONBASE ALTAIR

A chill ran down my spine, but then I shrugged. What was one more sealed exit anyway? I had plenty of air and, despite the sealed doors, I had a feeling that I wasn't trapped.

The slight vibration continued as I stepped further into the room. The walls and ceiling began to glow.

"Lights off."

The computer shut my helmet lights off. The glow from the walls created a twilight effect. I could see, but the lights seemed dimmer than they should be.

A brighter shimmering light began to appear about ten feet in front of me. It coalesced into a shape—the woman with the turquoise eyes. She wore the same diaphanous gown that matched her eyes. I hadn't noticed before, but she sported a set of pointed ears. She hovered over the floor and then slowly floated toward me.

Despite my fear, I held my ground. She didn't appear threatening, and this was why I had come all this way anyway.

*Hello, Charlie. We've been waiting for you.*

"Are you a ghost?" I extended my arm. It passed right through her.

*Stop it. That tickles!* The apparition moved back, out of my reach. She chuckled. *Just kidding, Charlie. I'm no ghost. I'm a hologram.*

"With a bad sense of humor."

She smiled. *Why don't you take off your helmet and relax?*

I shook my helmeted head. "Like I said, a bad sense of humor. You might not need to breath, but I do."

*Well then you'd better take off your helmet. You've been leaking oxygen for some time.*

"What?" I glanced down. The level of oxygen in my suit had gone into the red. I tore off my backpack and pulled out the spare bottle. It too was in the red.

"What the—?" Then I remembered. I'd turned the volume all the way down on the alarm system. Must have damaged the tanks when I'd fallen jumping up on the rocks. The hologram just continued to stare at me.

I looked around the room. The dust had begun to swirl around. That wouldn't happen in a vacuum. As my dad always said, "In for a penny, in for a pound." I loosened the clasp on my helmet and slowly pulled it off. There was no whoosh of air that there would have been had I been standing in a vacuum. I took a sniff. Didn't smell bad. A bit musty, like walking into an unused room at your grandparents' house.

"Ok, so how about explaining all of this to me?"

The apparition nodded. *Follow me.* She drifted toward the far wall of the room. As she approached it, the wall shimmered. An image of the Earth appeared on it. Only the continents didn't look right. A large continent that I didn't recognize sat right in the middle. I recognized Tierra del Fuego at the end of South America, and then New Zealand.

I pointed out what I'd discovered. "This is South America and this is Australia and New Zealand, but what's the continent in the middle." I paused. "It's Antarctica." I glanced at the beautiful apparition. "Where's the ice?"

*Very good, Charlie. I'd expect no less from you.* She looked at the map. *This is the way that Antarctica looked 1.2 million years ago. Back then we called it Atlantis.* She paused as I stared at the map, speechless.

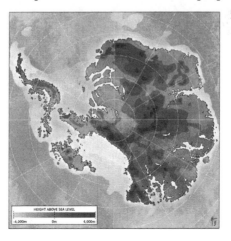

*Your parents were right, Charlie, there was a thriving civilization known as Atlantis. We built a technological civilization that* Homo sapiens *have yet to match. This base, Altair, is evidence of that.* She extended both arms.

"How do you know my name, and how do you know so much about me?" I looked into her eyes.

She smiled. *Ah, the impatience of youth. We've waited centuries for your arrival.*

"What do you mean?" This was too surreal. Maybe I was home in my bed in Seattle, dreaming. I squeezed my eyes shut, hoping for my mother's touch on my shoulder, waking me up for school.

*Open your eyes, Charlie. You're not dreaming.*

I opened them. The beautiful apparition was looking down at me, concern springing from her almond eyes. She smiled.

*Yes, I can read your mind, at least on its surface. Our children receive training to guard their thoughts, but you . . .*

"But you're a hologram, how . . ."

*Can I read your thoughts? Simply put, I am a hologram, but I am also far more than that. By the way, you don't have to speak. Just think your questions instead. Now, sit. Let me tell you a tale. I've waited a long time to tell it.*

I heard a scraping sound behind me and looked back. A chair was sliding in behind me. I sat.

*I am an Atlantean. My true name is too hard to pronounce in your language. I have been known as Isis to the Egyptians, Athena to the Greeks, Minerva to the Romans, Frigga to the Norse, and Nantosuelta to the Druids, but none of those seem to suit any longer.* She seemed to concentrate as I felt a tickle in the back of my mind. She smiled. *Galadriel. That's a fine name. Galadriel shall be my name for this Age.*

I guess she really could read my thoughts.

*Your parents were right, Atlantis did exist, and it is underwater, but that water is ice, not ocean.*

She pointed at the image of Antarctica.

*I am from our capital city, Solterra.* The image zoomed in on a city on the coast. It was like zooming in via Google Earth, but much more detailed. Tall, elegant spires of skyscrapers stretched high, while, lower down, pyramids dotted the cityscape. The zooming stopped in a wide-open park in the middle of the city. Golden fountains spouting multi-colored water dotted the lake. To one side I saw a little girl and her father. The girl had an enormous smile on her face, as her father flipped a shiny metal disk into the water. The girl had almond-shaped turquoise eyes flecked with gold. She had braided blond hair and her ears came to a pronounced point. I reached up and touched my left ear.

The hologram smiled. *One of my favorite memories, the fountains of Atria. My father used to take me there every Saturday after visiting the zoo.*

*That was long, long ago. We lived exceptionally long lives, but had very few children. We covered the globe, but preferred to reside on our home continent, Atlantis.* Home sapiens *had yet to arrive on Earth, but another group, very closely related to Atlanteans, challenged us. They called themselves Lemurians and lived on this island in the Pacific.*

The image shifted to a large island northeast of New Guinea, in the middle of Micronesia. I knew my geography. There was no island there now.

*The Lemurians were a young and brash race, much like* Homo sapiens. *They came to despise our control of the planet. They attacked us several times, but we beat them easily. We had little interest in expanding around the globe, and to assuage their egos we entered into a treaty with them, ceding them the area from their island to what you now call China and India. They were a very aggressive species, but impatient and short-lived. Even before our biotechnology blossomed, our lifespans were ten times theirs. When we expanded that to centuries, and then millennia, they claimed we had the secret to eternal life. They wanted that secret desperately. Our scientists tried, and we managed to extend the Lemurians' lifespans to centuries by modifying our nanites to their biology. We thought that they were satisfied, despite living far shorter than us, but they weren't.*

*I grew up in a golden age. The last Lemurian war had ended centuries before and we were expanding beyond the globe. I was young and jumped on the chance to come to the Moon. We were building a starship to expand out into the cosmos.*

*We were at peace with the Lemurians, traded with them, lived with them and, even though most Atlanteans looked down on it, intermarried with them. While children were rare, we were close enough genetically for children to be born. A faction within Lemuria argued that if Atlanteans and Lemurians could have children, why didn't our secret of longevity work on Lemurians? We were, after all, genetically similar enough to interbreed.*

*Atlantean and Lemurian scientists worked hard, but something in their genetic makeup prevented Lemurians from living beyond a few centuries. When*

I had transferred to the Moon, there were rumors of monstrosities created by the Lemurians, of demons that lived forever, but the Lemurian High Counsel ridiculed the rumors. Most Atlanteans relegated tales of secret labs and mutant Lemurians to our version of cheap horror movies.

When the schism within the Lemurian High Counsel happened, few Atlanteans paid attention. We should have. A civil war broke out in Lemuria. We ignored it. Many Atlanteans looked down on Lemurians as inferior, barely worth note. After all, they bred quickly and lived short lives. Their existence had little bearing on Atlantis.

Our news agencies reported that the Lemurian High Counsel had gained the upper hand in the war. That's when the rebels struck. They nuked the capital, killing the entire Lemurian High Counsel, the Atlantean Ambassador and his family and a handful of Atlantean businessmen that lived in Lemuria.

The use of a nuclear device horrified us all. In the past, we had used small nuclear devices for mining projects and had tested their use for spacecraft, but we had never dreamed of using them against people. War was a thing relegated to our distant past.

That's when they struck.

The map zoomed out, and brilliant flashes of lights rained down around Solterra, similar to what I'd seen in my dream of running on the lunar surface.

While our technology was great, we were a peaceful people. We didn't have a way to stop the attack. A nuclear barrage vaporized our capital.

Galadriel's head drooped momentarily.

My parents, my family and most of my friends were gone in an instant. I survived here, in base Altair with just over fifty other Atlanteans and a handful of Lemurians. The Lemurians were our colleagues and were devastated by the loss of their capital and the wanton attack on ours. They even struck us here on the Moon, despite a handful of their own people being up here. Since the Moon has no atmosphere, we used a modification of our gravitational lens drive to divert asteroids and meteorites from this base and our other Lunar facilities. Even our suits had their own versions of the shields. Unfortunately, the power supply in the suits was limited and we suffered one casualty from the attack. The astronaut whose body you found belonged to our chief pilot, my husband.

I lowered my head. I'm sorry.

She nodded. After their surprise attack decapitated our government, they sent a naval task force to demand the capitulation of Atlantis. What was left of our government relented and told the Lemurian dictator that we *would grant the Lemurians full access to our biological research facilities so they could learn our secret of longevity. Being a geneticist and the exobiologist on our team, I knew that the Lemurians could learn nothing from our lab. Despite being able to interbreed, their genetic code was different enough from ours so that the genetic engineering on us would not work on them. I feared that another wave of devastation would follow when they reached our shores and took over our research labs.*

*That's when it happened. Somebody in some research lab tied to our space program must have gone crazy with grief. He used a ZPEG to enhance our gravitational lens drive system and turn it into a weapon.*

ZPEG? What's that? I had kind of followed her to that point.

*ZPEG is a zero-point energy generator. The physics are extremely complicated. Even I don't understand them, but it helped us power our gravitational lens drive with enough energy to get us to another star system in less than one lifetime.*

I remembered hearing something about zero-point energy in a sci-fi movie, but hadn't paid attention. I nodded and thought, Did the attack succeed?

The hologram pointed at the image of the Earth. It zoomed in on the island of Lemuria. One minute the island rested peacefully in the Pacific and the next some massive force literally ripped it from the ocean floor, hurling it into outer space. I couldn't take my eyes off the image.

*What the designer of Atlantis's wrath did not account for, or perhaps they did and simply didn't care, was what would happen when you gouged a fifty-thousand-square-mile island out of the middle of the Pacific.*

I watched, fascinated, as the ocean rushed in to replace the mass that had been hurled away from the Earth. Giant waves rushed in, slamming together and then flowing rapidly outward. The waves devoured the Lemurian fleet and went on to swallow one island after another. When the wave reached Atlantis, it swept around the island continent faster than sound, scouring all the low-lying areas in its path.

*We thought that the worst was over as the initial waves receded. We tried to establish communications with the space port located in the highlands of Bendarsk and succeeded. Damage reports were horrendous. Our society had just about been wiped out. We were talking with the survivors at the spaceport as the true disaster began. When the gravitational lens ripped Lemuria from the*

Pacific, not only did it cause a mega-tsunami, but it caused the entire Pacific plate to shift. The first step was the eruption of multiple volcanos, including a long-dormant super volcano off the northeastern coast of the north island of New Zealand. We put on our suits and walked out on the surface to watch as the massive volcanic cloud enveloped our beloved Atlantis. We could see the lightning bolts in the clouds from the Moon with our naked eyes. It was horrible and spectacular at the same time. Within forty-eight hours, clouds from the eruptions had enshrouded the entire globe.

I watched the scene play out on the display.

How long did it last? I was starting to think of the hologram as a person.

The clouds began to dissipate in year three. By year four the third and final disaster revealed itself—a polar shift. Our island had always been near the southern polar region. My parents had a ski condo along the slopes of the Volentian range in the south. Now, the South Pole had shifted to the center of our island. The beautiful lowlands where I had grown up had been scoured by the tsunami and now were covered in ice. Our island nation had become what it is today, Antarctica and the South Pole. We tried to reestablish communications with someone, anyone, but were unable to do so. Finally, as our food supplies and hydroponics began to fail, we decided to return to the Earth. She paused as if in thought.

Where did you go?

She didn't answer. Instead she came closer to me and looked me in the eye. Charlie, we've detected gravitonic emanations from a remote area in Antarctica. The gravitational lens system must still be operational.

I stared into her eyes. They reminded me of my mother, the soft, loving looks she used to give me. I was about to tear up, so I looked away. And it still works? It could go off?

She nodded. If they can find and link a ZPEG to it, there's no telling the damage they could cause. It could be the end of your species. She paused to give me time to let what she'd said sink in.

The end of my species? I thought about the images of Lemuria being ripped away from the surface of the Earth. If that happened again, it would be catastrophic. Images of Hollywood disaster movies swarmed through my brain. Tsunamis would wipe out the coastlines, including my hometown of Seattle. I pictured the space needle toppling over as a giant wave came ashore. Mariner Stadium, where I'd spent many happy days with my father, would be inundated moments later. Inland cities would survive, but if volcanos ripped loose and clouds enveloped the Earth, hardly anyone would survive. It would be nuclear winter without nuclear weapons. I then remembered the disaster flick about Yellowstone. If it triggered the super volcano, the United States would be a goner. My stomach churned as my head drooped.

Galadriel placed her diaphanous hand on my shoulder. I could almost feel it. I lifted my head. *We need you to stop it. With your almost pure Atlantean blood, the holographic controller in the lab should recognize you if it is still functioning. If not, you will need this.* She pointed to one side. A hologram of an elaborate scepter appeared at her side. A golden ram's head crowned the top of a silver tube. The tube narrowed in the middle and then widened at its base. The base ended in a glowing crystal about the size of a baseball.

*Where will I get it?* Before she could answer, I felt a vibration through the floor and a small gust of wind blew my hair back. A strobe light began to flash as a siren sounded.

*Charlie, you've got to . . .* Galadriel faded away.

# CHAPTER 12
## LEMURIANS

G aladriel, come back! She didn't. The lights began to fade. I ran over to the huge vault-like door that had sealed me in the room. The air was definitely moving toward it. I had no clue where to go or what to do. I desperately pushed the buttons on the machine behind where the hologram had stood, but nothing happened. I looked at my air gauge. I only had a few minutes of air left in my suit.

I started gasping for breath. Was it my imagination?

"Calm down, Charlie. Think," I said to myself. The breeze blowing toward the big vault door had picked up. If it was blowing toward the door, then the leak was in that direction. The air must be coming from somewhere. I moved against the breeze. It led me to a small panel that might be a door. As I extended my hand forward, the familiar blue glow appeared. I tried to move my hand farther, but couldn't. A circle of clouds seemed to envelop me. I remembered the feeling, just like back at the Dome. Sure enough, the face of Trolga appeared in front of me. She laughed as her face morphed into the blend of a hawk and a human.

*Not leaving are you, Charlemagne? We will be with you momentarily.*

I struggled to free myself from the vision. The clouds cleared momentarily, and I saw the wall with the blue glow in front of me. The clouds swirled and then she was back.

*Growing stronger, aren't you. I like that.*

I focused as hard as I could and her face seemed to strain, but I couldn't break free. They had me. I felt something in my hand. I looked down. It was a baseball.

*Throw it, Charlie!* My uncle's voice!

I took my two-seam grip, did my wind up, and unleashed the hardest fastball I'd ever thrown. The expression on Trolga's harpy-like face suddenly changed to fear. Just before the ball reached her, the clouds evaporated.

*Go, Charlie, go!* I heard my uncle's voice as if he was right behind me. I didn't look back. I thrust my hand against the blue glow. A door slid open. I ran through. It shut behind me. I found myself in a long hall. I could breathe, but the air seemed thin. Something inside me drove me forward. I jogged down the corridor, passing several panels. They were probably doors, but I didn't stop. Another vibration shook the ground, this one larger than the last. The lights flickered. There. An open door at the end of the corridor. I sprinted for it. I made it through the door just as the lights went out. I turned back and looked down the corridor. Darkness had enveloped it. I stuck my hand against the wall. Nothing happened. The door wouldn't close.

I flipped on my suit's chest lights and looked around. The room was empty, but on the opposite side stood another airlock door. I struggled to catch my breath as I moved toward it. I rubbed my hands together and blew on them. My breath formed crystals in the air. I extended my hand and the faint blue glow appeared. I pressed my hand against it. Nothing. Then I heard it, the hiss of an airlock. The door swung open and I walked through. It was a small room with another airlock on the other side. I glanced back over my shoulder. Lights flickered off the wall of the corridor. Helmet lights.

I pushed the airlock door closed. It wouldn't seal. I tried the hand trick again against the wall. It didn't work. Maybe the pressure was off. It was getting hard to breath. I put my helmet on.

"How much oxygen do I have?"

The computer responded, "Six minutes and forty-three seconds at present consumption."

I flipped on the helmet lights and looked around. There was no panel against either door. The Atlanteans must have built in sensors that detected a hand, even through a space suit's glove. Frost began to gather on my face mask.

"What's the temperature?"

"Minus four degrees C and dropping."

Something had clearly screwed up the life-support system that I'd triggered when I'd first entered the cavern. I leaned against the airlock door and felt a click through my shoulder. It seemed to have finally sealed.

I scanned the room. Five Atlantean space suits hung along one wall. The helmets sat on a shelf above them. They looked just like the one the ancient alien had been wearing. I remembered how the meteorite hole that killed the astronaut had sealed itself and that it still contained air after a million years.

"Oxygen failure in two minutes," the computer droned in its monotone voice.

I didn't have much time. I tried to remove my helmet. It wouldn't budge.

"Computer, release helmet lock."

"The pressure is too low to permit you to remove your helmet safely."

"But I only have enough air for another minute! What does it matter?"

The computer didn't answer. Damn fail safe.

"Computer, emergency override. Unlatch my helmet!"

I felt a click, reached my hands up, yanked my helmet one quarter turn to the left and lifted it off. I took a deep breath. Cold needles burned my lungs. I had managed to hold my breath for over two minutes during diving class in the Bahamas. It would take almost that long to get the suit off. I popped my gloves off first and then deactivated the magnetic seam down the front of the suit. I pulled it apart and stepped out. I took a tentative sniff with my nose. There was at least some air here, but not much. I grabbed the suit that looked the closest to my size. When I touched it, the front pealed opened. I stepped in feet first and then pulled my arms through the sleeves. The suit sealed itself back up. Good sign. Maybe the air system would still work too.

I was starting to see stars. The helmet seemed out of reach. My feet were sliding out from under me. I focused, stretched my hand up, grabbed the helmet and slipped it on.

The next thing I knew, I was lying on the floor. I didn't hear any noise, but I was breathing again. It smelled like ocean air at a beach. I jumped for joy, which only resulted in banging my head against the ceiling. Fortunately, the helmet absorbed the shock or I'd have had quite a headache.

I looked through the small porthole in the door. Three space-suited figures approached the door. Two of them wore Clarksville security suits. Their visors were clear, and one of the men spotted me. He smiled, revealing a missing tooth. It was one of the men that I'd escaped from.

I moved to the other door and extended my hand. Now that the first door was sealed, this one opened slowly into a large space whose only illumination came from the open door behind me. I looked back. The three men from Clarksville had entered the space-suit room behind me. I shut the door. The only light shone through the door's porthole. I moved to one side so the Clarksville team wouldn't be able to see me. As I waited my eyes adjusted to the light. I began to make out shapes in the cavernous room. The Clarksville team tried the door. It didn't open for them, but I had no doubt that they'd blow it if need be.

I squinted, looking around. Several doors punctuated the wall to my left, but that wasn't what caught my eye. A perfect replica of a B-movie flying saucer rested in the middle of the large space. Disk-shaped, the edge of the ship sloped up toward the center, where a rounded bump rose up like a giant metallic pimple. The ship had no visible openings. I moved toward it. I'd covered half the distance when I heard banging on the airlock door. I loped quickly toward the saucer. I ran around it, but couldn't find a door or any other type of opening on this side either.

I leaned against the slope of the hull, not knowing what to do, when I felt a vibration through my feet. I looked back. The porthole in the door had shattered. One of the men was pointing a barrel through the broken porthole. Something pinged off the saucer next to me. A bullet! I ran around the saucer to put its bulk between me and the Clarksville guards.

As I entered the shadow of the saucer, I tripped and did a flip in the air. I flailed my arms and came down past the shelter of the saucer. I tucked and went into a roll. A poof of dust erupted in front of my face. I shoved myself back behind the bulk of the saucer and rolled into a ramp. It hadn't been there before. I ran up the ramp and into the saucer. As I entered, I glanced back. The ramp had retracted behind me. The lights flickered on down a hallway. It seemed to slope upwards. I followed the lights. A door slid open in front of me. I stepped in and the lights came up.

I stood at the edge of a round room about thirty feet across. Save for a large chair in the middle that looked as if Captain Kirk should be sitting in it, the room was empty. As I contemplated what to do, the seal on my suit popped. I began to panic, trying to hold the suit together. Then I realized that the suit's automated systems must have detected an acceptable atmosphere. I pulled the helmet off and took a deep breath. The air was chilly, but smelled good, with the same hint of a sea breeze I'd smelled before. I walked around the room, running my hand against the wall, hoping that my touch would activate something. Finally, I gave up, walked over to the control chair and sat down.

The chair molded to my body. It fit like a glove. I heard the sound of distant pings. I assumed that was the sound of bullets hitting the skin of the saucer.

I thought to myself, *I wish this thing had windows.* Immediately an image appeared in front of me. I could see the door to the hangar blown open and the three suited Clarksville men walking around the perimeter of the saucer. One held up his gun and shot at the saucer again. I heard another ping. One reached into the pouch at his side and pulled a rectangular block out. He started to put it against the skin of the saucer, but one of the other men yanked it away. Explosives! One of the men wanted to blow an opening into the saucer, but the other men were arguing with him. I didn't know what would happen or whether the saucer's skin would survive, but I didn't want to take a chance.

I wasn't sure what to do. I needed help. I looked around the room. An apparition appeared before me. It was similar to the woman that had appeared to me earlier, but the face was different.

The image spoke. "Do you have questions?"

I didn't have time to ponder the apparition this time. "Can you get us out of here?"

"To where?"

"There are guys out there that are about to blow a hole in the side of this craft. Anywhere."

The apparition smiled but did nothing.

"Up. One thousand feet straight up."

I settled deeper into the chair, but felt nothing but a slight vibration.

"I said up."

The apparition replied, "We are one thousand feet above the hangar."

I hadn't felt anything. "Are you sure?"

"Yes." The apparition nodded.

"What should I call you?"

"Whatever you like."

"Don't you have a name?" The apparition didn't reply. "Galadriel named herself, but I guess I'll have to do that for you. Shannon. I'll call you Shannon. Shannon, what are the men doing in the hangar?"

The holographic image reappeared and zoomed in. They were staring up at the saucer. One raised a weapon and fired. This time there was no ping.

I cringed, but heard nothing. "What happened to the bullet, Shannon?"

"The gravitonic drive repulsed the bullet. Might I suggest that we move away from this location?" Shannon gave a smug smile.

"Sure. Why?"

"The station autodestruct countdown is near completion."

"What?" I lifted myself out of the chair.

"The Lemurians triggered the station auto-destruct when they penetrated the control room."

I remembered the strobe light flashing in the lab and the apparition disappearing while she was trying to tell me something.

"Move us to a safe distance." I gripped the arms of the chair, waiting for the acceleration. Nothing.

"Done."

"How far are we?"

"We are 10.237 of your miles to the north of our last position."

"Show me." I pointed to where the holograms had appeared.

The holographic image reappeared, this time showing the Lunar surface. I couldn't make out where the station was and didn't see Clarksville.

"Where's the station?"

A red dot appeared in the hologram.

"How long before the self-destruct is complete?"

Red lights appeared next to the red dot indicating the station. They were changing very rapidly.

"Can you translate the numbers into seconds so I can understand?"

Shannon nodded, and Arabic numerals replaced the indecipherable red lights. Six, five, four, three, two, one, zero. A crater suddenly appeared where the red dot had been, and a small cloud of dust rose up.

# CHAPTER 13
## WHERE'S NIM?

I stared. Given the distance, I couldn't fathom the extent of the damage.

"Is the base gone?" I thought about the beautiful apparition and about all of the knowledge and information lost and cringed. My parents had spent their lives looking for evidence of Atlantis, and I had stumbled into an Atlantean base only to watch it get blown to smithereens.

Shannon closed her eyes. When they opened she smiled again. "Sensors indicate that the antimatter totally destroyed all evidence of the station."

"What about the people that were shooting at me?"

"The Lemurians have been liquidated."

That smile appeared again. Shannon was very different than the prior hologram—much less alive, much colder.

"You mean dead."

"Yes."

Despite the Lemurians having chased me out of the Atlantean base, I felt bad about it. But I was starting to think about them as Lemurians rather than as Clarksville security. I looked at the holographic image of the lunar surface.

"Where's Clarksville?"

The image shifted slightly, and then the lights of Clarksville appeared on the screen. I could make out the glow from central Dome.

"Can they see us on radar?" I pictured red lights flashing at the spaceport as a UFO appeared on their radar.

That smile appeared again. "I have scanned their systems. They cannot detect us."

I breathed a sigh of relief.

"I do detect a severe radiation leak in the northwest quadrant of Clarksville."

"What? Zoom in."

The university complex filled the screen. The lab where my uncle had examined the Atlantean was in a section highlighted in red. Much of the city around the university was in yellow.

"Zoom out." I wanted to see the whole city.

The hologram zoomed out. A yellow stain crept toward the heart of the city.

"What does the red and yellow mean?"

"Red is a severe hazard zone where most humanoid life cannot survive unshielded for more than twelve hours. Yellow is a moderate hazard area where humanoid life can survive unshielded for up to a week."

I shuddered. All my friends were down there. Rhea was down there. I noticed several flares by the spaceport—ships taking off. It looked like they were evacuating Clarksville. There weren't enough ships to get everyone away. They'd have to evacuate in phases. I hoped the evacuation went by the old "women and children first" adage and that my friends had gotten away. I remembered the safety lectures that I'd gotten my first week on Clarksville. Each part of the city had storm shelters for severe solar flares. They were heavily shielded and had supplies in place for over a week. That should give the people some protection while ships came to evacuate them.

What caused the leak? It had to be Trolga and her cronies.

Shannon appeared in front of me. "I detect an Atlantean signal just outside of the red zone."

"What? Where?"

The holographic image of the city zoomed in on a spot on the lunar surface a klick or so away from the university hangar. The image appeared to be getting nearer.

The Atlanteans had been gone for millennia. How could there be an Atlantean signal? "Let's go take a look."

"We are already on the way. Protocol 3847.12 requires that the ship investigate any Atlantean distress signals."

We closed the distance rapidly, even though I felt no acceleration. As we did, the image resolved into a space-suited figure pushing a hand sled forward. Unfortunately, a pool of red expanded rapidly toward him. It would envelop him within minutes.

"Can we go down there and save him?"

"Protocol requires that the protection of those on the ship override the distress call. Shutting down the graviton drive will stop shielding from radiation and risk discovery by the humans in the adjacent city."

We got closer to the fugitive. Something looked familiar. "Zoom in!"

The hologram zoomed in on the fugitives. It was my uncle! I recognized his suit.

"Rescue them now!"

"My programing . . ."

"I don't give a damn! Land now and save them."

Shannon just stood there. Nothing happened.

I thought for a minute. "That's a command, Shannon. Do it. Now!"

The ship descended toward my uncle. As we approached, he looked up. I grabbed my suit and helmet and ran out the door. "Show me the way to the airlock and let me know when we land." I ran down the halls as glowing arrows led me back to the airlock and the ramp where I'd entered the ship. I stepped into the suit and pulled it up. It sealed itself.

Shannon appeared in front of me. "We have landed."

I slipped on the helmet. I felt a slight pressure change as it sealed itself. "Open the door and lower the ramp." I didn't have long to wait and loped down the ramp. My uncle was about fifty yards away. I made it to him in a couple of bounds.

"Uncle Merl!" He made no response. "Computer, can the suit radio broadcast over human frequencies?"

"Yes, if you provide the correct frequency."

I didn't know the frequency, but did know that the radiation was bearing down on us. I grabbed his arm and pulled, but he wouldn't let go of the hand sled. Rather than argue, I got behind it and we both pushed it toward the ramp. Good thing we were on the Moon, because it felt like a couple hundred pounds. I have no clue how my uncle had gotten this far. We pushed the sled up the ramp and got it aboard. The door shut without a command.

Shannon was there, waiting. "Up. Get us out of here." I didn't feel anything, but assumed that we were moving away from the danger zone.

I pulled my helmet off, the suit released, and I stepped out of it. I walked behind my uncle to help him unlatch the helmet. It came off, and my uncle shook his grey hair around.

"Good to see you, Charlie." He grabbed me in a bear hug. "You had to know the radiation was close. Why didn't you abandon the sled?"

"I couldn't." He went to the back of the sled, opened the compartment and pulled out a large airtight box. He unlatched it and then hit the unseal button. As the door hit the floor, a blur jumped out, banged against him, and then sprang into my arms.

"Nim!" I held onto the cat, and this one time she actually let me give her a hug. Knowing not to press my luck, I gave her a quick rub behind the ears and lowered her to the deck. "So . . . what happened? Last time I saw you, security was taking you away."

Uncle Merl looked me in the eye. "I'd rather hear your story first. After all, you landed in a flying saucer, rescuing me and Nim from almost certain death!"

"But how'd you have an Atlantean signal, since that's what we picked up?"

My uncle smiled and pulled the damaged Atlantean helmet from the sled. "I couldn't leave this behind, now could I? Guess it sent out a distress beacon when it detected your ship. Damn impressive technology, what?"

I nodded. Unbelievable was more like it. As we headed for the control room, I started to tell Uncle Merl my tale about the Atlanteans, the Atlantean base and Galadriel. My uncle stopped suddenly. He stuck his hand out against the wall. A door slid back.

I gave my uncle a quizzical look. He shrugged and walked into the room. I followed. "Thirsty?" He stuck his hand against the wall again. A gap appeared in the wall with a glass in it.

I pointed, "how'd you do that?"

"All in good time, lad." He took the glass, tasted its content and frowned. "Water. I'd wanted a bourbon and soda. Maybe the technology's not that great."

I placed my hand against the wall, thinking Coke. All that it dispensed was water as well. But then, the ship was a million years old.

"Now, Charlie, tell me, did Galadriel ask you to do anything?"

I gave him a quizzical look. "How do you know about her?"

He just shrugged and said nothing. After a minute of silence, I gave up. "She did."

My uncle bent down. A chair appeared below him. "And . . ."

My Uncle clearly knew more than he was telling me. "Well, she told me that someone had discovered the device that destroyed Lemuria. She said that if they activated it, the device could wipe out mankind. Is that true?"

My uncle pulled on his beard. "That's serious. Are you sure that's what she said?"

I nodded. "She wanted me to shut it down. She showed me a picture of something that looked like a ram's head scepter, but before she could say any more, sirens sounded and she disappeared."

My uncle appeared lost in thought. He mumbled something that I didn't catch and left the room.

I followed behind him. "Maybe we should ask Shannon about the scepter?"

"Shannon?" He kept walking.

"She's a hologram of the ship's AI, I think."

When we entered the control room, Shannon shimmered there, waiting for us.

I addressed her. "Shannon, do you know Galadriel?" She did not respond. "You know, Galadriel, from the base. Almost six feet tall, blond hair, almond-shaped turquoise eyes. You know, Galadriel."

"No data available about base personnel." Shannon's expression did not change.

"How about a ram's head scepter?" I thought about the image of the scepter and it appeared in front of me. "That's it!" I pointed. "Shannon, what is it?"

"I have no data on that object."

"Then how did you display it?"

Shannon did not respond. My uncle frowned.

"She's definitely not like Galadriel. Galadriel acted like a real person." I kicked the ground in frustration.

"Perhaps Galadriel was more than a mere holographic interface to an AI, which is what Shannon seems to be." Uncle Merl walked around Shannon. She turned her head and watched, but did nothing else. He stopped by me and waved his hand through her. Still no reaction.

"Shannon, show me where we are." Uncle Merl used his stern voice, but Shannon did nothing.

He turned to me. "How did you get her to do anything?"

I shrugged. "Don't know. I just talk to her and she seems to do what I ask." I turned to Shannon. "Display where we are."

Instantly a holographic display appeared in front of us. We were looking down on Clarksville from a great altitude. Several ships appeared to be launching from the spaceport.

My uncle walked toward the display. "Zoom in on this section." He pointed to the area around the university. Nothing happened. He turned toward me with a quizzical look.

I shrugged. "Guess she only answers to me. Shannon, zoom in where my uncle pointed."

She instantly complied.

"See the vapor pouring out from the reactor building?" He pointed as I walked closer to get a better look.

I nodded.

"The bastards scrammed the reactor. Left me locked in the control room."

"How'd you get out?"

Uncle Merl waved his hand at me dismissively and walked back to Shannon. "Charlie, introduce me to Shannon."

"What?"

He extended his hand toward the hologram. "Introduce me."

I cleared my throat. "Shannon, this is my uncle, Dr. Merlin Ambrose. Uncle Merl, this is Shannon."

Uncle Merl stepped forward. "A pleasure to meet you, Shannon."

She looked at my uncle. "Uncle, Dr. Merlin Ambrose, you are now recognized by my systems."

"Thank you, Shannon, and please, call me Merl."

Shannon did not reply.

"Well, Charlie, you've had quite the adventure, and I have a feeling it's just beginning." My uncle smiled like the Cheshire Cat.

"What do you mean?" I didn't like his smile.

"Well, you've found out that you are an heir to Atlantis. I suggest that we find out more about this scepter and your quest. The Lady actually said it could destroy mankind?"

I nodded. "She mentioned a ZPEG and something about a gravitational lens device." My uncle said nothing and continued to pull on his beard. "Do you know what a ZPEG . . ."

"Of course, of course. It's been lost since she took it so many years ago. If the Lemurians find it, and if they use it to start a gravitational lens . . ." My uncle paused again, staring off at the side of the ship.

"So, you take what Galadriel told me seriously? What if I was just imagining her? What if this is a dream and I'll be waking up in my bed in Bothell soon?"

My uncle let loose a guffaw like a truck driver and slapped me on the back. "Good one, Charlie. Now get serious. We've got . . . Shannon, how long until you can get us to near Earth orbit?"

"Four hours and thirty-one minutes."

"You've got to be kidding. It took me three days, four if you count the stop at the Hilton in geosync, to get here."

Shannon was at least smart enough not to respond. She just stood there.

Uncle Merl sat down in the control chair and Nim jumped into his lap. He pointed to his right and a chair appeared up out of the floor next to his.

"Amazing technology these Atlanteans had, wouldn't you say? So, we've got a couple of hours. Charlie, did you bring your rucksack?"

I nodded. I'd gotten used to my uncle calling a backpack a rucksack. I looked around the control room, but didn't see it. I was sure that I'd dropped it next to the control chair when I'd first walked in.

"What's wrong?" My uncle was frowning.

"I left my backpack in here before running out to get you. But it's not here." The room had no furniture in it other than the two chairs we were in, and no furniture or drawers to speak of. In fact, it was so empty, it was a bit creepy.

"Shannon, where's my nephew's rucksack?" The hologram pointed to the wall behind us. A door in the wall lifted up and my rucksack slid out. There'd been no seam or indication of a door before. It was just like the ramp and the chairs.

"Bring it to me, boy." My uncle waved his hand at it. By the time I reached it, the door had closed. I felt the wall—no seam. I carried the rucksack over to my uncle. He opened it up.

"Jif peanut butter!" He pulled the jar out. "This is mine, isn't it?" He looked accusingly at me, but screwed the top off, stuck his index finger in, scooped out a big blob and shoved it in his mouth. He gave me a sideways glare, but then made the yummy sound.

"Remember, you told me to get a sandwich for you. The guards shoved it in my backpack when they grabbed me."

He nodded and handed me the jar. "Don't worry, boy. Just kidding. Glad you had something to eat. Have some."

I shrugged and slid my finger around the edge of the jar. I slipped it into my mouth and sucked the peanut butter off my finger. My uncle was dumping everything out of my backpack. The baseball from my no hitter rolled toward me. I picked it up and flipped it upwards. I almost missed catching it since it came down much quicker than it would have on the Moon. In fact, it came down as fast as if we were on Earth. I realized that I actually did feel heavier.

"Ah, here it is." My uncle picked up my mother's Atlantis journal. "Your mother showed me this years ago and I seem to recall . . ." He flipped through pages. "Right here." He pointed and held out the open page to me. There was a drawing in my mother's hand of a ram's head scepter. Under it mother had written, "Scepter of Apollymi?"

My jaw dropped open. "Damn. That's it!" I turned to Uncle Merl. "Who's Apollymi?"

Uncle Merl's eyes weren't focused on me. It looked as if he were focused on something off in the distance. "She's the goddess of life, death, war, wisdom and destruction in Atlantean lore, and the wife of Archon, the chief Atlantean god."

He mumbled something under his breath about Nim. I looked around but didn't see Nim.

Uncle Merl's eyes refocused on me. "Well, don't just stand there, boy, put all of your crap back away."

# CHAPTER 14
## RETURN TO EARTH

The Earth grew rapidly in the viewscreen.

"So, where are we heading?" I stared at the approaching Earth.

"That's what I'm trying to figure out." He squinted as he read my mother's journal.

"According to your mother's notes, the Scepter of Apollymi first appeared in ancient Egyptian lore. It was said to be a gift from the sun god, Ra. The Egyptians referred to it as the Scepter of Ammon Ra and left it in the temple of Ra in Heliopolis. It is said that Alexander the Great examined the scepter on his march from Pelucium to Memphis, and that an aura surrounded his head when he touched it. Shortly after Alexander's visit, the scepter disappeared from Heliopolis.

"It reappeared in Rome at the time of Julius Caesar. Some say that Cleopatra gave it to Caesar as a gift. Emperor Trajan was said to have taken it with him in his campaign against the Parthians."

I hated when my uncle got into one of his historical digressions, but knew better than to interrupt. The ship seemed to have entered a geosynchronous orbit, awaiting instructions.

"Hadrian then took the scepter with him to England where a slave allegedly stole it. It didn't reappear until Sir Galahad delivered it into the hands of Arthur Pendragon, claiming to have won it from a witch in battle." My uncle looked up and his eyes appeared to glaze over after his mention of Arthur Pendragon. "Exca—"

I tapped my uncle on the shoulder. Something had whizzed by the view screen.

"What?"

"Something almost hit us."

He looked up from the journal. "Why that's ridiculous. There's no way that this ship would get close to another ship or satellite. It's totally invisible to current technology."

As he spoke the ship shuddered. "Shannon, what was that?"

The hologram appeared in front of us. "An energy discharge from a plasma cannon."

I'd only heard of plasma cannons in sci-fi movies. "Plasma cannon? Can it hurt the ship?" I looked at my uncle with concern.

The craft shuddered again and Shannon flickered.

My uncle didn't need Shannon to answer. "Take us down, emergency trajectory!" The ship lurched forward. "Damn, the hit's damaged the inertial compensators." My uncle looked over at me, giving me a half-hearted smile. "I guess your friend Trolga somehow knows you're on this ship."

"How?" Trolga had attacked me several times and I guessed that she had sent the guards after me. "She's Lemurian?"

My uncle nodded. "I had hoped that she wouldn't figure out your heritage, but your bloodline is too pure. You're the closest thing to a true Atlantean that has been born in millennia. I sensed that you had the 'gift' when I first held you as an infant, but neither of your parents had exhibited any special Atlantean abilities. Your mother must have had some latent ability because she obsessed so about Atlantis."

The ship shuddered once again. Shannon flickered in and out. I glanced at the screen. We were much lower, skirting the upper atmosphere over the Indian Ocean.

"Manual controls, Shannon." A console rose out of the floor in front of my uncle.

He looked at me. "In case we lose the telepathic link to the ship's systems."

Another jolt shook the ship, rattling my teeth. The lights flickered.

My uncle stared intently at the controls. I watched the screen. A beam of light flashed from a spot north of India just before it slid behind us. The screen went dark. The ship shuddered again.

My uncle studied the controls in front of him. "Damn, that was too close. Northern India, as I suspected. Our orbit's lower now so we should be out of range. Shannon, how's the hull integrity?" No answer. "Shannon?"

An image flickered into existence, but then faded away.

Uncle Merl shook his head. "The neural interface is shot and I'm no pilot. Charlie, buckle in. This could get rough." A seat-belt-like strap and two shoulder straps looped over me, securing me into the seat.

"Can you get the screen back up?" I didn't like just sitting looking at the white wall.

My uncle didn't answer. Perspiration glistened on his weathered brow. The ship bucked a few more times.

"We're going in fast and steep. We should make it to the Pacific Northwest before I have to set her down. Grab your stuff." The seat belts released. My backpack was on the ground in front of me. I got out of the chair and crawled on the floor, grabbed my mother's journal and the baseball that had been rolling around, and shoved them back in the backpack. I then climbed back in the chair and the seat belts looped around me again.

The screen popped back to life. "Computer interface working again?" I asked hopefully.

My uncle shook his head. "Nope. Just like to see where I'm going. No point before because the ionization of reentry would have blocked the view."

I could see the Pacific below us, the coastline approached much more rapidly than if we were in a jet. I couldn't tell where we were along the coast.

"Are you going to be able to land?"

My uncle didn't answer as the craft began to buck like a mechanical bull. He looked over at me, pushed a button, and a bubble popped up over me. His lips didn't move, but I heard him in my head: *Don't worry, Charlie, it's a survival pod. It will fill with hyper-oxygenated fluid to cushion the g-forces. You'll be able to breathe.* Fluid began to fill the chamber. I panicked, struggling against the restraints as it reached my chest. I banged on the bubble, glaring at my uncle. He looked back at me, calmly.

I shut my mouth, holding my breath. It was over my head. *Open your mouth and inhale, Charlie. Don't fight it.* We must have hit a rough patch, because the room tilted, bucking my uncle against his restraints. I felt nothing in the bubble. I was still holding my breath, but couldn't for much longer. Looking over at my uncle, I took a deep breath. It felt really weird, like inhaling warm Jell-O. I thought I'd gag, but didn't. I exhaled and then inhaled again. The fluid was warm. Breathing it gave me a feeling of well-being.

*This is where you get out, Charlie. Complete the quest. I'll join you if I can.*

I could hear nothing, so assumed that my uncle was speaking telepathically again. *What do you mean, I'm getting out? Aren't you landing?*

He smiled at me and gave a brief salute. The floor opened below me. The next thing I knew, I was outside the ship, rapidly dropping away from it. I looked down. Nothing but trees.

# CHAPTER 15
## THE IRIDESCENT SPHERE

An iridescent sphere hovered above the spot where Uncle Merl had ejected Charlie's escape pod. As the light from the setting sun hit it, a cascade of colors shimmered across the sphere. Inside the sphere a tall woman with flaxen hair watched as the Atlantean ship piloted by Merl Ambrose bucked back and forth and drifted closer to the treetops.

*He is going to make it.* The Lady Galadriel projected her thoughts to the woman in the sphere.

While the thought had sounded like a statement, Nimue knew it was really a question. *Of course. Despite what he said to his young charge, Merlin is an exceptional pilot.* As if in answer the ship stabilized just above the tree line, hovered and then shot off to the east.

Galadriel breathed a sigh of relief. *Yes, yes, I know that, but this brazen attack...."*

Nimue felt Galadriel's mental shudder. *You're growing weaker. They know it.*

Galadriel let out a mental sigh. *They seemed willing to wait it out, to not challenge us.*

*But if Charlie's the one, your breakthrough, then they have no choice. They can't risk that your genetics program has succeeded.* The bubble ship bobbed up and down in the light breeze. Nimue took a moment to look to the west, toward the setting sun.

*You're probably right. Rusha and her minions are getting aggressive. Their scout ships have even ventured close to my enclave. As to Charlie, he's related to Merlin. He has latent abilities and our technology recognizes him. He must be the one, but he's sooo young.*

Nimue nodded. *And untrained.* She paused, staring off toward where Merl's ship had vanished over the horizon. *Rusha's plan is bold. I can envision its tendrils stretching off into the future.* Nimue projected images of a world shrouded in shadow. Bones of what once were the proud structures of mankind littered the coastlines of the world. The shattered remnants of mankind foraged for food and shelter as nightmarish creatures rushed in, snatching up any stragglers. An image of a demonic head smiling with a lamprey-like mouth, straggly threads of what was once hair and piercing red catlike eyes overlooking a herd of malnourished humans, appeared in front of Nimue. The demon lifted a polished human skull, drank from it, letting blood drip down her chin, and laughed. She seemed to be staring right at Nimue.

Galadriel emitted a mental sigh at the image, an image she'd seen centuries before when she'd stopped Rusha from capturing Charlie's great-great-grandmother. The Lemurian solution to longevity beyond that of the Atlanteans was ghastly. At least Galadriel and her fellow Atlanteans had managed to keep Rusha and the other Lemurians in check until recently. But now Rusha was thumbing her nose at Galadriel. The Lemurians knew that Galadriel and the few other surviving Atlanteans were growing weak. *You know what they plan and yet you don't intervene. You could help us—help Charlie.*

Nimue shook her head. *You know I can't. Kronos engineered that into my DNA.*

*But your craft deflected one of the plasma bolts.*

*Did it?* Nimue raised an eyebrow.

*We've worked together for millennia. Isn't that intervention?* Nimue had helped save Aku Brugal's ancestors from the onslaught of *Homo sapiens*, leading them to safety in old Atlantean bases and away from aggressive human tribes.

Nimue shook her head. *What appeared like intervention to you was merely an effort to keep things as they should be. I do what must be done.*

Galadriel took a deep breath. *What makes you the judge of what must be done?*

*You should know better than that. After all Kronos, Epaphos and Philipus oversaw my genetic design. Didn't they share it with you. Besides, didn't the Greeks model Themis, the Goddess of Justice, after you and not me? They must have had a reason.*

Galadriel brushed the comment to the side before it revived too many memories. *You are not a robot and you still have free will.* Galadriel's thoughts sounded irritated.

Nimue shook her head. *Free will is exactly the point. You, above all, should know that. I will not intervene as you did when engineering* Homo sapiens *and* Homo sapiens atlantean, *let alone me.*

Galadriel felt as if she were fencing with a master. It exhausted her. *But the Lemurians have engineered monsters. They killed your siblings at Toba. If Rusha succeeds, she will destroy all that we have worked to create.* Galadriel broadcast an image of Rusha sitting on a huge golden throne. She pointed into a herd of humans. A huge hulking creature covered in matted white fur drove the selected human forward with a cattle prod. When the victim, a young male, reached Rusha, the hulking beast forced it to its knees. Rusha pick it up by the neck. It thrashed and struggled, kicking its legs, but Rusha's one-handed grip did not slip. She lifted it, bit into its neck and sucked until its legs stopped kicking. She then dropped the husk to the ground and pointed to another before the image faded. *How can you let them fulfill their plan?*

Nimue shook her head. *You didn't doubt yourself when you saved me after Toba. You must be more exhausted than I thought.* There was a hint of sadness in Nimue's thoughts. *You and your compatriots have done well. Have faith. Your plan seems to be coming to fruition.* Homo sapiens *is robust, while the Lemurians are ancient with an exhausted genetic line.* Homo sapiens atlantean, *while in its infancy, may prove even more robust and a worthy steward for this world.*

*But you could guaranty that. Charlie is young—untrained. He needs help. Rusha and her minions could crush him.* Galadriel projected an image of Charlie standing in front of her in the lunar base. With his hair in a braid and his pointed ears he looked every inch an adolescent Atlantean.

When Nimue didn't answer, she continued, *You took the Scepter when Charlie's ancestor threw it in the lake. Wasn't that intervention? Why can't you at least guide him to it or hide it where it will never be found?*

Nimue shook her head. *Accepting a gift is not intervention. And I did what had to be done. Rusha's cousin, the Baobah Sith, almost took the Scepter before it was given back to me. It is safe. If it is Charlie's destiny to find it, he will.*

*But Rusha may beat him to it or find another ZPEG.* Galadriel took a deep breath and coughed.

Nimue shook her head. Their conversation had taxed Galadriel's strength. She shielded that thought and projected another. *Trust yourself and trust young Charlemagne. Faith, free will and instinct are wonderful things. What should happen will happen.* Nimue's thoughts faded as the sphere started drifting up and then shot away from the forest.

# CHAPTER 16
## SASQUATCH

Idropped like a stone. Even with the fluid to cushion the impact, there was no way that I'd survive. Just before hitting the branches, the pod jerked to a halt. I passed out. When I came to, I was lying on a mossy carpet below a giant spruce tree. I sat up and looked around. There was no evidence of the escape pod, my clothes were dry, and I felt like I had just awakened from a great night's sleep. Had I been dreaming? I stood up, picked up my backpack and looked around. Broken branches surrounded me. I looked up. Sure enough, I could see a pathway of broken branches where the pod had descended. I looked down. I could just make out a slight indentation in the moss and leaves. I touched the middle of the indentation. It felt wet. I rubbed my fingers together. They felt slick, but as I rubbed them, the slickness disappeared, kind of like that instant hand sanitizer we used instead of soap on the Moon.

I took stock of my situation. We'd been over the west coast, but I could be just about anywhere. Huge trees surrounded me. It was starting to get dark. I could be in a valley or it could be late in the day. I couldn't tell. I put my backpack down and opened it. I had about half a jar of Jiff peanut butter, a quart of water, a couple of generic energy bars from the cafeteria, a flashlight, a small Swiss army knife my father had given me, a T-shirt and pair of underpants, my mother's journal, the game ball from my no hitter and my glove. I took a sip of water and repacked my backpack, putting the knife in my pocket. Too bad I didn't have a compass, but, even if I did, I would have no clue which direction to go in. I started walking toward the light, assuming that would be west. If I could find a creek, I could follow it down and, hopefully, reach civilization.

After trudging forward for half an hour, I decided to make camp. No point in breaking an ankle wandering around in the dark. I'd seen on a survival vid that a human eye can see the light of a candle for over thirty miles away from a mountaintop. The trees were in the way, but maybe I'd get lucky and see lights off in the distance. I put my backpack down between two huge roots and began to wander around, looking for leaves that I could use for bedding. The ground was wet so I doubted that I'd be able to build a fire. I didn't have any matches and didn't think I'd be able to start a fire by rubbing two sticks together anyway. Fortunately, it was late May and shouldn't get too cold. Also, my clothes were well insulated and made to wear under a space suit. They should keep me warm.

I'd dumped the first pile of brush in front of my backpack and was going to gather more when I caught some movement out of the corner of my eye. I froze. I listened. Nothing. I collected more leaves and moss. I heard something. I whipped out my flashlight and shone it into a pair of glowing eyes. I laughed as the squirrel scampered up a tree.

I sat down and began to fluff the leaves and moss into a make-shift bed against one of the large tree roots. When done, I leaned back against the tree root and took a deep breath. While dark, my eyes had acclimated enough to see the outline of the trees around me. I looked up and could see a bright star through a gap in the trees.

I thought about Uncle Merl and Nim and wondered what had happened to them. The ship had been in trouble or my uncle wouldn't have forced me into an escape pod. I remembered the image of my uncle in my head telling me what to do in the Atlantean base on the Moon. If I was telepathic, maybe I could contact him that way. I leaned against the root, closed my eyes and began to concentrate, trying to focus on an image of my uncle. Nothing. I balled my hands into fists and tried to shout in my thoughts. Still nothing. I began to think about Rhea and Jamie, to wonder where they were and whether they'd been evacuated. Would I ever see either of them again? My eyes began to cloud over, but I bit my lip.

Leaves rustled to my left and then stopped. Must be that squirrel again. I grabbed my flashlight and stood up.

"Ok, Mr. Squirrel, come out, come out wherever you are." I shone the flashlight and walked forward. I didn't see anything. I heard something to my right and whipped the flashlight around in that direction. Again, nothing. My steps made a huge racket no matter how quietly I tried to walk. I heard it again. I shone the light, but still nothing. Could be something small under the leaves. When it's deathly silent, a beetle can sound like a grizzly.

I turned back to my makeshift camp, but felt like Peter Parker with my spidey senses tingling. I heard another rustle of leaves behind me, but didn't turn. I stopped, inhaled deeply three times and then jumped around, the beam of the flashlight whipping through the darkness. It went past something, so I swung it back around. I nearly dropped the flashlight. The beam outlined a creature covered in fur from head to foot, standing nearly seven feet tall. His mouth opened to reveal long, yellowed canines. I wanted it to be a bear, but no, it had to be—Bigfoot!

I backed slowly away from the creature when I heard something rustle behind me again. This time, I turned slowly. Another one. This one, while shorter, appeared even bigger. I looked from one to the other. Neither was making a sound or a move toward me. I moved forward, glancing from side to side to see if either sasquatch would make a move toward me. They didn't. I wondered how fast a 'squatch was, hoping that I was faster. I would make a break for it when I reached the large tree in front of me. As I approached the tree, another one stepped out from behind it, blocking my escape. He opened his mouth, almost as if he were smiling, but I focused on the size of his canines. Even though I grew up in the Pacific Northwest, and despite my parents' stories of seeing one, I'd never believed in Bigfoot. Now I wondered why they'd never been proven to exist. Maybe it was because they killed and ate anyone that observed them.

I turned and looked back at the tree. My backpack lay against it. I might just be able to run up the huge root like a ramp, jump and reach the first branch. It didn't look like these brutes could climb, so getting up the tree might be my only means of escape. Doubt crept into my mind as I remembered jumping on the Moon. Here on Earth, my muscles were weak, but I had to try. I was about to dash toward the huge root and vault up into the tree when another 'squatch casually walked out from behind the tree. I was surrounded.

I looked around. Too smaller 'squatches had joined the others, blocking any possible avenue of retreat. While smaller, these 'squatches were still six inches taller than me. They appeared to be females, but, then again, with all that fur, it was hard to tell. I rubbed the sweat off my palms on my pants, feeling the Swiss army knife in my pocket. I pulled it out, knowing that it wouldn't do much good, but still feeling a little better.

At that, the large 'squatch near my backpack took a huge stride forward. He was wearing a pair of Wayfarer sunglasses! He lifted his hand and pointed something at me.

"Excuse me, old chap, but that wouldn't happen to be a light?"

I was too stunned to reply.

"I say, is that a lighter in your hand. Seems my pipe went out and I'd sorely like a light." The huge 'squatch bared his teeth in what I hoped was a grin.

After the momentary shock wore off, I started laughing. I couldn't seem to stop, even as the circle of sasquatches closed in around me. All of them seemed to be wearing sunglasses of various brands, the smallest, a pair of Gargoyles like the Terminator.

"What's so funny, lad?" The large 'squatch tapped a pipe against the palm of his hand and pointed it at me again.

"I crash-land a flying saucer in the middle of the Pacific Northwest to be surrounded by a family of sasquatches with British accents wearing sunglasses at night, one looking for a light? Where are the cameras? Who's yanking my chain?" I shouted, "Uncle Merl, come on out." I looked around.

The large 'squatch stuck the pipe between his teeth, took an ineffective puff. "Damn, I really need that light. Don't get to smoke below ground much." He took the pipe out of his mouth and put it in a pouch at his side. "Now, by Uncle Merl, you wouldn't mean that old reprobate, Merlin Ambrose?"

This couldn't be real. "So, you know my uncle?"

"Of course. Known him since I was a mere pup, about your height."

"By the way, these are some awesome costumes he got for you. What do you do, work in Hollywood?" I grabbed a bunch of hair at the 'squatch's midsection and pulled.

"Stop that." He batted my hand away and took a step forward, stopping inches in front of me. He leaned forward. For the first time, I smelled something. It wasn't the grotesque smell of the infamous skunk ape, but a hint of jasmine. "No reason to be insulting, young man. We would never work in Hollywood. Not since George Lucas rejected my uncle for the roll of Chewbacca."

I stared up at him, wide-mouthed.

"He was in the running for the role, but told Lucas he thought the character's name should be Chimichanga, not Chewbacca!"

I stood there, speechless, until he pounded my back and let out a frightful guffaw. "That's a joke, lad." All of the 'squatches seemed to be laughing. He put his arm around my shoulder and rubbed my head with his other hand.

"Stop that!" I knocked his arm away.

He stepped back and let out a roar. "If he's going to be rude, maybe we should just par-boil 'im and eat 'im!" I stepped back, bumping into one of the smaller 'squatches. She gave me a gentle shove forward. The big 'squatch grinned. "Another joke, lad. You clearly don't have your uncle's sense of humor. But you're right. I've taken too many liberties even though we have not been properly introduced. My name is . . ." He let loose with a long and loud ululation that hurt my ears. "But since you might have trouble with our language, call me Aku Brugal."

"Ok . . . Aku Brugal. My name's Charlie Thomas." I extended my hand. His hand swallowed mine, but, fortunately, he did not squeeze too tight when he shook it.

"Pleasure to meet you, Master Thomas." He smiled and put his arm around me. "I bet you're hungry."

I nodded. He whipped out another pair of Wayfarer sunglasses from a pouch at his side and handed them to me. "Put these on and follow me."

"Why sunglasses?"

"Just put them on."

The rest of his tribe disappeared into the dark. I shrugged and put them on. Immediately the forest brightened up as if it were day.

"Night vision?"

Aku Brugal nodded. He strode forward as I struggled to keep up.

"Why Wayfarers?"

"Because I'm a *Risky Business* fan."

I wasn't sure what he meant by that, but he headed off at a quick pace. I struggled to keep up.

# CHAPTER 17
## UNDERGROUND

We trudged through the forest for over half an hour. Breathing heavily, I could barely keep up. We arrived at a creek about eight feet across. Aku Brugal jumped it like a gazelle. My legs ached. No way I'd make it. I searched for a minute and saw a few large stones that weren't too far apart. I hopped from one to the next. Aku Brugal was waiting for me, leaning against a tree, holding the unlit pipe between his lips. He pulled it out, tapped it on his palm, slipped it in his pouch, and started off again.

He muttered under his breath, but the only word I caught was "humans."

His long loping strides outpaced me again. I'd thought I was in good shape, but months on the Moon must have atrophied my muscles. I ran, but couldn't keep up. He disappeared in front of me, but had left a trail of broken branches along a narrow game trail that even I could follow. I spotted a glow in the distance and headed for it. When I caught up with him, he was leaning against the face of a cliff that rose roughly forty feet up, puffing on his pipe.

He blew a smoke ring toward me. "Found a match, thank goodness. Can't smoke at home. He took one more puff, blew out another smoke ring, tapped the tobacco out on his palm and put the pipe away.

"Ready?" He asked.

I was still breathing heavily. I tilted my head up. "Up or around?"

He laughed. "Neither. In." He placed his hand against the cliff face.

"After you." He gave me a bow and extended his hand toward the cliff face.

I walked forward and reached toward the face of the cliff. My hand passed right through the rock!

A large hand pressed into my back and, the next thing I knew, Aku Brugal shoved me through. I stumbled into a perfectly rectangular corridor hewn directly into the living rock. When I looked back, I could see Aku Brugal at the edge of the cliff, stepping in. When he was in the corridor, he pressed his hand along the wall. I didn't see any changes, but I walked back and pressed my hand against the entrance. Even though I could see out, the wall was solid and felt like a cool sheet of glass.

"Cool, isn't it? Hologram and a force field. After all, can't have anything just wandering into our home now, can we?"

I merely nodded.

"Let's go, but stay close. We don't get humans down here very often, and some of my friends might be hungry." He smiled and patted me on the back. He started to walk off and turned around. "Seriously, it is dinner time, but the stench of humans would ruin anyone's appetite." As he wandered down the hall I heard him mumble under his breath, "And they call us skunk apes!"

The corridors were well lit, though I couldn't identify any light sources. We passed a number of doors, but he kept going. The walls were smoother than concrete, but it appeared that they were natural rock because the colors of the walls varied and I could see veins of quarts, amethyst and other colorful minerals and crystals. Finally he paused by a door, pressed his palm against the wall next to it, and the door slid open. I walked into a small room.

There appeared to be a window looking out over the forest. I walked up to it and touched it. The image blurred where my finger touched it.

I turned to ask Aku Brugal about it, but there was now a sink along one wall and a table and two chairs in the middle of the room.

"This is your room while you stay with us, Charlie. Whatever you like in the way of furnishings, the room will supply it."

"What do you mean?" I pulled one chair back and sat down.

Aku Brugal scratched his head. "Ok. For example." He pulled back the other chair. "This chair is clearly too small for me and I'd prefer an upholstered chair with cushions." The chair became fuzzy around the edges and then began to blur entirely. Moments later a large upholstered chair had replaced the utilitarian cafeteria chair.

Aku Brugal sat down and crossed his legs. "Now, that's more like it."

"What did you do?" To paraphrase a line I remembered from a sci-fi book I'd read years ago, one man's science is another man's magic. This appeared to be magic, but after what I'd seen on the Atlantean saucer, I was sure that this was some kind of technology.

"You're telepathic, right?"

I nodded, somewhat unsure.

"Well, just think what you want and the artificial intelligence that runs our humble abode will get what you want—within reason of course."

I thought about the recliner in my old bedroom. Sure enough, the air sparkled in the corner of the room, then clouded over. When it cleared, there was a chair.

"Unbelievable! Your people did all this?"

Aku Brugal shook his head. "No, we can use it, but we didn't invent it. Those we serve built all this. Which reminds me, you need a shower and a new set of clothes. The Lady would like to meet with you in an hour."

"The Lady?"

"Don't worry. She likes you and you'll like her." Aku Brugal stood and headed for the door. The chair began to evaporate.

I followed him out.

When he realized that, he turned around. "Where do you think you're going?"

"Thought you were taking me to the shower."

He shook his head. "Nope, shower's in here. That's why these rooms are so small. When you're done with something you get rid of it and replace it with what you need, a bed, a table, a shower, whatever. See." He pointed to the corner of the room. A shower head had appeared out of the ceiling and a drain in the floor.

"If you get hungry, just think up something you'd like and I'm sure that the AI will be able to get it for you."

I nodded as Aku Brugal walked out and the door slid shut behind him. It had been a while, so I stripped off my clothes and stepped in under the showerhead. Problem was, there weren't any knobs. I thought about what Aku Brugal had said. I thought: *Water on.*

Cold water doused me. I jumped. *Shut off.* The water shut off. I was shivering. I looked for my clothes, but they were gone. *Towel.* A towel pushed up out of the floor. It was blue with my initials on it,

Legacy of Atlantis

just as I'd pictured in my mind. I wrapped it around me and thought about a warm shower. Water poured out of the showerhead again. I slipped my hand in. Perfect temperature. I dropped the towel and stepped into the shower. It felt great. My first one-G shower in a long time. Now all I needed was some soap and shampoo. I pictured a bar of Ivory soap sitting in a soap dish in the wall. Sure enough, it appeared. I picked it up. It even smelled like Ivory. I stepped out of the streams of water and soaped up. I then stepped back under the water and rinsed off. I pictured a bottle of shampoo next to the soap. It magically materialized. It had a coconut scent just like the shampoo my mother used to get me. I'd never enjoyed a shower quite so much.

I thought *off* and the water stopped. I dried off with the towel. My clothes had not reappeared. I pictured a pair of boxers, blue jeans and a Mariners T-shirt. After a brief shimmer, a handle appeared in the wall. I pulled on it. It was a drawer. It contained boxers in my size, blue jeans and a Mariners T-shirt. I slipped on the clothes and then realized I was hungry. I hadn't had a hamburger in ages, so I thought about a Big Mac and an order of fries. Sure enough, a burger and fries appeared on a plate in a gap in the wall. I eagerly reached in and grabbed the plate of fries. Not up to fast food standards that I remembered, but not bad. I then picked up the burger. It looked ok, but didn't smell right. I took a bite and spit it out. Tasted like cardboard.

I looked up. Aku Brugal stood at the open door.

"What's wrong, don't like our cooking?" He stepped in, grabbed the burger and took a bite. "Delicious. Perfect veggie burger." Another bite and it was gone.

"But I asked for a hamburger."

"You asked for meat?" Aku Brugal wore a shocked expression.

"Yeah."

"We don't eat meat."

"But I thought you said . . ."

"About eating people. That's a laugh. We're vegans, boy."

"Guess I'm out of luck then."

"Looks like you've got some fries." He grabbed a handful and popped them into his mouth. "Personally, I prefer sweet-potato fries, but these aren't bad." He grabbed another handful and popped them into his mouth. He then picked up the plate and handed it to me. "Here, this is your dinner."

I ate a couple more fries and another plate appeared in the wall. There were sweet potato fries and two sandwiches on white bread. Aku Brugal took the plate, grabbed a few sweet-potato fries and handed the plate to me. "Grab one."

I gingerly picked up a sandwich and sniffed it. Smelled like peanut butter. I took a nibble. "Peanut butter and strawberry jelly!" I took a large bite.

"We might be vegetarians, but we're not uncivilized. One must have the occasional peanut butter and jelly sandwich."

I nodded as I devoured the sandwich.

Aku Brugal had already finished his plate and returned it to the wall. "Now, if you're ready, the Lady's waiting for you."

I ate a couple of the sweet potato fries and slipped the plate in the shelf in the wall. "Ready."

"I said we're civilized. Don't you need a pair of shoes?"

The floor felt so good to my feet that I'd forgotten. I thought about a pair of Nike sneakers in my size. Sure enough, a drawer handle appeared. When I opened it, a pair of Nike's was waiting for me. The swoosh looked real, but there were no markings on the inside. I slipped them on. They felt perfect.

"Ready."

"Good." The door opened, and Aku Brugal led the way down the hall.

# CHAPTER 18
## LADY GALADRIEL

We reached a large, ornately carved wooden door. Aku Brugal turned the brass handle, opened it and signaled for me to enter. Gilded antique furniture that looked like it belonged in a museum or, better yet, a palace, filled the room. Despite the age of the furnishings, the air smelled fresh and clean, not at all fusty. A fire blazed in a fireplace surrounded by a marble mantelpiece. Mythical creatures were carved into the marble, including a serpent with the head of a ram in the center. Above the mantelpiece hung a painting. It looked like an impressionistic depiction of the park in Atlantis's capital city, Solterra. Shelves of leather-bound books adorned one wall and, on the others, hung a series of paintings of men and women dressed in garb from Egyptian to Greek to Roman. A gilded desk rested in front of a leaded-glass bay window. The window looked out over a beautiful mountain glade. The view was not of any forest in the Pacific Northwest. The trees looked—different.

I looked over at Aku Brugal. "Is the Lady here?"

He shrugged. "She keeps her own counsel. She merely requested that we meet her here."

I nodded, walked over to the fireplace and extended my hands. The heat felt good. I'd expected a hologram. I looked up at the painting. The fountains of Atria were off in the distance. I glanced at the signature. Claude Monet. One of my mother's favorite artists. I reached out to touch it.

"It's real, Charlie. I'd prefer you not touch it. I commissioned Claude to do it for me. I merely described it to him from memory. An amazing artist. One of the best ever."

I turned sharply. Galadriel stood by the desk. She smiled, her turquoise eyes welcoming me.

"Have a seat." She extended her hand toward two chairs by her desk. By the sizes, I knew which one to sit in. Galadriel sat behind the desk as I lowered myself into the chair. The chair next to me creaked as Aku Brugal sat down.

"Go ahead, Charlie, ask me your questions. I can feel them ready to burst out."

Charlie leaned forward. "So, you're the same as the hologram on the Moon?"

Galadriel laughed melodically. "Not quite the same. I find it difficult to project myself that far anymore."

"Project yourself?" I'd thought that she was a holographic image designed by the computer at the lunar base.

She chuckled. "Like all Atlanteans, I'm telepathic. I inserted a picture of myself in your brain so you would see me as I am. Given the distance to our former lunar base, my image appeared somewhat like a hologram."

"And you're here, now, in the flesh?" She looked real enough.

She sighed. "In a manner of speaking, yes, but I'll get to that later. I'm glad that you and your uncle were able to escape from the Moon and make it here in one piece. I tried to thwart the Lemurian attack as you passed over their territory, but was unable to do so. Fortunately, your uncle got you close enough to us so Aku Brugal could go out and recover you." She nodded at the big 'squatch.

"Thank you, mi Lady." Aku Brugal tipped his head.

I glanced over at him. "But why's he here and what's he got to do with Atlanteans?"

Galadriel smiled and looked affectionately at me. "The inquisitiveness of youth. It's been so long I'd nearly forgotten." She stood and walked over to the window-like display. She pointed toward the idyllic park at the center. "I spend too much of my time looking at the past. And you, my child, are the future.

"When we first returned from the Moon, we came upon a broken land. Lemuria was gone and Atlantis had become the new South Pole, with tons of ice covering our old homes. The only technology left was what we brought back from the Moon and a few isolated outposts, such as this, around the globe. We used our satellite capabilities and our telepathic abilities to track down those of our people that had survived. Tragically, very few had survived the cataclysm brought about by the Lemurians. Of those that did, many lost the will to live. We tried to work with the Lemurians that had served with us on the Moon, but they were so dejected that they wandered off, seeking their own kind. They couldn't accept that civilization had fallen.

"As a geneticist, I realized that we didn't have enough survivors to maintain our species. Genetic drift would wipe us out within a few generations at best. One of my colleagues had been a student of the *hominids* that populated the continent you now call Africa. We knew that we and they shared common ancestors. He suggested that we modify the genetic codes of these *hominids* to make them viable to accept our DNA. That way, we Atlanteans could survive as a species.

"Since our average lifespan extended well beyond a hundred generations of the *hominids*, we had the ability to adapt the *hominids* into new species similar to us. Our good friend, Aku Brugal, is a result of those manipulations—as are you. You call his ancestors *Homo neanderthalensis*."

I turned to Aku Brugal and looked him over. "You're a Neanderthal?"

"While I resent the derogatory nature of your species' use of Neanderthal, that is partially correct." He grinned widely, baring his canines. "If it were up to your species, we would have been wiped out. Thanks to Lady Galadriel and her kind, she adapted our genetic code and saved our species. Given their lack of numbers and physical limitations, we have lived in symbiosis with the Atlanteans for more generations than I can count."

The Lady sat and turned her chair to face us. She brushed her hair back and I saw her elf-like ears for the first time. "That's right. We engineered the branching apart of Neanderthals and humans a few hundred thousand years ago. We have followed and continued to work with both branches. Neanderthals proved more malleable given their telepathic abilities, but, like us, they breed very slowly. As a result, modern humans overtook them, practically wiping them out. Were it not for the few enclaves that we created, they might have gone extinct."

"So, Neanderthals are Bigfoot?"

Aku Brugal had his pipe out again, fiddling with it. "My feet aren't so large, but, yes, we have been spotted occasionally."

"Then why haven't you ever been uncovered."

Aku Brugal pointed his pipe at me. "Because you humans are so dumb!"

I looked at Aku Brugal and then at Galadriel. She began to laugh first, then Aku Brugal broke into his guffaw.

Galadriel smiled at me again. "Child, it's only because you have Atlantean telepathic abilities that Aku Brugal's telepathic camouflage failed to work on you. Very few humans have the ability to see a sasquatch since the sasquatches can detect their mental presence from quite a distance. If they do get close, the sasquatches can use active camouflage to make themselves look like ordinary humans, bears, or to blend in with their surroundings. Of course, telepathy can't trick cameras, but they are very careful, and we have technology for that."

"What about the famous videos of 'squatch hunters?" I looked over at Aku Brugal.

"They're almost all fakes. I actually joined a group of 'squatch hunters in my youth. Had quite a bit of fun with them, too. My brother would make 'squatch calls from a distance, throw rocks into camp and leave false trails for the hunters to follow. It was a blast."

I chuckled as I pictured the big ape standing behind the cameras laughing at the searchers.

"Charlie, I've assigned Aku Brugal to assist you in your quest. Now that the Lemurians know about you, you will need his assistance."

"And you want me to disarm the gravitonic weapon before it's used again, right?"

"Unfortunately, yes. Our sensors have shown that someone has located an old base below the ice in Antarctica. You need to reach it and disable it before it is activated. You saw the destruction of Lemuria and what happened to the planet then. Think what would happen to the Earth, to your species, if a huge section of Antarctica was ripped away and hurled into space."

I thought back to the hologram that Galadriel had shown me on the Moon. Antarctica was much larger than Lemuria had been. Mega tsunamis, super volcanos and years of unrelenting cloud cover. It sounded like the script for a Hollywood disaster flick. If only it was. A mega tsunami originating in Antarctica would not be limited to the Pacific. It would sweep into the Atlantic, Pacific and Indian Oceans. I'd read somewhere that close to fifty percent of the Earth's population lived within fifty miles of the coast. They'd be toast within a day. And they'd be the lucky ones. Khrushchev's quote that the living would envy the dead would come true. Civilization would collapse in an instant. The whole ecosystem would soon follow. It would be the sixth great mass extinction. It might be worse than the Permian mass extinction where north of ninety-five percent of all species went extinct.

I shuddered as a weight descended on my shoulders. "Why me? Why can't you fly there in one of your spaceships and deactivate it?"

"Because I can't. No Atlantean can." Her shoulders drooped. "We are old, Charlie, very old."

I could see the sadness in her eyes. "But you don't look old, you look—beautiful."

She smiled and shook her head. "I told you before when you asked if I was here in the flesh that I am, in a manner of speaking. My mind is here, but my body's not. A team of trained sasquatch scientists keep me and the other eleven surviving Atlanteans alive."

"You're a million years old?" I asked.

Galadriel smiled, but shook her head. "Even our longevity and our science can't keep us 'alive' for a million years. We developed hibernation chambers when we were heading out to explore the stars. We brought them back to Earth with us. We numbered over fifty when we first returned from the Moon. We would take turns in the hibernation chambers, keeping a small number of us awake as we would have were we traveling to the stars. Now, with only twelve of us remaining, I am the only one currently awake. I have waited a long time for you. Once your task is complete, I will rest and another will replace me.

"Your way will be difficult, but I know you can do it. You are the first true Atlantean born to this new world in millennia." She pulled out the drawer to the desk and lifted out something wrapped in red satin. She walked around the desk and handed it to me. It weighed a little more than a baseball, but was about the same shape and size. I unfolded the red satin and peered at a crystal sphere. It felt good in my hand. I flipped it up in the air and caught it.

"What is it?"

"It's an educator, something that all Atlantean children use for training. Focus on it, look into it. It will help you to hone your mental abilities."

I glanced up at Galadriel and then looked into the crystal ball. It felt alive in my hand. I gripped it tighter. All of a sudden, I felt it pulling me in. It reminded me of when the image of Trolga had assaulted me in Dome Park, but this somehow felt right. I floated in a sea of clouds. I looked up and saw a swath of clouds across the horizon. One left the heavens and slowly descended toward me. As it got closer, it became a face, the face of my mother. I could feel her voice inside my head. She leaned down and kissed my forehead. I could even smell the scent of her perfume. I reached out to hug her, but she evaporated. I was back in the room with Aku Brugal and Galadriel.

"What was that?" I wiped sweat from my brow.

"The educator bonded to you. It can't be taken from you without your free will now. While it will assist you in learning to control your telepathic and telekinetic abilities, you can also call upon it to amplify those abilities. But be warned, it is not a toy."

I decided to try it out. I thought, *I understand.*

Galadriel nodded, but Aku Brugal thought, *A bit loud, boy. You need to learn some control.*

*Fortunately, you will be going with him, to teach and protect him,* Galadriel thought back.

"I was still hoping to parboil him, but perhaps I'll still get the chance. What, boy, no laugh? You need to learn to laugh if you're going to be around me." Aku Brugal let out another guffaw, but I still didn't laugh. I slipped the educator into my pocket.

"Going? Where will I be going?" I looked up at Galadriel.

"You need to find the Scepter of Apollymi and then shut down the gravitonic generator in Antarctica." She smiled as she looked at me.

She seemed supremely confident, but I wasn't. An image of Atlas holding up the world flashed through my mind. I'd seen his statue once at Rockefeller Center. I imagined him signaling me to come over. When I did, he lowered the world onto my shoulders and walked away with barely a second glance. But I was not Hercules.

The Earth pressed down on me until it slipped out of my hands. As it fell, I imagined it cracking like an egg. "Are you sure you can't go? You could shut it down, right?"

She frowned and shook her head. "I am no longer physically capable of travel, and it must be shut down in person by a genetic Atlantean. You are the only one that fits the bill."

"But you look fine—unbelievable, actually." Galadriel looked to be in her twenties, thirties at most.

"That's how I like to remember myself, and how I'd like you to think of me. But you deserve to see me, to see us, as we really are. Aku Brugal, on the way out, take him through where I rest."

"You are certain, mi Lady?" The chair creaked under AkuBrugal. While I hadn't learned to read 'squatch facial expressions, he looked surprised.

Galadriel nodded.

"Ok, no time like the present. Besides, I've got Mariners' tickets for tomorrow's game."

"We're going to a baseball game?" I had thought that my quest would begin by digging through row after row of musty old books or, perhaps, information disks like from *The Time Machine*. "No research or time with"—I lifted the educator—"this?"

AkuBrugal shook his head. "Nope." He glared at me. "Don't you like baseball? Thought I saw a mitt and ball in your knapsack."

I nodded, but then I asked, "You went through my backpack?"

He shook his head. "No, they spilled out on the floor when you put it down. Come on, kid, let's not leave the Lady waiting." He stood, gave Galadriel a brief bow, and headed for the door. I looked up at Galadriel and she nodded. I followed quickly since he'd taken off at his usual loping pace.

"Hey, wait up." I missed my ability to take giant strides on the moon as I struggled to keep up.

The hairy 'squatch stopped and turned around. "I forget how slow you *Homo sapiens* are." He waited, hands on his hips.

I caught up, out of breath. "Can't help it. Too much time in low gravity. I feel like I weigh a ton—which I guess you do!"

Aku Brugal bared his teeth and raised his hand as if to swat me. I thought, perhaps, my smart mouth had gotten the better of me, but then he laughed and ruffled my hair. "I like you, kid. Glad I didn't eat you."

I smiled at the big ape, although I'd never call him that. Wookie, perhaps, but not ape. "So, what should I call you when we're out and about? I can't very well call you Aku Brugal. What kind of name is that anyway?"

"A very old and distinguished name is what it is. Kind of like yours, Charlemagne. Any ideas, Charlemagne?" He slapped the back of my head.

"How about AB? That sounds good, and if we run into anyone, I'll tell them that you're a former student of my uncle's."

"AB's fine with me and I am, actually. A former student of your uncle's, that is. Studied with him for a while. Taught mathematics. I heard that he was in hiding for some reason or another. Damn good calculus teacher, though. Used to tell us that he learned it directly from Isaac Newton. Never did figure out whether that was a joke or not."

I could only shake my head. With his warped sense of humor, I never knew whether AB was telling the truth or not. As for my uncle, I had learned that he was much more than I'd been led to believe. But Isaac Newton? No way.

I shoved all of my stuff into my backpack while AB ordered a bunch of sandwiches for the road. Instead of carrying them, he handed them to me.

"Here, stick these in there. Might get hungry on the way."

I looked at the sandwiches but didn't recognize anything. Looked like lots of green stuff on bread. "Did you get anything for me?"

"Didn't even think about it. Why, you hungry?"

I shook my head.

"You will be when I pull into McDonald's on the way to the ballgame. Come on, kid, I'm here to take care of you. You do like McDonald's?"

I nodded and actually started getting hungry. Hadn't had a real burger since I'd left Seattle, let alone a Big Mac. Don't get me wrong, the Lunar garden burgers were good, but they got old fast.

We arrived at what appeared to be an airlock at the end of a corridor. AB placed his palm against the wall. The door slid open and we walked in. The room filled with light and the door shut behind us. A smaller 'squatch with rust orange/brown hair, wearing a lavender lab coat, matching surgical pants, and blue cloth surgical shoes rose from behind a monstrosity of a desk and approached us. She gave AB a hug but eyed me warily.

"Charlie, meet my little sister, Laika."

I walked over and extended my hand. "Pleasure to meet you."

AB nodded at her, and she extended her hand toward mine. I shook it.

"Laika doesn't like to speak, so concentrate and think clearly."

I nodded, stuck my hand in my pocket and held the educator. I then thought, *Nice to meet you, Laika.*

She smiled condescendingly. *A bit loud, but most humans have to resort to guttural vocalizations.* She walked back over to her desk and grabbed two badges. She clipped one to my shirt and handed the other to AB. *The Lady instructed me to let you see her in person. You must touch nothing and stay on the illuminated red path. DO NOT leave the red path.*

Her lips didn't move, and yet I heard her in my mind as if she were speaking. A red path did indeed appear in the floor.

AB and I stepped forward. I turned to him. "What's this about?"

Laika shook her head. AB said, "Ignore her. She's a bit of a snob."

I felt a hot wind brush past me, and AB yelled, "Ouch!" He gave his sister a glare. As if off in the distance I heard, *If you weren't my sister . . .* Then AB turned to me. "Let's go. I'm anxious to get to my apartment in town before morning."

A door slid open, and the red path glowed off into the distance. AB stepped forward, and I followed. No other light illuminated us, and the glow from the floor didn't seem to penetrate the darkness other than along the path itself.

*Quite the honor, kid. I doubt even your Uncle Merl got to meet the Lady in person.*

I felt a faint tingle in my forehead. Was that an indicator that AB had thought to me? Now that I wasn't getting headaches from the telepathy, it was hard to tell the difference.

A blue glow appeared in the distance, off to our right. As we approached, AB turned to me. "Don't leave the path. It creates a barrier that separates us from the ancients."

I nodded. "So if I were to fall or stick my hand out, my germs might infect them?"

AB shook his head. "No, if you were to stick your hand out, it would be vaporized. Nothing's permitted to violate the safety of the ancients."

I walked more carefully. As we approached the blue glow it appeared to be a glass tube filled with glowing blue liquid. AB took a knee and bowed to the tube. "My Lady." He signaled me to kneel as well. I did.

I squinted as a form moved forward in the liquid. It was hairless and shriveled like a raisin. It stopped a few feet from the edge of the tube. *Hello, Charlie. Now do you see why I can't go back home?*

I didn't know what to say. She looked more desiccated than the mummified Atlantean I'd found on the Moon. I leaned forward, but AB stopped me.

"Galadriel?"

*Yes, Charlie. This is what I really look like. We are long-lived, but millennia and multiple trips in the suspended animation tanks take their toll. I can't leave this chamber other than with my mind. A few of us have abandoned reality for our dreams, unwilling or unable to accept this final stage, yet unable to terminate our lives. I try to communicate with them on occasion, but while I can read a fleeting thought or two, they remain in their own worlds.*

*We have worked long and hard trying to bring back Atlantis, but I know that isn't going to happen. Rather your kind, our legacy, will create its own Atlantis. But remain vigilant. The Lemurians are beginning to suspect our weakness. They want to enslave humans and eradicate the Atlantean genome that we have so judiciously nurtured over millennia. Your quest can stop their plans.*

*You, Charlie, have all of the abilities to combat them. With dear Aku Brugal's help, you will succeed. I'm sure of it. Now go. I must rest. Moving through the tank is taxing.*

I nodded as she retreated further into the tank. She was gone. I turned to AB. "But what if I need her?"

Her voice slowly faded from my mind. *Use the education device, Charlie. I will be able to hear you if you think clearly enough.*

AB grabbed my shoulders and looked me in the eye. "Quite the burden, eh? Let's forget about it for now and go watch a ball game."

# CHAPTER 19
## ROUGH ROAD

We got to a garage of sorts. AB grabbed a set of keys and headed for a vintage red-and-white Ford Bronco. I threw my backpack in the back seat and climbed in as AB started the engine. I yawned.

"You can thank me later, but I came prepared." AB reached behind my seat, pulled out a pillow and handed it to me. "You may as well sleep. We've got a bit of a drive and it's the middle of the night."

I put the pillow against my seat and the window and leaned against it. I felt a mental nudge and then a thought. *Buckle up. Some of these roads are a bit rough.* I reached down and put on my seat belt. I was out before we made it out of the garage.

A lurch and a jolt woke me up. "Watch the pot holes, will you?" I was about to lay my head back against the pillow when AB swerved the wheel sharply. The tires slid off the road and began shooting gravel up against the wheel well like machine-gun fire. I looked around. A beam of light carved a trench in the road where we would have been but for AB's swerving.

"What's going on?" I looked around. Nobody was following us as we sped down a tree-lined road in the dark.

A thought pierced my brain. *Shhh, got to concentrate.* AB maintained a tight grip on the wheel. He swerved so sharply the seat belt dug into my lap painfully. Another beam of light hit just next to us, peppering my window with rubble.

I looked around, but saw nothing. "What . . ."

AB turned, bared his teeth and snarled at me. I shut up. Another swerve and another shot that just missed us. I pulled the educator out of my bag and held it in my palm. I closed my eyes. My senses opened up. I could feel white heat next to me in the shape of

AB. Above and behind us, I saw a glowing oblong craft hovering. It looked a bit like a Tic Tac. AB swerved as another beam of light lanced down at us. I focused on the craft. As I did, the sides of the craft became translucent. Two glowing shapes appeared inside. One remained focused on driving the craft while the other appeared to be looking down at AB. A thin thread of light seemed to connect them. The beam briefly intensified as AB let out another snarl and swerved, almost losing control of the Bronco.

I focused and stretched out to try to reach the Lady Galadriel. *Lady Galadriel, we need your help. We're under attack.* I sent a picture of what I had seen in my mind out to her. I felt a warm sensation as her voice seemed to be stretching out to reach me when a searing beam of light erupted in my skull. I dropped the educator and grabbed my head.

Dots swam in front of my eyes, but AB had turned his head and smiled at me. "Thanks, kid. You distracted that Lemurian SOB for long enough so I could stun him. They're dropping back, but they'll attack again, and now they know you're a threat . . ." He looked in the side-view mirror, as did I. I didn't see anything, but even without the educator, I felt a cloud descending over me like when Trolga had first attacked me on the Moon. I could sense that AB was battling the Lemurian, but a needle of light was slowly moving toward my right eye. I tried to back my head up, but couldn't. Heat radiated from the needle as it approached. I started to scream as heat sizzled my brow. Then it was gone. A brilliant flash of light erupted in the air behind us, followed by a thunderclap. The windows rattled and several trees crashed across the road behind us.

I rubbed my temples. "What just happened?"

"We were attacked, that's what. Lemurian patrols don't generally get this close to the fortress. They must have sensed something. When they attack, they use both physical and mental weapons. I swerved every time I sensed a shot coming. I had tried to contact the fortress, but was unable to do it and avoid their particle beams. You, my boy, distracted them. Once you picked up the educator, they sensed you as the larger threat and focused on you. That gave me time to stun them."

"So you knocked them out of the sky with a mere thought?"

AB let out a massive guffaw. "No, Charlie. Nobody can do that. You must have reached the Lady with your plea and she used the fortress defense systems to vaporize the Lemurian craft. That's why they don't usually get this close to the fortress."

I looked back, but saw no evidence of the destroyed saucer.

"If any humans saw the craft destroyed, they will assume it was a meteorite that exploded. The fortress's main batteries would have left nothing to be found. You did a hell of a job there, kid. But I'll need to teach you how to defend yourself. You were too open for a counterattack."

I nodded.

"Go back to sleep. That will help with the headache. We've got a few hours before we hit the outskirts of Seattle."

Despite the excitement, my head bobbed down and my eyes drifted shut. I sensed AB in my head, but didn't fight it. I could tell he was merely helping me go to sleep.

Several hours later I stretched my arms and yawned. Looked like we were about to hit the 405. Between Earth's gravity and the thirty-year-old springs in the seat under me, I was feeling achy like an old man.

AB looked over at me. "Good thing you snore. I was getting a bit sleepy, but your sawing wood managed to keep me up."

I stretched again. "Sorry, didn't know I snore."

AB smiled, revealing his large canines, and slapped me on the back. "You don't. Just yanking your chain. We 'squatches are nocturnal, don't ya know."

It felt as if I had a wad of cotton in my mouth. I started thinking about a Coke. We had them on the Moon, but they just didn't taste the same. Maybe the gravity.

"Chick-fil-A coming up in about a mile. You can get a Coke there."

I looked over. "What?"

*Don't vocalize, think. The Lady told you to practice.* His lips hadn't moved.

I thought, *Ok.*

He smiled. *See, no headache from last night.*

*Seemed more like a dream than reality. Did we really...*

*Get attacked by Lemurians? Yes. Let's hope we lost them last night. I activated a thought cloaker once you went to sleep, just in case one of their patrols came close.*

I nodded, but little of it made any sense to me. I started to think about a Chick-fil-A biscuit and some waffle fries.

*Ok, now you've done it, got me drooling. I may have to try one of those.*

"Sorry." When I spoke, AB frowned. I thought this time. *Sorry, didn't know I was projecting my thoughts.*

*You were, and strongly too. Not many cubs like you can project senses via thought. But you'll need to practice with the educator to be able to control your thoughts leaking out and to block out thoughts you don't want to hear.*

I nodded, thinking about Trolga and the attack last night. That alone was incentive enough to practice hard. I picked up the educator.

AB turned onto the exit ramp. *And, as much as I want you to practice, in public we must communicate the old-fashioned way. Sometimes it's hard to do, which is why not many of us 'squatches are allowed out in public.* AB turned into the Chick-fil-A drive thru. He spoke this time. "Now, what do you want to order?"

I thought of a Chic-fil-A biscuit as I slipped the educator back into my backpack. AB ordered me a chicken biscuit, waffle fries and a Coke. He passed me my drink and the bag of food. I opened it.

"Six biscuits?"

He reached down and grabbed one. "Thought you might like an extra." He unfurled a wrapper and shoved a whole biscuit in his mouth. He grabbed another.

"I thought you were a vegetarian?"

"I am on Mondays, Wednesdays and Fridays. Good thing we met on a Monday!" He smiled and took half of the next biscuit into his mouth.

I shrugged and started on my breakfast. I surprised myself and ate two of the six.

# CHAPTER 20
## BASEBALL REUNION

We got to the ballpark at 1:45. The game started at 3. I smiled. My dad always used to bring me early so we could watch warm-ups to shag a home-run ball during batting practice.

*You ever catch a BP home run?*

I wasn't sure that I liked AB's ability to read my thoughts. I'd have to practice trying to hide them. I couldn't seem to read his thoughts no matter how I tried.

*No. You?*

He shook his head. *Maybe today'll be our lucky day.*

We approached the ticket gate and AB pulled two tickets out of the pocket of the windbreaker he was wearing. I glanced at him. He still looked like a big furry 'sqautch to me, but nobody else seemed to give him a second glance. I spotted a couple of cameras by the gate. I grabbed AB's arm to slow him down. He stopped.

*What about the cameras? You can trick people's minds, but not cameras.*

AB laughed. *Won't be a problem.*

*You mean you can trick cameras with your mind?*

He shook his head and chuckled. *Now that would be a real trick. Were that the case, you humans would be working for us!* He pulled a tube of Chap Stick out of his pocket. *When cameras started to be a problem, the Atlanteans gave us the plans for these.* He held the tube up. *It generates a field that creates an electromagnetic distortion. Cameras can't get a clear image of me.* He pulled the top off and applied a bit of Chap Stick to his lips as well. *Also keeps me from getting chapped lips!* He thumped me on the back.

The seats were in the outfield and batting practice had just started.

*Want a hot dog or something?*

I glanced over at him. "I haven't had a hot dog in ages." *Thought we were supposed to talk normally in public.*

"Quite right, lad. What do you want on your dog?"

"Just mustard—and a Coke."

He nodded. "Catch me a home-run ball while I'm gone."

I nodded. I'd come here many times, but had never had a home run come close to me. I looked around. The park was fairly empty, but that wasn't surprising given that game time was over an hour away. The Mariners new third baseman, Chavis, was warming up. He'd only been in the league a couple of years and I'd heard that he had some real power. He stepped into the box. He lined the first pitch past third. The next few he popped up. I glanced to the dugout. My favorite player, Johnny Vance, began running out to center. He was almost in position when I heard that sweet crack of the bat. Vance accelerated and looked over his shoulder. He was running right toward me. I glanced up. The ball was still rising. It was always hard to judge a ball from dead center, so I glanced back down at Vance. He'd stopped running and was looking up toward me. The ball was coming right at me. I got ready to make a grab for it. I shifted a seat to the right. Wished I had my glove. What a hit. I was ten rows deep and it was going right over my head. I willed the ball to slow, hoping I could make the catch. I pulled my hat off and jumped. It hit my hat dead center. I had it. I pulled the ball out of my cap. Johnny Vance was looking up at me. He tipped his hat. I smiled and nodded my head.

*Not a good idea, kid. That ball should've gone a good ten rows deeper. Good thing it's a windy day. They'll think a gust of wind caught it.* AB was walking slowly down the aisle with a box of food and two drinks.

"I see you got one, kid."

I nodded. *What do you mean?* I slipped the ball into my pocket.

AB shrugged and handed me my Coke and my hot dog.

"Thanks." I glanced over. He had a brat with sauerkraut, a barbecue sandwich, a pretzel and a beer. "Eating meat again, I see, and plenty of it."

"What, it's Tuesday isn't it?" He grinned and took a bite. Mustard squirted out and stuck on the fur at the side of his mouth.

I heard another loud crack of the bat. The ball was heading right for us again. I quickly put my Coke down and got ready, but this time Vance kept coming. He climbed the wall and snatched away a home run. As he trotted back to center, he glanced back at me. I smiled and tipped my hat to him. He threw the ball up to me and ran back toward the dugout.

"Damn, kid, two balls in one game. Who'd have thunk?"

I was grinning ear to ear. I slipped the ball in my other pocket, sat back down and took a sip of my Coke. I finished my dog at about the same time as AB finished his brat and his barbecue. We sat back and watched more BP, but the Mariners were about done. I glanced around. The stadium remained fairly empty.

"How about we hit the pitching machine? I haven't thrown a pitch in over a year." I started to stretch my arm to loosen it up.

AB took a huge bite of pretzel, finishing it. "Ok, as long as you don't do anything stupid." AB wiped the mustard off his fur and got up. I followed him.

There wasn't even a line at the pitching machine. I tapped my iLet against the pay terminal and three balls rolled out. I stretched again, picked up the first ball and hurled it at the target. 74 mph. I'd thrown harder than that when I was thirteen. I picked up the second ball. 76. Better, but not where I used to be. I loosened up some more, toed my foot against the rubber, bent into my crouch and AB's voice in my head made me stand up. *I know that look. Don't put anything extra on it, if you get my drift.*

I looked over at him and nodded, even though I wasn't sure what he meant, and got back in my crouch. I broke my hands, extended my arm, pushed off the rubber with my right foot and threw. 84. Fastest pitch of the day. I smiled.

"Nice pitch, kid." Two men in sunglasses and dark jackets stood behind AB.

I smiled. "Thanks."

"Now, if you and your friend would come with us, we'd appreciate it."

A hint of worry passed over my face, but AB seemed unconcerned.

"Why? We need to get back to our seats." I stepped out of the pitching cage.

"You and your friend are getting a nice seat upgrade, kid. Just follow us." They turned and didn't wait. I looked over at AB. He shrugged and followed them. I did as well.

*Any clue what they want?* I telepathically asked AB.

*You want me to read them after I've eaten? You do it.*

I focused on the back of one of the men's heads. I began to get dizzy as seemingly random thoughts sprang into my head. I stumbled. The men looked back, but continued walking. I felt a bit queasy.

*See what I mean?* thought AB. *These humans are dense and hard to read. It can make me sick to my stomach.*

We reached an elevator manned by a lady in a navy blue jacket with an official Mariners' badge over the breast pocket. She said hey to the men, pushed the button, and the elevator opened. We all got in. The elevator moved up and then opened on the suite level. The men walked toward the home-plate corner. Before we got there, they stopped in front of a box with a grey-haired cop sitting outside. The brass plate on the door read "Mariners' Box." I wondered if this had something to do with my catch.

The guard opened the door. "Come on in, come on in. Name's Joe. If you need anything just let me know."

AB nodded his head. "Thanks, Joe. Appreciate it." The suite had a large bar and a spread of food against one wall. Two rows of seats faced the field, separated from outside by glass doors. I glanced out. We were over the first base line. Two more rows of seats were outside the glass doors. One person stood and turned. I froze. I knew him.

Richard opened the glass doors and walked right up to me. "So, Charlemagne, the last time I heard, you were a wanted man in Clarksville." The two men that had escorted us up to the box walked up right behind me.

I had no clue how to respond. I looked over at AB for support, but his large body was bent over the buffet table getting more food.

"Richard, good to see you. How's it going?" I said tentatively. I could feel the two bodyguards behind me. They seemed almost as big as AB.

"Considering that you stole my girlfriend, then somehow caused a meltdown of a nuclear reactor on the Moon, forcing me to evacuate and potentially costing my family billions, I guess I'm better now that you're here."

He motioned to the guards and each grabbed one of my arms. I glanced over at AB again, but he remained at the buffet.

"Mark, Eric, you can let him go." The men released my arms. Richard started laughing. He pointed to the window. Rhea and Imee were standing outside, looking at me, smiling ear to ear. They ran up the couple of steps and came in the room. Rhea gave me a big hug.

"I thought I'd never see you again. When the rover came back without you we all thought you were dead." She squeezed me again and let go. Imee then gave me a smaller hug. "What happened?"

Richard put his arm around Imee. "We can catch up out in the seats. It's almost time for the first pitch. Let's grab a plate and get in our seats."

Richard headed to the buffet. Imee grabbed a plate and got in line behind him. Rhea grabbed my hand and pulled me to the buffet.

"By the way, who's your big friend with the healthy appetite?" Richard was looking at AB with a mountain of food on a plate. AB set his heaping plate down, grabbed a carrot and took a big bite.

"AB's a former student and good friend of my uncle's. My uncle left me with him when we arrived from the Moon." AB walked over and extended his hand. "Nice to meet you, Richard." Richard's hand disappeared in AB's as they shook. "Any friend of Charlie's is a friend of mine." AB turned toward the girls. "Particularly the pretty ones."

The girls blushed, but not as deeply as I did. I turned and grabbed some chicken nuggets.

"Your father's Arthur DeMarco, right? The owner of the team?" AB looked appreciatively around the suite.

Richard nodded tentatively. "You know my father?" he asked more softly than usual.

AB shook his head. "No, just a big Mariners fan."

"Let's head outside and enjoy the game." Richard's voice boomed as he reached for Imee's hand. Imee took it and gave it a squeeze. "There's room for you too, AB."

AB waved his hand. "No thanks. I'll let you guys catch up. Besides, I'd hate to be that far away from all of this wonderful food."

Richard nodded and walked out to his seat. Imee trailed right behind him. I smiled at Rhea and extended my hand for her to go in front of me. I followed and sat down next to her. The Oakland As were on the field warming up.

I looked over at my friends. All three looked quite happy. Imee was holding Richard's hand. "So, how're you guys holding up in Earth's gravity?"

Imee looked over. "I feel like I'm wearing a fat suit. Still not used to it. I miss the floating feeling when you step. Each step's an effort."

Richard gave me a glare. "If we'd had time to spend in the acclimation gym working out before coming to Earth, we'd all feel better. But somebody had to go and trigger a meltdown in the university's reactor."

"Look, I didn't have anything to do with the reactor. I wasn't even in Clarksville when the reactor started acting up."

"Yeah, I heard. You stole a rover after beating up Jamie."

Rhea answered before I could. "Look, Charlie didn't have anything to do with Jamie getting hurt. We'd both been with Jamie about twenty minutes before he went to the infirmary. He was fine."

"As if I believe that Charlie could get through security and scram the university reactor. That's a laugh." Richard gave me a wry smile.

"I'm glad you believe me."

"Believe that you didn't have anything to do with the reactor or with Jamie's injuries, yes. But you were up to something fishy. Before being evacuated, I went to Dahak Mining to contact my dad. I didn't get him, but security was tracking a rover not too far from where you'd disappeared on the field trip. My guess is that you were on it."

I looked over at Rhea. She gave me an almost imperceptible nod.

*Careful, Charlie.* I glanced back at AB. He looked normal, chomping on a piece of pizza.

"Come on, Charlie, tell me. I, for one, am glad that we had to evacuate. I was sick and tired of the Moon, but my father insisted. I'm grateful to whomever or whatever caused the reactor to leak." Richard looked sincere.

"But your father's company, the mining operations . . ."

"Will go on. Clarksville's still open. They contained the leak and have merely shut down the university section. Mining will go on. Besides, my father's onto something new, something he claims will be bigger than helium-3. He's hoping it will make him the first trillionaire in the world!"

I knew Richard was rich and that he liked to show off his wealth, but a trillion? I shook my head. I couldn't conceive of that much wealth.

Rhea leaned over to me. "I'll tell you about Richard later, but for now . . ." She leaned over and kissed my cheek. She then turned to Richard. "You're right. Charlie was up to something."

I was about to say something, but she squeezed my hand tightly. "Remember the field trip when Charlie's faceplate cracked?" Richard nodded. "Well, Charlie found a metal artifact that day."

Richard had that "yeah, right" look on his face. "And you saw it?"

Rhea shook her head. "No, but . . ."

Richard turned to me. "Just wanted to impress her, huh?"

"No, I really did find a medallion, but Trolga took it from me."

"And why'd she do that?" Richard crossed his arms.

"Jamie figured it was because she didn't want to slow down mining operations in the area." I glanced over at Rhea.

"So now Jamie's part of it. Maybe you made it up, Jamie decided to tell Rhea the truth, and you beat him up." Richard had a smug look on his face.

"We found a body, a dead astronaut!" Rhea blurted out.

"What!" Richard shouted. People in the next box looked over.

I grabbed Rhea's arm. "Why don't we go inside and close the doors so we can talk—privately."

Richard stood and pulled Imee up. "Good idea." He walked inside, signaling for the security guards and the hostess to step out of the suite. As we walked in, he pointed to AB. "What about him?"

"AB's good to go. He knows the entire story." It was Rhea's turn to stare at me.

"Look, AB not only studied under my uncle, but he's a student of Atlantis as well."

"Atlantis? You've got to be kidding!" With the hostess out of the room, Richard poured himself a bourbon on the rocks. He then made Imee a screwdriver. "Anyone else before we hear this wild tale?" He took a sip of the bourbon, put the glass down and crossed his arms.

I shook my head. I'd had a few beers in my day, but still remembered my promise to my mom. Rhea declined as well. AB, the only one of drinking age in the group, grinned and picked up his beer. *You adolescent humans and your mating rituals. Quite entertaining! I thought you were interested in the one called Rhea. She appears to be appealing, although nowhere near buxom or hairy enough for my taste. Why not get her a drink like the other male did?*

*Shut up, AB! I need to think.* I looked away from him. "Look, Richard, we got off on the wrong foot and we really don't know each other that well, but if Rhea's willing to trust you, I will too. We did find the body of an ancient astronaut. We took him to the university hangar and met my uncle and Dr. Betrys. They examined the body and determined that it was from Earth about one million years ago. The body's a genetic cousin of humans, a much closer match than chimps. We all left before my uncle and Dr. Betrys finished. Next thing I knew, I was being taken away by security. After my uncle's cat attacked the security guards, the sirens from the reactor leak started blaring. I bolted. I took off in a rover at the university hangar. I met my uncle at his ship and he flew me back to Earth. He dropped me off with AB." I paused. Richard's arms remained crossed.

"My parents disappeared searching for Atlantis." I opened my backpack and pulled out their Atlantis notebook. I opened the page with the drawing of the ram-headed serpent. "The medallion and the suit both had the same ram-headed serpent as this." I showed the picture to Richard.

Richard turned to Rhea. "And this really happened? He's not full of it?"

Rhea nodded. "It's for real. We dug the body out of the regolith. It looked like it had been there forever. And I heard what Dr. Ambrose and Dr. Betrys said about the body. It came from Earth." Rhea slapped her forehead. She pushed a button on her iLet. A hologram of Jamie and me digging out the astronaut popped up over her arm.

Richard stared at the image. He looked over at Rhea. "Damn. Looks like you're telling the truth." He glanced at Imee. "Sounds a whole lot more fun than spending the summer with my mother's family in Long Island. What say we help Charlie on his quest to find Atlantis?"

AB grinned at me. *Doesn't hurt to have the backing of a billionaire on a quest now that the cat's out of the bag.*

I nodded. "Fine." My eyes darted over at Rhea. "I could use the company. AB and I are planning on heading to Nassau tomorrow.

My mother found a ram's head serpent image underwater near Bimini. Seems like a good place to start. Why don't all of you join us?"

"Not a bad idea, but bag going commercial. I'll call dad's pilot and we'll fly down on the Gulfstream. We can stay on the *Sarah Charlotte*. Dad usually likes to cruise the Bahamas in her this time of year, but he's tied up with some new project. She should be moored off Lyford Cay."

"Sounds awesome, Richard." Imee gave him a hug.

I nodded. "It's a plan."

# CHAPTER 21
## GREEN-EYED MONSTER

After the game, AB and I pulled the Bronco around to the player's lot and parked next to Richard's limo. We got our stuff out of the Bronco and dropped it in the trunk of the limo. Richard leaned against the limo, chatting with Duke Mitchell, the ace pitcher for the Mariners. Imee and Rhea stood right behind him. I'd pictured myself as Duke Mitchell during many a trip to the mound in little league. I ran back to the limo and opened the trunk. I dug through my backpack and pulled my perfect game ball out. I turned, but then looked down. I couldn't. I slipped the perfect game ball back in my backpack.

*What about the ones you caught today?* AB stood there flipping a ball up and down in the air. He tossed it to me.

*Thanks.* I looked back over at Duke Mitchell. He was posing for a picture with Imee and Rhea. He had his arms around their waists. They finished the picture and he started chatting with Rhea, but his eyes kept drifting downward. Rhea didn't seem to notice—she was all smiles and giggles. I turned away, squeezing the ball. Chavis was walking out of the locker room straight toward his car. Nobody paid any attention to him. He'd gone 0-3 before being pulled from the game. Two of the balls were pop-ups to the wall, and one had been a line drive that would have been a double but for the diving catch by the A's all-star center-fielder, Johnny Vance. Not bad at bats, but no hits. I walked toward him. "Mr. Chavis?"

He paused and looked up. "Yes?"

"Caught this home run ball during BP. Would you mind?" I held it out toward him.

"You made that catch? Hell of a play. I should give you my agent's number." He smiled and extended his hand. I handed him the ball.

"Got a pen?"

I reached but didn't have one. AB came to the rescue. "Here's one, Charlie." He handed it to Chavis and smiled.

Chavis grabbed it, wrote on the ball and handed it back.

"Thanks, sir."

Chavis shook his head. "Charlie, I'm only a couple years older than you. It's Mike. Look me up next time you want to watch a game. I'll have tickets waiting for you."

"Thanks, Mike."

He nodded, walked over to a Chevy quad cab, jumped in and drove off.

I looked back over. Rhea was standing on her toes, hugging Johnny Vance. My face reddened.

*Don't do it Charlie!*

I ignored AB and tried to get into Rhea's head. A searing pain gripped me. I staggered, letting out a yelp. AB grabbed me, supporting me. He helped me toward the limo. *Told you so. It's a defense mechanism. It's almost impossible to read the minds of the opposite sex—particularly ones that you might consider as a mate. It's evolution. It was hard enough for me to stay married to my first three wives. If they'd been able to read my mind— Then again, probably would have saved me three marriages . . .*

I glared at AB and pulled my arm away. *I don't—*

*Hard to lie telepathically, Charlie, so don't try. Besides, DON'T interrupt me when I'm on a roll!*

He grinned at me again, baring those huge incisors.

"Charlie, you all right?" Rhea had come up behind AB and was standing next to him.

"I, I'm fine. Just tripped. AB caught me." She was looking at me as if she really cared. I looked in her ruby-red eyes. My anger evaporated. Then I noticed Johnny Vance walking away, looking this way. I thought about the training device in my bag and then focused on Vance.

I saw through Vance's eyes, which were staring right at Rhea's ass. *Man, would I like to . . ."*

*Charlie! STOP.*

Suddenly I was back in my body.

"You ok?" Rhea asked as AB helped me into the car. "You suddenly went pale."

I nodded as I sat down in the Limo. AB slid in after me and Rhea next to him. "Got a little dizzy. Must be getting acclimated to a full Gee again."

AB glared. *There are risks and responsibilities with telepathy. I know you weren't taught like we are as young pups, but there are certain things you just don't do. It's rude and dangerous to enter someone else's mind. Guess we should have stayed in the fortress so I could teach you properly.*

I shook my head. *No time. Besides, I'm a quick study. Rule one, don't try to read the thoughts of potential "mates."*

*You'd better make that "don't try to read the thoughts of any girls roughly your age." I was your age once, and from what I see on TV, you humans are worse than 'squatches when it comes to mates.*

I ignored him, but he was partially right. Imee sure did look good too. I shook the thought out of my head. *Rule two, don't read thoughts unless invited or in dire need.*

*Not bad. I'll have a few more for you once I come up with them. Since you humans aren't generally telepathic and can't shield your thoughts, the rules will have to be somewhat different.*

AB was so big that I couldn't see around him to talk with anyone else. I sat forward and glanced around AB. Rhea and Imee appeared to be playing a virtual game while Richard was talking on his mobile. I sat back and pulled my parents' journal out of my backpack. I flipped to the pages about Bimini. My mother had circled eleven spots around Bimini. Most of them had Xs by them.

I remembered diving over the Bimini Road and being intrigued by the rectangular blocks running underwater for about half a mile. The large blocks sure did look like a road to my ten-year-old self, but, then again, there were so many more fun places to snorkel around Bimini. After about an hour, I finally convinced my parents to leave and head to the Three Sisters where there were far more fish and where I could swim through an underwater arch. I did it several times with my dad while my mom stayed in the boat making notes in her journal. After about the third time through, my dad pointed around a corner. I thought he'd seen a shark, but he swam toward the spot. I followed. When we rounded the turn three huge eagle rays with white spots all over their wings glided through the water. They turned when they saw us and slowly swam toward us. We swam over them, getting a perfect look at them below us. Two of them were bigger than me. It was the highlight of the trip, even beating out catching that eight pound. bonefish on a fly the next day.

My mother had placed an X in the journal next to the Bimini road. As a kid, I'd thought that the X marked the spot for buried treasure, and I'd always kept my eye open for a glint of gold underwater. Whether it was pirate booty or coins from the lost civilization of Atlantis, I didn't care. I just wanted to find something exciting. My parents would occasionally get excited and bring up some overgrown chunk of coral from the bottom, but, after a brief examination, they always threw it back. I glanced at the other spots, but had only snorkeled with my parents at the spots where there were Xs. Those Xs must mean that there was nothing interesting in those spots.

We came to a stop and I leaned forward to look around AB. Rhea noticed and gave me a big smile. I smiled back. After the unflattering clothes we'd had to wear on the Moon, I couldn't wait to see her in a bikini. Starting with the Bimini Road and the Three Sisters would let me take the lead since I'd been there before. The road would get them excited about Atlantis, and Rhea would love the multitude of tropical fish at the Three Sisters. I pictured myself following her through the coral arch and smiled. Wouldn't hurt to have a bit of fun first. We could then head south toward some of the other spots circled by my mother that she hadn't marked off.

We pulled up to the airport and a gate opened in front of us. The limo pulled up to something that looked like it was right out of a sci-fi movie. Sleek and shiny, its wings came straight back out of the nose. There was no tailfin, but, instead, two small fins came out of the sides of the fuselage just over the back of the wings.

"Sweet, isn't she?" Richard was smiling at us like the cat that had just swallowed the canary. "She'll do Mach 4 once we get up over 60,000 feet! Fastest private plane made."

Imee walked forward, her jaw down. Richard walked up behind her and put his arm around her. "Flight time for commercial is just under eight hours. We'll be there in just under two."

Rhea was a math whiz and I could see her doing the calculation in her head. Evidently Richard could too. "It'd only take an hour, but we have to go very slow at takeoff and landing."

The door was almost seamless and there were no windows, even in the cockpit. I started to point, but Richard had been through this drill before.

"As you've probably noticed, she's got no windows. Given her cruising altitude of 80,000 feet and her Mach-4 speed, the engineers couldn't design windows, but she has high-tech fiber-optic sensors that will give us whatever view we want on her screens."

Wouldn't Richard be surprised if he knew about the Atlantean craft that I'd come down in. Its doors weren't almost seamless, they *were* seamless, and I doubted that his state-of-the-art view screens could match the almost perfect holographic images that the Atlantean ship had provided. I heard an almost imperceptible hiss as the door swung down.

AB walked up behind me. *Not bad for humans. Door's a bit small, though.*

*Guess you'll have to duck, then, you—* I tried to cut my last thought off, but I think that *"big ape"* leaked out. I heard a whisper in the back of my mind.

*Humans are genetically much closer to apes than we are.* AB bared his canines. I still wasn't used to this telepathy stuff.

Richard led Imee toward the stairs. AB headed for the stairs, but I stopped him and signaled for Rhea to go ahead.

AB grunted, but Rhea smiled. "Didn't know you were such a gentleman, Charlie. Thanks."

*Gentleman, my ass. You just wanted to look at her rump. Not big enough in my opinion.*

*AB!* I really needed to practice with the educator. I hadn't said anything, but with AB, I didn't need to. *Thought you weren't supposed to be a peeping Tom!*

*There's an exception between master and padawan. Besides, I'm fascinated with your mating rituals. For example, Richard is—*

*AB, enough. I don't want to know!*

I boarded the aircraft right behind Rhea. AB boarded behind me, ducking to get in the door.

# CHAPTER 22
## BARSOOM

T he interior of the plane surprised me. Instead of sleek and ultra-modern, the place looked more like the living room of a palace with gilded furniture and art in gaudy gold frames. Imee ogled one of the paintings, but my eye went right to the two pictures hanging on the rear wall of the cabin. One looked vaguely familiar, like an ancient navigation map, while the other showed the same image, but in ultra-high definition using modern technology. I sat down and pulled out my mother's journal and flipped through a few pages. I had remembered it: the old map was pasted in my mother's journal. Next thing I knew, Richard was standing over me.

"What're you looking at?" He glanced down at the journal and then back over his shoulder. "Ah, so your parents knew about the Oronteus Finaeus map."

The name seemed familiar. I nodded.

"Go—take a look. That's the original. Believe it or not, it cost more than all of these other paintings."

That got Imee's attention. She moved away from a print with four images of the same person, all in different hues.

"More than the Warhol?" she asked.

Richard nodded. "Yep, more than the Warhol and the Pollock put together. My dad had to build an entire new wing for the museum he bought it from."

"It looks like Antarctica, but without any snow or ice." Imee looked at the print of the satellite image on the other side. "So does this satellite picture. What's the big deal?"

Richard grinned and put his arm around her. "The big deal, Imee, is that the Oronteus Finaeus map, and its sibling, the Piri Reis map, were drawn way before explorers knew Antarctica existed, let alone showing it with no ice."

"According to my mother's notes, the map was drawn in 1532, while the Piri Reis map was drawn in 1513."

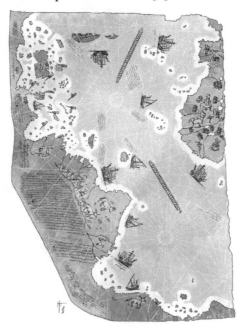

"Both were supposedly based on much older maps that are said to no longer exist." I turned to Richard. "Why'd your father buy them?"

Richard fignored my question. "Wait 'till you see this." He hit a button on the side of his seat and an image appeared in front of the Oronteus Finaeus map.

I leaned forward. It was another ancient map of Antarctica without snow or ice.

Richard pointed, "The DeMarco map's much older than the Piri Reis map. It was unknown until an archaeologist on my father's payroll found it in an Etruscan tomb."

I whistled. The Etruscans predated the Romans in Italy. "That'd make it well over two thousand years old!"

"Older." Richard gloated. "It's drawn on papyrus. My father's scientists think it's originally from Egypt's twenty-fourth dynasty." Richard paused. "That makes it almost three thousand years old!"

Imee walked up and touched it. Her hand went right through the map. "Hologram?"

Richard nodded. "Way too fragile to be on display. My father's got it in one of his vaults."

I was about to get up and take a closer look when a chime sound-ed. "This is the captain. Mr. DeMarco, please fasten your seatbelts."

The plane began to roll forward.

Richard sat down. He patted the seat next to him and Imee sat down with him. AB grabbed the seat across the aisle from Richard as Rhea sat down across from Richard. I hesitated when *Don't be an idiot* sounded in my head. *And don't bother me. I need a nap.* I sat next to Rhea as AB leaned back and closed his eyes.

I noticed the five point seat belt similar to the one I'd used when I took off for the Moon on the lunar shuttle. That seemed like an eternity ago now. I started to strap in when I noticed Richard put on the lap belt only.

"We don't really need these fancy restraints for this flight."

The rest of us followed suit.

"Captain Paul'll give us a smooth ride and will warn us if he ex-pects to run into any turbulence." We all nodded.

Richard flipped a button and a hologram began to float in the air behind him. I turned around and saw the same one behind me. They both showed an image of the runway in front of us.

"Cool technology, huh?" Imee and Rhea nodded. AB looked to be asleep. I nodded as well. The hologram would have been very im-pressive but for the much better Atlantean ones that I'd just seen. The image changed. It was of the aircraft from above. We were sec-ond in line for takeoff.

"How'd you manage that?" I asked almost instinctively.

Richard smiled. "We've got a computer on board that's one gen-eration ahead of the one the university had on the Moon." He point-ed to a sensor dot on his left temple. "I can control it through this interface. I wanted to see where we were in line and watch the take-off so I had the computer pull up a satellite view of the runway." The plane in front of us took off and we turned into the runway. "Ready." He grabbed Imee's hand. "Not like a vertical rocket launch, but fun."

We sped down the runway and then took off, climbing much more steeply than a normal plane. The satellite image stayed focused on the plane as it climbed. The airport and then the city quickly disappeared. The Pacific Ocean appeared below us. The satellite must have been re-directed to follow our takeoff. I knew that Richard was a spoiled brat, but I was just starting to learn how rich Richard's father really was.

"We need to get fifty miles offshore before Captain Paul can punch it and take us through Mach 1. Once we do that, we'll quickly climb to our cruising altitude of 80,000 feet."

I felt a brief shudder. Imee grabbed Richards's hand. "That was just the plane breaking through Mach 1." He patted Imee's hand. I glanced over at Rhea. She seemed fine as she smiled at me.

She leaned forward. "So, Richard, did I hear that this plane's made of graphene?"

I'd heard of graphene being used for small applications but didn't know anyone was making it in large enough quantities for aircraft.

"Sure is, at least a fair chunk of it. One of my father's companies has patented a way to make graphene in large sheets. It's one hundred times stronger than steel and weighs far less than paper." He picked up a large ball in front of him and flipped it to Rhea. It drifted toward her much more slowly than you would expect. Rhea bobbled it and it dropped in her lap. She picked it up.

"It's as light as a feather." She looked up in surprise. She flipped it to me. I almost bobbled it because it was so light.

Richard smiled. "Squeeze it."

It felt as thin as tissue paper. I thought it would crumple in my hand. I squeezed gently. Nothing. I squeezed harder. Still nothing. I flipped it back to Richard.

"Hard to believe."

Richard smiled again.

"We're flying in a paper airplane?" Imee appeared scared, but I'd had her in one of my classes and knew she was smart.

Richard leaned over and kissed her cheek. "Nothing to worry about. It's unbelievably strong."

Imee smiled. "Any other surprises for us?"

Richard smiled. The floor below us disappeared. We all gasped, lifting our feet up involuntarily.

"Don't worry, the interior of the cabin's got a flexible screen painted onto it—another invention of one of my father's companies. Imee, didn't you say you liked *A Princess of Mars*?"

She nodded.

Suddenly, the ocean below us disappeared and we drifted over a landscape of ruddy red desert. It looked like we were skimming slowly over it. We came up on a cluster of men, but, when we got closer, you could see that they were green and had four arms. They appeared to see us and began hurling spears at us.

"That's amazing." I looked up at Richard.

"Yep, we're cutting a deal with Hollywood now. We can put these screens anywhere and you'll be able to load whatever image you want on them." The scene below us changed from Barsoom to an open plain. Off to one side a beam of light illuminated a large white city. In the other direction, dark clouds roiled toward it. The image seemed to bank as we headed under the roiling clouds.

Rhea spoke up. "Minas Tirith, right?"

Richard nodded.

A glow appeared ahead of us. "And you've got us heading toward Mordor." I watched as the glow began to illuminate the volcano below it. "Mount Doom?"

"Yep. But here's the part that really creeps me out."

The plane continued toward a dark stone tower. An orange/yellow spotlight seemed to sweep the plain below us from the apex of the tower. Suddenly, as we approached, the light swung toward us. Rhea leaned toward me.

Imee screeched, "Shut it off, shut it off!"

I was glad when the image disappeared. "The Eye of Sauron. That's a hell of a lot scarier than the movie."

"Like I said, creeps me out." He patted Imee's leg. "Sorry about that. How about we go back to my dad's suite. I've got a scene with Dejah Thoris and John Carter that I think you'll like."

Imee nodded her head, still clutching at Richard.

When Richard got up, Imee winked at Rhea. Richard walked to the back of the cabin to the door between the two maps and opened it. Imee followed.

"What're they up to?" I turned to Rhea.

"Don't be so dense." She hit my arm. "Now, take me through your mother's notebook. I'd like to find out more about our long-dead astronaut."

As she leaned against me to look over my shoulder at my mother's journal, I felt guilty about not telling her more.

# CHAPTER 23
## NASSAU

As we pulled up to the terminal, the hologram showed us pulling up to a Mercedes stretch limo. We came to a stop and the hologram dissolved. Richard and Imee emerged from the owner's suite in the rear of the plane. They had both changed into shorts, Hawaiian shirts and flip flops.

"I've booked us a room at Atlantis." Richard smiled. "See, wasn't too hard to find."

*How droll.* AB grinned at me as he sat up and stretched. He'd napped through the entire flight. I didn't reply.

I gave Richard a wry smile, but otherwise ignored the lame joke. "Thought we were staying on your boat?" I slipped my mother's journal into my backpack as Rhea stood up.

"We were, but she's delayed in the yard in Lauderdale. She'll be here tomorrow. That'll give us time to enjoy the famous water slides."

Imee smiled. "I hear they're better than the ones at Disney. Went once when I was a kid in LA, but—"

Rhea walked up to Imee. "Those pearls are gorgeous. Where'd you get them?" She lifted them off Imee's chest to look at them.

Imee beamed. "Richard just gave them to me. Said I needed something for the tropics."

Rhea turned to Richard and then back to Imee. "He never gave me anything like that when we were dating."

Richard started to say something, but Captain Paul came out, unlatched the door and lowered the stairs. "Watch your step as you exit and don't touch the exterior of the plane. Graphene's an unbelievable conductor and the temperature of the skin is still a bit high from our rapid descent."

He stepped back and let the ladies leave first. Richard leaned over to me as Imee and Rhea walked down. "She's got quite an ass, doesn't she. I sure took a step up when I dumped Rhea."

He elbowed me in the ribs and then walked down the stairs without waiting for my reply. While Imee had a good figure, no way would I trade her for Rhea. There was just something about—

"Uhmm. Can you get a move on it, lover boy, I need to stretch." AB gave me a shove to prod me down the stairs. I gave him a glare. He'd actually said that out loud. I turned to the captain who had totally kept his composure despite my reddening cheeks.

"Captain Paul, thanks for a great flight."

"My pleasure Mr. —"

"It's Charlie. Looking forward to the next flight."

"Thanks, Charlie. Same here."

With that, I headed down the steps to the limo. AB followed. The ride to Atlantis took just over half an hour. The driver was a typical loquacious Bahamian, giving us a running dialogue on New Providence Island as he weaved in an out of traffic. Size seemed to matter since, as he "judiciously" laid on his horn, small cars seemed to part like the Red Sea in front of him. Once the gap opened, he'd shoot through. Rhea cringed several times, leaning into me, as we came within millimeters of scraping against other cars. Richard and Imee, sitting in the rear seat, seemed not to notice at all. They were all lovey-dovey, with Imee fingering her new pearls, smiling and hugging Richard. AB, Rhea and I sat around the horseshoe seat going along one window up to the partition to the driver's cabin.

We passed an old hotel in downtown Nassau that the driver explained was once owned by the owner of the New York Yankees. He then shifted from his tourism dialogue to baseball and how the Yankees might be the team to beat this year. I glanced at Richard, but he said nothing.

We crossed the bridge to Paradise Island, which, per our driver, used to be known as Hog Island, and headed down the boulevard to the main gate to Atlantis. When we pulled up, more friendly Bahamians descended on the limo, dressed in white uniforms with turquoise stripes down each leg.

Richard got out first and a man rushed up to greet him. Imee went next, then Rhea, me and AB. A lady dressed in a brightly colored junkanoo gown and headdress held a tray of drinks for us. Richard grabbed two and handed one to Imee. He took a sip.

"Umm. Goombay Smash. They don't have these on the Moon." He smiled. "Grab one."

AB didn't hesitate. He grabbed two, handing one to Rhea. I thought about reaching for one, but my head buzzed.

*Alcohol and learning to control telepathy don't mix.*

*Party pooper.* I saw another lady behind the first holding a tray. Looked like she had a tray of soft drinks. "Ginger ale?"

She nodded.

I grabbed one. "Don't think my stomach can handle alcohol after that roller-coaster ride from the airport."

Richard took a big gulp, put his now empty first back on the tray and grabbed another. "Suit yourself. More for the rest of us." He turned to the genuflecting man that had run up to us. "Lead on."

"Yes, sir."

We entered the lobby.

"If you will follow me, we have the Presidential Suite ready for you. As you requested, we've sent clothes up to the suite for all of you to pick out." He eyed AB's large frame. "I will have more sent up for your large friend shortly. No offense, sir, but I didn't anticipate your healthy stature."

"No offense taken." AB smiled. "I typically wear a size 66L suit and my waist is a 46." He reached into his pocket and pulled out a wad of cash and a credit card. He started to hand the credit card to the man. "This should take care of the bill."

The man shook his head. "No, sir, this is already taken care of, complements of the house." The guy looked over at Richard and gave him a smile.

AB turned toward Richard. "Richard, thanks for setting this up. Charlie and I hadn't planned to travel so we don't have anything to wear."

"Don't worry about it. My father's what they call a whale. He loves to gamble and they always treat us right. Besides, my father's on the board of their principal lender. Everything'll be on the house."

The man smiled. "Mr. DeMarco, your credit line is set up. The route to your suite is through the casino. We would be happy to set up a private table for you and your guests should you like to stop before getting to your rooms."

"No thanks." He glanced over at Imee. "We'll change and hit the slides first."

Imee smiled, clearly pleased.

AB was glancing out the windows. "Mind if I wander outside for a bit. Want to stretch my legs after the flight. I hear they've got a huge sawfish in one of the tanks outside."

The manager smiled. "Yes, sir, just follow the signs and they will lead you to George. He's been a resident with us for over thirty years. But, before I forget." Another man rushed up to him and handed him a white and turquoise folder. He opened it and pulled out a handful of wrist bands. He passed them out. "These will give you access to all of our facilities. They are charge cards and will grant you elevator access to the penthouse in the Tower. Just tap it against the reader in the elevator and it will take you directly to the penthouse."

"Great, then I'll head out and stretch my legs." AB headed away from the casino and out the door in the back of the lobby. *Too many cameras in casinos. I'll go see George and meet you later.*

*Ok.* I gave him a mental nod.

*Keep your eyes and mind open. There may be some surprises waiting for you.*

*Will do.*

We headed into the casino, following the manager. I felt a tingle in the back of my mind and started to look around. Maybe nothing or just paranoia created by AB's warning. We passed the craps tables and headed down the long bank of blackjack tables. That tingling started again. It seemed associated with the second-to-last blackjack table. There were several people at the table, but my eyes focused on a long grey ponytail hanging out the back of a baseball cap. As if he knew I was watching, he turned to face me as we approached.

"Uncle Merl!" I darted ahead.

My uncle got up to receive my hug. He rubbed the top of my head. "Great to see you, Charlie." He glanced around. "Looks like you brought a few of my former students with you. Ms. Harte, Ms. Castillo and Mr. DeMarco, if I'm not mistaken."

"Yes sir, Dr. Ambrose." Rhea stepped forward first. "Good to see you. I suspect it was a bit of an adventure for you and Charlie to get off the Moon." My uncle nodded.

"Lucky you had your own ship." A frown creased her face. "What happened to your cat? She didn't . . ."

"No, of course not. I'd never leave Nim behind." He glanced around, leaned in between me and Rhea and whispered, "She's here, in my room."

"You're kidding?" Several people looked over and the manager gave us a scowl.

"In fact, why don't the two of you come on up to my room. I've got something for you, Charlie. You don't mind, do you, Mr. De-Marco?" My uncle used his professorial stare on Richard. For the first time since I'd run into Richard at the Mariners game, Richard looked uncomfortable.

"Of course not, sir. Charlie and Rhea know where our suite is. We'll see you out in the park. Let's meet at the slide of terror in an hour?"

I nodded. "Thanks, Richard."

Richard shifted his feet back and forth. "Want to join us for dinner, Dr. Ambrose? On me?"

"No thanks, young man. Other plans." My uncle smiled. Richard stood uncomfortably.

Imee nudged him. "Let's head to the room. I can't wait to see the clothes the hotel sent up." She smiled at Rhea. "This way, I'll get first dibs over Rhea."

Relieved, Richard turned to the manager waiting at a polite distance. "Lead on."

Uncle Merl signaled to the dealer. "Color me."

The dealer took his stack of chips, counted them and handed him back far fewer chips. Uncle Merl grabbed them, but dropped several on the floor. I quickly leaned over and picked them up. They were $5,000 each. I started to hand them to Uncle Merl.

He shook his head. "No, no, keep them. Got plenty. Besides, you may need the money for your quest. Don't want you to have to rely on the largesse of Mr. DeMarco."

"But it's $15,000!"

My uncle waved his hand dismissively. "Now, young lady, want to head up and see Nim?"

"Yes, sir."

My uncle turned and headed toward the elevators.

# CHAPTER 24
## UNCLE MERL'S TALE

Uncle Merl handed me his key card when we got to the room. I opened the door. He signaled us to go in first. I walked in and a ball of fuzz flew toward me. I caught Nim in my arms.

"Nim! How are you, kitty?" I rubbed behind her ears and she purred. Rhea walked over and petted her.

"Hello, girl. Glad you're safe." Nim jumped down, rubbed up and down on Rhea's legs and then leaped onto the bed.

"Seems like Nim's adjusted to Earth gravity much quicker than we have." Rhea turned toward Uncle Merl. "Did she do any exercises on the Moon?"

Uncle Merl laughed. "Get a cat to do other than what she wants, particularly a first-generation serval cat? No way. You'd need to be a magician."

Nim glanced up at Uncle Merl and walked into the little kitchen area.

"I think she wants to eat. Mind feeding her?"

Rhea answered, "Love to."

"There's food and a bowl on the counter, and thanks."

Uncle Merl headed to the window and I followed him. He glanced over at the kitchen, sat down and signaled me to sit as well.

He spoke telepathically. *So, where's Aku Brugal?*

*You knew they'd be waiting for me. Why didn't you warn me?*

*A bit busy if you recall. The ship was damaged and I had the devil of a time getting you out anywhere near Aku Brugal and the Atlantean colony.*

*That's another thing. If you knew about Galadriel and the Atlanteans, why all of the stink on the Moon about finding the Atlantean astronaut?*

*You needed to find out on your own. Some things are much better learned if experienced. He shook his head. The impatience of youth.*

Rhea popped her head around the corner. "Mind if I have something to drink?"

"Not at all. Help yourself, but could you bring me a Diet Coke? Charlie?"

"I'll take a Coke."

*By the way, they've all met AB—that's what I call Aku Brugal. He's here, but he's avoiding the cameras in the casino.*

*Smart 'squatch, that one. I remember teaching him . . ."*

Rhea retuned with our drinks.

"Thanks, Ms. Harte." Nim followed her in. "Nim's taken a liking to you and she's picky about her friends. Aren't you ready to head out and take advantage of this beautiful weather?"

Rhea frowned briefly, but then answered, "Sure. I'll head up to Richard's suite, get a bathing suit and head out. See you out there, Charlie—soon?"

I nodded, but stood, a bit confused as Rhea left.

My uncle smiled, "Jedi, am I not, but mind games, can I play."

"So you can make people do what you want?"

"No. Just skimmed the surface of her mind and placed an image of the beautiful weather in her head. A mere suggestion that reinforced what she wanted to do. Rhea's a sweet girl, but I need to share a few things with you privately."

"That's ridiculous. She helped discover the Atlantean astronaut."

My uncle held up his hand and shook his head. "Have you told her about AB, your telepathic abilities or the quest the Lady Galadriel, gave you?"

I shook my head.

"There's a reason for that. Trust your instincts. She's an exceptional girl, but there's something else about her. A powerful aura, and I'm having difficulty penetrating her thoughts."

"Why would you do that anyway?"

"It's an old survival instinct. Wouldn't be the age I am if I hadn't followed my instincts. How old do you think I am, Charlie?"

I looked at my uncle. Long grey hair draped his shoulders and age spots dappled his wrinkled skin. "My mother's forty-two and you're her uncle, so seventies should be about right. But if that were true, you wouldn't be asking."

My uncle smiled, but didn't give anything away. "How old do you think AB is?"

I shook my head. "No clue, but I would guess middle age for a sasquatch—thirty-five?"

"He'd be pleased to hear that. The normal lifespan of a sasquatch is 150. Given Atlantean technology, AB can expect to live to be close to 400." He paused and wrinkled his brow. "AB's 142. Not quite middle age yet."

My jaw dropped. AB didn't look or act old, let alone ancient. Then it hit me that Uncle Merl had taught AB when he was a mere cub. "But that would make you at least 175! Maybe older." My eyes narrowed. "AB said that you learned calculus from Isaac Newton. Did you?"

Uncle Merl laughed. "No, I wasn't in England when Isaac Newton was working on calculus. But I did learn geometry from Euclid!"

I stared in disbelief. "That would make you over two thousand years old!"

He just looked at me and began to laugh again. "Just kidding, boy. I'm not that old. But we do both have a lot to do, so pull out that educator of yours and we'll get to work."

I reached into the backpack and pulled out the crystal sphere. It began to glow when I touched it.

*Hand it to me.*

I did. Uncle Merl flipped it into the air. It stayed there, glowing.

*Now, focus on the glowing orb and on my thoughts.*

I focused on the orb as it glowed. It slowly started to spin. The room faded around me. Uncle Merl started to glow. He became brighter and brighter. I had to shut my eyes.

*Use your mind, Charlie. You need to learn to control your mental vision. Shield yourself from the glow of my aura. Think about a rheostat.*

A what? The bright glow from my uncle was starting to hurt. It reminded me of the pain from the Lemurian attack on me and AB after leaving the Atlantean fortress.

*A switch that lowers the light in a room. You probably use your iLet. Picture that feature and then turn down the volume.*

I thought about the switches on my iLet and how I controlled them. I tried. The light dimmed slightly. My head began to ache. Suddenly the light dimmed.

*I did that. But you need to learn to block the inflow from my aura. I'm not even trying to penetrate your mind. This is my natural aura. Were I trying to, I could make you do anything, like those zombie ants in the Amazon. That's what Trolga was going to do to you if I hadn't intervened. Now, focus!*

Uncle Merl's aura brightened again. My friends controlled almost everything by thinking at their embedded iChips. Maybe this worked the same way. I thought, *Light, shut off.* Nothing. I pictured flipping a switch off. That didn't work either. The light from Uncle Merl's aura started to brighten and shift from a yellow-white to crimson.

*Come on, boy, you've got talent and the Atlantean gene. You can do things that I can't. Remember your ability to control the ship.*

*But that was a hologram and I just talked to it.*

*It was more than that, boy. Now, focus!*

I tried again, but nothing.

*Come on or I'll march you around the room like a puppet!* The aura brightened more and a focused beam came out of the middle, grabbing hold of me. I took a step and then another.

*Now, do an Irish jig.* I could feel my uncle's laughter as I danced around the room with my arms crossed.

*No. Stop!* I grimaced.

*Make me.* My uncle continued to laugh. He reminded me of a schoolyard bully that had preyed on one of my best friends. He stopped when I stepped up and punched him in the nose. I took my licks, but he and his buddies left us alone after that.

*Stop!* I focused, trying to block the beam of light emanating from my uncle.

*Better, but not good enough. They'll chew you up and spit you out. Now, let's see. I think I'll get Rhea to come up here and watch.*

A thin tendril extended from my uncle and shot through the door. Part of my consciousness flew out the door with my uncle. The tendril approached Rhea. She was walking toward the pool with Imee, laughing. Suddenly, she stopped, turned around and began walking back to the lobby. I reappeared in the room, but was looking through my uncle's eyes now. I looked ridiculous dancing around the room like a leprechaun.

*Now, take off your pants. I want Rhea to see you dancing a jig in your underpants. That'll stop any romance between the two of you.*

I stopped dancing and sat down to take off my shoes. I placed them and my socks neatly under a chair and then undid my belt and took my jeans off. Then I was back up dancing a jig.

*She'll be up here momentarily and that will be that.* My uncle rubbed his hands together as if washing them.

I heard a knock at the door. *Noooo!* I pushed as hard as I could. I felt something snap and I tumbled to the floor. When I looked up, my uncle was seated, rubbing his head. I picked up my pants, slipped them on and then went to open the door. Nobody was there. I closed the door.

*Now, that's more like it. Haven't had my head banged like that in over a hundred years.*

*Where's Rhea?* I'd balled my hands into fists.

*Outside with your friends. I just made you think she was on her way up here to give you the right motivation.*

*Screw you.* I turned to leave, but my feet wouldn't move.

*This is a lesson that only I can teach you, boy, and you need to learn. Now, do you need another dancing lesson?*

My foot began to move involuntarily. I clenched my fists tighter. My aura expanded outward and pressed against my uncle's.

*Not bad, kid. I was beginning to doubt AB's assessment of your abilities. You'll have a fighting chance unless you run up against a full-blooded Lemurian. Now, let's take a break. You've given me quite a headache.*

*Good. You shouldn't have done that to me.* I stuffed the glowing orb back into my backpack.

"Sorry about that, kid, but I had to get you over the hump in a hurry." He'd actually spoken this time.

"Why should I listen to you?"

Uncle Merl sighed and sat down. "Because I'm your oldest living relative and I have asked you to." He pointed to a chair. "Have a seat."

I refused.

"Fine. Have it your way." He sat down, took a sip of tea and sighed. He then focused his eyes on me. "I was born in a small Celtic village around 382 AD. I'm not certain of the date because my memories of my early childhood are remote and sketchy. I do remember hiding behind my mother's skirt as a cohort of Roman legionnaires marched through my village. The Romans were leaving Britain, and that event lets me estimate the year of my birth."

I slid down into a seat, my anger replaced by curiosity. "But that would make you—"

"Around 1,700 years old." Uncle Merl nodded. "Yes, I have the Atlantean gene just like you. One of the blessings and curses of that gene is extreme longevity."

"Then I'll live—"

"Only if you quit interrupting a tired old man. Otherwise—" Uncle Merl's aura darkened into an angry deep red.

I sat back in the chair as Uncle Merl's aura lightened into a pleasant blue.

"Now, where was I?" He took another sip of tea.

"The Romans marching through your village."

"Ah, yes. Anyway, my father was a cooper, so in terms of our mud-encrusted village, he was wealthy. We had a copse of old oaks behind the village that generated the perfect wood for kilderkins, barrels and hogsheads. He would sell his barrels to all of the surrounding villages and towns. In fact, he used to brag that some of his hogsheads had made it all the way to Londinium—London now.

"As a result of his wealth, he married one of the prettiest girls in the neighboring towns, my mother, Erwana. I was one of seven children, but only three of us lived to adulthood." Uncle Merl's aura darkened momentarily. "I didn't know my mother very well. She died giving birth to my sister, Robyn. My mother loved birds and named us after them. My older brother Peri's full name was Peregrine, after the falcon. She named Robyn about a week before giving birth to her when a bright red robin landed on the rail while she was rocking me on the porch. Somehow she knew Robyn would be a girl.

"Since I was so small at birth she named me after the smallest and one of the fastest of the falcons, Merlin. They didn't think I'd make it, puny and small as I was as a child, but, then again, look at me now."

While not tall, Uncle Merl did stand a full six feet. That must have been very tall back then. Then it dawned on me . . . "You're Merlin—the Merlin—King Arthur's Merlin?"

My uncle smiled and nodded. "Close your mouth, lad. A fly might fly in."

I hadn't realized I'd opened it.

Uncle Merl continued. "There's a grain of truth to every legend. I am that grain."

"And King Arthur?" I leaned forward.

Uncle Merl chuckled. "Yes, I remember the young lad. One of these days, I'll tell you about him and about your namesake, Emperor Charlemagne. But those are tales for another day.

"Now, where was I?" He grabbed a pipe out of his pocket, packed it with tobacco and then looked back at me, drawing me in with his eyes.

"One afternoon, Robyn and I were cleaning out some old barrels when old man Dagfinn's dogs started going nuts. Robyn and I glanced down the muddy lane and saw a dozen figures in hooded robes enter our village. As they walked up the lane toward our house, mothers shooed their children into their houses and shut the doors. The visitor's heads were recessed in their hoods so far that you couldn't see their faces. We glanced at each other, nodded and decided to head for our secret glade in the woods we'd found years before. Robyn took off. I tried and tried, but couldn't move. When Robyn made it to the edge of the woods, she looked back. I wanted to yell to her to keep going, but couldn't.

"My father came out of his workshop, wiping his hands on a rag. He spoke in a booming voice, louder than normal. I could hear the tension in it. He looked over at me and tilted his head to one side for me to go, but I still couldn't move. After a heated discussion, he looked over at me. One of the figures took several steps toward me. Pulling back her hood, I was surprised to see a beautiful woman with long flaxen hair. I was taken aback by her beauty, never having seen its like. She motioned with her index finger for me to come forward. I did.

"When I reached her, she rubbed my head and bent down and spoke to me. 'Merlin, is it? A fine name for a young lad. How would you like to come with us on an adventure?'

"I looked up at my father. He nodded uncomfortably. I found that I could speak again. 'But this is my home,' I said. She answered, 'Yes, but there's a very large world out there. We'll teach you about it. Come, join us.' I looked into her eyes. Something about them drew me in. I wanted to go with her. I nodded. 'Yes, I'll go.'

"I heard my sister wail as she ran toward me. One of the hooded men stopped her. I looked over at her. Deep inside I wanted to go to her, but somehow I couldn't. I took the lady's hand and started to walk off with her. I heard weeping. My sister. Then I heard my father say, 'They're Druids, lass. He's been chosen. There's nothing we can do.' Their voices faded as I looked up at the lady and smiled.

"We traipsed through the woods for several days before we came to a cave. I had to duck to enter the dark and damp cave. We passed a large she-bear and two cubs. I wanted to cower and run, but the Druids walked right past them without a second thought. We continued around a bend and, to my shock, the cave opened up into the largest room I had ever seen, larger than what I imagined a throne room for a king would be. Immaculately clean and furnished with chairs and tables nicer than anything I had ever seen or imagined. Before getting started, they introduced me to running water and a shower. I was totally shocked when warm water poured down over me.

"After I had showered and changed into a Druid robe, Nimue brought me into the presence of the Lady you call Galadriel. She hovered above the floor in the middle of the cave. I tried to bow down to what must be a goddess, but Nimue lifted me back up. The Lady studied me briefly and then invited me to walk with her. Clouds enveloped us, and the next thing I knew we were walking along a shaded path next to a pristine lake in a place she called Atlantis. She told me that the blood of the gods flowed through my veins and that I had certain powers and abilities that ordinary mortals did not have. She explained that she had much for me to do, but that first she would leave me in the care of the beautiful Druid, Nimue, to educate me. When we returned to the cave, she took her leave of me, turning me over to Nimue.

"I stayed in Nimue's cave for many years learning math, science, history, Latin, Greek, Atlantean and even Lemurian. The Lady Galadriel would appear periodically to check on me. We walked through her memories of Atlantis many times, and I learned of the war between Atlantis and Lemuria and of the Atlantean plans for *Homo sapiens*. In addition to providing me with a classical education that would be the envy of an Oxford don, Nimue honed my telepathic and telekinetic abilities.

"I don't know how long I studied. Time didn't seem to pass within that cave. I grew into adulthood seeing little of the outside world.

One day, Galadriel came to me and told me that it was time to leave. My training would help me watch over others that had the blood of the gods flowing through their veins and protect them from the Lemurians. With my almost pure Atlantean blood, the Lady assigned me the task of watching over my family and their descendants. She had high hopes that this blood line would lead to their goal of recreating Atlanteans in humans. Unfortunately, my gifts couldn't be passed on because I was like a mule. Genetically both human and Atlantean, but sterile. This bloodline would have to flow through my siblings.

"I left the cave to return to my village. The next time I saw my younger sister, she was forty-two years old, sitting on our old porch, holding her granddaughter in her arms. Her husband had taken over our father's business and they lived in the house I'd grown up in. She didn't recognize me because now I wore the grey-hooded robe. As much as I wanted to, I didn't reveal myself to her. She looked ancient while I still looked and felt like a young man. She eyed me with fear and suspicion as I passed by. I have kept an avuncular eye on your ancestors since that time, keeping them safe and hidden from the Lemurians. I am your uncle, but many, many times removed."

I didn't know what to think. Uncle Merl—Merlin the Magician—and he was ancient—older than Methuselah! I sat there, dumbfounded.

Uncle Merl sat back in his seat, pulled out some matches and lit his pipe. He breathed in the smoke, blew out a smoke ring and sighed. "One of the things I really missed on the Moon was smoking." He took another puff. "What, cat got your tongue?" As if on cue, Nim walked in and rubbed up against my leg. I reached down and scratched behind her ear.

"The Lemurians know who you are. They know the stakes. You need to understand them." Uncle Merl made a circle with his finger in front of him and then blew a puff of smoke. The smoke coalesced into an image of the Earth. A black shadow swallowed India, Pakistan and swelled toward the Far East and China. As it did, additional shadows appeared and then expanded throughout Mexico into the United States, Peru, throughout South America, northern Scotland into England, and Russia into Europe. The shadows quickly enveloped the entire globe. My shoulders slumped.

Uncle Merl brushed a finger through the globe and the vision disappeared. "I think you're starting to understand the stakes. It's not just you. It's Rhea and your friends, your parents, everybody. You need to be able to defend yourself. That's why I grabbed hold of you and forced the breakthrough that generally takes years. I had no choice—and neither do you." He put down his pipe as Nim jumped into his lap. "Now, forgive me?"

I nodded. "You could have told me."

His eyebrows rose. "Could I?"

I thought about it. "Guess not. But why can't you find the scepter and do it yourself. You can defend yourself. And you have Atlantean blood." I pictured shifting the world off my shoulders and onto Uncle Merl's. If anyone could keep it from falling and cracking like an egg, he could.

He shook his head and blew out a puff of smoke. "Wish I could, but just as the hologram on the spaceship didn't recognize me until you introduced me, the scepter will not work for me. Your genetic code is that much closer to a true Atlantean. While it won't work for me, it will work for you."

The weight shifted back to my shoulders. But then I focused more on his tale. I had so many questions for him about the Atlanteans, my mother and father and their disappearance, but didn't know where to start. Questions filled my head about my mother and father.

Uncle Merl shook his head and shifted back to telepathy. *No. They must've felt something in their gut, but they had no knowledge of their heritage.*

*Do you know what happened to them?*

*No, but—*

A knock at the door interrupted his answer. He got up to open the door, but turned to me. I focused my thoughts on the door. I sensed someone out there, but they were blocking their thoughts. I thought about the orb and focused on it. While I still couldn't read his thoughts, I felt his aura. It was large, jovial and familiar. "AB!"

My uncle nodded and opened the door.

AB sported a big grin below his Wayfarer sunglasses and wore a tacky pair of boarding shorts with blue and green hula girls on them. He held a tall glass with a big chunk of pineapple on its rim.

"How'd you find us?" I asked.

AB nodded to me, but turned to Uncle Merl. "It looked like a storm up here. Any telepath would notice. What were you thinking?"

Uncle Merl blew another puff of smoke. "That's what I'm counting on." He pointed the stem of the pipe at me. "Olga Larsen's here. She's following you."

I felt a moment of panic, thinking back to when she grabbed hold of my mind.

"How'd she find me?" I paced back and forth.

AB answered. "She picked us up in Seattle. I sensed something at the ball game. After we were attacked coming out of the fortress, we knew she'd have her agents tracking us down."

I looked over at Uncle Merl. His image started to waver. All I could see was a blur. When he came back into focus, I felt that I was looking in a mirror.

"How'd you do that?" I asked in disbelief.

He laughed just like me. "I've been around a long time." He sounded just like me. *AB, how do our auras look?*

*Not bad. You could fool me from a distance, and I know you both.*

*Good. Charlie, stay here and practice with the teaching device. Should be safe for you to leave in a few hours.*

I shook my head as I looked at myself smiling. I watched myself walk to the door. *When will we meet up again?*

My doppelganger gave me a wink, walked out and closed the door. The door became transparent and I watched a shimmering image of myself walk down the hall. *If you work on it and focus hard enough, Charlie, your thoughts will always reach me. Good luck with your quest. Now practice!* As Uncle Merl's thoughts faded, the shimmering image of myself walking down the hall faded out as well.

# CHAPTER 25
## TROLGA AND JAMIE

A B just stood there. I shifted my feet back and forth, waiting for him to say something. Finally, I couldn't stand the silence. "So, how's the pool?"

*Practice your telepathy, my dear boy. As to the pool, a bit hot and got tired of looking at all of the bare-skinned humans. If you don't have a good coating of hair to show off, why take off your clothes in the first place. All they'll do is burn that sensitive* Homo sapien *skin of theirs.*

I must have been getting better at the telepathy game because not only did I "hear" AB's words, but I could see an image of the pool. Girls in bikinis swarmed like gnats around the pool. AB had focused on Rhea and Imee sitting in lounge chairs, chatting. Then his eyes had shifted around the crowd. Several guys were focusing their attention on Rhea and Imee. One of them was Richard. I didn't like the way he leered at Rhea, but then maybe he'd been looking at Imee.

*Hold on there, cowboy. I held the image so you could take a quick look around and practice looking through other people's eyes. Get your hormones back in control and look again. Search through my memory of the images at the pool.*

I did, looking back into AB's prior thoughts. It was harder than reading current thoughts. Were AB not cooperating, I doubt that I could have done it. As it was, I replayed his time at the pool. After his eyes left the girls, he focused on the water slide that shot through a shark tank. I saw something familiar. I reran the memory and froze the scene with the waterslide. Jamie. I hadn't seen him since the Moon.

*That's Jamie. How'd you know he was here?*

*I wasn't talking about Jamie, but interesting you managed to pick him out. Must be a smart guy based on that pelt of hair on his back. Now, look back and see if you notice anything else.*

I did and followed AB's glance up to the top of the water slide. There were several kids up there, but something looked fuzzy. I tried to focus on it and the fuzziness slowly faded. Trolga. AB's eyes then followed her gaze to the hotel. She was looking at my window. As AB had said, I could see a pyrotechnic display of auras while Uncle Merl had tested me. AB glanced back up to Trolga, but she was gone. That was when he quickly headed to Uncle Merl's room.

*We've got to go. Now. She'll be here any minute!* I picked up my backpack.

AB shook his head. *Your uncle will take care of that. He'll make sure they see him and will make a run for it. They'll follow. Besides, the educator provides for time dilation. Look at your iLet.*

I glanced down. Barely five minutes had passed since I'd entered the room. It had seemed like an hour or more.

*That's an advantage of the educator: your brain works much faster when you use it. He knew Trolga was watching. But we do need to get moving. We don't know the extent of the resources that Trolga and the Lemurians have brought to bear. Given their attack on your spaceship and their attack on us leaving the fortress, they're pressing hard.*

I nodded as my iLet rang. Rhea.

"You coming down?"

"Yes, my uncle just left. Be down in a minute. Hey, by the way, Jamie's here."

"You're kidding."

"Nope. Saw him on the shark slide a little while ago—" I realized my mistake. "With my uncle's new binoculars. He couldn't get them to focus. I spotted Jamie on top of the slide—but then I saw Trolga."

"You sure?"

"No way I'd mistake her ugly mug. We need to leave for Bimini ASAP."

Rhea paused. "That may be a problem. Richard's at the crap tables. Imee's mad, but you know how Richard is."

I didn't know Richard that well, but, unfortunately, Rhea did. I believed her. "How the hell's he gambling? He's too young."

"And we're all too young to drink but they served us. When you've got his kind of money, age mustn't matter."

"Let's meet in the lobby in five."

Rhea paused. "OK. See you in a sec."

I disconnected and picked up my backpack. "You coming?"

AB nodded.

When we arrived at the lobby the elevator door slid open and a guy in a wet bathing suit backed into AB. I couldn't believe it—Jamie! He was chatting with a group of guys. Jamie looked up at AB.

"Sorry, mister." He continued chatting with his friends. I tapped him on the shoulder.

Jamie turned. "I said I was sorry."

I smiled. "To him, but not to me."

Jamie stared at me for a second and then his lips broadened into a grin. "Charlie!" He threw his arms around me and gave me a hug. "What the hell are you doing here?" The elevator door started to close. Jamie waved to his friends and got off the elevator with us.

"Visiting with Rhea, Imee and Richard. By the way, the hulking beast that you bumped into is AB."

AB extended his massive hand. "Nice to meet you, Jamie."

Jamie looked a little tentative. "Same here."

"AB lives in the Seattle area. He's a former student of my uncle's. When Richard invited me to Atlantis, my uncle agreed if AB came along to chaperone."

AB grinned. "How could I say no to a free trip to the Bahamas?" *You're getting quick with those lies, Charlie—taking more after your uncle every minute.*

I ignored AB. "Have a second to catch up?" I looked at Jamie closely. The last time I'd seen him was when he'd left during the middle of my uncle's examination of the Atlantean astronaut. Something about him had changed, but I couldn't place my finger on it.

He nodded. "Sure."

We walked over to a set of chairs in the lobby with nobody around. I sat down and Jamie sat in the chair next to me. AB stood there.

"If you don't mind, I'll wander outside for a bit." I nodded as AB drifted off.

*I'll be on the lookout for Trolga and any of her minions. Even if she took your uncle's bait, she probably left someone behind. By the way, look at Jamie's aura. You need the practice.*

I leaned forward. "So, Jamie, what happened to you? Last I heard you'd accused me of having put you in the hospital." I focused on Jamie. I could barely make out a blue-green haze around him.

Jamie shook his head. "Don't remember that. Last thing I remember was leaving you and Rhea watching your uncle and Professor Betrys work on Spock."

"So, you don't remember accusing me of having beat you up and put you in the hospital?" Jamie's aura expanded and darkened, but quickly changed back to a bright blue-green.

"I don't remember that time at all. Must have bumped my head or something." Jamie gave me a blank look.

I could see the hole in Jamie's memory. He wasn't lying. "Trolga must have gotten to you and done something."

"What do you mean?" Jamie fidgeted in the chair.

"They tried to arrest me. I think Trolga wanted the astronaut. She somehow scrammed the university reactor and caused the evacuation. I had to take off toward where we found the body. Had my uncle not found me, I probably would've died out there."

"Damn, you're kidding." His eyes widened. "I think I saw Trolga. She's here, at Atlantis!" He glanced around.

"I know. We're heading to Bimini on Richard's boat as soon as possible."

"Richard—thought you hated him."

"Guess I misjudged him. Ran into him at a Mariners game. Did you know his father owns the Mariners?"

Jamie nodded.

"Anyway, Rhea blurted out about the ancient astronaut we found. Richard's agreed to help us track down Atlantis."

Jamie didn't hesitate. "I'm in." He leaned forward. "How're things going with Rhea?"

I ignored his question. "Don't you need to check with your parents?"

"Nah. Came down with friends. I'll text my father that I ran into some friends from the Moon that invited me to go for a cruise on a yacht. He won't care. He wants me out of his hair to spend time with his new wife." Jamie's aura darkened again.

"Well, glad you're here."

AB's thought interrupted me. *The girls are on the way with Richard in tow.*

"We can catch up on the way to Bimini. The run should be a couple of hours at least." AB walked in one door as Rhea, Imee and

Richard walked in from the casino entrance. Richard was grinning from ear to ear.

He spotted Jamie and headed his way. "Well, well, look who's here. The gang's back together." Richard stared at Jamie.

Jamie's head drooped slightly. "Hey Richard."

"Don't look so happy to see me." Richard pulled a chip out and flipped it to Jamie. "Here's $1,000. Just made over $500,000 in an hour at the tables. My new record."

Jamie caught the chip and looked at it. He started to hand it back to Richard.

Richard shook his head. "No, keep it. I meant it."

Jamie looked uncomfortable. "Thanks."

Richard clapped his hands together and rubbed them. "So, Imee's ready to do a bit of snorkeling. Anyone else ready to bail on the wonders of Atlantis to snorkel and search for, well, the wonders of Atlantis?"

"I—" A man in a suit walked over to Richard, interrupting me.

"Mr. DeMarco, I'm terribly sorry, but would you mind coming with me?" The man stuck his finger under his collar as if to loosen it.

"I do mind. We're not here for long and we'd rather not take the time. Where's Jackson?" Richard glanced around. "He'll take care of anything."

"I understand, sir, but Mr. Bonier has left for the day. Please, this will only take a moment." He leaned forward and whispered something in Richard's ear.

Richard's face reddened, but then he regained his composure. "I think I can handle this myself."

The man nodded, but said, "Why don't your friends come as well. I have food and refreshments in the room, compliments of the house. They can eat while you address the matter at hand. Now, if you will all follow me, please." The man headed toward the southwest corner of the lobby and entered a door marked "Office." Richard followed him, and we followed Richard.

*Spidey senses are tingling, Charlie.*

*What?*

*Never mind. Something doesn't feel right. I tried to skim the man's mind but ran into a brick wall. That's extremely unusual for you Homo sapiens. I also get the hint of—* AB entered the room last. The door closed behind him. *Yet—!*

My link to AB's thoughts abruptly terminated.

I heard a guttural growl. I'd heard it before, a few days ago when I'd met AB. I turned. Two huge men grabbed AB's arms.

Ignoring the melee, Richard looked anxiously around the room. "Where's the phone?"

A smile erupted across the man's face. "Sorry to deceive you, Mr. DeMarco, but you see, we needed to get all of you away from the myriad of cameras in the hotel and casino. What better reason than to imply that your father was deathly ill."

"Is he?" Richard leaned forward.

The man shook his head.

"Then why?" Richard looked confused, as did everyone but AB. While he'd quit struggling, he looked taut as the string of a compound bow.

Ignoring Richard's questions, I shot AB a quick thought. Nothing. I pictured the teaching device and felt myself connect to it. I then focused on AB and the two burly men holding him in check. They began to blur and then refocused. They were slightly taller than AB and even stockier. Their brows were thicker and, when one noticed me looking, he cracked a smile. Long yellowed canines protruded from under his lip. As their business suits faded away, I could see that dirty white fur covered them. Yeti—that's what AB had thought before getting cut off.

Hazy lines, like heat radiating from sand, began to wiggle around the man conversing with Richard. I focused harder and the man's image faltered even more. A blood orange aura began to creep around the edges of the man. I felt a droplet of sweat drip down my temple. I pushed hard. Suddenly the image of the man disappeared. Trolga!

She stopped talking to Richard and focused on me. *I see you've learned. Good. You'll make an even better prize.* A wave of thought slammed into me. My vision blurred. I stumbled.

Rhea grabbed my arm. "You all right?"

I nodded, but my head spun. The lights in the room briefly dimmed. When they brightened, Trolga stood in front of us.

"Sorry for the little deception, students, but class is back in session!" she said, arms crossed.

All eyes in the room focused on her. "Now, I'm sure you're wondering how I got here. It seems your buddy, Charlie here, has not been totally forthright with you." Several more men entered through a back door, carrying handguns.

Richard and the others looked over at me. Rhea squeezed my hand.

"First of all, as to Charlie's friend, AB. Just take a look behind you and see what he really looks like." Trolga extended her arm toward the back wall.

Everyone turned. AB's and the yetis' mental camouflage had evaporated. Imee gasped and grabbed for Richard. Rhea squeezed my hand harder.

I cleared my throat. "AB's a sasquatch. I met him when my uncle dropped me off in the forest outside Seattle. The two creatures holding him appear to be yetis." I turned and faced Trolga. "And Dr. Larsen here has been pursuing me since we discovered the body of the dead Atlantean astronaut. Lemurian, correct?"

Trolga tilted her head slightly. "I guess I'm a good history teacher."

Richard cleared his throat. "Lemurian, huh. What the hell's that? Thought you were a Damn Yankee."

Trolga nodded her head, and one of the men put his pistol away and walked up to Richard. "Extend your hands."

Richard gave him the ultimate in disdainful looks.

"Fine, have it your way." He pulled out the pistol, looked at Richard, turned rapidly and pistol-whipped Imee. She screamed as her head snapped to one side. The man pulled the slide back on the gun and pointed it at the whimpering Imee. "Now, do I put a bullet in her or do you—" he looked around the room, making eye contact with each of us "—all of you, agree to cooperate."

I'd never seen Richard look so shocked.

"Now, stick your hands out, you spoiled little shit. We need you intact, but we don't need her"—he pointed the gun at Imee—"or her"—pointing the gun at Rhea—"or him"—pointing the gun at Jamie.

Richard docilely extended his hands.

The man pulled out a plastic tie and tightened it around Richard's hands. "Next."

I looked around and stepped forward, but Trolga stepped in front of me.

"So, little Charlie's brave. Let's save him for last. Do the 'squatch now."

I looked closely at Trolga. Beads of sweat had formed around her brow. I closed my eyes, reached out to the educator and focused on Trolga and AB. The room appeared in my mind. I saw the aura of each of the people. Richard was closest to me and he glowed an angry orange, mixed with a hint of something else. Confidence? I shook my head. I was new to reading auras. Imee, next to him, extended a hand toward Richard. She glowed an odd shade of orange. Not what I'd expected. No fear there. Rhea's aura seemed to pulsate with a mixture of orange and violet, but a thin tendril of silver extended from just under her belly button toward me. Jamie was hidden behind the glowing blast furnace of deep orange-red surrounding AB. A shell of mucus-green slime encased his aura. Much of the slime oozed from the yetis standing on either side of him. Their auras seemed far weaker and more primitive than AB's. They couldn't be restraining him. I then noticed diaphanous tendrils of glowing slime that lead back toward the bright-green aura that radiated from Trolga. She was bolstering the energy of the two yetis to control AB. That was why AB couldn't talk or even issue one of his guttural growls.

I reached out with my mind, picturing my hand karate chopping through one of the tendrils leading from Trolga to AB. I felt a searing pain, but I'd broken the tendril. Another searing pain shot through my head, severing my link to the educator. My knees buckled, but Richard and Rhea held me up. My head throbbed, but at least Trolga was rubbing her left temple. AB smiled at me.

"Try that again, boy, and see what happens." She nodded her head toward me. One man yanked me up, while another pulled my hands behind me. The plastic cuffs dug into my wrists.

"Hey, that hurts!"

The man behind me leaned forward. "I was gentle. Next time I won't be." He shoved me forward. "Next."

After they'd cuffed all of us, Richard addressed Trolga. "Professor Larsen, if you're looking for money from my father, there's no need. Just set us free and I'll get you all the money you could want."

Trolga snorted. "Of course you think this is about money." She shook her head.

"Then what?" Richard questioned.

"You'll learn in good time." She motioned her head toward the rear door. "Take them. I'll join you at the airport." A shimmer appeared around her again and she transformed back into the assistant manager. She exited the door back into the lobby. I glanced over at AB and his yeti guards. They, too, had transformed back into their human appearances.

One of Trolga's henchmen opened the back door. "Move it." He shoved Imee forward. She tripped.

Richard moved forward, picking her up. "Now then. No need for that. If you treat us right, I'll make it worth your while."

One of the men hesitated, but the henchman who'd cuffed my hands took control. "Move 'em out. Now!"

We marched down an interior corridor that seemed to run a long way. We passed several doors, but didn't stop. We turned a corner. The hall ended in double doors. In typical Bahamian fashion, the E and X in the Exit light were broken, and a gap of sunlight shone through a rather large crack between the two doors. The leader held up his hand.

"Joe, make sure the truck's ready." One of the men with a machine pistol opened the door. A bright blast of sunlight and heat greeted him. When the doors shut it took a minute for my eyes to adjust.

A blast of light shot in again. "All clear."

"Ok, people, move it. Take the 'squatch first and chain him in the front."

AB and his twin yeti guards ducked as they walked through the door. The rest of us followed. We were on a loading dock, away from the prying eyes, and cameras, of any tourists. The only people I saw were a couple of locals shifting boxes around. AB and his yeti guards ducked as they entered the box truck. Richard was next in line. He looked back over his shoulder at the rest of us and winked. I thought it strange, but then a searing pain shut out all other sensations. I slipped to the ground.

# CHAPTER 26
## DAMN YANKEES

I floated in a cloudy fog. The fog cleared and I saw Trolga talking with a creature that looked like a walking corpse. Its back was to me and it appeared emaciated. Little patches of long grey hair seemed to barely cling to the blotchy-grey skin that hugged the skull below it. I tried to move away, but Trolga spotted me. The walking corpse turned and glared at me. It smiled, showing a mouth full of lamprey-like teeth. It pointed at me with a boney finger. Trolga laughed and nodded.

The creature's eyes bored into me. As they did, its appearance morphed into the image of a goddess, with beautiful blond hair, an alabaster complexion, ruby lips, porn star tits and burning dark-red eyes. Her eyes drew me toward her. I tried to break away but couldn't. As I approached, she pointed to her left. My head turned involuntarily. The clouds in front of me parted.

I looked down on a baseball field. My old teammates were lined up along the first base line, hats over their hearts, waiting for the pledge of allegiance. It was one of those pristine days in Seattle with beautiful blue skies unblemished by clouds. My best friend, Steve Reynolds, looked up, but he wasn't looking at me, he was looking behind me. Black clouds roiled up out of nowhere. I glanced over my shoulder as the winds picked up to hurricane force. Our coach yelled, but he couldn't be heard over the roar behind me. The sound became deafening. The entire baseball team ran. I covered my eyes with my hands, knowing what was coming. The wave crested right over the top of me, crashing down on my teammates, sweeping them away. Tears filled my eyes and I tried to scream. Nothing came out.

I closed my eyes tightly and thought about the Lady Galadriel. A white ball appeared next to me. I focused on it. The roar of the waves diminished. When I could no longer hear the waves, I dared to open my eyes. Shafts of light that looked like what my mother called the fingers of God pierced the ugly black clouds that had enshrouded me. An image appeared in the light. The Lady Galadriel. She appeared calm and seemed to be looking through me. She walked toward me and then right through me. I followed her. She was looking at a map of the globe. She raised her hand and the map zoomed in on an area north of India. She seemed to focus for a minute, and then the globe shifted rapidly to Antarctica. Spots glowed under the ice. One in particular flashed red. She looked up suddenly, seeming to see me as her image faded.

I heard a droning in the background. I slowly opened my eyes. I found myself lying in a small bed in a dark room. I sat up. My head felt as if it were going to explode. I lay back down slowly. The last thing I remembered was seeing AB enter the truck in front of me. A searing pain followed that memory. I glanced around. My backpack sat on the end of the bed. I slowly sat up and reached for it. My head didn't hurt too badly if I moved slowly. I pulled it toward me. My mother's journal and the educator were both in it.

I realized that I wasn't tied up. If I were a captive, they sure were being nice. Given Trolga's demeanor earlier, that didn't seem likely. The floor seemed to be swaying back and forth slowly. Somebody had taken my shoes off. They sat neatly on the floor. I reached down slowly, my head still aching, and slipped them on. I tried the door, half expecting it to be locked. It wasn't. I cracked it open and peaked outside. There was a wooden door across from mine, and a short wood-paneled hall with several more doors along it. Brass lights alternated along each side. The hall ended in a larger door at one end and a stairwell at the other. The humming seemed to be coming from the larger door, while light came down the stairwell.

Over the humming, I heard muted conversation. I couldn't make out who it was, but it sounded like it was coming from upstairs. I walked toward the stairwell. The floor seemed to be shifting slightly under me. I had to put my hand against the wall to steady myself. Grabbing the rail, I slowly made my way up the stairs. The voice sounded like Richard. The stairs made a right turn halfway up. I could see light through a window at the top. I made my way up slowly. Richard was laughing. When I got to the top, I saw him talking with a man in a white uniform. They both turned as I walked into the room.

"Well, well, I didn't expect you to be up and about yet." Richard signaled the man in uniform. "Let Captain Steve help you to a chair."

I shook my head and took a couple of steps but didn't pull away when Captain Steve led me to a chair and helped me down. "Anything else, Mr. DeMarco?"

"How long to Bimini?"

"At this pace, a couple of hours."

Richard nodded. "I'll let you know once everyone is up and about so we can pick up speed. Thanks, Captain."

The captain left the room.

"Glad to hear we're headed for Bimini, but why the surprise that I'm up?"

Richard smiled. "To the point as usual, Charlie." He walked over to a fridge built into a cabinet, pulled out a Coke and brought it to me. He handed it to me and then reached into a pocket and pulled out a bottle of pills. He popped open the top and shook a couple of pills onto his palm. "Here, take these. Doc says they'll help with the aftereffects of the hypersonic cannon."

I took the pills, popped them in my mouth and drank some Coke. I then sat back since my head still hurt. We seemed to be rocking gently. "We're on your boat?"

Richard nodded. "I was going to wait until everyone was up to avoid explaining twice, but since your up . . ."

I took another swig of Coke as Richard sat in the chair next to me. "Being the son of the wealthiest man on the planet, I have a security detail assigned to me. I used to bitch like crazy about them, but my dad always insisted. One reason my dad sent me to the Moon was to get me away from threats and give me some freedom. Thanks to you, I'm back.

"My security detail monitors my location at all times via my subcutaneous iChip. Mine is a specialized version of the retail one that came out last year. My dad agreed to keep the monitoring at a minimum, but they do monitor my vitals and my location. When I realized that Trolga was a threat, I waited for an opportunity to use my code phrase, Damn Yankees. Once I spoke that, the team moved into position. They tracked where I was, set up an ambush outside the loading dock, and zapped everyone with the hypersonic cannon."

My head was feeling much better. The pills must have been working. "How'd you avoid the ill-effects?"

"Since my detail is required to use non-lethal force except in extreme cases, I have sonic earplugs built in. They can filter out extraneous noises and can even allow me to hear over greater distances. Since the hypersonic cannon's the weapon of first use by my team, the earplugs totally filter it out. I heard no more than a slight humming while the rest of you dropped to the ground."

I nodded. "Then what happened? Did your team get all of us to your boat?"

Richard laughed. "Not many people would call this high-speed yacht a boat, but that's ok. I'm beginning to like you, Charlie. Life was getting boring until you entered it."

He walked to the fridge and pulled out a beer. "Kalik, the beer of the Bahamas. Want one?" He took a sip.

I shook my head. "Headache." I'd had my first experience with beer after a ballgame at a friend's house. He was my catcher, my next-door neighbor and my best friend. He'd found a case his older brother had left behind. We'd gone through a fair number of them before I managed to stagger home. I got sick as a dog. My mom, smelling the beer, made me clean up my own mess. I also had to sit out the next two ballgames. I'd promised my mom that I'd at least wait until I was eighteen. Now that she was gone, I couldn't break that promise.

He sat down. "Once everyone was out cold, my security detail came in, loaded us up and brought us to my boat."

"Did they get everyone?"

Richard laughed. "You think I'd leave a sasquatch behind? I can't wait to hear the truth about your friend AB."

"Did he look like a 'squatch when he was out cold?" I worried about Richard or his people having proof about sasquatches. They'd stayed secret for so long.

"By the time my team got there, both he and his two yeti guards just looked like huge NFL players. Glad my father wasn't around or he might have tried to get them to try out for his team. That camouflage of theirs must work on an unconscious level."

I nodded. "Good. I'd hate for AB's secret to be out. What happened to the yetis?"

"My team loaded us into two cars. By the time they finished, all of Trolga's men, including the yetis, were gone. No way they got up and walked off. When my team radioed the news to me, I had Captain Steve take off post-haste. Didn't want to run into Trolga again. She seems to have more resources than the mafia. Closest I've come to getting kidnapped. Quite elaborate, really, for them to have planted Trolga on the Moon and then followed me here."

Just like Richard to think that Trolga had tried to kidnap him. At least his arrogance meant that I could dodge any questions about why Trolga and the Lemurians were trying to stop me.

"I thought this adventure might be fun. Now with sasquatches, yetis and Lemurians involved, I'm beginning to feel like Indiana Jones. Wish I'd brought my fedora." He glanced around.

AB appeared, rubbing his head. "Man, do I have a headache. I feel like Maz Kanata slipped me a mickey." He glanced around when nobody laughed. "Hell, you're all too young I guess." He looked at Richard. "Ooh, that a Kalik? Mind if I try one?"

Richard pointed to the cabinet with the fridge. "Help yourself."

AB was already heading in that direction. He looked back. "Hair of the dog, you know."

Richard pulled out the bottle of pills and dumped two in his hand. He held them up for AB. "But you'd better take a couple of these with that beer. Hypersonic cannon hangover can be quite painful."

AB grabbed his Kalik, took the pills, popped them in his mouth and followed with a long pull from the bottle. "So that's what happened. I thought it was the smell of those damn yetis. Talk about skunk apes! I hope you have them in chains."

Richard shook his head. "When my men went back, they were gone."

AB finished the beer and got up for another.

Richard looked over at me. "I like this guy." He turned to AB as AB sat down with another Kalik. "Now, why the aggravation with the yetis? Aren't they like cousins or something?"

AB bared his canines and almost let out a snarl, but then settled back in his chair. He took a pull from his beer. "How would you feel if I called an orangutan your cousin! We sasquatch are an old race, evolved from the mutual precursor to your species and to Neanderthals. Yetis are descendants of *Gigantopithecus*. They're dumber than orangutans and are under the total control of the descendants of the Lemurians. If they weren't so dumb they might realize that they're slaves."

"Sorry, man, didn't know." Richard grabbed another Kalik.

"They're nothing more than trained monkeys. The only thing we have in common is telepathic psychotropic camouflage. Ours is vastly superior, by the way. We both evolved a telepathic ability to camouflage ourselves from the prying, and deadly, eyes of a brash young race that burst upon the scene a few hundred thousand years ago. That species lives short lives, breeds like rabbits and saw us, *Gigantopithecus* and a few unlucky species such as the poor, dumb Neanderthals, as competition. They hunted us down and tried to kill us. We used our superior mental acuity to focus our telepathic abilities on psychotropic camouflage while the new species spread across the globe like a plague. *Gigantopithecus*, whose camouflage is inferior to ours, moved into the Himalayan massif to hide out. Their combination of physical and psychotropic camouflage enabled them to survive. But they were so dumb that even there your kind might have slaughtered them but for the Lemurian agents that began using them as bodyguards and slave labor. They were a passive, friendly, omnivorous species. Now they're vicious and aggressive. Thank God those guards were females." AB took another sip of beer. "Man, that stuff really worked. My head's feeling better."

Richard shook his hand. "Just a minute. Those huge hulking beasts were females?"

AB nodded. "Yep, the male yetis grow to just over nine feet tall and are much more aggressive. Seen a video of one ripping a snow leopard to shreds. Uhhh." AB shook his head from side to side. "Brutes. I hope to never meet one."

Richard nodded. "Not unless I had a sonic cannon handy."

AB pointed his beer bottle at Richard. "Those things really work, but you wouldn't want to be around once they woke up."

Richard nodded. "They can do far more than merely stun."

AB kicked his feet up on an adjoining chair. "So, we headed to Bimini?"

Richard nodded. "I've had the captain take it slow. Didn't want to wake you sleeping beauties prematurely. We can dock at Cat Cay, just south of Bimini, or head on up to Bimini."

I recalled the map of the area from my mother's journal. Most of the spots had been Xed out. "Let's head to Bimini. We can hit a few spots on the ocean side of the north end of Bimini, including the 'Bimini Road,' and then move into the harbor for the night, unless this boat's too big to get into the harbor."

Richard shook his head. "This is the *Runaway*, Dad's fast tender. It'll do seventy-five knots in a pinch. We use it to scoot around while the *Sarah Charlotte* stays at anchor."

I looked around the room and shook my head. If this was a tender . . . "Good. I thought we could start at the Three Sisters and then move on to the Bimini Road. I've been to both. Doubt we'll find anything, but a good place to start and get our feet wet."

Nobody laughed at my rather lame joke. I was glad that Rhea hadn't been around to hear it. Then I had a thought. "You do have snorkeling gear on board?"

Richard laughed. "I texted Captain Steve from the plane. He picked up everything we need. We even have an old hookah rig."

I was about to comment, but AB jumped in. "Last time I used a hookah rig was at Mos Eisley Cantina. As I recall, Han told me it would make my hair stand on end."

Far lamer than my joke, yet I heard giggles from the stairs. Rhea and Imee were making their way up. They wore new bikinis with sheer coverups that spurred my imagination. I shook my head, knowing what AB would say.

Richard walked over to them, his hand extended with a couple of those pills. "Don't make them laugh, AB, at least not until they get these down. Bet you both have wicked headaches."

They both nodded.

I got up to get them a drink. "What do you want to wash those pills down with?" I'd started to reach for a Coke, but wasn't sure.

"Water," Rhea said.

"Me too," Imee chimed in.

I grabbed two cold waters and handed them to the girls. They popped the pills and sat down.

I was about to say something, but Richard took charge. Now that the ladies were present, his demeanor seemed to change. "We're heading for a spot just off the north end of Bimini. Charlie tells me that it's on the short list his mother put together of

Atlantean sites. While I doubt anything's there, it will let all of you try out the gear."

"How long before we get there?" AB went for another Kalik.

Richard brought his hand to his temple. The front wall of the cabin came to life. An image of the bow of a dark blue boat gliding through turquoise waters filled the screen. Along the port side it displayed digital compass headings, speed, depth and water temperature. The speedometer showed that we were moving at around 42 mph. I could feel a bit of vibration, and had felt a slight rocking when I'd first gotten up, but it didn't feel like we were moving that fast.

"Looks like we're on the Bahama Bank, right?" I asked.

Richard nodded. "Since you're all up, and since the waters are calmer now that we're on the Bank, I'll have the captain pick up the pace."

Richard touched his temple again. "I suggest you all take a seat. While the stabilizers are great, the acceleration is quick and there's an outside chance that the captain will have to dodge a coral head."

Richard sat on the sofa and patted the spot next to him. Imee took the hint and joined him.

# CHAPTER 27
## HOT DOGS AND LOBSTER

I had just finished reviewing my mother's journal when the vibration of the engines lessened. I felt a surge of deceleration. I was amazed at how quick the trip had been from Nassau to Bimini. When I'd made the trip before in a sailboat with my parents, it had taken all day.

Richard flipped off the television and jumped up.

"Let's head up to the flybridge. The view of Bimini harbor's spectacular."

I nodded. I remembered the mix of colors from deep blue to turquoise blue to shades of green when I'd first sailed into the harbor with my parents. I set the journal in my backpack and followed. Richard led the way up the spiral stairs with Imee right behind him. Rhea followed her and I jumped up to climb up behind Rhea. Unfortunately a large hulk jumped in front of me.

AB grinned. *The view's outside, laddie. Focus—no distractions!*

I glanced up as Rhea turned the corner of the stairs in her bikini.

Jamie pushed past me, intentionally bumping my shoulder. "She obviously likes you. You'd better do something about it before I ask her out myself." He headed up the stairs after AB. I followed in the rear.

As I got to the top of the stairs, the wind caught my hair. The girls had already started to ooh and aah at the colors as we pulled into the harbor. I assumed we'd be making our way to the large casino and development at the end of North Bimini, but the boat turned into a small marina near the entrance to the harbor.

Richard noted my quizzical look. "Ernest Hemingway used to stay at this marina. My mom was a huge fan, so my dad bought it for her as an anniversary present." He smiled weakly as a hint of sadness crossed his face. "Anyway, let's eat while the crew gets the dive boat ready."

At the mention of food, AB headed for the staircase.

"I'm glad somebody's looking forward to eating, but they'll bring the food up here. Sit."

We all sat around a u-shaped seating area with a large dark-wood table in the middle. Richard sat at one end. Given his size, AB took the other end.

"So, I hope you're all hungry. I've taken the liberty of ordering Bahamian fare. We're having conch chowder and conch fritters for appetizers and then fresh Bahamian lobster for the main course."

"Don't tell me that the crew made lunch while we were running?" Knowing AB, he was probably hungry and wondering how long it would take.

"Don't be silly. I called ahead. They're bringing the appetizers up from the marina's restaurant right now."

Even as he spoke, several Bahamians walked up the stairs.

"Mr. Richard, how good to see you again. It's been a few years."

Richard nodded. "Yes, Jackson, too long. In fact, I've been thinking about your conch chowder and fritters for some time."

"Yes, sir. You'll have them in a minute."

Jackson walked over and opened a cabinet under the bar while another Bahamian offered us drinks. Jackson then came over and served us. The smell of conch chowder brought back memories of sailing with my parents.

*Sea snails. All we're going to get is sea snails?* AB had already drained his cup of chowder and had popped several fritters in his mouth.

Even at his size, he ate more than I'd expect. 'Squatches must have a much faster metabolism than humans.

"This chowder's great, and the fritters are almost as good as my mother's."

Jackson beamed at my compliment. "Thank you, sir."

*Stop complaining, AB, there's plenty to eat.*

*Yeah, if you're a pescatarian.*

*A what?* Leave it to AB to try to improve my vocabulary. Guess he learned that from my uncle.

A tray of lobster arrived. Quite a change from the limited fare we'd had on the Moon. Of course, Richard had both fried and

broiled with butter and honey mustard for dipping. What came out
next brought a smile to AB's face. A tray of hot dogs wrapped in bacon. AB rudely grabbed one before the tray got to the table.

*Yes, real food at last!*

Richard smiled. "Jackson, you remembered."

"Yes, sir. You can't have lunch without our cheese-stuffed hot
dogs wrapped in bacon."

All of us grabbed a dog. AB had already finished his first.

Smacking his lips he asked, "How'd you get the bacon so crispy?"

Jackson grinned broadly, his teeth shining through his lips. "We
deep fry it, maan."

At that, the girls put down their dogs, but AB grabbed another
and a fried lobster. "What's the matter? Doesn't fried food keep you
young?"

The girls shook their heads, but Richard laughed. "Knew I liked
your friend, Charlie."

Richard sat back and put his arm around Imee. "So, Charlie,
where should we start?"

I took a sip of Coke and put my plate down. "Let's stick with the
plan we discussed: dive the Three Sisters rocks and then move on to
the Bimini Road."

"Good. We'll leave in about an hour."

Jackson and the other Bahamians had discretely cleaned up and
left the flybridge. Richard eyed AB. His natural camo had drifted
away. "Besides, I got gear for all of you, but I don't have anything
that'll fit AB."

"No worries. I don't like to swim, maan. I'll stay aboard and catch
up on my reading, maybe get some sun and chillax." He pulled out a
pair of Wayfarer sunglasses, grabbed a Kalik beer and sat down. "By
the way, mind if I smoke?" He pulled out a briar root pipe, tapped it
several times on his palm and stuffed it in his mouth. He dropped
his camouflage and propped his feet up on the table.

I couldn't help myself. I started to laugh. The girls, Richard and
Jamie, after a bit of shock, started laughing as well.

"What's so funny?" AB slid his sunglasses down over his nose
and looked out at us.

"Oh, you mean besides a pipe-smoking, sunglass-wearing sasquatch? I don't know."

AB bared his teeth and let loose with a bit of a growl. I kept laughing, but the others quit.

I pointed at AB's feet. "Richard, you think there's a pair of flippers on the island that will fit those?"

AB gave me a glare, but then he started to chuckle. Everyone else joined in.

"Damn, it's hard enough to get used to AB being a sasquatch, but picturing Bigfoot wearing flippers, that's just too much." Richard was laughing harder.

AB pulled his pipe out of his mouth and pointed it at Richard. "Enough already. If I wasn't so civilized and a vegetarian, I might just have to get up and take a bite out of you for being so rude!"

Everyone else laughed even harder when AB's camo suddenly came up. He again looked like a large human. He tilted his head toward the spiral stairs. Richard turned. The captain popped his head up.

"Sir, I've got your father on the line." He handed a portable phone to Richard.

"Yes, Father, I'm fine." Richard walked down the stairs and headed for the bow. "How's Antarctica?"

I froze. Richard's father was in Antarctica? And the gravitonic device Galadriel had mentioned was also in Antarctica. And the Piri Reis map in the plane . . . it couldn't be a coincidence. I shook my head as my thoughts became muddled.

Jamie turned to the girls. "Probably a good time to get your shopping in. Not sure when we'll have another chance. Charlie and I can do a bit of exploring. I've never been here, but Charlie's a veteran."

Rhea and Imee nodded their assent, but I just sat there.

"Charlie, ready to go?" Jamie elbowed me.

"Sorry. Yes. AB, want to go with us?" I asked.

AB took a puff from his pipe, blew out a huge smoke ring and smiled. "No, I'll just stay here and chillax in the sun."

I got an image in my mind of Gandalf blowing a dragon-shaped smoke ring.

*Nice. I like that.* AB tipped his pipe at me. *Wish I could do it.*

I shook my head, still not used to this telepathy stuff. I'd have to learn to block my thoughts. "Great. We'll meet back in about an hour and then head for the Three Sisters."

# CHAPTER 28
## THREE SISTERS

A light breeze gently pushed the turquoise clouds over our heads as we headed out of the harbor in Richard's dive boat. The girls sat on the cushions in the bow, their hair blowing in the breeze.

Rhea looked up. "Why are the clouds such a pretty color?" She looked over at me.

I smiled. "The color of the water reflects off the clouds. Beautiful, isn't it?"

Rhea and Imee nodded as Richard cut the boat around the reef at the mouth of Bimini harbor, accelerating. I held onto the rail of the center console and watched the girls on the cushions in the bow.

The trip to the Three Sisters only took a couple of minutes. Richard pulled up on the south side of the southernmost coral outcropping, pushed a button and dropped the anchor. The boat automatically played out line until the anchor held.

Richard turned to me. "Charlie, tell Jamie and the girls what to look for while I get out the snorkeling gear." Richard walked around the center console and watched the mate pull bags of snorkeling gear out.

I wasn't really sure where to start. "Look, first of all, have you snorkeled before?"

Imee raised her hand, but Jamie and Rhea did not.

"Richard, flip me a mask and snorkel." He did. They were one-piece unicorn masks and seemed denser than the ones I'd used in the past. "With these"—I turned the mask over in my hand—"you just slip them on, swim on the surface and breath normally. If you dive under to see something close up, the snorkel seals itself so no water will get in." I glanced at Richard and he nodded.

"As to what to look for, I've been to this spot lots of times with my parents. We never found any artifacts here, but it's close, it's a good place to learn to snorkel, and the fish are unbelievable." I smiled.

Imee raised her hand. "What about sharks?"

"Other than possibly a nurse shark, I doubt we'll see any here, but if we do, they're generally harmless. If you see one hold your hand up like a fin, like this." I held my hand up in front of my face, making a fin. "Don't make any sudden movements or take off for the boat. Stay with your buddy. We'll swim slowly back to the boat."

Richard appeared at my side, a mask and flippers in his hand. "Good, the girls are my buddies. You get Jamie." He chuckled and slapped my shoulder. "My boat, my gear, my choice." With that he sat on the side of the boat, pulled on his flippers and slipped his mask and snorkel over his head.

Before sliding in, he looked over at the mate. "What's your name and where's Miguel?" Just like Richard not to notice when we first got on the boat.

"Miguel's wife got sick. He left about a month ago, sir. My name's Pavel."

"So you know where everything is?"

Pavel nodded. "Yes, sir."

"Pavel has your gear up front. Come on, girls, where's it hung up?" With that Richard slipped into the water and went under.

"I guess that's it, then." Imee headed for the bow, but Rhea stopped next to me. "I'm sure you know more about the fish than Richard, and I'd like you to show me that tunnel." She smiled and walked to the bow. She turned her head back. "Catch up."

Jamie had his flippers on and walked awkwardly toward me. "No biggie, bro. Richard's just being his usual self. We'll all stay together."

I nodded and looked around. Where was Richard? He hadn't come up for air yet. I walked to the side nearest the outcroppings and looked around. Despite crystal clear water, I didn't see Richard.

"Where's Richard?" I kept scanning the water. He'd been down too long.

Imee and Rhea were sitting on the edge of the boat about to slip over the side. They looked around. Jamie waddled to the side of the boat. The only person seemingly unconcerned was the mate.

"Pavel, where's Richard. He hasn't come up for air!"

Pavel smiled, one front tooth missing. He pointed down. "Under boat."

Imee walked over to him. She started rattling off in Russian. I couldn't follow any of it, but Pavel wilted against her verbal tirade and then finally replied. Imee's shoulders relaxed. She looked at the screen on the center console. Just then I heard a splash and looked over. Richard held a large conch over his head. He slipped his mask off.

"Forgot to tell you, these masks and snorkels are the latest thing. They've got a built-in rebreather. You don't have to come up for air like a normal snorkel so ignore what Charlie told you. You can stay underwater for around twenty minutes." He swam to the boat and handed the conch to Pavel. "Come on in. The water's crystal clear and I spotted a few eagle rays circling the islands."

Imee slid over the side and joined Richard. She swam up to him and lightly slapped him on the cheek.

"That's for scaring the crap out of me. Now, how do these things work?" The mask sat on the top of her head.

"Simple, just use them like a normal snorkel, but you can take breaths underwater. When a red light appears in the top right of your mask, you have to come up to recharge the rebreather."

Richard looked up at Rhea. She slid over the side as well. She glanced back at me.

"Hurry up, Charlie." She smiled and then turned and followed Richard and Imee. My eyes followed her swim away.

Jamie elbowed me and handed me my mask. "Stop looking and start acting. Let's go." Jamie slipped over the side.

Richard was taking the girls around the north side of the island. I grabbed a set of gloves and slipped into the water. I quickly caught up with Jamie. He seemed mesmerized by a school of yellowtail drifting in front of him. I tapped him on the shoulder and pointed up. We surfaced.

"Follow me. I've got a shortcut."

Jamie nodded and I took off. Ignoring the myriad of colored fish, I shot through the tunnel and looked back. Jamie was almost through. I had to force myself to take a breath through the snorkel rather than go to the surface, but after doing it once, it became easy. We swam northwest along the Sisters, buzzing past some big blue runners that swam by in the deeper water. I spotted a large grouper lurking around a coral head over forty feet away. In front of me teeming schools of fish swam around the coral and the purple sea fans. We made our way toward the giant brain coral near the northwest corner of the islands. Richard and the girls should be coming around from the other side soon. I tapped Jamie on the shoulder and pointed to the brain coral. He headed over there. I swam to the edge. The coral was large enough to hide both of us from Richard and the girls.

I peeked around the corner. Sure enough, I could see Richard leading the girls. They were taking their time chasing after a school of blue, green, red and turquoise parrot fish. I swam back to where Jamie waited. The yellow caution light appeared in my mask. I surfaced and recharged the rebreather. Jamie rose up next to me. We floated around, looking at the fish drifting beneath us. Jamie grabbed my arm and pointed. A three-foot cuda lurked in a shadow, waiting to pounce on an unsuspecting fish. While they looked scary, they almost never attacked divers. I gave Jamie a thumbs up and led him slowly away from the cuda.

The green light came on indicating the rebreather was full. I pointed down at another large coral head sitting in the sand about thirty feet away from the edge of the Three Sisters. It would give us a great ambush point. We swam down and looped behind the coral head. I glanced back. A shoal of fish was following us from the Sisters toward the outcropping of coral. Very strange. They usually stuck close to the safety of the coral islands. It reminded me of the fish trailing me as I walked through the underwater tunnels in Atlantis.

I looked back. *Shoo.* I waved my hand.

The shoal of fish scattered and quickly swam back toward the Sisters. Glancing forward at the coral head, I noticed several black sticks wiggling under one corner. I pointed them out to Jamie, but he shook his head. I dove down and stretched my hand under the rock as quickly as I could and squeezed. I felt something struggling in my hand. When I pulled it out, an eighteen-inch-long lobster wiggled in my hand. Jamie's eye's bugged out. The lobster flexed its tail, struggling to get away. I held tight. I wanted to surprise Rhea with it.

Richard, Imee and Rhea came around the corner. Imee pointed at a pair of bright bug-eyed orange squirrelfish swimming in front of them. I glanced back, signaled to Jamie behind me and swam forward, holding the lobster in front of me. I was halfway across the open sand area when Rhea turned around. At first she smiled, but then her eyes darted to one side of me. She pointed behind me. Richard held up his palm in the sign of a fin. I sensed something behind me, but it wasn't a sense of danger. It was more a sense of homecoming. I turned slowly.

Instead of a shark, a dolphin swept in behind me. He came so close that he spun me around, almost knocking my mask off. When I got my bearings again, the dolphin lazily circled me. Jamie came up behind me, putting me between him and the dolphin. I signaled him that everything was ok, but he remained right next to me. As the remaining members of the dolphin's pod came into range, he grabbed my arm. I shook my head and gave him the thumbs up. I wished that Richard's masks had built-in radios as well.

I felt a brief tingling in my head and then felt a presence. *Is that for me?*

What? I looked around. I knew AB wasn't here, but it felt just like telepathy.

*That delicious-looking lobster. You must have gotten it for me!* A dolphin looked squarely at me.

*Sure.* I let go of the lobster. It flipped its tail, heading for the sand. It didn't stand a chance.

The dolphin pounced on it. *Yummy! Quite a treat for this time of year.*

I floated there shocked. Telepathy with a sasquatch and now with a dolphin! I came to my senses when Jamie grabbed me again and tried to drag me toward Richard and the girls. They had surfaced with the islands behind them.

I pointed to them and then pushed Jamie toward them. I followed.

The dolphin swam alongside me. *Your friend's quite nervous.*

*He's never been snorkeling. He thinks you're a shark.*

The dolphin shot up to the surface, jumped and landed on his back. He then darted over to his family. *That human thinks we're sharks. Let's scare him!*

*NO! Don't.*

The leader came back toward me. *Ok, ok, just don't shout. That hurt my head.*

I started to pick up on some of the thoughts from the other dolphins in the pod. The young ones wanted to leave to go to a hunting ground. A picture of a big fat mullet appeared in my head. I could almost taste it. I shook my head. I didn't want to taste a mullet!

I swam toward my friends. *Excuse me, I need to check in with my human friends.*

*No hurry. We'll be in the area. The mullet will WAIT.*

The dolphin zipped past the young ones. The pod followed, disappearing into the distance.

When I surfaced, Richard was laughing at Jamie, who looked pissed. Jamie shoved his hand, splashing Richard.

"What's going on?" Rhea swam next to me.

Jamie glared at Richard. "When Richard put up his hand like a fin, I was sure that the huge shape charging us was a shark. I practically crapped in my bathing suit."

Richard laughed again.

Jamie tried to dunk Richard, but he darted away. "Asshole."

Rhea leaned her head toward me. "So where'd you find that lobster?"

"Under that coral head out there. I was bringing it over to show to you."

Rhea smiled. "That was pretty cool to see the dolphin shoot right past you and then dive on the lobster the minute you let it go."

I nodded.

"I wonder what they were thinking. They're supposed to be pretty smart."

I started to answer, but Richard butted in. "They're fairly intelligent, and can be trained, but that's about it. They're just animals."

Imee hit him. "Richard, you're such a buzz kill."

Richard turned to me. "Now that we've all made it around the island and we know you can swim, what now, hot shot?"

I looked off into the distance. "I have a feeling those dolphins are coming back. Why not hang out for a while and see?" Richard seemed to be getting bored.

"That sounds great." It was Rhea. "I think it would be cool if the dolphins came back. Can you find another lobster?"

"I saw a few at the edge of the tunnel, but they're too close to the nurse shark on the bottom."

"Shark?" Jamie looked shocked. "But we swam through that tunnel."

"Nurse sharks are harmless. There's usually a three-to four-footer sleeping on the bottom of the tunnel."

"Let's take a look. Sounds more fun than waiting around for the dolphins to reappear." Richard took off for the tunnel. Imee followed right behind him.

"Mind if I join Richard's group?" Jamie gave me his wingman look. "I'd like to see this shark."

Rhea and I treaded water for a minute in silence. She smiled at me.

"So, um, want to head back and get the metal detectors?" I glanced at her eyes and my heart seemed to skip a beat. I looked away.

She reached down and grabbed my hand. "Sure, let's take our time, though. I'd like you to take me through the tunnel to see that nurse shark."

We stayed on the surface, snorkeling the old-fashioned way, looking at the teeming schools of fish. Rhea continued to hold my hand and I wasn't about to let go. I pointed out a large triggerfish outlined in iridescent blue, nibbling at the coral. She squeezed my hand and we stopped to watch. I looked over at Rhea as she looked down at the fish. She was far more beautiful than all of the reef fish in the ocean. She squeezed my hand again and pointed. The only fish I find prettier than the triggerfish, a queen angelfigh, swam below us. Rhea's eyes were wide with pleasure. I looked down, wishing it would come closer. It did, drifting lazily beneath us. Rhea watched as a triggerfish joined it. I glanced over. Rhea's eyes seemed almost the same shade of red as the bright red dot on the forehead of the queen angelfish. I didn't recall ever seeing one with a red dot before.

As the queen angelfish drifted off, I pointed toward the tunnel and we took off. Just as we got to the tunnel, a fever of spotted eagle rays slid below us, their wings flapping at a leisurely pace. The rays, Rhea and the beautiful reef fish almost made me forget why we were here. But as the rays glided away from us, something flashed in the water below them. I kept my eyes on the spot. Sure enough, another shaft of sunlight hit it just right and I saw the glint again. I squeezed

Rhea's hand, pointed and swam over to the spot. I slid my mask on top of my head. Rhea lifted her mask onto her forehead.

"I can't believe how beautiful these fish are. No wonder you wanted to come to this spot."

I nodded. "The fish are amazing, but look down." I pointed just below us. She put on the mask and looked down. The glint in the white sand appeared again. She lifted her head.

"What is it?"

"No clue, but it's not natural. I'm going to dive down and find out. Stay up here." I put my mask back on, took a deep breath, turned down, kicked my flippers and shot down toward the sand. Based on the pressure on my ears, I figured it was almost twenty feet deep. When I got down to the bottom, I swam carefully over the spot to avoid stirring the sand too much. I didn't see the glint. I looked up at Rhea to get an idea of where the glint was and started swimming around where we'd seen it. I was ready to give up when I spotted it. I reached down and carefully pulled at the tiny bit of what looked like gold sticking out of the sand. Hoping to see some ancient Atlantean relic, I was disappointed when it turned out to be an earring with three gold hoops. I held onto it, turned upwards, kicked hard and surfaced next to Rhea.

"What'd you find?" Rhea's face looked full of expectation.

I opened my palm and showed her. "It's only an earring. Some diver probably lost it years ago."

Rhea picked up the earring and held it to her ear. "How's it look?"

"Great." What else was I going to say.

"Good, well I may wear it tonight! You're quite the treasure hunter, finding an ancient disk on the Moon and now finding a gold earring in the middle of the Atlantic Ocean!" She pulled the earring down, but it caught in her hair and slipped out of her fingers. "Oops!"

"Watch it drift down. We should be able to find it again." Both of us put our masks on. As we watched it, Rhea grabbed my arm and pointed down. Some sand had moved where I'd taken off with a kick of my flippers earlier. Something was now poking out of the dimple in the sand created by my kick. The earring drifted down and settled next to the dimple.

I turned downward and swam quickly to the bottom. I grabbed the earring and slipped it in the small pouch in my bathing suit. I then grabbed the thing we'd seen from the surface. It was slick with encrusted sea growth. My fingers slipped, so I slid my hand under the sand next to it and tried to scoop it up. It wouldn't budge. I was about to give up when Rhea appeared at my side. She pointed at her mask and took a breath. In the excitement I'd forgotten about the masks. I took a deep breath as Rhea dug at the other side of the object. It came loose with a sudden pop. We headed to the surface with it.

Rhea slid her mask up on her head. "What is it?"

I shook my head. "Don't know. Too much gunk on it. Let's get it to the boat."

Rhea nodded.

"Follow me. The tunnel's the quickest way." We slipped our masks back on and took off. I glanced back. Rhea kept up easily. We swam through the tunnel quickly. The boat floated about thirty-five feet away. Richard, Imee and Jamie were already aboard. We swam up to the ladder.

Rhea climb aboard first. "Help Charlie. We found something!"

Richard reached down over the gunwale. "Let me take it."

I shook my head. "Get the net. It's slippery." Richard scowled, but Jamie came back with a net. He lowered it into the water and I placed the disk in the net. They pulled it up as I swam to the ladder and climbed aboard.

Richard had placed the object on the fish cleaning table. He picked up a hose and sprayed it. Not much of the gunk came off.

"If this is Atlantean, it's been down there a long time," Rhea said.

Richard scowled. "Atlantean my ass. Looks like a large metal washer used in marine construction."

I picked it up. It was about eight inches in diameter and weighed around a pound. One side seemed raised more than the other, but lots of coral had grown on it.

"You may be right, Richard, but we're here looking for clues to Atlantis. Think positive." I reached out to hand it to Richard. He stuck his hand out, but the disk slipped. It fell with a thud to the deck.

"Damn, Charlie. I hope you didn't damage the deck." He bent down to pick up the disk. A piece remained behind. Richard moved the piece, looking at the deck.

"Deck's ok, but looks like you broke your washer." He set it on the fish cleaning table and bent down to pick up the broken piece. I picked up the disk. When I flipped it over, it glinted in the sunlight. The coral had broken away, revealing a silvery surface. While most of the disk remained covered in coral and sea slime, I could see a pattern peeking out. I pushed the sea slime away, but couldn't pry the rest of the coral off.

"Do you have a hammer?" Richard shook his head. I looked over at Pavel. He nodded and bent down, opening a hatch. He pulled out a small hammer.

"I use it to get conches out of their shells."

I grabbed it. I tapped on the growth of coral. It was stubborn, but I didn't want to damage the disk.

"Here, let me." Richard grabbed the hammer out of my hand, elbowed me out of the way and banged it down on the disk.

"Careful, you might break it," Rhea said.

Richard shook his head as he tapped the disk on the fish cleaning table. The coral fell away. He held up the shiny disk. One stubborn clump of coral and a few wisps of green slime remained, but, for the most part, it was clean.

He held it up and examined it with his eyes and his hands.

"Guess you were right, Charlie, this isn't a marine washer." He flipped the disk over to me.

I caught it. Sure enough, it had a slightly raised ram's head on one side. The other side had nothing on it, but seemed to shimmer iridescently in the sunlight.

Rhea stepped up behind me. "What do you think it is?"

I handed it to her. "No clue."

Richard plucked it from Rhea's hands. It filled his palm. "Too big to be money." He flipped it to Imee. She caught it.

"The shimmering reminds me of an old DVD, but it's way too thick for that."

"Well, I'm guessing it's Atlantean. It's got a ram's head just like the disk on the Moon and just like the drawings in my mother's journal."

"Sure, it's probably a fake. Somebody planted it." Richard picked it up over his shoulder like he was going to throw it back into the water.

"Don't." The girls squealed in unison.

Richard laughed and flipped the disk to Jamie. "Just kidding."

Jamie caught it and looked down. Rhea stepped next to him and I did as well.

"You saw the disk that Charlie found on the Moon. Is it the same?"

Jamie turned it over in his hand. "Seems a bit larger, but the disk on the Moon had the same ram's head on it." Jamie handed it over to me.

I held it up and nodded. "Pavel, can you get me one of those metal detectors?"

He nodded, reached into a waterproof gear bag and handed one to me.

I turned it on and waved it over the disk. Nothing happened. I did it again. Still nothing.

"Did you turn it on?" Richard looked like he was about to snatch it out of my hand.

I glared at him and showed him the green light on the handle. I then waved it over the chrome steering wheel. It beeped and flashed.

"Why doesn't it work?" Rhea lifted it out of my hand and tried.

I shook my head. My uncle knew about the Atlanteans. Maybe he'd modified the magnetometer that he'd assembled on the Moon to be able to detect Atlantean metal.

"Well that sucks. How're we going to find any other relics?" Richard now had two open Kaliks in his hands. He handed one to Imee.

I shrugged. "The old-fashioned way. We do a grid search around where Rhea and I found the disk, using our flippers to move the sand out of the way."

"An air cannon would work much better. I'm sure that I could get one shipped over here by morning." Richard tapped on his iChip.

"Don't," I said. "Everyone'll think we've found a treasure. The Bahamian government and treasure hunters will swarm around here."

Richard nodded. He took a long pull from his beer and put it down. "We've got a couple of hours of light. Let's take a look around." He picked up his mask and flippers and looked back. "Well, where's it hung up? Let's go."

# CHAPTER 29
## THOR

We'd been snorkeling for about half an hour but hadn't found anything else. Pavel had moved the boat around the Three Sisters and anchored near the spot where Rhea and I had found the disk. Jamie tried to dive down, but he couldn't get past ten feet before his ears started killing him. He was supposedly watching us and would help if we found anything.

I glanced over at Richard. He'd begun to swim behind Imee rather than look around. I knew that if we didn't find anything soon, Richard would declare it was time for happy hour and head in. I glanced over at Rhea. She was still searching, but turned her head as if she'd known I was looking her way. She smiled and waved.

I dove back down and felt around in the sand. I'd flip my flippers, look again, and then move on to the next spot. I doubted we'd find anything else. We'd been lucky to find anything at all. At least the disk seemed to prove that we were on the right track. I was digging in the sand when I felt a nudge in my side. I jerked sideways. It was a dolphin.

*What're you looking for?* The dolphin had backed off a few yards and floated near me.

*You scared the crap out of me, coming up behind me like that!*

*I know. I can smell your fear in the water. Looking for another lobster? I know where some are hiding.* The dolphin zipped through the tunnel.

*No, I'm looking for relics from Atlantis.*

The dolphin appeared around the edge of the Three Sisters and headed back my way. A school of yellowtail darted out of his way.

*Don't know what those are, but there's no treasure around here. I've watched humans look before.* The dolphin darted behind the boat and then came back.

I turned and watch him zip around. *You know these waters pretty well?*

He nodded his head back and forth. *Yep, my pack's lived around the big island forever. Good hunting. We've also traveled a good way down south to hunt for crabs when the humans dredge.*

I knew that there used to be large dredging operations in the small chain of islands well south of Bimini. I'd sailed past it on a trip with my parents about five years ago. *Hold on a second. I want to show you something.* I swam toward the boat.

*Got another lobster on the boat?*

I ignored the dolphin and climbed halfway up the ladder. Jamie stood drinking a Kalik and staring out over the turquoise waters. "Jamie, hand me the artifact." He didn't respond. Seemed zoned out. "Jamie!" Finally, Pavel nudged him.

He smiled at me sheepishly and shrugged his shoulders. Jamie just hadn't seemed right since we'd left the Moon.

"Hand me the artifact." I extended my hand.

He hesitated, but brought it to me. "Careful. We already lost the one you found on the Moon. Richard'll go ballistic if we lose another." He glanced behind me as a large dark shape rapidly approached. He pointed and reached down to grab me.

"Don't worry. It's that dolphin again. And I won't drop the disk." I carefully held the disk in both hands and swam away from the boat. *Ever see anything like this?* I held the disk out so the dolphin could take a look.

The dolphin shot over. I felt something funny as he was looking at it, as if he was looking through it.

*Many times. That is the metal of the . . . . . . . . .*

*The Atlanteans?* An image of Galadriel appeared in my head.

*Yes, yes, the Atlanteans.*

I wondered how he knew what an Atlantean might look like.

*We remember. We committed to always remember.*

I began to think about what the dolphin had said, but an image of the Atlantean disk appeared in my head. *How do you know just by looking at it?*

*I used my > > > > > > > > > >.*

Evidently, the word did not translate telepathically.

*Your > > > > > > > > > >?*

*Yes. I can see what the object is made of with my > > > > > > > > > >?*

I thought for a minute. *You mean sonar!*

*Yes, that's what I said.*

*You can see through the coral growing on it?*

*Yes, yes. I also see that there's an injured > > > > swimming on the oth-*er side of the island. A picture of a blue runner appeared in my head. Guess I was establishing a better connection with the dolphin. *Back in a minute.* The dolphin took off.

I returned the disk to Pavel and dove back down.

The dolphin darted back. *Mmmmm.*

*So . . .* I didn't know what to call him. I couldn't just call him dolphin. *What's your name?*

All I heard was a high-pitched squeal.

*Mind if I just call you Alpha?*

The dolphin nodded its head. *Sure. We don't need to use names much.* But I like Alpha. The dolphin dashed away so quickly he disappeared in the distance.

*Hey, where're you going?* I swam back to the spot where I'd stopped my searching.

*Back in a minute. Get me a lobster, will you?*

The dolphin darted off as a picture of a spiny lobster drifting in open water entered my mind. I looked down at the sand and then off at the others, searching. What the heck? We hadn't found anything in over half an hour and I could see the spiny antenna of several lobsters poking out from under a nearby coral head.

I swam over and approached from behind the coral head. I reached down as quickly as I could and came away with another lob-ster. I held on tight and swam back over toward the others. Rhea and Imee were separated by about ten feet, looking down at the sand. Richard was behind them, looking at them rather than at the sand.

*So, you did get a lobster for me?*

I looked around but didn't see Alpha.

*Over here.*

I looked to the north and, sure enough, the shape of a dolphin approached rapidly.

*Hold onto that sucker and I'll make you a trade.*

Alpha was in front of me in no time. He shook his head up and down. He was holding something in his jaws.

*Take it before I drop it and grab that lobster out of your hand.*

I reached out with one hand, but the lobster gave a wriggle and slipped out of my other hand. Alpha didn't wait. He dropped the thing in his mouth and dove for the lobster. I didn't see him chomp on it because I was too busy trying to catch the object. I surged down and forward with a strong kick, grabbing the disk before it reached the sandy bottom. It looked just like the other one.

I headed toward the boat. *Where'd you find it?* I didn't see the dolphin, but had learned that he could be a decent distance away and my thoughts could still reach him.

*There're a few where I found it, but I know another spot where there's a lot more metal like that.*

I was almost to the boat when I felt something grab my ankle. Startled, I let the disk slip out of my hand as I turned.

Richard was behind me. He was pointing up toward the surface. I pointed down and watched the disk hit the sand. Fortunately, it didn't bury itself when it landed. I surfaced next to Richard.

Richard pulled his snorkel out of his mouth. I did the same. "Find anything?"

"As a matter of fact—" Something yanked my foot again and pulled me under. Richard went under too. We both surfaced to the girls laughing at us.

"How 'bout we head in?" Imee looked over at Richard. "I could use a beer."

"Me too." Richard and Imee started toward the boat. "Have you ever seen a slippery dick?" Imee pushed Richard away and he laughed.

I knew that a slippery dick was a small but beautiful fish that lived around reefs like this, but it seemed as though Imee didn't.

"What is it, Charlie?" Rhea could see I was a bit pissed.

I shook my head. "When Richard grabbed me from behind. I dropped the other disk."

"You found another one?"

I nodded. "Fortunately, it didn't sink into the sand." I pointed down and then dove toward it. One good kick and I was there. I picked it up and headed back to where Rhea watched from the surface.

Rhea smiled. "This'll really piss Richard off."

DANGER!

"What?" I said aloud rather than telepathically.

Rhea chuckled. She took the disk carefully. "This will piss Richard off."

THOR! *The other side of the island.*

"Get to the boat. Quickly." I pushed Rhea toward the boat.

"Why?"

"Go!"

Rhea slipped the disk in her dive bag and took off. I followed behind her.

*Who's Thor?* I pictured a Norse god with a hammer in his hand.

An image replaced that image. A huge hammerhead shark.

Alpha darted up to me. *Go.* He took off. *It's Thor! I've got to tend to the younglings.*

Rhea was almost to the boat when a huge black shape loomed on the other side.

*Hey, over here asshole!* I swam toward the coral island, keeping my eye on the shark and Rhea. I knew not to swim fast, but it was very hard not to. The damn shark looked so big.

A distant thought reached me. *He's after you, not the female.* It was Alpha.

Sure enough, he swam right under the boat, ignoring Rhea's dangling legs as they tried to pull her up. I reached the edge of the Sisters and swam slowly toward the tunnel. My heart pounded in my chest. I kept heading toward the tunnel. He was huge, maybe bigger than the boat. Some bubbles shot through the water close to the shark and I heard several muffled reports. Richard must have been shooting at the beast, but to no effect. I'd almost reached the tunnel when another shadow passed in front of me.

I thought it was another shark, but the shadow spread around me. A huge shoal of reef fish. They zipped around me and got between me and Thor. They were so densely packed that I couldn't see the shark on the other side of them. I bagged swimming slowly and kicked as hard as I could. I was almost to the tunnel when I felt a swoosh in the water. I glanced back. The hammerhead had plowed through the curtain of fish. I kicked as hard as I could, willing myself to reach the safety of the tunnel. I turned into it when something yanked me back, hard, jerking me out of the tunnel. I felt no pain as I jerked violently back and forth. Suddenly, I was free. I looked back. My rubber flippers were shredded! I kicked and pulled to get into the tunnel.

I stopped in the middle of the tunnel and looked out. Sure enough, the beast drifted by, one huge eye glaring from the side of his hammer. He turned and darted toward the tunnel. I froze. Thor's lips lifted as it opened its maw to grab me. The teeth got within two feet of me, but no further. I drifted back. He thrashed his tail, trying to squeeze into the tunnel. Thank God he was just too big. He twisted from side to side until blood began to pour from tears on his thick hide. Finally he gave up, backing away, leaving a bloody trail behind him. He disappeared. Next thing I knew, he was at the other end of the tunnel. He darted in, but it was even narrower. The sharp coral must have dug into one side because he backed out quickly.

I was safe. I looked down at my feet, pulling off the tattered remains of my flippers. If they brought the boat up close to the edge of the tunnel, maybe I could get to the boat before the shark got to me. But without flippers, I'd be swimming much slower. I swam to the northern edge of the tunnel and glanced out, trying to see where the boat was. It hadn't moved. Maybe they thought I was dead, or maybe they didn't want to tempt me to make a mad dash for the boat. The shark came around the corner of the island and shot forward when it saw me at the edge of the tunnel. I darted back, but without flippers I felt as if I was swimming through pudding. I just managed to get beyond the shark's reach.

Sharks were supposed to be instinct predators, and this shark should have gone away once I got in the tunnel, but it kept swimming from one entrance of the tunnel to the other. I wasn't bleeding, so there was nothing to keep it around. I caught motion out of the corner of my eye. I swam over to the northern side of the tunnel. Something shiny drifted to the bottom. The guys on the boat were trying to get something to me. Unfortunately, without flippers, I'd never get it and get back to the tunnel before Thor got me.

Another shiny thing was drifting down, this one closer to the mouth of the tunnel. It might just be within reach. I glanced out. Thor was back. I backed up as he swam along the edge of the tunnel. A yellow light in my mask caught my attention. My oxygen level had almost dropped into the red. I only had a few minutes of air left.

I'd either have to make a dash for it or drown in this tunnel. Neither sounded good. While death in the jaws of a shark seemed worse, I might escape Thor. No way could I cheat death if I ran out of air in the tunnel. As I thought, the indicator turned red. Next time Thor was on the south side of the tunnel, I'd dash out of the north side, push off the bottom with my feet and swim for the boat.

I spotted Thor swim by the south side of the tunnel. This was my chance. I pushed off the bottom, angling out of the tunnel toward the boat. I saw the anchor line and headed for it. Without flippers I could pull myself along it quicker than I could swim. I didn't look back, but caught a black shape out of the corner of my eye. Thor. I redoubled my efforts and reached for the anchor line. Something hit me. I blacked out.

I drifted in a haze, wondering if the shark had gotten me. If he had, there'd been no pain. I was glad of that. I reached out with my mind and felt the presence of AB not too far away. Further off, I detected Uncle Merl. He appeared to be hiking up a mountain somewhere. Farther off I saw a light in the distance. I drifted toward it. As I got closer, I could see the Lady Galadriel in her projected form. She smiled at me.

*Charlie. Glad you are communicating with the* > > > > > > > > . A picture of Alpha appeared in my head. *The* > > > > > > > > *have always been friends of Atlanteans. We helped them gain sentience long ago. Beware. Thor is an agent of Lemuria. They will stop you at all cost.*

Galadriel faded away. I floated over Richard's boat. Richard was talking with Pavel. Rhea, Jamie and Imee seemed to be leaning over something in the bow. My vision clouded as a bright light began to sear my brain. I shook my head and opened my eyes. A mistake. I shut them quickly.

"Charlie." I felt Rhea squeeze my hand. My head throbbed.

"Sunglasses." I felt them slip sunglasses on my face. "Thanks." I cracked my eyes open. The sun burned, but a shadow replaced it. Rhea was leaning over me. I smiled.

"You scared the crap out of us." Rhea reached down and touched my cheek.

I rubbed my temples. "Help me up, slowly. I have a splitting headache."

They helped me up and sat me down on the seat under the T-top of the boat.

"No wonder you have a headache." Richard walked up. "Better than being fish food, though. Biggest damn shark I've ever seen."

I nodded, head still throbbing.

"Lucky for you I had a hypersonic cannon on board. We had to use it at almost full strength to drive that beast away." Richard handed me a couple of pills. "Here, take these. They should help with the headache."

I took them and washed them down with a Coke.

"It was the Harbormaster." Pavel looked through the windshield at us.

"The Harbormaster? Never heard of him." Richard walked around the center console and took the controls from Pavel. He started the boat.

"And?"

Pavel eyed Richard, but quickly looked away when Richard looked toward him. "He's a legend. The locals were talking about him at the End of the World the other day."

"The End of the World?" Imee walked back and stood next to Richard. He put the boat in gear and began to idle away from the Sisters.

"It's a bar. Maybe we'll stop by tonight."

Imee smiled. "Sounds like fun. Wonder if they have a shirt that says 'I survived the End of the World'?"

"If they do, I'll buy it for you." He smiled at Imee with a grin that kind of looked like a shark. "Now, Padder, finish the story."

"It's Pavel, sir. I thought they were pulling my leg: a hammerhead over twenty-four feet long. They say it's been lurking around these parts for over fifty years. I shook my head, but they pointed to a picture of a dark shape and a huge fin next to a small fishing boat. The bartender said his father had taken the picture."

Richard continued to putter away from the Sisters in idle. "Never heard of an attack on a diver around here."

"No, sir. They told me that the Harbormaster had been seen by divers off in the distance, but he'd never been aggressive."

"Well, he's aggressive now." Richard pushed the throttles down. The boat jumped forward as the engines roared. The vibration hurt my head, making me feel nauseous. I leaned against Rhea.

She spoke over the hum of the engines. "Lie down. Put your head on my lap."

I didn't argue.

# CHAPTER 30
## HERBAL TEA

Those pills must have been strong because I passed out with my head on Rhea's lap. Next thing I knew I heard Rhea gently saying my name: "Charlie. Charlie."

I opened my eyes to Rhea's smile. I sat up, but felt dizzy. I laid my head back down and closed my eyes.

"Slowly, Charlie. We're almost to the *Sara Charlotte*." Rhea gently stroked my hair.

I felt a bump as we pulled alongside the yacht. Richard must have still been driving. I lifted my head slowly and sat up next to Rhea. I started to get up, but she held me back.

"Take it easy, Charlie. We'll get out last."

Richard walked up the gangway, while Imee followed right behind. Jamie looked back at us, gave me a wink as Rhea looked down at me, and then followed up the gangway.

I lifted my head up slowly. It still throbbed. At least I no longer felt as if someone were driving a hot poker through my eyeballs. I sat for a moment as Rhea stood. She extended her hand. I took it and lifted myself off the seat. My eyes began to blur. I wavered, almost falling. An arm reached under my arm and lifted me.

"Let me help." Pavel smiled.

I nodded carefully. "Thanks." With Pavel on one side and Rhea on the other, I made my way to the gangway. It was too narrow for them to help me, so I took my time, feeling like an old man, carefully placing one foot up on the next step as I gripped the rail, my head swimming. Sweat dripped off my forehead by the time I got to the top. I felt like an idiot. I glanced over at Rhea, expecting her to be exasperated, but she smiled, slipped her arm around me and helped me to my cabin. I lay down on my bed, my head feeling like a helium balloon about to explode.

Rhea fixed my pillow behind my head. She closed the drapes, darkening the room.

"Thanks." Maybe Rhea was better than my uncle's tonic.

"You were very brave today. Splashing to get the shark to come after you."

I shook my head. "It was after me." She nodded knowingly, shook her head slowly, leaned down and kissed my forehead. I smiled weakly. The door opened and a shaft of light shot in. I winced. Rhea's head whipped around.

"Close the door!" The light faded as a large body blocked the hall light. I felt AB's presence and sent a tendril of thought toward him. It hurt.

*No. Words only.*

"How's he doin'?" AB walked up behind Rhea. She brushed the hair off my forehead.

"All right, I guess. Richard said that those sonic cannons could cause some damage."

I tried to lift my head, but it hurt too much. "Ask me, I'm right here. And I'm fine other than a splitting headache."

AB chuckled. "Right. Good thing I know your uncle's home headache remedy."

Rhea looked alarmed. "Richard gave him Tylenol with codeine earlier. I don't think he should have anything else." She reached for the steaming mug of tea, but AB stopped her.

"No need. This stuff's much better: tea with honey and special herbs. Charlie's had it before."

I nodded, hoping it was the same stuff that my uncle had given me on the Moon. "I'll prop him up and you give him this." He handed the mug to Rhea.

She sniffed it. "Tea?" Rhea looked skeptically at AB. She took a small sip. "A bit sweet for my taste. What kind of tea?"

"Special herbs." He slid the hairy four by four he called an arm behind my shoulders and lifted me up. "Remember?"

I nodded. "Hope it works as well as last time."

Rhea lifted the glass to my lips. I took a sip. It had the same sweet flavor I remembered. I drank it down. "Hope you got Uncle Merl's recipe right." I yawned.

"He stole the recipe from my grandmother." AB smiled. "I got it right."

I nodded. Another yawn escaped my lips. I settled my head into the pillow and closed my eyes. I could feel the herbs that AB had put into the tea working already.

AB's and Rhea's voices drifted away.

I walked down a path through a grove of tall evergreens. They weren't redwoods or sequoias, but they seemed to reach for the sky. The air smelled fresh and clean, better than the canned, recycled air that I'd gotten used to on the Moon. I looked down, surprised at the smoothness of the forest path. Instead of dirt, roots and bumps, I walked on a path of weathered stones. Despite their obvious age, they were perfectly level with each other.

I came to an open area with a lake to my left. I stopped. Water cascaded down several fountains near a beach about eight hundred yards across the lake from me. I did a double-take as skyscrapers loomed over the forest behind the beach. The buildings seemed spindly and unnatural, yet they had a slight familiarity to me. They were taller than the tallest buildings that I had seen, yet seemed less solid. I looked back at the beach and the handful of kids frolicking in the water as their parents watched.

I looked down the rows of trees. Something was wrong. They looked cultivated, but, given their height, they must be nearly a thousand years old. I continued down the path, away from the beach. The trees created a shaded canopy over my head. Several large squirrels chased one another under the trees. I smiled as they scampered up a tree. I breathed deeply. A familiar scent drifted on the slight breeze. It smelled like honeysuckle, but I couldn't quite place it.

I followed a bend in the path. A marble pavilion basked in light from a clearing ahead. I walked toward it, my feet seeming to have a will of their own. As I entered the clearing the sun hit me. The warmth felt good. Under the pavilion stood a tall, thin lady in a diaphanous gown. She was looking down into a round pedestal in the center of the pavilion. As I approached, she seemed to sense my presence. She turned.

"Hello, Charlie." She smiled and reached her hand toward me. Her almond-shaped turquoise eyes seemed to bore right into my soul.

I reached out, taking her hand. "Lady Galadriel?"

She chuckled. "Yes, Charlie. It's easier for me to communicate with you during your dreams."

I looked down. My clothes looked like nothing I'd worn before. It looked as if I was wearing a translucent toga, not too dissimilar from Galadriel's gown. "Where are we?"

She smiled. "I implanted an image of Atlantis as it was in your dreams. I want you to understand what we lost."

I nodded.

"Come forward."

I did. She extended her arm over what appeared to be a large bird-bath. A silvery liquid filled it. I could see the roof of the pavilion in the reflection. Blue sky peaked through the circle in the top of the pavilion. I watched as the reflection of a large bird flew over the circle.

I looked up. "What was that?"

She glanced up. "I didn't see it, but from the shadow I bet one of my favorite birds, a frigatebird, flew over the oculus."

"Oculus?" I glanced up.

She chuckled. "Yes, the circle in the dome is called an oculus. We used them frequently in our architecture. We like the feeling of openness. Besides, the light coming through it helps to charge the quicksilver." She pointed to the font. "We called these fonts the mirrors of the soul. Legend tells that by staring into this font filled with quicksilver, the great Atalen became the first of our kind to develop telepathy. We have used them since as a place of reflection and meditation. Go ahead, look into the font."

I leaned over and peered down. At first my reflection stared back at me, but it wasn't my reflection, it was something else. The face looked like mine, but I had a long braid of hair wrapped around my shoulder. My eyes appeared almond-shaped, like Galadriel's, but they were green, not turquoise.

I looked at Galadriel questioningly.

She smiled. "That's how you appear on the inside. Despite your outward human appearance, your soul is Atlantean. Look again, only relax and open your mind."

I looked back into the font, beyond my reflection. At first, all I saw was the reflection of the fresco painted on the ceiling of the pavilion. I hadn't noticed the fresco before. Images of elephants, lions and even a Tasmanian tiger covered one quarter of the ceiling. The animals morphed into mythical creatures and then transitioned into sea life.

Dolphins frolicked in the waves. Galadriel's voice faded out. *Learn from your visions, but remember, they are only shadows* . . . A whale breached just outside the reef line. In front of it the sickle-shaped dorsal of a giant hammerhead cut the water just inside the reef. The images mesmerized me. I looked at giant turtles crawling ashore as the seascape segued into the land again. Then motion in the corner of my eye caught my attention. The hammerhead was swimming, circling around just above me. My skin began to crawl. It felt as if the hammerhead was searching for me. Then I noticed the nick in the hammerhead's dorsal fin. It was Thor. How?

As if on cue, it darted away, swimming hard. It was making for the shallows around shore. I hadn't noticed before, but a young Atlantean was playing along the shore with a pod of dolphins. They didn't appear to see Thor heading their way. I tried to cry out a warning, but couldn't. At the last second, the dolphins scattered and the boy turned. The hammerhead charged him. The boy didn't panic. He didn't even seem concerned. He merely raised his hand. The shark became confused. It began swimming erratically in circles. Whenever its circling took it close to the boy it was as if it bounced into an invisible barrier and turned away.

I breathed a sigh of relief. The boy turned and walked ashore. The scene shifted and a young man now walked in a desolate winter wasteland. He seemed to be searching for something. He stopped to think. Yetis materialized out of the swirling snow, surrounding him. Again, he showed no fear. The yetis closed in on him. When they got within the range where he could smell the foul stench of their breath, he closed his eyes. The yetis charged, but he floated upwards, out of the reach of their yellowed claws. He smiled and looked down, reveling in his escape. To his shock, the yetis had captured several people. He floated above them, trying to see who the yetis had captured. He couldn't make them out. They wore white winter parkas with their hoods up, making them almost invisible. From their shapes, two appeared to be female and two male. Suddenly, a feline shape darted in from one side as blue sparks erupted from one of the captives' hands. One of the male captives darted through a gap in the ranks of the yetis created by the vicious surprise attack of the feline.

The yetis started to give chase, but a small figure stopped them. She smiled and glanced up at me. Trolga. She pointed up at the floating figure and then pointed at her captives. One of the captives looked up. It was me. I was looking at myself. Vertigo struck. I plunged downward toward the waiting arms of the largest yeti. He snarled as I approached, his yellowed fangs protruding from his lips. I cringed, but fell right through him and right on through the snow. I came to a stop in a large cavern. I started walking toward a light in the middle of the cavern. It seemed eerily familiar to me. As I approached I could see that the glow came from what appeared to be a large bubble in the middle of the cavern. The light from the bubble cast long shadows from the people surrounding it. They had set up a mobile lab around the bubble, with tables, computers and all kinds of devices that I didn't recognize. Something that looked like a throne sat in the middle of the bubble. Threads of energy seemed to pulse from it. As I looked, the threads stretched out toward me, wrapped around me and drew me forward. I tried to stop, planting my feet and leaning backward, but it drew me in like a black hole. I left the ground and shot forward. I screamed and sat up, sweat dripping from my brow.

# CHAPTER 31
## HAMMERHEAD CAKE

"Charlie?"

Rhea sat on the corner of my bed, holding my hand. A look of concern creased her brow. I smiled up at her and squeezed her hand.

"Nothing, just a bad dream." I sat up. "In fact, I'm feeling much better." As I said that, my stomach groaned. It felt like an empty pit. "And I'm starving."

Rhea laughed. "Well, it's just about dinner time, so you're in luck."

"Guess I got a good nap in since getting back to the boat."

Rhea frowned. "A good nap? You've been asleep over twenty-four hours. I was real worried, all of us were, but AB assured us that you needed the rest and that your uncle's tea would keep you asleep for at least that long."

I nodded, slid up in the bed and stretched. "I do feel much better. Headache's gone, but a bit stiff. That stuff really works. Knocked me out the last time too." I remembered my headache after my first confrontation with Trolga.

A ding sounded over the boat's intercom. Rhea stood up. "That'll be dinner."

I began to slide out of bed, but Rhea stopped me. "I'll meet you at dinner—after you get dressed."

I blushed as I realized that I didn't have any clothes on under the covers. "You . . . ?"

It was Rhea's turn to blush. She shook her head. "Your friend AB took care of it. See you at the dinner table. Weather's good, so Richard's got them doing dinner up on the flybridge." She turned as she got to the door. "By the way, I got you a present." She pointed to the foot of the bed.

Rhea closed the door behind her. I slipped on a pair of box-ers and shorts and then picked up the present. It was wrapped in ocean-blue wrapping paper with sailfish on it. I tore through the paper and opened the box. I pulled out a rash guard dive T-shirt. I laughed when I flipped it around. It had a picture of underwater ruins with the caption "Atlantis—Mysteries Revealed." I slipped it on and headed up to the flybridge for dinner.

Richard sat in the center of the horseshoe-shaped sofa that wrapped around the rear of the flying bridge. He had one arm around Imee. Jamie sat on his other side with Rhea next to Jamie. Richard was laughing at something when he saw me.

"Ah, the sleeper has awakened."

Jamie chimed in, "*Dude!*"

Richard shook his head. "Not bad, but let's put the trivia game on hold. So, Charlie, how do you feel?"

"Much better. A bit sore." I rubbed my temple.

"You know you're lucky to be alive. Good thing I thought about using the hypersonic cannon. Saved your life."

I nodded my head. "Thanks, Richard. I'd be chum if you hadn't done that."

Rhea came to my side. She gave Richard a scowl. "Charlie's the real hero here. He lured the shark away so I could get away. That was the bravest thing I've ever seen." She leaned over, gave me a kiss on the cheek and grasped my hand. "Come, sit by me."

I squeezed her hand and followed her to the sofa, sitting down next to her.

Richard leaned forward. "So, Charlie, did you piss yourself when that shark came after you?"

Imee hit Richard in the arm. "You've got to be kidding. What a stupid question." Imee looked sympathetically at me. "What were you thinking! That thing looked as big as a submarine. And it was fast."

I shook my head. "I wasn't really thinking. I knew my only chance was to get in the tunnel. Thor's head was so huge that I hoped he wouldn't be able to get to me."

"Thor?" Richard looked at me. His eyes widened. "Got it. Makes sense, the hammer and all." Richard picked up a drink and took a sip.

"Anyway, he was much faster than I thought. He got a chunk of my flippers before I got deep enough into the tunnel. That screwed up my chances. Even with both flippers, I'd have to have a huge head start to get to the boat. I'd hoped he'd circle the islands and that would give me time to get to the boat, but he kept going back and forth from one opening of the tunnel to the next."

Imee chimed in. "We saw blood. We thought it had gotten you."

I nodded. "I was afraid of that. Thor cut himself thrashing against the coral."

Richard shook his head. "Very strange. I've seen sharks press into a hole in a coral reef to get to prey, but when they can't get to it, they usually head on around the reef and don't come back." Richard finished his drink. "Pavel, get me a Kalik."

Pavel went to the fridge and came back with several Kaliks in his hands. He handed the first to Richard and then shoved one in my direction.

I shook my head. "No thanks."

Rhea smiled and took two. "Thanks, Pavel." She handed one to me. How could I say no. She lifted the beer. "To Charlie, the bravest guy I know."

Everyone responded. "To Charlie."

She held her bottle up to me. I clicked it and did the same with the others, and then took a gulp from the bottle. Rhea put her beer down, turned to me and placed her hands on my cheeks, her ruby-red eyes looking right through me. My heart thudded in my chest. She leaned over and kissed me on the lips. Her lips lingered momentarily and then she pulled away. My cheeks flushed.

"Way to go, Charlie. Next time, I'll jump in and wrestle the shark." Jamie smiled at both me and Rhea.

Richard looked over at us and then at Imee.

She leaned over and kissed him, lingering longer than Rhea had. She pulled away. "You're my hero. You saved Charlie." She lifted her bottle. "To Richard."

Bottles clinked together again. "To Richard." I meant it. Richard had saved my life. The headache had been a minimal price to pay. Richard looked a bit irritated despite the toast and the kiss from Imee. He glared at me. I wondered if I'd taken the spotlight off him or whether he still felt something for Rhea. I started to probe his mind but my thoughts seemed to bounce back.

AB walked up onto the flybridge. "Smells great in the galley. Dinner's coming up right behind me." *That's a big no no, Charlie. Remember the rules. Resist temptation.*

I nodded.

*You also need to learn some control. Your thoughts were leaking all over the place when Rhea kissed you.* AB mentally shook his head and a thought leaked out. *Cubs are so challenging when they reach sexual maturity.*

*I heard that!* It was bad enough that AB had read my thoughts. Thank goodness none of the others could, particularly Rhea. I looked over at her as my thoughts strayed again.

AB strode forward as only he could and reached out and grabbed a handful of egg roll off the appetizer tray. "I'm starving. How's sleeping beauty feeling?" He picked up another handful of eggrolls and flipped one to me. *See what I mean? We learn not to read thoughts without permission.*

I caught the egg roll with ease. "I am hungry." I took a bite and then another. "And I do feel better. No more headache."

AB nodded, sat down and looked over at Pavel. "How about a beer?" He shoved another egg roll into his maw. I reached out and grabbed one as well.

Richard glared at AB. "Guess they don't teach sasqu . . . " Imee elbowed Richard and darted her eyes over at Pavel ". . . manners in Saskatchewan."

AB pounded his chest and let out a long, deep burp. "Guess not. In some cultures, including Saskatchewanian culture"—he smiled and his canines edged over his lips—"it's polite to belch when food is enjoyed. And as I've told Charlie many times, good thing I'm a vegetarian." He smiled at Richard, forcing his canines to show even more.

Richard paused momentarily, but then laughed and stood up. "Glad you brought ol' AB along, Charlie, he's the life of the party. Dinner's ready. Let's eat."

After a delicious but uneventful dinner, everyone started to get up from the table.

"Hold on." Richard's words stumbled out of his mouth. He'd been drinking a lot. "I've got a surprise for Charlie."

We all sat back down. *AB?*

*No. Let it be a surprise.* "I can't wait. Hope it's something to eat." AB rubbed his huge hands together.

"You mean you didn't have enough?" Rhea looked over at AB's plate littered with broken stone-crab claws and two giant T-bones literally gnawed to the bone.

AB began to beat his chest.

"Don't you dare!" Rhea chastised him. AB somehow refrained from burping but did manage a toothy smile.

A beautiful brunette who I hadn't met walked onto the flybridge with a large covered silver tray. She lifted the top with a flourish. "Voilà."

Several oohs and aahs followed. A cake the shape of a swimming hammerhead shark rested on the tray. Scoops of ice cream surrounded the shark.

The brunette extended a silver cake knife toward Richard, but he shook his head. "No, no. Charlie's honor. Since Thor didn't eat Charlie, Charlie gets to eat Thor!"

I couldn't believe it. Sometimes Richard was a complete ass and other times he acted like my best friend. "This is amazing. How'd you do this?"

"Nothing but the best for my father. Not only is Terri hot"—Imee elbowed Richard, but he ignored it—"but she's a cordon bleu chef. Besides, due to your sleeping-beauty imitation yesterday, she had plenty of time to work her magic."

I smiled and looked up at Terri. "Thank you. This looks amazing." Everyone nodded.

"Wait until you taste it before you thank me." She pointed to the knife. "Please, do the honors before the ice cream melts and the shark swims away."

That got a chuckle out of everyone. "Thanks." I cut into the center of the shark, just below the dorsal. I carved out a piece and handed it to Rhea.

"That's ridiculous. A niggardly piece if I've ever seen one." Richard grabbed the knife.

"Richard!" Imee hit him.

"What? Niggardly, that means a small piece. It's got nothing to do with race."

"Even so . . . "

"Fine." He decapitated the shark with one swipe and then cut off one side of its hammer and handed it to Imee." He quickly butchered the rest of the cake, doling out pieces to all of us. He, of course, kept the largest piece for himself.

"Terri, how about a glass of my father's favorite cognac?"

"You know what your father said last time."

"What my father doesn't know won't hurt him—and you're not going to tell him." Richard stared at Terri.

She smiled. "Of course not, sir."

"Can I have a glass?" Imee rubbed icing off her lip, stuck her finger in her mouth and sucked the icing off.

"No." Richard shoved a large bite of cake into his mouth.

Imee hadn't expected the rejection. "Why not?" She did a fake pout.

"Because this cognac costs over $10,000 a bottle. You don't have the palate for it."

Imee looked pissed, but she composed herself. "Do you have something else for me?"

"Sure. Terri, get Imee a glass of the XO my dad keeps for guests. In fact, bring the bottle up and a few snifters."

"Yes, sir." Terri departed down the stairs.

*Man, what a snob. I was about to ask for a glass. Glad I didn't. XO's not bad. I'll settle for it.*

I looked over at AB. He grinned as he picked up the knife and cut himself another piece.

*And don't get any ideas. You're not having any. In fact you shouldn't have had the beer after the sonic cannon.*

But— I started, but AB didn't let me finish.

*I know, you couldn't say no to the female.* He shook his head.

Her name's Rhea and—

*Sorry. Didn't know you were sooo sensitive.* He stuck another piece of cake on my plate as if in a peace offering.

Man, did AB know how to get my goat. Guess that was one of the negatives of telepathy. *You're one to talk. How many beers did you drink while I was battling Thor?*

*I'm well over one hundred, and you're a mere pup. Besides, alcohol and my grandmother's tea don't go well together. Watch it.*

I shook my head. Terri returned bearing a silver tray with crystal snifters. She handed the first to Richard and then passed them out. When she got to me, I declined. "Take it to my big friend over there. I'm sure he can handle another."

Terri turned, and AB quickly grabbed two snifters off the tray. "Don't mind if I do." He elaborately swirled the goblet in his right hand and then brought it to his nose. He sniffed tentatively and then put it to his lips. He took a small sip, curled his lips back as if in displeasure, and then downed the whole thing.

Richard laughed. "I guess that's one way to drink a fine cognac." He lifted his snifter, swirled it around, took a sniff and then a small taste. "Ahhhh. Nectar of the gods."

AB took a sip from the other snifter. "It's not a cognac."

Richard looked at him with his best upper-crust glare. "What do you mean?"

"Just what I said. This"—AB brandished the glass—"is not cognac."

"Then what is it?" Richard sniffed at his cognac again.

"Larressingle XO—Armagnac. I'd say bottled in 2021."

Richard looked shocked. He glanced over at Terri. She nodded. "I never would have thought that a sasqu— gentleman from Saskatchewan would know his cognac. Charlie, your friend's full of surprises."

AB walked over to Richard and extended his hand. "May I take a sniff?"

"By all means." Richard handed his snifter over.

AB lifted the glass up to his eye level and looked through it. "Nice snifter. Baccarat?"

Richard could only nod.

AB swirled the cognac around in the Baccarat snifter and slowly raised it to his nose. He tilted the snifter slightly and inhaled slowly. He handed the snifter back to Richard.

"Now that's a fine cognac. Your father has exquisite taste. If I'm not mistaken that's from a bottle of Croizet Cuvee Leonie, bottled in 1858. I didn't know there were any bottles left. I think the last one sold at auction to a Saudi prince for just under $800,000."

Everyone stared at AB and then at Richard. Richard took a sniff from the glass and then looked up. "You are full of surprises. My father bought six bottles before I was born. He's down to the last three." Richard looked over at Imee. "Now do you understand why I didn't share? Each sip costs a small fortune!"

Imee smiled coyly. "You're right. I'd much rather have this and a diamond bracelet than a glass of that."

I looked over at AB. *For real?*

He nodded. *Yep. A vice of your uncle's. He's been packing away cognac now for several centuries. Once you're of age, I'm sure he'll give you a few tastes.*

Richard lifted his glass. "Terri, bring AB a small taste. I think he's earned it."

"Thank you, Richard. I've smelled it, but never tasted it. I'm wondering how it compares to Henri IV Dudognon Heritage."

"You've had that?" Richard looked shocked.

"Yes, about—" he glanced over at Terri as she made her way down the stairs "—a hundred and twenty years ago, an old acquaintance who loves cognac let me have a small taste. As you said, nectar of the gods."

Imee looked over at Richard. "But yours is better, right?"

Richard shook his head. "Henri IV Dudognon is the best, most expensive cognac in the world. The last bottle sold for just under $8 million. My father, of course, had the winning bid, but he won't let me near it,"

"Damn. That's ridiculous. This is just fine with me." Jamie took a sip of his Armagnac. "Warm, tasty and does the job."

The sonic cannon and herbal tea must have muddled my brain. We were sitting around, drinking and talking about absurdly expensive liquor. Ridiculous. We were not here for a party. That weight settled firmly back between my shoulders. I looked around. Everyone seemed relaxed. Other than AB, they didn't know what was at stake, but I did. I gave AB a glare. He at least put down the snifter of cognac.

"What about the disks? Did you find out anything while I was out? Did you go back and try to find more?" I looked around. Even Richard seemed to avoid my eyes. "I guess not. Anybody think about what we should do next?" Still silence.

I stood up and began to pace. "This isn't a vacation. We shouldn't be sitting around drinking and eating." I glared at Richard and Imee.

They turned their eyes away. "We've discovered an ancient civilization, been chased off the Moon and almost killed in the process, kidnapped by yetis, robbed, and attacked by sharks. This is serious!" I looked around. Even AB looked sheepishly at me. Rhea stood and came over to my side.

"Charlie, you're right, but we were waiting for you to get better. None of us really has a clue what to do." The sun was about to set over the Gulf Stream. It really was beautiful. "It's easy to get distracted and forget given the setting. I never would have thought about being on a fabulous yacht in the Bahamas searching for an ancient civilization. This whole thing's surreal." She took my hand. "I think I can speak for all of us and say that we were concerned about you and were waiting for you to get better."

*The scenery's quite distracting, and none of them know the real story. To them this is just an adventure.* AB glanced over at Rhea. She squeezed my hand as her ruby-red eyes looked into mine. *Give her a break. She really cares for you.* AB gave me a toothsome smile.

As my anger grew, I pictured Trolga laughing at me. I'd never blown up like this before. I took a couple of deep breaths and squeezed Rhea's hand. As I calmed down, the vision of Trolga seemed to evaporate. "Sorry. I appreciate your concern. But this isn't a vacation. It's deadly serious. If any of you want out, I understand."

Rhea squeezed my hand. "I'm in, all the way."

Jamie stood up and extended his hand. I took it. "Me too. Trolga came after me with both guns blazing. I have a score to settle."

Richard raised his cognac. "In for a penny, in for a pound. Got nothing better to do for the summer."

AB crushed an empty can of Kalik and made a perfect free throw into the trash can ten feet away. "Your uncle charged me with keeping an eye out for you. As much as I'd like to kick back on this lovely yacht, drink beer and eat lobster all day—" AB paused, letting out a loud belch "—you're stuck with me. Besides, I have a feeling we're going to get another crack at those yetis. I'd have taken care of them if Richard's sonic cannon hadn't."

Imee looped her arm through Richard's. "Me too. So, what's the next step?"

All eyes turned to me. To be honest, I hadn't really thought about the next step. I was just frustrated with our inaction. Alpha had said that there was a spot to the south where he'd seen a lot more metal like the two disks we'd found. My mother's Atlantis journal also had a couple of spots marked to the south of Bimini. I'd bet that Alpha's location was close to one of them.

"I hadn't mapped anything out yet, but I think we should try a couple of the spots to the south outlined in my mother's journal. After all, we did find the disk at the Three Sisters which she'd marked in her journal."

Richard chimed in. "Not a bad idea. Never liked Bimini that much, and Cat's swarming with little kids for the summer. Just need to check my weather app."

Of course Richard had the newest subcutaneous iLink. He looked off in the distance, focused on the 3D image projected in front of his optic nerve. I'd heard about them and seen demos on line, but I had the old fashioned iLet on my wrist. Richard nodded. "Good. No hurricanes or other significant blows coming in the next week or so. We should be good to go. I'll have the captain make sure we are provisioned for a couple of weeks in the outer islands and we can head out tomorrow."

"Great." I looked around. After my little bit of an outburst, everyone looked a bit uncomfortable. Richard sipped at his ridiculously expensive cognac and AB grabbed another beer.

Imee looked a bit antsy. She nudged Richard. "Remember the show."

Richard smiled. "I'd almost forgotten. The *Weapon Shops of Isher*'s about to start." He looked around. "I promised Imee we'd watch on the 3D projector in the master cabin." He sounded sheepish, but I knew that he really wanted to watch. We'd read the book in English class on the Moon, and Richard had really gotten into it. Knowing that Hollywood was producing a mini-series had gotten more people interested in the book.

They got up. "See you in the morning."

I looked over at Rhea. She pointed to the horizon. The setting sun glinted off the horizon. "Let's go up to the bow to watch the sunset." She grabbed my hand.

I turned to AB and to Jamie. They shook their heads. "I think we'll go below and watch *Isher* in the main salon."

# CHAPTER 32
## THE GREEN FLASH

We went forward of the flying bridge and took the spiral stairs down to the main deck. Rhea led me forward to the cushioned lounge in the bow of the boat. She crawled on and I crawled up next to her. She put her arm around me and nuzzled her head against my shoulder. My heart hammered in my chest.

I looked to the west. An orange glow crept across the water as the sun settled down toward it. I hoped we'd see the green flash together. I'd never seen it. I'd heard about the green flash from my sailing trips with my parents, but had never seen one. Some people claimed that it was a mirage, but my parents had seen several. As we had watched one evening my father had explained that as the sun . . .

Rhea picked up her head. "What're you thinking?"

I looked into her ruby-red eyes and smiled. "I was thinking about the green flash."

"What is it?" She nuzzled her head further into my shoulder.

I wanted to lean down and kiss her, but her head was below mine. I sighed. "When the sun drops behind the ocean, the final beams of light refracted by both the atmosphere and the surface of the ocean can create a brilliant sparkle of green. Conditions have to be just right, but if they are, mother nature provides a beautiful, but brief, light show. But it's rare. You have to be lucky." I leaned over slightly and kissed the top of her head.

Rhea squeezed my hand and looked up into my eyes. "Well maybe you'll get lucky tonight." She glanced over at the sun. It was just about to hit the water.

I looked at its orange ball descending into the water. I cupped my hand to my ear. "Hear it?"

"Hear what?" Rhea turned to me.

"The sizzle of the sun hitting the water."

Rhea hit my arm as I laughed. We both grew quiet as the sun dropped below the water. One tiny glint of yellow remained and then disappeared.

"I guess . . . " A dazzling burst of green interrupted me. It only lasted a moment, but man, it took your breath away.

Rhea lifted her head off my shoulder, scooted up and turned her head toward me. Her lips were only inches from mine. "That was beautiful."

I looked into her eyes. They sparkled in the twilight—a red flash. I leaned forward slightly. Rhea closed her eyes. Our lips touched. My body tingled all over as if a weak electric current had passed through me.

I pulled back. I spoke softly. "Not as beautiful as you."

Rhea put her arm around me and leaned forward. Our lips touched again. I reached my arm up along her back, running my fingers through her hair and softly supporting her head. Rhea wrapped her arms around me. Time seemed to slow as I leaned toward her. She pulled me on top of her as our lips stayed pressed together.

I reached my arm down her side and slid it up until it hit her bikini top. She wiggled a bit. I yanked my hand back. She pulled back and smiled.

"I thought that a baseball player would know how to slide into second base." I chuckled and she kissed me. "Richard . . . "

I pulled away. "Richard? Richard what?" I slid off the cushioned lounge. "You'd rather be here with Richard? Is that it? This is his boat." I paced back and forth.

Rhea sat up. "No. Charlie, come back. I didn't mean anything."

"Yeah, right." I leaned on the railing looking to the east.

"Charlie, I'm here with you, not Richard. Your pulling back is one of the reasons I really like you."

I turned and looked at her. The light of the fading sunset sparkled in her auburn hair. She was gorgeous. What would she want with a guy like me?

"Richard was an ass. You're cute, smart and you saved my life." She patted the lounge next to her.

My anger faded and I took a step toward her.

She lowered one spaghetti strap on her bikini. "I didn't do this for Richard." She lowered the other strap and pulled her bikini top down.

I couldn't believe my eyes. Her breasts were perfect. Much nicer than the ones that I'd seen while surfing the net.

She laughed. "Close your mouth and come lay your head down on my chest."

I jumped back onto the lounge.

That was when we heard the big splash.

Rhea pulled her top up. "What was that?"

I smiled. "Probably nothing. Just a fish." I leaned up on my elbow toward her.

Another loud splash. Rhea pulled away and fixed her bikini.

I couldn't believe my bad luck. I got up off the lounge and looked around. Rhea got up off the other side. I walked to the bow rail in time to see a dolphin splash up again.

*It's about time. I've been yelling at you, but you didn't hear me. Thought you'd lost your ability to hear us. I almost left, but decided to make some noise first.*

*Alpha?*

*Of course. Told you I'd be back.* Alpha did a tail walk to show off.

Rhea walked up next to me. "That's the dolphin from the other day. The one you gave the lobster to."

I was a bit shocked. Maybe Rhea was telepathic. "How do you know?"

She pointed as Alpha rolled past the bow. "Look, just above the dorsal, he's got a slight scar, and there's a little nick in his dorsal. I'm pretty sure he's the same one."

I felt a presence behind me. I turned and almost went over the side. "AB, how the hell can you be so big and yet so quiet?"

Rhea looked back as AB grinned. He lifted one giant foot and wiggled his toes. "How do you think we've stayed hidden for so long?"

AB pointed. "What's he want?"

Before I could answer, Rhea said, "Probably another lobster. I think Charlie's spoiled him."

*Yes, yes, yes. A lobster. That would be great.*

I turned, but AB stopped me. *I'll go rustle one up out of the fridge. You stay here. Find out what Alpha wants.* "Think I need another beer. Be back in a minute. Either of you want anything?"

We both shook our heads.

We leaned over the bow rail and watched Alpha dart around the boat and the anchor line. Rhea reached her hand out. I took it, looked at her and smiled. She smiled back.

*Is the big guy getting me a lobster?*

*Yes. He'll be back in a minute. What did you come by for?*

Alpha spun on his back and hit his tail in the water. *I spoke with an elder from another pod and confirmed the location of the place of the Atlanteans. I'll guide you there tomorrow.*

Alpha continued to put on a show for Rhea as we conversed telepathically. He did a couple of flips and Rhea laughed and clapped her hands.

"Quite a show, first the green flash and now this dolphin."

I nodded. I hadn't mastered the ability to talk and telepath at the same time. *How far?*

*Not far. A nice swim. Might pick up a few blue runners or a snapper or two along the way.*

AB reappeared behind us, this time popping a beer so we would hear him. "Got the lobster. Want me to throw it to him?"

Rhea shook her head. "Let me."

"I'm never one to say no to a pretty girl." AB handed the lobster tail to Rhea. She held it up over the rail so Alpha could see it. He darted away and then back, popping his head up just in front of the bow. Rhea tossed the lobster tail to him. He caught it, gave it a couple of chomps and it was gone.

*Thank your > > > > > > > > for me.*

I didn't know what he'd said, but a picture of Rhea standing next to me appeared in my head. *I will.*

*See you at daybreak.* Alpha did one last tail walk and then headed out rapidly.

I thought about Richard and Imee. *That's probably too early for my friends.*

*No problem. Just head south when you're ready and call out to me. I'll find you.* Alpha's thoughts faded away.

"I guess he's gone." Rhea looked out over the water.

I nodded. "He'll probably be back. Dolphins are very smart, and I think he's got a taste for lobster."

AB stretched and yawned. "I'll head below. Sounds like we've got a long day ahead of us." He didn't wait for a reply.

The stars had started to come out. While you could see far more from here than you could from Seattle, the night sky paled in comparison to what we could see from the Dome in Clarksville. I could see the Milky Way above us. I looked over at the lounge and then, longingly, at Rhea.

She leaned over and kissed me again. I started to wrap my arm around her, but she pulled back. "Good night, Charlie. See you in the morning." She walked away slowly. I watched, savoring the lingering taste of her lips on mine. I smiled and looked back up at the stars.

# CHAPTER 33
## DOES BACON FLOAT?

I woke early, dressed in a bathing suit and the Mysteries Revealed rash guard shirt that Rhea had given me, and quietly headed up to the flybridge for breakfast. I expected to be the first one up, but AB greeted me with a smile and a forkful of bacon and eggs.

*Come, join me for breakfast.* AB pointed to a spot at the table next to him. *You've got to say that Richard and his dad don't skimp.*

AB had a huge plate full of food in front of him, but that huge plate barely made a dent in the spread of bacon, sausage, eggs, hash browns, English muffins, OJ, coffee and fresh cantaloupe laid out on the table.

He tasted the coffee and smiled. *That's a good cup of joe. Once you experience the siren song of coffee, you're addicted for life.* He smiled, put the coffee down and picked up a bottle of champagne from a bucket next to him. *Perrier-Jouët. Not bad.* He made himself a mimosa.

"What, drinking . . ."

AB shook his head. *Telepathy while nobody's around. You need the practice. You should have detected me before you got up here.*

*A bit groggy, I guess. Speaking of groggy, champagne before diving?*

AB stuffed a sausage in his mouth. *I'm staying here. Sasquatches don't make good divers. Don't like getting my fur wet.*

An image of a soaking wet sasquatch appeared in my head. I laughed. I could see why AB didn't like getting wet. *So, what're you going to do, relax and watch baseball?*

*Not a bad idea, but I need to communicate with my family back home. Communicating at that distance will require deep meditation. After you leave, I'm going to go to my cabin and start meditating.*

I pictured AB, legs crossed in the lotus position, hands held above his knees in the om position, levitating off the floor.

*Not a bad image. Good practice. Sending an image is harder than sending words.*

*So you can . . . levitate?*

*Don't be ridiculous. Telepathy comes naturally to us and so does our ability to detect other sentients and camouflage ourselves, but levitation or telekinesis?* He shook his head. *I wish. Sit, have some breakfast.*

I grabbed a plate and sat down. I inhaled deeply through my nose. The breakfast spread smelled heavenly. A breakfast like this was extremely rare on the Moon. I reached for some bacon, but AB grabbed my wrist, stopping me.

*Now you, a descendant of Atlanteans, should be able to do telekinesis. Picture that piece of bacon in your head and try to lift it to your lips.*

*You kidding?* I searched AB's enigmatic face for that grin that popped out when he pulled a fast one on me. Nothing.

*You want it. Try.* AB closed his eyes and sent me an image of a piece of bacon floating in front of me.

*Fine.* I stared at the bacon, willing it to lift from the plate.

AB shook his head. *That's the wrong way. Don't strain. Relax and make it happen. Think of the flavor of the thick-cut hickory-smoked bacon dissolving in your mouth.*

I sat back, closed my eyes and tried to visualize the bacon. I could smell the odor of freshly cooked bacon mingled with the smell of fresh-brewed coffee. I could even taste it. I slowed my breathing and focused on the bacon with my mind's eye.

"What are you doing?"

I opened my eyes. Richard and Imee stood at the top of the stairs leading to the flybridge. AB had a slice of bacon in his hand.

"If you're still tired, go back to bed. We can head south later." Imee looked concerned.

"I'm fine. Just thinking." I looked over at AB. He winked.

"Well stop thinking and start eating." Richard grabbed a plate and started scooping scrambled eggs onto it.

I shrugged and did the same. Maybe AB had been pulling my leg, but, then again, I remembered the rock I'd thrown at Richard on the Moon and how it had rapidly decelerated when I'd panicked.

With a mouth full of food, Richard turned to me. "So, Charlie, where to?"

I took a sip of OJ to clear my throat. "I looked at my mother's journal. There're a couple of larger islands and a few small coral islands to the south that she's marked. I dove a couple of caves with my parents years ago. Never found anything, but we never got very deep into the cave systems. We just didn't have the equipment."

"And I take it that you think I do."

I nodded as I swallowed a bit of scrambled eggs with American cheese. "Those new masks and snorkels with built in rebreathers will work great. If fully charged, they should give us what, fifteen minutes underwater."

"Twenty. And I have charge packs that we can take with us that'll give us an additional ten minutes."

Rhea had walked quietly up the stairs. She hit Richard's arm and then crossed her arms. "Then why the hell didn't you throw some down to Charlie when he was trapped by the hammerhead!"

Richard rubbed his arm and looked up at Rhea. "Because, dear Rhea, I didn't have any on board the dive boat. Besides, they're lightweight patches and float. Even if we'd had them with us, we couldn't have gotten them down to Charlie."

Rhea took a breath and relaxed. "Sorry." She sat down next to me, leaned over and gave me a kiss on the cheek and patted my leg. "Sleep well?"

I nodded and blushed. Her question had triggered a recollection of a dream she'd been in last night.

"Damn, Charlie, it was just a kiss. No reason to blush." Richard picked up what looked like a Bloody Mary and took a sip.

Imee smiled. "It's cute that you blush, Charlie. I can't think of the last time that Richard blushed."

I changed the subject. "So, Richard, drinking before diving?" I pointed at the Bloody Mary.

"As much as I might like to party, I'm not stupid. Virgin Mary. Want one?"

I shook my head. Didn't like the taste of tomato juice.

Jamie wandered up, with Pavel right behind him. Pavel walked over to Richard as Jamie sat down.

"We're ready to go any time you are, sir."

"Your mother didn't put any GPS locations down in that journal of hers, did she?" Richard polished off the Virgin Mary.

I shook my head. My mother and father seemed to like to do things the old-fashioned way. "My dad had an uncanny ability to find a spot without GPS. He rarely used it."

"Too bad. Guess we'll have to do a bit of searching."

I nodded. I really wasn't sure how to deal with following Alpha right to the spot. They'd learned a lot about AB, but not that I was telepathic. I didn't want to tell them about being an Atlantean or my ability to communicate with dolphins.

"What do you guys say? Ready to go find some more traces of Atlantis?"

I glanced over at Jamie. He looked rough. It wasn't like him. He'd always been up before me, ready to go. "I'm ready, but let's give Jamie time for breakfast."

Jamie waved his hand. "I'm fine. Just a cup of coffee and I'll be good to go." He poured a cup and took a sip.

"Ok, then." Richard addressed Pavel. "We'll meet you at the transom in thirty. That'll give everyone time to get ready. Take sandwiches and plenty of drinks. We don't know how long we'll be."

"Very good, sir."

# CHAPTER 34
## HIDDEN CAVE

Pavel had the dive boat waiting at the transom. I got there first and started looking around for Alpha. The girls came out next, with Richard behind them. His eyes were on the girls' bikinis walking in front of him. He almost tripped because he wasn't paying attention, but, in typical Richard fashion, he smiled and made an obscene gesture and pointed at the girls. I merely shook my head.

*Don't hold it against him. From my study of you human adolescents, his behavior is typical. And don't say you never look. You young male humans are always rutting.*

I glanced up. AB waved from the back of the flybridge. *I thought you were going to go meditate or something. Go!* I looked up and Rhea was staring at me. I helped her on board.

"Why the scowl?"

"Oh, nothing, just thinking."

"Well start thinking good thoughts. No more scowls." She and Imee put towels down across the cushion in the bow and lay down.

Jamie came out last, looking a bit pale, but better than he had when he'd come to breakfast. I guess with everything going on, I hadn't paid as much attention to Jamie as usual. He nodded and stood behind the center console.

Richard took the helm. "Ready to cast off?"

Pavel nodded. He cast off the lines as Richard put the engines in gear.

*Alpha, you around?* I really wasn't sure where to go if Alpha didn't show up. Could I really rely on a dolphin? After all, he seemed more into lobster than anything else.

Richard swung us around and headed south, plowing through the light chop kicked up by the gentle breeze. He pushed a button and a holographic image of everything in front of us popped up on the windshield. It showed all of the small islands to the south in surprising clarity. Richard would have the best and the latest.

"So, Charlie, where to?"

I looked up at the screen. The detail amazed me. It showed each island, the air temperature, the water temperature and our speed of sixty knots.

"Are we really doing sixty knots? Doesn't feel like it."

Richard nodded. "I set the autopilot to take us to this island." He pointed at a small coral atoll. A red dot appeared next to it. "From what you said before, the most promising spots are south of Sandy Cay, so I set the autopilot to take us to a spit of land south of there."

I nodded and pulled out my mother's journal from my water-proof pouch. I flipped to the dog-eared page with the islands south of Bimini. I needed to buy some time. "I can't quite make out the spots designated by my mother relative to the islands plotted by your Garmin."

I looked down as if to study the chart and then looked up at the hologram of our route. I shook my head.

Richard grabbed the journal and held it out in front of himself.

I reached for it. "Careful with that."

"Here." He handed it back.

"Why'd you grab it?" I carefully closed the volume and put it back in my waterproof pouch.

Richard smiled and then pointed as a handful of red dots appeared on the hologram. "The computer interpreted your mother's notes and overlaid them with the chart. The red dots are all of the spots indicated in your mother's journal. Now, which one do we head for?"

I looked at the chart. Without Alpha, all I could do was guess.

"Wow! Look there." Imee pointed to starboard.

We all looked over as a dolphin leaped out of the water and spun to land on his back, showing off his pink belly. He was so close that the splash almost reached the boat.

"That's amazing," Imee said. "Where's my camera?"

"Don't worry." He pointed up. "Got the latest Go Pro installed on the T-top. I've got it recording." Richard eased back on the throttle so the girls could watch the dolphins.

Imee nodded. "Where'd they go?" She and Rhea were looking out over the bow. Richard slowed the boat a tad more.

*You out there, Alpha?* I thought that this must be Alpha's pod, but there were lots of dolphins in the area. An image of a lobster appeared in my head. I had my answer.

We were all focused ahead and to starboard, but then we heard Jamie. "They're coming up behind us."

Sure enough, a handful of dolphins shot through the turquoise waters right behind us. They started surfing our wake.

"Looks like they're having fun." Rhea smiled as they effortlessly darted back and forth.

*So, Alpha, where too?* I looked around, but couldn't spot Alpha in the group.

*Just follow me.*

*But where are you?* I looked at the dolphins dancing in our wake.

*Out front, scouting. Those are some of my pups behind you.*

I nodded, looked forward and watch Alpha roll about a hundred yards in front of the boat.

"Can we stop and get in the water with them?" Imee looked coyly over at Richard.

I started to say something, but Richard shook his head. "No. This is not a vacation." He looked over at me. I nodded and looked at the hologram. We were only a couple of miles from the first red dot.

"Richard's right. This is deadly serious. I've almost been killed and they kidnapped all of us. We've got to find what they're trying to stop us from finding." I still hadn't figured out how to tell them what the Lady had shown me. I was hoping that we'd find the scepter and that would be that.

"So, Charlie, which dot do we head toward?" He nudged the throttle forward.

I took a deep breath, not sure what to say.

"Can we at least follow the dolphins for the time being?" Imee looked hopeful. Of the members of our quest, she seemed the least interested in moving forward.

Rhea looked back at me. I could tell that she wanted to follow the dolphins as well. Imee batted her eyes at Richard. "Let's follow them for a while."

"What the hell, why not. It's not much farther to the first couple of marks on the map. Since you seem to be unable to make a decision, let's leave it to chance and see where the dolphins go." Richard inched the throttle back. "We'll have to go a bit slower to let them keep up." The speed settled on fifteen knots.

The dolphins moved up into our bow wake and the girls moved forward, leaning over the rail to watch. Richard was obviously enjoying the view. I didn't mind him leering at Imee, but Rhea was right next to her.

A tap on my shoulder startled me. Jamie smiled. "Nice view."

After a brief pause, I nodded."Hard to beat it."

Richard smiled. "Damn right."

We were in about ten feet of water on the Bahama Bank. The turquoise waters sparkled ahead of us. The clouds had picked up the color of the water again, glowing a light turquoise in the sky. Imee and Rhea were laughing as they leaned forward, watching the dolphins surf our wake.

Richard pointed at the hologram. It switched to a live feed from the mini Go Pro mounted on the T-top. He zoomed on the dolphins rolling in the wake and then shifted slightly, with a zoomed-in view of the girls leaning over the rail. They were both beautiful and it was a hell of a view. A bit crass of Richard, but what the hell.

We were all so focused on the girls that we didn't notice that the dolphins had darted out toward deep water.

*Charlie, this is it, but we need to get to the deep-water side of the island.*

The mate stepped forward and pulled the throttle back to idle. "Sorry, Mr. DeMarco, but there's a flat on this side of the island."

Richard looked angry at first, but then laughed. "Guess I shouldn't be driving while distracted. Take the helm, Pavel." Richard didn't wait and walked around behind Imee. He glanced down at her butt. When Rhea turned around and scowled, he slid his arm up around Imee's shoulder, gave her a kiss on the cheek and then extended his arm to starboard, indicating with his hand that we should follow the dolphins.

Pavel turned and headed out toward deeper water. I glanced ahead, noticing that we'd gotten within a hundred yards of the flats. I hadn't noticed the flats either. Richard wasn't the only one distracted. I watched as Rhea pointed toward the pod of dolphins.

*Is this the spot, Alpha?* I was afraid that the dolphins had gotten tired and decided to take a break. I didn't know how I would explain the delay to everyone. Maybe Richard would give in to Imee's desire to swim with the dolphins.

*Just a bit further up the island. I'll take you to the spot. How long can you >>>>>>>>>>?*

The last word didn't translate in my brain. *What?*

*I know that even you Atlanteans can't stay >>>>>>>>>> for too long, but I worry about the humans.*

*Send a picture. Not sure what you mean.*

Alpha paused, but then a picture of me in the cave at the Three Sisters appeared in my head. *How long can you stay . . . in my element?*

*Underwater?* I pictured myself underwater.

*Yes.*

*Only a few minutes without assistance.*

*What's a minute?*

Our concept of time was probably very different. *Let me think. I can swim three lengths of this boat.*

*That's not long. Even our youngest can stay under for much longer. But how did you stay under when you met Thor? You didn't have those metal tanks.*

*The mask gave me air like a small tank.*

*You will need the masks to get where I am taking you.*

*We've got them aboard.* We headed south along the island. The coral rose up over the ocean around fifteen feet. The edges looked razor sharp. I remembered how sharp when I'd tried to grab ahold of a rock years ago. I looked down, still carrying the scar from the slice on my hand. Fortunately, only a light chop washed against the coral wall on this side of the island. We wouldn't have to worry about being pushed up against it by the surge of waves or current.

The girls were watching the dolphins that still danced in our bow wake. Richard and Jamie were watching the girls. Pavel stood behind the wheel, but he seemed to be watching the girls out of the corner of his eye now.

I scanned the shoreline to see if I recognized anything. We had just passed one of the red dots in my mother's chart. Pavel looked over at me. I nodded and looked back at the shore. A couple of scrub pines dotted the top of the island. One lone coconut palm stood above them, its fronds moving back and forth gently in the wind.

*Anchor your boat where I do my tail walk.*

Before I could respond, Alpha came out of the water in front of us and glided back across the water on his tail, eliciting several oohs and aahs from the boat.

"I hope you got that on camera, Richard. I'd like to post." Imee looked ecstatic.

Richard nodded. "Of course. Filming everything."

I waited a second as we approached the wake created by Alpha's tail walk. "This should be it." I signaled to Pavel to cut the throttle.

Richard looked back at me. I nodded and turned to Pavel. "Drop the anchor here."

Pavel looked at Richard. Richard nodded and Pavel dropped the anchor. I walked around the center console.

"So, this is it?" Richard looked around. "We're in around fifteen feet of water."

I nodded. "And there's a beach around the other side of the island."

"Ready to do some diving?" Jamie had already opened the front hatch and started pulling out masks, snorkels and flippers. He handed a set to Rhea and to Imee.

*Alpha?* I grabbed the mask, snorkel and flippers that Jamie gave me.

*There's a cave at the base of the island. I'll lead you in there.*

Richard got his own gear out. I had no doubt that it was a step above what we were using. "Doesn't look like much. Why here?"

"I remember that palm." I pointed to the lone palm on top of the hill. "We dove around here and found a couple of caves. My dad wanted to go in, but my mother wouldn't let us. They'd planned to come back with scuba gear." I looked down at my feet thinking back to the last time I'd been here. "We should take extra charge units for the masks."

Richard held a handful up. "Ahead of you, as usual."

Rhea ignored the comment and looked over at me. "Have you ever been in this cave?"

I shook my head. "No, but nothing to worry about. The tide's almost slack and the waves are small. It'll be easy getting in and out. Besides, I'm hoping we can hitch a ride, make the trip quicker."

"What do you mean?" Rhea asked.

I glanced over at the dolphins lolling alongside the boat. "They seem very docile. I don't doubt that we can grab their dorsals and let them pull us in like Flipper."

Richard laughed. "Yeah, right. You've got a Bigfoot for a friend and now you're claiming that you're a dolphin whisperer. What d'you want to bet you can't hitch a ride with a dolphin?"

I thought about it, but shook my head.

"What, you scared? How about if you do? I'll let you and Rhea have the master suite tonight."

My cheeks began to burn. I'm sure they were beet red!

"Richard!" Imee hit him hard as daggers shot from Rhea's eyes.

"What, they obviously like each other. They must be doing it." He shrugged.

My fists balled up, seemingly on their own. I took a step toward Richard, but Rhea grabbed my shoulder.

"Just because you're a cad doesn't mean that Charlie's not a gentleman."

"Richard, apologize to Rhea right now." Imee looked fit to be tied. Richard just stood there. "If you don't, you'll be by yourself in that master suite for the rest of this trip!"

"Sorry," Richard said in the quietest voice I'd ever heard him use. I looked over at Rhea. She smiled and nodded. "Apology accepted. Now, Charlie, I'm looking forward to you showing me how to get towed by a dolphin."

Richard could be such a prick. To think that I'd started liking him. Imee and Rhea climbed down the ladder built into the transom and got in the water. They started to swim toward a shoal of fish swimming along the base of the island. I followed. The temperature felt like a bathtub, and I could see them swimming through the crystal-clear waters in front of me.

*Alpha, we're in the water. Where's the cave?* I looked around, but didn't see Alpha or his family group. I swam after the girls. I started thinking about Richard's bet. Especially after last night, but . . . My mind clouded at the thought that she and Richard . . . I shook my head. I looked at Rhea and Imee swimming in front of me. Imee and Richard made no bones about sleeping together. Had Rhea?

A pressure wave slammed into me, startling me out of my reveries. I spun around. *Alpha?* After the incident with Thor, I didn't want to take any chances.

*Yep, tried talking, but you weren't listening.*

*So, where's the cave?* I looked to the south and saw several dolphins swimming toward us. I kicked harder to catch up to the girls. Didn't want them to be frightened. The dolphins got to us first and darted in and out around us. Fortunately, the clarity of the water let the girls see them coming.

Rhea tapped me and pointed at them.

Rhea slipped off her mask. "You think they'll let us touch them?"

"They seem pretty friendly. Besides, they like me. I gave them several lobsters the other day."

Rhea looked quizzically at me. "How do you know this is the same pod?"

Before I could answer, something grabbed my ankle and yanked me underwater. I turned around, expecting to see Richard laughing. I'd had just about enough of Richard. If I didn't need his resources . . . Since my mask wasn't on, I surfaced and looked around. Jamie trod water, smiling like a cat that had eaten the canary.

"You . . . "

"I know, you thought it was Richard."

I nodded. Rhea splashed Jamie as Richard swam up with Imee.

"So, where to?" Richard looked up at the island.

"A bit to the south. I'm going to hitch a ride." *Alpha, can you give me a lift to the cave?* I splashed the top of the water, pretending to try to attract a dolphin.

*Sure, and my family can help too. You surfacers are so slow in the water.* Alpha swam up next to me and I grabbed his dorsal. As I did, I noticed a triangular nick in the back of it.

*Hang on.* Alpha took off. His dorsal was slick, but I managed to hang on. I'd never gone so fast in the water. We slowed and stopped after a minute. I looked around, but couldn't see any of the others.

*Where's the cave?* I looked toward the island, but all I saw were a few coral heads, sand and then the sharp dead coral of the island.

*Not here. Behind us a bit.* Alpha circled playfully around me. A couple smaller members of his pod came up behind us. As they came into view, I noticed that Rhea had hitched a ride with one of them. They weren't going as fast as Alpha had.

*Look down.* Alpha swam down to a spot on the bottom, pointing with his bottle nose. Pieces of an old wooden boat lay coated in a thin layer of sand below us.

*Lobster?*

*YES. Me and my family need something in exchange for our help!*

*All right, all right. As soon as my*—I looked back at Rhea—*mate, I mean friend, gets here, we'll get you some lobster.*

*Great.* Alpha shot out of the water and splashed back down above me.

When Rhea arrived next to me, she let go of the other dolphin's dorsal. She had a huge smile on her face. I pointed up and we both surfaced.

"Wow, that was a blast. Awesome." She hovered right in front of me. "How'd you get them to do it."

"I've always had a way with animals, but I think it was the lobster."

"But how do you know these are the same dolphins?"

Alpha obligingly swam close to us. *Lobster?*

"His dorsal. Just like you noticed before."

Rhea nodded.

"Where are the others?" I looked back in the direction that we'd come from.

Rhea shook her head. "Not sure. I didn't wait. When one of the other dolphins stopped beside me, I grabbed its dorsal and off we went."

"That was brave of you."

Rhea smiled. "No big deal. After all, you did it!" She then splashed me.

I laughed. "Hey, want to get some lobsters for our rides?"

"Sure. How?"

I pointed down. "Looks like part of an old wooden boat about ten feet below us. I bet there are a few lobsters under it."

"I hope so. How do we get them out? You don't have a lobster spear."

I hadn't thought about that. I looked down. "Doesn't look too heavy, and we both have gloves on. Let's see if we can lift it."

"Ok."

We put our masks back on and kicked down. *Ready Alpha?* Rhea and I hovered just to the side of the boards. I glanced around. Sure enough, Alpha and several other dolphins circled us. One thing I really liked about telepathy was being able to communicate underwater. No need to surface to talk. I looked over at Rhea, pointed down and then bent down and slid my hands under the boards. Rhea did the same. We both started to pull up. The boards came up much more quickly than we'd thought. As they came up about a dozen lobsters shot out from under it.

Alpha and his family shot down, grabbing the lobsters, and gulping them down as fast as possible. Rhea and I watched. The lobsters didn't stand a chance. One darted toward a coral head, but before it could get there, Alpha was on it. Sand swirled around us after the feeding frenzy.

Alpha stopped and hovered in front of us.

*Had enough?*

*Delicious. So glad we came down here.*

*Good. Now, what about the cave?*

*Not too far. Just grab hold and we'll be there in a few.*

*What about my friends?*

*They're on the way.*

I looked over at Rhea. I pointed to the dolphin next to her. She nodded. I grabbed Alpha's dorsal and he took off. I managed a glance back and saw that Rhea was right behind us.

We darted back north for a couple of minutes before Alpha began to slow. He stopped. Rhea pulled up alongside us. I looked around.

*So, where's the cave?*

*Right in front of you.*

I looked toward the island, but didn't see a cave. There were several large coral heads and what looked like a landslide of rock where part of the coral from the island had collapsed. I didn't see anything.

*Are you sure. I don't see anything.*

*Yes. It's right there.* Alpha swam toward the landslide. *Can't you see it?*

I shook my head. *Nope. Don't see it.*

*Right behind the big coral head.* Alpha paused. *I forgot. Even you Atlanteans don't have sonar. It's behind the coral head.*

*Ok. Thanks.*

*It's a long cave. I'll give you a ride.*

I nodded. Letting Alpha get me through the passage quickly would save energy and air. As I learned on the Moon, having a good air supply is important. I looked over at Rhea and pointed up. We surfaced.

"That's fun. I hope they let us ride back to the boat."

I looked north toward the boat. Looked like Alpha had brought us a mile or so. "I hope so. Looks like a long swim."

Rhea tilted her head and looked at me quizzically. "By the way, if I didn't know any better, I'd say that you're communicating with that dolphin."

I shook my head. "What? How could I?"

"Oh, I don't know—your best friend's a Bigfoot. Anything's possible when it comes to you, Charlie Thomas." She leaned forward and gave me a peck on the lips. "Now, where are the others?"

"Alpha told me they're on the way." I smiled.

Rhea looked blankly at me and then smiled. "You!" She splashed me.

I looked up at the island and pretended to look around. The lone palm was just to our north. "This is about where the cave was."

"How can you be sure. It was what, five years ago?" Rhea looked up at the island. She was right. There were very few landmarks up there.

"I think it's right here. There was a landslide to one side of the cave. See where there's a recent slide in the side of the cliff." The razor-sharp coral rose up steeply about twenty-five feet to the top of the island.

"Ok. Let's take a look. It'd be a good thing to find the entrance before Richard gets here. By the way, if it's a cave, did you bring a flashlight?"

I shook my head. Didn't think of it.

"Good thing I did." She held up a small underwater flashlight. "That means I get to take the lead." She dove down and started swimming toward the landslide. I followed behind her. She turned around the coral head, stopped right in front of the cave and started looking around. I gently grabbed her arm and pointed to the cave. She shook her head. I pointed up and swam out from the cave and up to the surface.

I pulled my mask off as Rhea surfaced beside me. She pulled her mask off as well.

"What were you pointing at?"

"The cave."

"What cave? I didn't see a cave."

I thought Rhea was kidding me, but she kept a straight face. "It was right in front of us."

"You kidding?"

"No. It's right down there." I pointed down and slipped on my mask. Yep, just below us to the west. I could see the top of the mouth of the cave, but the rest was blocked by the coral head.

I looked up. Rhea slipped on her mask and looked where I pointed. She came up shaking her head.

"There's nothing there."

"Very strange. I can see it and you can't. Maybe it's like that cave on the Moon."

"What cave on the Moon?"

"Never mind. Richard and the gang'll be here soon enough. Let's go down again. You point the flashlight and I'll slip into the cave. Ok?"

She appeared skeptical, but said, "Ok."

I dove down. She followed. When I got to the mouth of the cave I pointed. Rhea shook her head. I started into the cave, but she grabbed my leg. I turned around. She signaled that we should surface.

She had her mask off when I came up.

"You disappeared! I grabbed your leg, but couldn't see the rest of you. Freaky."

"For some reason I can see the cave but it's camouflaged from you. Very strange. Why don't I go explore it with Alpha. You wait for Richard, Imee and Jamie."

"You sure?" She looked worried.

I nodded. "This must be Atlantean, given the camouflage. I'll come right back."

"Ok." She leaned forward and kissed my cheek. "For luck."

I smiled, slipped on the mask and dove down. *Alpha, can you give me a lift?*

In answer, Alpha glided next to me. I grabbed his dorsal. We took off, zipping right into the cave. I was concerned about the speed, given the razor-sharp coral above the water line, but below the water, the coral was smooth. Erosion I guess. It got darker before I realized that I'd forgotten the flashlight. I looked back as the light from the entrance receded behind me. Alpha darted to the left and I almost lost my grip. He'd dodged a large stalactite. We were going way too fast for visibility, but I trusted Alpha's sonar. In front of us a dim green glow appeared. It wasn't sunlight. The sides of the cave glowed with a greenish iridescence. The color reminded me of the glow wake sometimes makes at night in these waters. My dad had said it was caused by a special type of plankton.

*Almost there?*

*Yep.* In fact, Alpha had started to slow. I could see actual light coming from an opening at the end of the tunnel. As we approached, Alpha slowed more. The opening looked artificial. While covered in coral, the lines were too straight. The entrance looked fluted, like Greek columns. Alpha swam right past them. I'd have to check them out later.

As Alpha entered a pool of light, I let go and looked up. We were in a large cave with an oculus at the top. Galadriel had said Atlanteans liked them. There was a small beach on what I thought was the east side of the cave. It ended abruptly in the coral bones of the island. Like the coral on the outside, it appeared pitted and razor sharp.

I looked down where the shaft of light illuminated the water. The cave was deeper than I would have thought.

*Why do you come in here?* Alpha dove to the bottom. He came up next to me. He had something in his mouth. It looked like a giant roach.

*These are tasty.* He chomped down on it. *And I've never found them anywhere else. Our pod has visited this cave for generations eating these chitons.*

*Where do they come from?* I didn't see any on the bottom.

*Look around you. They live on the walls. We can only get the ones that happen to fall off. In fact . . .*

I spotted a handful where the water ended and a small beach began. They glowed iridescently in shades of green, turquoise and red, like an old-time CD wind chime that my mother had on our porch. They were beautiful, much prettier, and larger, than the brown/black roach-like chitons I'd seen before.

*I'll get you some later. We need to get back before my other friends show up.*

Alpha tilted his head to one side and seemed to nod. *Your friends are almost here. Grab ahold. I'll go fast this time.*

I thought he'd gone fast before. I looked over at the razor-sharp coral above the entrance to the cave. I grabbed Alpha's dorsal and we took off. He shot through the cave so fast I could barely hold on. The greenish glow faded quickly as light from the entrance brightened. We burst out of the cave, and Alpha darted to the right to avoid the coral head. I almost lost my grip.

He slowed and stopped. *Your female's just ahead with one of mine.*

I looked forward and could just make out Rhea hovering below the surface, tentatively reaching out to touch another dolphin. I surfaced to recharge the mask and swam over to her. She saw me, waved and surfaced.

"That was quick. I got a vid of you taking off, but didn't see you coming back."

"Too quick. I could barely hold on. Did you get a ride from the female?"

"I . . . Hey, how'd you know it's a female."

I didn't have a real explanation. "Smaller, so I assumed she was female. Besides, Alpha told me!"

"Yeah, right." Rhea scowled at what she assumed was a lame joke. I guess it does pay to tell the truth. "Remind me to upload the vid when we get back to the boat."

"I will, but don't post anything. It'd give us away."

Rhea hit my arm. "I'm not an idiot . . . but I'd better make sure that Imee hasn't posted anything."

"Speaking of Imee, I think I see them coming." I pointed north. A large wake pushed rapidly toward us. I slipped on my mask and ducked below the surface. It looked as if three torpedoes had us targeted. They were moving fast. Several dolphins swam alongside, seeming to struggle to keep up. They would be on us momentarily. Leave it to Richard to not tell us about another one of his gadgets.

One accelerated as it approached. It jetted right alongside us, spinning me and Rhea around in its wake. We surfaced. Imee and Jamie floated alongside two short, fat tubes. Another breached like a whale next to us—Richard. His ride came all the way out of the water, pulling him three quarters of the way out. He then belly-flopped down, his wake rocking the rest of us.

Alpha breached a moment later right next to him, splashing him. *Humans! They used these noisemakers instead of letting us guide them.*

*It's ok. You can guide me and Rhea into the tunnel and I'll get you all of the treats in the cave that you can eat.*

I noted excitement in Alpha's mind. A picture appeared of him and other members of his pod chomping on chitons.

"You guys should have waited. I had two more cuda scooters on board. Pavel was going to lower them down."

Rhea gave Richard a cold look. "Charlie and I had a great time riding with the dolphins. Much more fun than a scooter."

As if on cue, Alpha leapt over the five of us, turning as he did. A jet of water shot out of Alpha's underside, hitting Richard as he passed over him. He then slid into the water, barely making a splash.

Richard ducked underwater and then popped back up. "That dolphin just peed on me!" Richard started looking around. His hand went to his belt and a dive knife.

*Alpha, stay away!* I didn't want Alpha within Richard's arm length for a while.

Imee laughed, leaned over and kissed Richard. "That's unbelievable good luck in Filipino culture. I've never seen it."

Richard relaxed and smiled. "Guess a bit of harmless good luck is the way to start a treasure hunt. So, Charlie, where do we go from here?"

I glanced over at the island. "There's a cave just below us. I think that's what we've been looking for."

"How do you know?" Richard rolled his eyes in his typical fashion.

"Because while we were waiting for you one of the dolphins gave me a lift. There's a long tunnel at the entrance—I'd guess over a hundred yards long. We'll need those extra breathing cannisters that you brought just in case we have to swim in and out on our own."

Richard tapped the side of his scooter. "These are reliable. Not sure about your buddies, the dolphins."

Rhea looked over at me. "Charlie and I'll be just fine. Don't worry about us."

I smiled. "Ready to go?"

"Sure, just let me signal Pavel." Richard tapped his forehead. "He'll pull the anchor and anchor here in a few minutes. So, where's this cave?" Richard stuck his mask underwater and looked around.

"I had trouble seeing it too. It's behind that large coral head." Rhea pointed in the direction of the cave.

Richard turned to me. "Charlie, this is your expedition. Take the lead."

Richard had sounded facetious when he said expedition, but beggars can't be choosers. I had to remind myself that we wouldn't have gotten this far without Richard's help.

I nodded and splashed the water next to me. *Ready, Alpha?*

*Yep. I'll take you and my female will take your mate.*

Alpha appeared at my side, and a slightly smaller dolphin appeared at Rhea's side. We lowered our masks and I grabbed Alpha's dorsal.

*Not too fast. My friends need to keep up.*

*Don't worry. I'll go slow. Like what I did to the big one?*

A picture appeared in my mind from Alpha's perspective of him peeing on Richard's head. I laughed inside. *Yep, but it was dangerous. He can hurt you.*

*I'm not dumb. Knew he didn't have anything with him to hurt me. Ready?*

I nodded mentally. Alpha kicked his tail and we took off. Sure enough, we went slower this time, slow enough for me to glance back without having my mask ripped off. Rhea was behind me, with Richard leading the group of scooters. We dove into the tunnel. The tunnel arched downward a couple of degrees before levelling off. A small nurse shark rested on the bottom in a bed of sand. Purple sea fans had attached to the sides of the tunnel and swept back and forth with the current. Small fish of all colors swam in and around the coral and the stalactites. I felt as if I were swimming through a huge aquarium. As Alpha approached, the fish shied back deeper into the protection of the fans and corals. While the colorful corals and sea fans gave the tunnel a natural look, it was dead straight—too straight to be natural. The only natural tunnels I'd ever heard of like this were lava tubes, but there were no volcanos in the Bahamas.

The green glow began to appear on the sides of the tunnel, adding visibility. My eyes had time to adjust. This time I noticed a small side tunnel. As we passed, the head of a green moray eel darted deeper into the hole. In a couple of places the coral had fallen off. The wall appeared smooth, artificial. The glow of white light appeared ahead. As we approached the entrance to the cave, I looked for the columns I'd seen before. While covered in coral and sea fans, they were there, definite columns. I could clearly make out the fluting, despite the deep growth of coral. I looked up at the top of the tunnel. A large block traversed the top. It looked like a capstone, but, knowing Atlantean technology, it was probably more decorative than functional. Although coral encrusted it, the faint lines of a ram's head with the tail of a serpent seemed to jut out from the center of the capstone. I hadn't noticed it before.

Alpha surfaced in the pool in the center of the cave. Rhea popped up next to me. Richard, Imee and Jamie surfaced behind her. This time, the cave appeared bigger. The pool had plenty of room for all of us, including the dolphins. The light from the oculus had shifted slightly. I swam over to the beach and crawled ashore. The others followed.

"This is amazing! Did you see the columns at the entrance?' Imee gawked as she looked around. "Look!" She pointed up. In one section of the roof, the coral had fallen off. A scene of a fountain in the foreground with otherworldly buildings behind it covered the clear section of the roof. It looked like the images of Atlantis that Galadriel had placed in my head. Unfortunately, most of the fresco was covered by coral, but it was an astounding testament to Atlantean technology that any of it remained.

"That can't be Atlantean. I've seen Roman and Greek frescoes and they're all worn out. If, as you said, Atlantis is a million years old, there's no way this can be Atlantean." Richard looked dubious. "Must be a fake. People dive here all the time. Someone would've found the cave."

Rhea shook her head. "This is fantastic! Richard, look around. No way can this be a fake. Besides, if the Atlanteans were on the Moon a million years ago, their technology could be way more advanced than ours." Rhea walked to the edge of the sand and looked down. The water dropped off rapidly, but was crystal clear. The shaft of light from the oculus reflected off something on the bottom. "Look." Rhea pointed into the water. Suddenly, brilliant flashes of multi-colored light sparkled through the water, lighting up the cavern. The flashes faded quickly.

"Beautiful. It looked like an underwater disco ball." Imee looked down at the water. "Wonder what it was?"

"Something artificial, I hope," I said. *Alpha, any clue what caused that sparkle of light?*

*Lots of Atlantean metal on the bottom. It's happened once before when I've been in the cave. What about some food?*

"So you've become a master of understatement. I'd like to see what's down there." Richard began walking toward his scooter. "Imee?"

"Hold on." I looked around at the wall. Several of the iridescent chitons that Alpha wanted had anchored themselves to the coral just above and below the water line.

"And who made you the boss? Imee, let's go see what's down there."

I gave Richard a glare. "Do you have a flashlight?"

Richard walked over to his scooter and popped a little hatch, pulling out a flashlight. "What, don't you? I guess your ride didn't have one." He chuckled. "Once the sun moves a bit, we'll need one. I've also got a small dive bag and a dive knife. What about you?" Richard held his hands on his hips. "I thought not. Now, who should be in charge?"

He was right. I'd forgotten all about the equipment we'd probably need.

"Good thing three of us have the proper equipment." He popped open the compartment on Jamie's scooter and pulled out another underwater micro flashlight and collection bag.

"Jamie and Rhea can cover the eastern half of the underwater section of the cave, while Imee and I cover the south, where the disco ball seems to be. We'll come up in about twenty minutes to recharge the rebreathers. You can explore this little beach area." Richard extended his arm. "Maybe you'll find something interesting while we dive."

Richard popped the hatch on Imee's scooter and handed her a flashlight as well. "If we find anything interesting, we'll flash the laser three times." Richard pulled out the micro flashlight, turned it on and then flipped a switch. The tight beam of a red laser shot out at the wall, flashing three times."

I fumed, feeling like a real idiot.

Richard handed one pen light to Jamie and one to Rhea. "Now, be careful with these. Setting one is a flashlight, two is a pointing laser and three"—Richard turned the setting on his pen light, pointed it at the wall of the cave, and pressed down—"is a cutting laser." While no light came out, the wall cracked and a piece popped off.

Everyone seemed adequately impressed. Rhea and Jamie looked down at the settings.

Richard smiled. "Don't worry, there's a safety that needs to be held down on setting three. You can't accidentally activate it." He gave me a sneer. "Sorry I don't have a spare."

I wasn't sure whether I was more pissed at myself or at Richard. "Can I at least borrow your knife?"

Richard put his hand on the knife at his belt.

"Don't worry. Take mine." Rhea reached down to her ankle and pulled out a blunt-nosed dive knife with a light-blue rubber handle. I hadn't noticed she had one. She handed it to me and gave me a brief smile. "Let's go. Light's wasting." She turned and dove into the water. Richard and Imee followed.

I shook my head. "Damn it! I'm such an idiot."

Jamie turned to me. "Don't be so hard on yourself. We wouldn't be here if not for you. Best time I've had since first getting to the Moon. Don't let Richard get to you. If you piss him off, how'll we finish your quest to find your parents?"

I looked up at Jamie. My quest was to find the Scepter of Apollymi and stop whatever the Lemurians were up to. The quest everyone else thought we were on was to find Atlantis, or at least evidence of it.

"We're here to find Atlantis, and I think this was part of it."

Jamie shook his head. "We both know that's not the real reason." Jamie's eyes bore into me. "Look, I've been your best friend since you got to the Moon. I know you want to find your parents. They disappeared looking for Atlantis, and now you've found proof of Atlantis. They might have too. I'll help you find them. We're in this together." He stuck out his fist. I gave it a fist bump.

"Good. Better catch up with Rhea. She swims like a fish." We both looked down at Rhea cruising along the bottom.

I nodded. "I'll look around up here."

Jamie dove into the water. I watched him swim down, spooking a shoal of blue-and-yellow-striped grunts. I looked up at the oculus.

Despite the dead coral that reached the ceiling, the oculus was perfectly circular. I wondered if my parents had been here. They'd left me with my travel ball coach last summer for a two-week sabbatical to follow up on what my mother had said were promising leads to Atlantis. I'd have gone with them but for my travel-ball schedule. I had hoped to pitch in college, but when my parents disappeared, somehow that no longer mattered. If I'd gone with them . . . I wiped my eyes and shook my head.

*AB, can you hear me? AB? Must be out of range.*

I heard a loud splash and looked over. *You're not out of my range. What about a crunchy chiton?*

I smiled. I thought that dolphins were supposed to be smart—maybe smarter than humans—but Alpha seemed to have a one-track mind.

*I heard that. You control your thoughts like a youngling. And if you compare me to mere humans again, you'll have a long swim ahead of you.*

I flipped the knife in the air and caught it.

*And you'll miss out on these crunchy chitons.*

*Touché.*

I walked toward the nearest wall. A handful of chitons had anchored themselves to the coral just above the water line. I'd seen chitons before. They inhabited the coral near waterlines and looked like big cockroaches, but these were the largest and most colorful I'd ever seen. I stuck the blunt end of the dive knife behind one and pried it off. It dropped to the sand. I picked it up. It was as big as my palm. I flipped it over. It had a mean-looking beak-like projection near the top end. It slipped and fell on the sand. It scuttled back toward the wall. I blocked it with a flipper. It tried to crawl over the flipper. I picked it up and quickly flipped it into the water. Alpha nailed it.

When I picked up the flipper, I noticed a chunk taken out of the rubber. Strange.

*Delicious. How about a few more?*

I noticed several more dolphins in the cave. *Ok, but just a few more for now.*

I found a handful of slightly smaller ones. I pried them loose and flipped them into the water. As each hit, one of Alpha's pack nailed it. As I stood, I noticed about a dozen more just outside my reach on the wall over the water. I hadn't noticed them before.

*Enough for now, Alpha. We'll be here awhile, so I'll get you more later. Can you stay close enough so I can call you when we need to leave?*

Alpha's head popped out of the water and he nodded. *See, I can copy dumb humans! Yes, I'll leave one of my younglings here. If you can't reach me, she'll be able to.* A smaller dolphin popped its head up next to Alpha.

*Can she hear me?*

*Of course she can, but she's a youngling and can't control her thoughts. Just talk as if you're talking with me.*

I nodded as they both ducked back underwater. I watched the wake as Alpha darted toward the opening of the cave.

I walked back over to where I'd pried the chitons loose, wanting to take a look at the wall. I stuck the knife in, but the coral appeared thick here. I walked around the shore, looking at the wall. There didn't appear to be any gaps in the coral. Given that Atlantis had disappeared in Antarctica over a million years ago, I had no doubt that this cave had been out of the water and totally submerged several times over. The coral had been growing here for a long, long time. It was a miracle that the cave had survived. At least on the Moon, there was little erosion. Here, the ocean had swept in and out over eons.

I looked up again at the section of the roof where the coral had fallen off. The fresco looked fresh and was much like the ones shown to me by Galadriel. The Atlanteans had to use something other than paint. Maybe they somehow bonded the colors to the metal.

I looked around. The beach was semicircular and covered the back third of the cave. I missed not having a flashlight and wished that I'd brought one, or at least gotten one from Richard. The light from the oculus left most of the cave in twilight. I approached the wall and started to walk along it, looking carefully for any gaps in the coral or hints of any rooms behind the walls. If this base was like the one on the Moon, I hoped that my presence would activate a door or something. Nothing happened.

I walked into the shallow water and looked over the edge. I could see Richard and Imee on one side of the cave and Rhea and Jamie on the other. They'd have to come up in a few more minute to recharge their rebreathers. No point in using the spare canisters unless they really needed them.

I sat down to think, dangling my feet over the edge into the deep water. I closed my eyes, picturing the cave around me. I tried to relax, breathed in deeply and then exhaled. I pictured the fresco on the roof and then thought back to the one that Galadriel had shown me in Atlantis. I remembered the way the fresco had come to life, and quickly thought about the disco ball instead. I didn't want to invite Thor back into my life. I thought about the disco ball and then about the Scepter of Apollymi. The ball at the base of the scepter had been some kind of crystal. I squeezed my eyes tighter and tried to visualize the crystal more closely. *Zoom in,* I thought to myself. Nothing happened. I took a deep breath and pictured the scepter again. This time I started at the base. The crystal did appear heavily facetted. If the light hit it properly it could reflect the light like a disco ball. I nodded to myself as I felt a hard tug at my leg. I slid into the water and under.

Whatever had grabbed me released my leg. I rocketed to the surface, picturing Thor just below me. I shot out of the water onto the sand. Rhea and Jamie sat there, laughing at me.

I grabbed a handful of wet sand, ready to peg them, but they were doubled over laughing. Had it been Richard, I probably would have thrown the sand ball at him, but Rhea's laugh disarmed me. I dropped the sand and started to laugh as well.

"You should have seen the look on your face." Jamie pointed at me and opened his mouth and eyes as wide as possible. He then started laughing again.

"You're not mad, are you?" Rhea didn't let me answer. "You looked so peaceful, like you were asleep. We just couldn't resist."

I shook my head. "I'm not mad, but you almost made me crap my pants. I thought Thor had grabbed me."

Rhea's eyes widened. "I'd forgotten about that. Sorry."

By now, Jamie had stopped laughing as well. "Me too. I can imagine how you felt."

I shook my head. "It's all good. Find anything?"

Jamie pulled his bag up out of the shallow water and onto the beach. "Just a few more of those disks. There were some coral-covered humps down there that could have been desks, chairs or even computers, but we'd have to get hammers or something to bang through the coral to see. As to other rooms, there were some indentations that could have been doors, but coral totally encrusted them. The one open tunnel we saw had the biggest moray eel in it you've ever seen, so we didn't get close to it."

Rhea nodded. "I know it sounds like a disappointment, but these disks and this cave are clearly evidence of Atlantis." She smiled, holding a disk up in front of her.

"It is and will validate what my parents believed, but I'm no closer to finding them." The excitement of the quest had enabled me to bury my parents' disappearance into the recesses of my mind, but my talk with Jamie had brought them back to the forefront. I sniffled a couple of times and my eyes teared up.

Rhea hugged me. "It's ok, Charlie. We'll keep searching. Did you at least look for footprints or evidence that someone else may have been here?"

I shook my head. My parents could very well have come back to this spot with scuba gear and entered the cave. Even the Atlantean camouflage at the entrance shouldn't have been an issue. After all, I was their child, so they had to each be at least one half Atlantean. I glanced around but didn't see any sign of disturbance in the sand.

"I don't think they've been here. They would've climbed out and the sand would have been disturbed."

Rhea hugged me. "Maybe, but maybe the tide came in and wiped out any footprints. We need to look harder."

I wasn't convinced. We had more chance of finding the scepter than my parents. They were probably dead. I put my head in my hands, trying to hold back tears. Rhea hugged me and patted my back. I hadn't cried about my parents in a long time. I didn't hear Richard and Imee emerge from the water.

"What's the matter, did Charlie stub his toe?" Richard laughed.

Rhea turned her head sharply. "No, you asshole." She leaned in and kissed me.

At least Richard's jibe ended my self-pity in a heartbeat.

"Fine, maybe you don't want to see this!" Richard blinked. A hologram appeared in front of him. I shut up and looked. A long thin object sat lodged in a bed of coral. At its top rested a large crystal sheltered by three ribbons of a coral-encrusted substance. While coral covered most of the object, the crystal remained free of coral and undersea growth.

"That's really cool." I couldn't believe it. They may have found the scepter.

Imee squealed with glee. "The crystal must've made the disco ball effect when the light hit it. Richard headed in the direction he thought the reflections had come from, shining his flashlight. It took a while, but finally I saw a glint to our right. We swam that way and Richard shone his flashlight again. A rainbow erupted against the wall in front of us. We headed for the spot." Imee looked over at Richard. He nodded. "We tried to pull it out but couldn't. Richard even tried cutting at the bottom with his laser."

I cringed, thinking that they may have damaged it.

The hologram disappeared. "It must be pretty long because I cut around it, but still couldn't pull it free. Not sure if we'll be getting it out without some heavier equipment."

I nodded. "Before we do that, let's go down. I'd like to see it and maybe, working together, we can pull it loose."

Richard looked skeptical. "I doubt it, but you're stubborn as a mule." He nodded to Imee and slid into the water. Imee followed.

Jamie hocked up a loogy and spit in the sand. "He's a bit of a prig, but he'll come around." Jamie and I waited as Rhea slipped on her mask and dove in. We followed.

The warm water felt good after the dampness of the cave. We swam through a school of small jacks, their yellow tails glistening as they hit the light from the oculus. Richard and Imee were swimming alongside a large growth of coral near the middle of the cave. My ears popped. It was probably twenty-five to thirty feet below the surface. Our oxygen would run out sooner this deep.

Richard pointed to the object. A trumpet fish sat suspended, nose down, right in front of it. Richard then shone his flashlight in the crystal. A rainbow of color erupted from the crystal, causing the trumpet fish to dart away. Richard slipped on a glove and then grabbed hold of the object, right below the housing for the crystal. He tugged at it, but it wouldn't budge. He pointed to it. Jamie moved in and tried. It wouldn't budge. Rhea didn't wait and slid in. She studied it first, grabbed it below the crystal and tugged. Nothing. She looked over at me.

I swam around the scepter. I could see where Richard had zapped the coral with his laser. I looked at the coral, trying to find the best spot to grab it. Richard floated in front of me, his arms crossed, waiting for me to fail. I found a spot, planted my flippers on the bottom and wrapped my hands around the scepter. Immediately my hands began to tingle. I let the tingling energy flow into my body, took a deep breath, braced myself and pulled. The scepter slid free easily—too easily. I shot toward the surface.

When I got to the surface, I climbed out on the beach, took off my flippers and examined the scepter. Other than some coral encrustation on the metal, it looked just like the hologram that Galadriel had shown me. It continued to tingle in my hand and I felt energy flowing into me. I stared into the crystal and extended one finger to touch it. It sent a wave of energy through me, almost causing me to drop the scepter.

I hadn't noticed the others come up behind me.

"Damn, you shot straight up as if fired by a cannon." Jamie walked around to look at the scepter.

"I know. It came loose so much easier than I thought it would. You guys must have loosened it up."

Richard reached for the scepter. I pulled it closer to me, not sure what it would do if touched by someone else.

"Come on, Charlie, let us all have a—"

# CHAPTER 35
## THOR-ROR

I heard a high-pitched mental squeal, and then Alpha's young-ling flew out of the water. A huge grey crescent-shaped dorsal fin sliced through the water right behind where she'd jumped. Other huge fins churned up the water. The young dolphin jumped and dodged, but she didn't stand a chance. The space was too small. She darted, trying to beach herself, but a huge hammerhead grabbed her tail, dragging her back down. One more mental squeal pierced my psyche as blood filled the pool.

"Shark!" Imee shouted. Everyone stared at the pool where we'd just been diving. A flipper had floated off the beach and large fins circled around it. We backed away from the shore. With the blood clearing, we could see at least three hammerheads circling below us. Big ones. Not Thor, but the smallest was a ten-footer.

"They killed my dolphin." Tears trickled down Rhea's face.

*Alpha, can you hear me? Hammerheads killed your youngling.* I glanced up at the oculus at least twenty feet above our heads. *They've got us trapped.*

Very faintly I picked up Alpha's thoughts. *Thor . . ."* Then Alpha faded out. I looked around. Imee hugged Richard tightly, pulling him back away from the edge of the water. Rhea looked horrified. I put my arm around her. Her whole body shivered. Jamie seemed mesmerized. He just stood there.

"We've got to find a way out of here!" I looked around the cave for a loose rock or something. I spotted a small conch shell under a ledge and headed toward it.

"Why? It's high tide. The sharks can't get to us and they'll even-tually leave." Richard sounded confident, but his voice trembled as he looked down, kicking at a loose piece of coral.

I picked up the conch shell, positioned myself just right and launched the shell at the oculus. It sailed right for the opening, but somehow bounced back and dropped to the ground. I couldn't believe it.

"I thought you were some kind of superstar pitcher. How'd you miss?" Richard picked up the conch and launched it at the oculus. While not as accurate as my throw, it wasn't bad. It also impacted something and bounced back.

"I didn't miss. There's something up there blocking the opening. It looks clear but isn't." Richard continued to stare up at the opening.

Jamie finally seemed to come out of his funk, let out a scream and then collapsed to the sand. We looked over at him, but then something breached the surface of the pool.

I had to blink to believe what I saw: Trolga sitting astride Thor's immense sickle-shaped dorsal. She had a rope tied around Thor's massive hammer and seemed to be riding him like a horse.

*Surprised to see me, Mr. Thomas? You've led me on quite the merry chase, but now it's over.*

She looked around the beach as Thor circled in the pool. "Good to see you, Mr. DeMarco. Your father will be quite glad to see you again."

Richard seemed to be concentrating very hard on something.

"No use trying to call your bodyguards. Fool me once, shame on you, fool me twice, shame on me. Your signal's jammed." Trolga circled on Thor's back.

*AB, we need help. It's Trolga!* I concentrated hard and pushed my thoughts out, trying to focus them on AB.

Trolga turned rapidly to face me. "And your telepathy won't work either. I activated a dampening field before coming in."

"Telepathy?" Richard said it, but all eyes turned toward me.

I shrugged.

Rhea gave me a strange look. "So you were communicating with the dolphin. Were you reading my thoughts also?"

I shook my head. "That's not how it works." I touched her shoulder, but she pulled away.

"I guess Charlie hasn't clued you all in on what's really going on, has he?" Trolga laughed. She guided Thor over to the beach. Two thrusts of his massive tail propelled half his bulk up the sand. We all backed away as Trolga stepped off. Thor was huge, at least twenty feet, maybe twenty-five. The other hammerheads looked like gold-fish in comparison. Trolga petted his head and he wriggled back-ward into the water.

Everyone was glaring at me. "Look, I couldn't tell you every-thing. I just couldn't." Trolga just stood there smiling as several more people popped their heads up in the pool. They climbed out, warily staying as far away from Thor as possible. Their spear guns, while deadly, looked like toys next to Thor.

"Now, Charlie, hand over the Scepter of Apollymi." Trolga ex-tended her hand.

I clutched it tighter, feeling its energy pulse up my arm. I fo-cused on Trolga, trying to release a burst of energy at her.

She staggered back a couple of steps as Thor thrashed mightily, grabbing one of the smaller hammerheads in his jaws, chopping it in two.

"You've gotten stronger, boy, but not strong enough." Her assault started. I couldn't move. I focused my mind on the scepter and be-gan to wiggle my fingers. I could break her hold on me.

*Give it up, boy, or your friend will be shredded by Thor and his smaller friends.*

Two of the men had Jamie's limp body held up between them, ready to throw him into the water. The sharks began to thrash about as if the dinner bell had sounded.

"Don't." I extended the scepter. "Take it."

One of her men stepped forward, grabbed it with a gloved hand, slipped it into a waterproof bag and then handed it to Trolga. She nodded.

"Now, that wasn't too hard, was it. I'd hate to waste Jamie. He's been such a great tool, but I think his usefulness is over." She nod-ded her head and the men began to drag Jamie toward the pool. He had started to come too and began to struggle.

"No, don't!" Rhea screamed and took a step forward.

Trolga gave her Cheshire Cat grin as if she'd just gotten exactly what she wanted. She held up her hand and her men stopped. "Fine, but in exchange for Jamie's life, you will need to come with me."

Rhea stepped back toward me. "Why?"

"Why, dearie, just like Charlie's a pure genetic descendant of Atlantis, you're a pure genetic descendant of Lemuria. She has been following your progress just as the Atlantean scum have been nurturing Charlie."

"What?" Rhea looked around. "I don't feel any different and I'm certainly not telepathic." She gave me a glare.

"But you are Lemurian nonetheless. Your red eyes are but an outward sign of your heritage." Trolga reached into her eyes and pulled something out of each. When she did her eyes were a darker red than Rhea's. "Glad to get those out. Now, my mentor would like to meet you and, perhaps, train you. Just come with me." Trolga extended her hand.

Rhea, a Lemurian! I couldn't believe it.

"What about the others?" Rhea looked around at us.

"Richard'll be coming with us as well."

"What? What do you mean?" Richard looked perplexed.

"Why young Mr. DeMarco, we cut a deal with your father. We deliver the Scepter of Apollymi and you to him in Antarctica and get ten percent of his new venture in return," Trolga said, holding her hands at her hips.

"So you're kidnapping me and holding me for ransom." Richard crossed his arms. His arrogance seemed to be returning.

"Of course not. Your father needs the scepter to activate the Atlantean equipment that he's uncovered in Antarctica. With it he'll manage to tap into the infinite supply of zero-point dark energy that pervades the universe. As to you, why we're rescuing you from those who would try to keep him from his work." Trolga stared directly at me.

"That's ridiculous! Charlie and I have been trying to find Atlantis." Richard looked over at me. "Charlie?"

I glanced down at my toes in the sand and then back up at Richard. "I've been trying to find the scepter since we started. The Lady told me that someone has uncovered an ancient Atlantean science center in Antarctica and that should they succeed in turning on the equipment, it could mean the end of civilization. I didn't know it was your father."

"So you believe that crap and are willing to use my father's resources to try and stop his efforts? I can't believe this!" Richard looked over at Trolga. "I'm with you Trol ... Professor Larsen." Richard turned to Imee. "Come on, Imee, let's go."

"I'm sorry, Richard, but it's just you and Rhea now. Due to Charlie's attacking me, my ride"—she pointed down to the huge sickle cutting through the water—"is a bit agitated and I doubt anybody'll want to join me."

I glanced over at Rhea. She'd gone over to help Jamie up. He still looked dazed, but seemed to be coming around a bit.

A three-seat mini sub with a Plexiglas top surfaced in the pool. It slowly beached itself. "Ah, your ride's here. Richard, Rhea, please take the back two seats."

"Don't go. She threatened to kill Jamie," I said. Richard had already taken a step toward the sub.

Trolga laughed. "An idle threat, meant to get this"—she held up the scepter—"from Charlie. Richard, this scepter will make your father hundreds of billions. It will enable him to provide cheap energy to the world while saving the environment from fossil fuels. It will open up the solar system and create a new era of prosperity. And I'm going to tell him you found it and let you give it to him." Trolga smiled pleasantly.

I could see a tendril of red stretching from Trolga to Richard.

As she turned her gaze at me, she telepathed me. *You say a word and they're all dead, especially the pretty one. I know you like her.*

"I appreciate that, Professor Larsen. That's great. I'm sure my father will be pleased. Rhea, you coming?" Richard didn't even glance back at Imee.

She ran over to him and grabbed his arm. "Can't I go with Richard?" Tears formed in her eyes as she looked back at Trolga.

"Sorry, dearie, but no." Trolga's voice was firm.

Imee glanced at Richard and batted her eyes. Richard shook his head, patted her hand and said, "It'll be ok." He glanced at Trolga. She nodded. "I'll make it up to you. Promise. Something special." He kissed Imee.

She hugged him and, with a sob, stepped back.

Trolga had manipulated me, getting my friends to doubt me. I looked over at Rhea. She seemed stuck in place, her feet almost rooted in the sand.

"What about Charlie, Imee and Jamie? Will you send the sub back for them?" Rhea looked over at all of us and then back in the water as a large dorsal cut through the surface as if on cue.

"Of course, dear. Just need to take two at a time. You two are on the top of the list, which is why you're going first. Now, please step into the sub." Trolga walked over to it.

Imee and Jamie had both walked closer to me. "Go with them. We'll be fine." I nodded at Rhea.

She glanced over at me. I tried to give her a reassuring look and a slight nod. She nodded back and walked over to the sub. "And I'll be able to contact them later?" Trolga nodded.

Richard climbed in and she handed him the scepter. He gripped it tightly, staring down at it.

"Richard, I'm assuming they can stay on the *Sarah Charlotte*." Rhea sounded miffed as she climbed in next to him.

Richard stared down at the crystal at the end of the scepter. "Sure, sure." He waved his hand dismissively as Trolga closed the plexiglass top. She tapped on it and nodded to the pilot. He pulled into the middle of the pool, put a regulator in his mouth and gave a thumbs up to Trolga. Gas began to fill the sub. Rhea and Richard looked shocked momentarily, but the gas knocked them out almost immediately.

"What did you do to them?" I started toward Trolga, but her henchmen pulled up their spear guns. I stopped.

Trolga laughed her hyena-like laugh. "Nothing but put them night-night. I do need both of them, but I don't need any of you."

Imee's eyes widened. "So you're not going to let us go?"

"Of course not, dearie. But I'm not going to kill any of you." She signaled and another mini-sub rose from the depths. A wide-eyed Pavel sat in the back, tied up with his mouth taped shut. The sub pulled up on the sand and the Plexiglass top opened. Her men pulled Pavel from the sub.

"Now, I'm going to give you two choices—your pick." Trolga nodded. One of her men pulled out a machete and cut the rope tying Pavel's arms together. Two other men each grabbed one of Pavel's arms, spreading them. Pavel was strong, but he couldn't budge his arms. I concentrated. Sure enough, the two "men" were yetis, not men. They stood two feet taller than Pavel. Their camouflage must have totally dropped because Imee let out a gasp.

"I was going to do that, Mr. Thomas, but glad you wasted some of your energy doing it instead. Now"—Trolga walked over and grabbed the machete—"you probably think that I'm going to cut one of this man's arms off." She reached forward with the machete. Pavel squirmed and struggled, but he couldn't pull free. The machete cut a line along Pavel's left shoulder and then his right. "Good, I like a sharp tool." She stepped back, lifting the machete in the air. Instead of slicing off one of Pavel's arms, she threw the machete into the sand between his legs, like a game of mumbley-peg. He looked down with a relieved expression. But then the two yetis yanked hard at each arm, tearing poor Pavel's arms right out of their sockets.

Even through the tape, Pavel's screams reverberated throughout the cave. He dropped to his knees and toppled over. Thank God, it looked as if he passed out. Imee collapsed, and Jamie was puking his guts out on the sand. Bile rose in my throat, but I focused my hatred on Trolga, forcing the bile down.

Trolga nodded and picked up the machete. One yeti picked up Pavel and flipped him into the water. The sharks took no time whatsoever, churning the water into a red foam.

Trolga pointed. "That is option one."

Jamie looked up. "I'll run into the water before I let those yetis tear me in half."

Trolga laughed. "You misunderstood me. I'm not going to do anything quite so quick. We're leaving. You're going to need to pick between Scylla"—pointing to the sharks—"and Charybdis"—pointing to the wall of the cavern. One of the yetis tossed one of Pavel's arms over toward the wall of the cave. Blood began to ooze into the sand. As it did, those extra-large chitons I'd been feeding to Alpha scurried over to the severed arm. I knew chitons typically moved at a snail's pace, but these moved as quick as cats, covering the arm in no time. They shredded it to the bone like a school of piranha.

I stood, frozen. I didn't think the Atlanteans would create such insidious creatures. I remembered the one I'd fed to Alpha taking a chunk out of my flipper. That had seemed odd at the time, but now . . .

Trolga smiled. "Until you came through the tunnel, breaching the entry barrier, we couldn't get into this cave, but our creatures could. Lemurians were always great geneticists. We took ordinary chitons and modified them to be fast and carnivorous. Should a human somehow make it into the cave, we wanted to make sure they would be properly greeted."

Even as she spoke, the chitons seemed to be massing against the wall.

"I wish I could stay to see what you choose, but Rusha's waiting. While she'll be disappointed not to suck the lifeforce out of you, she'll be happy enough with the Scepter of Apollymi and with a pure-blooded Lemurian like Rhea."

"You bitch." I saw Rhea's knife in the sand where I'd dropped it. I dove for it, picked it up and heaved it at Trolga. It flew straight and true but she grabbed it out of the air.

"Thanks, Mr. Thomas. I'd been meaning to pick this up. Now I don't have to." She slipped the knife into her wet suit. She then took Pavel's other arm from her yeti and flipped it to the sub driver. "Take this with you and make sure to drop it next to their boat. I want to make sure that people think everyone drowned and their bodies were eaten by sharks." The sub departed.

She turned to the water. Thor dutifully pulled up onto the sand and she crawled on his back behind his dorsal. "Goodbye, Mr. Thomas. Sorry you'll miss out on all the fun of our new world order. I'd so much enjoy watching your reaction as we wipe out everything that you know and love. At least the look on your face will stay with me forever!" She put on her mask, and Thor thrashed his huge tail, pulling them both back into the water. As Thor departed, two large hammerheads remained to circle in the pool.

# CHAPTER 36
## SCYLLA OR CHARYBDIS

A s soon as Trolga left, Imee began to fiddle with her bracelet. While she seemed out of it, at least she wasn't crying.

The beam of sunlight through the oculus had shifted toward the wall. Soon the cave would lapse into twilight and then—darkness. I looked over at the mass of chitons, wondering if they were waiting for the dark so we wouldn't see them coming.

"We've got to do something before it gets dark," I said.

Jamie looked around. "What?"

I picked up the conch shell and threw it at the opening again. It bounced back, but this time plopped into the water rather than the sand. The sharks stirred at the splash, their dorsals cutting through the water.

I shook my head. "No. We'll make it out. We have to." I stared over at the pool where Trolga had submerged with Thor moments before. The large ripples had just started lapping up on the beach. A large sickle-shaped fin cutting through the water refocused my attention. I glanced around the cave. I could see the indentation in the sand from where I'd left my mask and snorkel. Trolga's men must have picked it up before she took off. There was a pair of flippers floating halfway across the pool. Trolga probably left that for us on purpose. Even without the sharks, there was no way we'd be able to swim through the entire tunnel holding our breath.

One of the chitons had gotten closer to us than the rest. It had crept up on Imee while she wasn't looking. I got an idea—not a particularly brilliant one, but perhaps something worth trying.

I ran past Imee and carefully picked up the renegade chiton. I held it upside down, its sharp beak snapping open and closed. Nasty creatures. I looked up at the oculus, pulled my arm back and launched the chiton toward it. It hit dead center. The oculus emitted a spark and the chiton fell back to the sand, landing upside down. I cautiously walked over. It appeared to be dead. I kicked it with my toe, flipping it over. Nothing. I picked it up and sniffed it. There was a slight odor of burnt ozone. That hadn't happened to the conch shells.

"It's dead." I threw it in the water. One of the sharks nailed it before it sank three feet.

"Good," Jamie said, "Now we've got a way to kill them and fill up the sharks' bellies so they'll leave!"

"Gallows humor?" I raised an eyebrow. "Must be feeling better."

Jamie nodded. "Other than a god-awful headache, I feel back to normal. Last thing I remember clearly was your uncle examining the Vulcan astronaut."

"I think Trolga took control of you. She made you say that I'd attacked you and then she used you to track us."

Jamie nodded. "It would explain a lot. Sorry about that."

"Not your fault. Trolga's evil. She uses her mind to control people."

"I told you they were Vulcans. Sounds like the mind-meld."

Imee started looking around. She was holding something in her hand. "Enough old home week, boys. We're in trouble. Either of you have any ideas?"

I gave Imee a look. She stared right back at me. "You don't really think I'm a dumb, vulnerable female, do you?" She placed her hands on her hips.

"Nnno." I stuttered a bit.

"Good, because I'm not. But if you ever tell Richard, I'll . . ." She left the threat open.

"Man, Imee, you're quite the actress," Jamie said. "And if Richard's father's the richest man in the world, how can I blame you?"

"I'm not a gold digger, either, but I do have my reasons, Jamie, so just watch it." Imee scanned the cavern.

Jamie nodded. Imee had fooled us both. Which was a good thing. I'd thought she'd be a basket case.

"So what's that about a new world order? Sounded like Trolga's been watching *Star Wars* reruns." Jamie looked over at me.

"It's a long story . . ." The cat was out of the bag and I was going to tell them about the scepter, Antarctica and that this was bigger than all of us, but Imee interrupted.

"No time right now. Let's focus on getting out of here. If we don't, everything else is irrelevant." Imee was unraveling her bracelet.

The light from the oculus dimmed as a cloud passed overhead. A few more of the chitons had started creeping toward us. I rushed over, grabbed the closest and flipped it into the water. Again, the sharks nailed it.

"Won't be able to keep that up once it gets dark," Jamie said.

I stopped at one spot. There seemed to be a line in the coral along the wall. I concentrated, hoping that, like on the Moon, a doorway would appear before me. Nothing happened.

"Charlie, lookout!" I glanced back. Imee had the flashlight in her hand. She depressed a button. A bright red beam shot right next to my foot. I looked down. A chiton lay smoking in the sand next to me. Must have crept out of a fold in the coral while I'd been concentrating.

"Thanks, Imee. Didn't know you still had that flashlight/laser."

"I forgot. Richard had thought it was funny, slipping one down the back of my bikini. I remembered when I saw the chiton getting close to you. Think we can cut a hole in the oculus with it?"

I glanced up. "Even if we did, how would we get up there?"

"Like this." Imee walked over to a large conch shell. She shot a hole through it with the laser and then fed a small string through it. She tied a knot in the end and then stepped back, extending the thread to its full length. She glanced over at me. "You should be able to throw this through the oculus."

I nodded. "I can, but it'll just bounce back."

"And that's the problem we need to solve." She looked at each of us. "Any ideas?"

Jamie stepped forward and started to grab the thread.

"Careful!" Imee pulled the string and wound it around her hand. "That thread's silk fiber woven over strands of graphene nanotubules. It has to be handled in just the right way."

"If that's the case, then how's it going to hold us if we try to climb out?" Jamie crossed his arms with a QED attitude.

"It's plenty strong enough to hold all three of us, but the nanotubes are very dangerous. We can't risk scraping the silk off it." Imee carefully started to tie loops in the line every couple of feet.

I remembered seeing something in a movie about monomolecular fiber being basically invisible. A bad guy had strung some up, managing to decapitate the good guy when he walked through it. "And it would be essentially invisible, right?"

Imee nodded.

"Could we use it as a weapon?" Jamie looked over at the sharks cutting through the water.

"Sure. If we could scrape all of the silk off, fix it across the water and get the sharks to both cross it, it would probably kill them, but how are we going to do that?"

"What about those things?" Jamie looked over at the chitons.

"Could we create a barrier around us with the graphene?" I looked hopefully over at Imee.

She shook her head. "Our best bet is to get through the oculus."

"AB will start looking for us at some point." Jamie looked over at me. "If he sees smoke, he'll know where to look for us." Jamie started to look around for stuff to burn.

Imee shook her head. "Not enough stuff here to burn. That's our way out." She pointed the laser at the oculus and fired it. She made a circle with the beam and then stopped. Nothing seemed to happen, no smoke or anything. Imee then turned and zapped the nearest chiton. "Throw it on up there, Charlie, right in the center. See if it goes through."

I kind of knew what was going to happen, but walked over, picked up the chiton and threw it at the oculus anyway. It hit right in the middle and fell back down. No spark this time, but perhaps that only happened to live creatures.

"Damn, I'd hoped it would work." Imee looked up with her hands on her hips.

Jamie picked the chiton up and lobbed it into the pool, feeding the sharks. "A hundred more or so and we should be good to go."

Chitons had crawled down on the sand all around us as the shaft of light continued to climb the wall.

"What about your telepathy? I've watched you and AB, and it seems that the two of you have been communicating without talking." Imee's eyes appeared to peer into my mind.

Imee, are you telepathic. I gently probed the surface of her mind to see if she could hear my thoughts. All I got was a jumble of thoughts about Richard, the cave and escape. AB had told me that I couldn't communicate with females about the same age as me.

"Charlie." Imee tapped her foot in the sand.

"Yes, I can communicate telepathically with AB."

"What about now?"

I shook my head. "Don't you think I already tried. Trolga said something about a dampener. It must block out thoughts."

"Then we're screwed." Jamie had been looking at Imee, but he shifted his eyes when I looked over at him.

Imee ignored him. "So, can you read my mind? What am I thinking?"

I shook my head. "AB explained it. It's very hard to read the minds of the opposite sex. Something about evolution and breeding."

Jamie chimed in. "Yeah, if my girlfriends could read my mind, I'd be in trouble. Can you read my mind? What's my favorite color?"

I let a tendril of thought drift toward Jamie. "Blue and green?"

"Damn, I was trying to trick you. What else am I thinking?" Jamie seemed to be having fun.

"Given the looks you've been giving me, even I can read your mind." Imee walked under the oculus and looked straight up. "But we don't have time for this."

"Agreed. How about giving me the laser?" I extended my hand.

"I'd prefer to hold onto it. Why? Have an idea?"

I shook my head. "Nope."

"So you think that since you're a guy and I'm a girl, you should hold the weapon. I guess you and Richard aren't that different." Imee gave me a glare.

"No, that's not what I meant. I wanted to see if I could figure out how much power's still in it. We're about to have to start zapping the chitons." I pointed over Imee's shoulder. She looked back. A dozen chitons had left the safety of the coral wall and were heading across the sand toward us. They were coming at us from all directions, but most were coming from where the walls met the waterline.

The last of the direct sunlight was now hitting the top of the oculus. The temperature seemed to have dropped a couple of degrees.

"Even though they're fast, we're much quicker. As long as we can see them we can avoid them. Let's wipe out as many as we can so when it gets dark, we'll have a fighting chance." To prove his point, Jamie dashed over to the lead chitons, grabbed one and hurled it into the water.

"That's the best plan we have? That's pitiful." Imee was eyeing the laser. "I hate to waste the power when we might have a better use for it later."

"I don't think the sharks will sit still long enough for the laser to kill them. Even if they did, we can't swim all the way through the tunnel without Richard's fancy masks."

Jamie sounded a bit dour. Either he had a hangover from Trolga's control or he'd lost his sense of humor. I had a thought. "I'm going to sit and concentrate to see if I can get in touch with the Atlantean technology. Since I have Atlantean genes in me, the technology should react to my telepathic contact."

Imee looked skeptical. "So you're just going to sit there and let us protect you?"

I nodded. "I've been able to communicate with Atlantean technology in the past. Perhaps there's a vestige still active on this base."

"Well, we have one weapon with an unknown amount of power. Imee can zap the buggers, but what can I do? Dance around and pick one up at a time?" To emphasize his point, he took off running toward the nearest pack of chitons. Before he got there, he tripped over a piece of coral sticking out of the sand and went sprawling toward the chitons.

"Jamie!" Imee yelled and pointed the laser. The chitons must have sensed something because they picked up speed, heading quickly toward Jamie. I jumped up and ran to Jamie, grabbing him by the shoulder. A beam of energy shot right past us, frying the closest chitons. I got Jamie up and yanked him away before a host of chitons reached where he'd fallen. They paid for their aggressive move with their lives as Imee fried them all, but there were hundreds more creeping out from nooks and crannies in the coral.

"Looks like you stirred the hornet's nest." Whether it was the fact that the sun had dropped down far enough that no direct light was coming through the oculus or the thud of Jamie's body on the sand, something had made the chitons start their march toward us. Imee got down on the sand and lined up the laser, killing four chitons with one shot.

"Looks like they're both carnivorous and cannibalistic." Jamie pointed as a bunch of the chitons had crawled atop their fallen brethren and started eating them. "Maybe that'll slow them down."

"I hope so. Look. Give me a few minutes. If any of the equipment in this base is still active, I may be able to find and open a door somewhere."

"Fine. Sit and meditate. We'll wake you before the first bite." Imee took a defensive position, holding the laser in front of her.

I sat in the sand and tried to relax and focus. Imee and Jamie stood on either side of me. The chitons approached from every direction but the water. We couldn't retreat far because the sharks had started circling closer to the shore, and we remembered how far up Thor had gotten. Maybe they sensed something.

I focused, trying to sense any tendrils of thought around me. I felt Jamie's and Imee's presence and blotted them out as best I could. I hoped that, as in the Lunar base, a computer was still working and had come active due to my presence. I had definitely felt power in the scepter. Perhaps its power had seeped into an old system in the station. I felt my mind leave my body. This was something new. I looked down at my seated self and Imee and Jamie. They were bright lights in my vision. The encircling army of chitons glowed a dull yellow. While there were hundreds on the sand slowing creeping toward us, there were many more in the cave, slowly moving toward the beach. I floated over the water, looking down on the sharks. From here, I had no fear of them. They too had a dull yellow glow emanating from behind their hammers.

I noticed a light down below a ledge of coral and dove into the water, right between the sharks. They didn't notice me. I hoped that the light meant that some of the base's systems were still working. I didn't swim, but rather drifted toward the light. It appeared to be getting dimmer as I approached. I moved more swiftly. The light emanated from a hole on a relatively flat surface. I looked into the hole and noticed the sharp-edged cuts in the coral around it. I touched it and felt a surge of power up my arm. When I pulled my hand away, the light faded out. This was where I'd pulled the scepter out. The power was residual.

I detected a glow down the tunnel. I headed through the gate and into the tunnel. Dots of light danced around me. It took me a minute to figure out the dots were fish. I saw a barrier at the entrance to the tunnel. It looked like a spiderweb of blue lines. As I focused on it, the blue lines began to waver. They faded out. I moved toward them, but heard something behind me, yelling. I felt a slap on my cheek and darted back through the tunnel and up out of the water much faster than Alpha had ever gone. I popped back into my body.

"What? I was . . ."

"I don't care what you were doing. The laser just ran out." I slowly regained my senses and looked around. Heaps of dead chitons lay around us in a semi-circle. Other chitons had slowed their advance to eat what we'd offered them. Unfortunately, it looked as if the second wave had just about finished off the first.

I looked up. I could see stars above the oculus. I must have been out of my body longer than I'd thought.

"Well, I hope you found something that can help us." Imee and Jamie both looked at me.

I stood, a bit stiff. "I'm not sure. When I got close to the entrance to the cave, the force field seemed to waver. If I could get close, perhaps . . ."

"Close to the entrance? What do you mean? You never left here." Jamie seemed skeptical. "Never mind. There's no way we can get you close to the opening, so that won't work. Any ideas?"

I shook my head. "If I could go back, maybe I could figure something out."

"Too bad for us. If you go back in your 'trance' the next thing you'll feel will be the beaks of these nasty little beasts." Imee picked one up and heaved it into the water.

Jamie looked at the bones of Pavel's arm and then back at the water. "I for one think I'll try swimming out rather than getting slowly pecked to death."

The light faded. Imee suddenly took off right at one group of chitons. As she approached them, she jumped over them, going into a roll. She dashed over to Pavel's arm bones and picked up the largest. A chiton came at her, but she batted it away, pivoted and dashed back, jumping over the chitons that had encircled us.

Imee kept the larger bone from the upper arm and dropped the bones from Pavel's lower arm onto the sand.

"That's gross," Jamie said, "but I guess we're better off armed." Jamie leaned down and picked both bones up, handing one to me. "Get it, armed?"

I nodded. More gallows humor. "I think we got it. Good thinking, Imee."

She nodded. "Now, stand back to back so we can knock the chitons away as they attack."

We pushed back against each other. A couple of the chitons, like an advanced guard, scurried forward as the mass held back. I whacked at one and glanced back as Imee nailed two, knocking them into the water.

"Nice shot, you should have been a baseball player," I said.

"Field hockey was my game." We focused on the horde.

"You know, this reminds me of *The Fellowship of the Ring* when they were surrounded by goblins in the middle of the Mines of Moria." It was getting dark, but we could still see the front lines of the encircling chitons. It looked like an army of giant cockroaches closing in on us. As long as they came at us slowly, the bones would give us a fighting chance.

"The arrival of the Balrog saved them." I remembered the scene vividly.

"So, where's our Balrog?" Jamie looked around.

"Wait," Imee said. "Didn't they have a problem getting the doors open to get in the mines?"

Jamie and I nodded. "Yep, Merry said 'speak, friend, and enter.' They just had to say the elvish word for friend."

Imee looked over at me and then looked up. "Maybe you just have to think friend or open or something like that?"

I hadn't thought about telepathically saying open. It might work. "I'll try." I concentrated, looking up at the oculus. *Open. Open the oculus.* Nothing changed. I shrugged. "I tried."

"But how do you know it didn't work?" Imee picked up a small conch shell and threw it up. It went through!

"It worked. Let's move!"

Imee started to uncoil the thread with the conch on the end. She whipped it around her head and released it. It banged against the edge and fell back. "Damn." She glanced over at the chitons as she pulled in the thread. They'd stopped moving forward.

"Let me try. I can throw, remember?" I took the conch from Imee's hand.

"Sorry, forgot." She dropped the coil of thread in the sand so it would play out when I threw the conch.

I glanced back over at the chitons—they'd started to close in again—and made my throw. *Open, open. Stay open.* I projected my thoughts as hard as I could. The conch arched up and through the opening.

"The string!" Jamie dove for the last coil on the ground. It lifted out of his grasp. Fortunately, Imee had tied the other end to her wrist.

She slowly pulled on the string, trying to see if the conch would catch on the jagged coral of the island. It seemed to catch. She pulled hard and it released. She started a slow retrieve again and it caught. She put her weight on the string. It held.

"Let me go up first. I'm the lightest." Imee didn't wait for a response. She grabbed the highest loop she could reach and began to climb.

Jamie looked over at me. "Ladies first, I guess."

I nodded. I could just make out the line of encircling chitons in the twilight. I picked up the larger bone that Imee had left behind and stepped forward, whacking several chitons into the water. "Hurry, Imee, they're closing in fast."

"Almost there." Imee had reached the top.

I glanced up. She'd paused. "What's the problem?"

"Coral's a bit sharp."

"So are the beaks on these damn chitons." Jamie leaned forward and whacked at the closest of the chitons.

I smashed down on one, hoping the others would delay to eat it, but they didn't. I glanced up. Imee was gone and so was our lifeline! "Imee." I shouted. I searched telepathically and knew she was still up there.

The chitons were getting damn close. "Think she screwed us?" Jamie and I were back to back, batting the chitons away as fast as we could.

"Don't think so." My doubts evaporated as the thread dropped back down next to us.

"You first." I batted away another chiton.

"No, you. You're more important. Go!" Jamie moved forward, whacking away at the chitons. He gave me a nod.

I grabbed the rope and started pulling up. Imee had made it seem easy. "Come on, Jamie, it'll hold both of us." I hoped.

The time on the Moon had weakened me, and I strained to pull up on the small loops Imee had tied. Fortunately, the fiber was tacky, so my hands and feet didn't slip. I dug my toes into one loop after the other and pulled with my arms. I was only a short distance from the top when I heard Jamie scream. I started to look down, but Imee yelled to me, "Don't look. Keep coming. Jamie's on the way up."

I redoubled my efforts, climbing to the top. I reached the edge, finding a handhold just over the top. I pulled myself up. Imee grabbed under my arms. I was up.

"No time! We need to pull Jamie up." Imee grasped the rope, her hands bloody.

Jamie screamed again.

"HOLD ON!" I shouted.

Imee yelled down. "Wrap the line around your arm."

Imee braced herself and started pulling. I grabbed as well, braced myself on a smooth rock, and started to pull.

Imee's face was screwed up in pain.

"What happened?"

"The coral." Imee bit her lip as she pulled. "I'm ok. Just pull!"

I nodded. We pulled. I strained as the line slowly came up, scraping against the coral.

I looked over at Imee. As if reading my mind, she said, "Don't worry. The coral can't cut the line. It'll hold."

Jamie screamed again. We kept pulling. Finally, his head popped over the edge of the oculus. He was dripping sweat, his face flushed and frozen in a grimace.

"Hold onto the line." Imee reached forward and grabbed Jamie's arm. We both pulled and got Jamie to the top.

"Get them off! Get them off!" Jamie screamed.

Two chitons had latched onto Jamie's left foot and ankle. I looked around for something to get them off with, but Imee was ahead of me. She carefully grabbed the end of the thread and manipulated it. It looked as if she'd snapped it in half. She held the end in one hand with another piece in the other, but it looked like there was no line in between.

"Jamie don't move!" She leaned forward over Jamie's leg.

Jamie gave her a pleading look and gritted his teeth.

She held the line and pulled the gap through the first of the chitons. The monomolecular line cut the chiton in half. She then carefully did the same to the other.

"You got the coating off and used the nanowire," I said.

Imee nodded.

I bent over Jamie's ankle and pulled the half chiton off. It looked as if the thing had bitten all the way to the bone. Imee pulled the other dead chiton off. Jamie's foot looked like a bloody piece of raw meat. Several bones on top of his foot showed through.

"How's it look?" Jamie gritted his teeth.

"Not bad." Imee looked up at me. *Wish you could hear my thoughts.*

I nodded. Shocked. *Can you hear me?* I tried to project my thought to Imee.

Imee seemed to wait and then started up again. *Guess this is one way. If you can understand me, nod.*

I nodded. "You'll be just fine, Jamie. Just catch your breath right now."

*We need to keep him quiet. There's a beach over there, but I doubt we can get to it barefoot even without carrying Jamie.*

I nodded, leaned forward and peered down the oculus. Although dark, I could make out a heap on the sand right below us. "Wish I had a grenade to lob down there."

# CHAPTER 37
## NEED A LIFT?

I sat looking over at Jamie, wondering what to do. Jamie's foot looked like a hunk of raw meat. I glanced at Imee. Her hands didn't look much better. They needed medical treatment—soon. Besides that, I needed to rescue Rhea and get the scepter back. I lowered my head into my hands. We were stuck on a desolate coral island miles from any habitation without any way to get help.

"Look."

I glanced up.

Imee pointed at a light rapidly approaching us.

"Could . . . be . . . Trolga." Jamie gasped between words.

I shook my head. "Don't think so." The light approached rapidly, much faster than a helicopter. It was coming in from the north.

*Need a lift?*

I recognized AB's thoughts immediately and smiled. "It's AB!"

"Thank God," Imee said.

*What, no comeback?*

*We're in trouble. Jamie and Imee are both hurt. Can you land close to us?*

*Will do. Be there in a minute. What about the rest of you?*

*Just get here. I'll explain once we're aboard.*

The light shot toward us and then stopped directly above us. It slowly grew as it descended. As it got close, I recognized the shape of an Atlantean spacecraft.

"That's a flying saucer!" Jamie pointed, excitement creeping into his voice for the first time in a while.

I nodded. *Uncle Merl?* It would be just like AB and my uncle to not announce his presence.

The saucer gently settled down next to us. *I was hoping to surprise you. You've had quite an adventure since I last saw you at the hotel.*

I gave my uncle a mental smile as the door began to open on the saucer. A short ramp extended outwards. I expected to see the big furry form of AB standing backlit in the doorway. Instead, as soon as the door cracked open enough, a small form darted out and shot right for me.

"Nim!" Nim leapt into my arm. She began purring immediately as I scratched behind her ears.

"That's your uncle's cat from the Moon?" Imee's eyes widened.

I nodded. "My uncle and AB are on board."

Jamie pulled himself up with a scowl of pain. Nim strutted over to him, rubbing up against Jamie's side. Jamie smiled, rubbing Nim's ears. "So, Charlie, what's the story behind the flying saucer?"

I shrugged. "A long story. When we have time, I'll tell both of you all about it."

AB appeared in the doorway holding a backpack. He strode toward us. Uncle Merl came out more slowly.

AB walked stiffly toward me and said. "Klaatu."

I frowned.

"Never mind. You're too young." He looked down at Jamie's feet and shook his head. "What the hell ran over your foot, lad."

Jamie looked down. "It's not too bad compared to the alternative." He gave a lame smile.

AB bent down to take a closer look, but Uncle Merl walked up behind him. "Make way, make way."

Uncle Merl bent down, pushed his glasses back up on his nose and looked at Jamie's injuries. He studied them for a moment, shook his head and then pulled a silver flask out of his rucksack. He opened the top and handed it to Jamie.

"Take a swallow."

Jamie sniffed at it, his nose wrinkling in disgust. He pushed it away. "That stinks."

"I said drink it, don't smell it." Uncle Merl handed it back to Jamie. "It will make the pain go away."

Jamie nodded, held his nose and drank. As he did, Uncle Merl picked up half of the carcass of one of the dead chitons. "This what bit you?" He gazed into Jamie's eyes.

Jamie nodded and let out a yawn. "Hurt like hell." He yawned again.

Uncle Merl turned to us. "Did either of you get bitten?"

I shook my head, as did Imee.

"What about your hands?" Uncle Merl walked over and looked at Imee's bleeding hands.

"That's from the coral." She winced as Uncle Merl inspected her hands and forearms.

"And she helped pull Jamie up even though her hands were torn up." I hadn't gotten a good look at Imee's hands until Uncle Merl inspected them. They were torn to shreds.

Uncle Merl looked at her over the edge of his glasses. "Brave girl. That must've really hurt."

Imee nodded.

He reached into his rucksack and pulled out a spray bottle. "Now this won't hurt—" he started to spray "—much."

Imee winced, but didn't cry out.

"Numb yet?" Uncle Merl asked.

Imee flexed her hands. "Not quite."

Uncle Merl nodded and glanced over at Jamie, who was having trouble holding his head up. Uncle Merl nodded to AB. "Take him into the ship. He'll be asleep soon."

AB lifted him as if he weighed nothing. I wished we'd had AB pulling Jamie out of the cave.

Uncle Merl watched AB carry Jamie into the ship and then turned back to me and Imee. "You sure you weren't bitten?"

We both nodded. "Why?" I asked.

"Because these beasties may be venomous." He glanced down at the beak, took out a pair of tweezers and pulled at it. With an eye dropper, he drew out a small amount of fluid and squeezed it into a vial. He carefully wiped the tweezers and the eye dropper and put them away. Then he lifted the vial and glanced at the fluid.

"Nasty critters." He shook his head and put the vial away. "Now, let me take a look at those hands."

He reached out, palms up, to hold and inspect Imee's hand. She pulled them back.

"Not until you tell us what's going to happen to Jamie!"

"Ok. Ok. He's fine for now. The tonic I gave him killed the pain and will slow down his metabolism. I'll have time to get him to my lab and concoct an antidote." He extended his hands again. "Now, your hands."

Imee extended them sheepishly.

"Let me know if this hurts." Uncle Merl turned her hands over and moved her fingers up and down. She didn't seem to be in any pain. "Good. Now flex your fingers, slowly." Uncle Merl lowered his face close to her hands to watch as she moved her fingers. "No pain?"

Imee shook her head. "The pain's gone. That's quite a painkiller you've got there."

Uncle Merl ignored the compliment. "Don't see any sign of nerve or tendon damage." He turned to his rucksack again and rummaged around. He came out with a tube of ointment. He squeezed some onto his fingertips and gently rubbed it into the cuts and scrapes on Imee's arms and hands.

"Any scrapes anywhere else?"

Imee pointed down to her stomach. "I did get a bit of a scrape as I pulled up over the edge of the coral."

Uncle Merl took some more of the ointment and gently rubbed it on her stomach.

"Charlie?"

I shook my head. "Imee found a smooth spot where I climbed out."

Imee looked down at her hands and wiggled her fingers again. "I can't believe the pain's gone."

Uncle Merl nodded. "You'll be fine. That ointment will speed up the healing process and kill any bacteria from the coral. You'll be good as new."

"I didn't know that you were a doctor, Dr. Ambrose."

Uncle Merl chucked. "But you just addressed me as doctor."

"I mean a medical doctor."

"I've dabbled over time. Trust me. You'll be fine." Uncle Merl looked intently into Imee's eyes.

"Yes. I'll be fine."

"Now, let's get on the ship. We've got to get Jamie to my lab in Scotland." Uncle Merl rose, not waiting for us.

It took a minute for what he'd said to sink in. "Scotland? But we've got to go after Trolga. She's got Rhea—" my voice caught in my throat "—and the scepter."

Imee caught up with us. "And Richard."

Uncle Merl stopped and put his hands on his hips. "If we do, the odds are that your friend will die." He looked back at both of us. "That's what I thought." He turned and walked into the ship.

# CHAPTER 38
## MERLIN'S CASTLE

I ran toward the control room, with Imee on my heels. When I got there, Uncle Merl was nowhere to be found. I knew from experience that we wouldn't feel the ship take off.

*Shannon, show viewscreen below the ship.*

A viewscreen appeared in front of us.

Imee gasped. "Where'd that come from?"

The turquoise blue waters on the screen receded as we climbed. Bimini appeared and then began to shrink rapidly. Once it appeared the size of a penny below us, we shot forward, passing over Grand Bahama island, which quickly shrank and disappeared to our south. The turquoise waters darkened into the deep blue of the Atlantic.

"Was that Grand Bahama Island?" Imee pointed down.

I nodded. "Think so."

"Then we must be going faster than Richard's hypersonic plane."

"Yep. This ship's fast. Made it from the Moon to Earth in just a few hours."

"Damn. That means it was doing 40,000 to 50,000 miles per hour. I don't feel anything. No acceleration."

"I think my uncle mentioned that the Atlanteans had something like inertial dampeners."

"So . . . the ship's Atlantean? And it still works?" Imee raised her eyebrows.

"Don't ask me how."

Imee nodded. "Their technology's way ahead of ours."

"Yep, they were about to leave for interstellar space when the war broke out."

Imee looked at me funny. "What war and how do you know all this?"

I smiled coyly. *Shannon, please show yourself and tell us orally how long until we reach Scotland.*

The air shimmered for a second and Shannon appeared as before. "We are approximately twenty minutes from our destination in the island that you call Great Britain."

Imee took several steps back and pointed at Shannon. "A hologram?"

I nodded. "Her name's Shannon. Shannon, this is Imee. Please answer any questions she might have."

Without hesitation Shannon answered, "That is not permitted."

I looked at her strangely. "Why not?"

Before Shannon could answer, my uncle entered the control room. *Shannon, leave.* He then smiled at me. *Not a wise idea, Charlie. Fortunately, Shannon's programed to only respond to those of Atlantean descent.*

"Well, Ms. Castillo, I see that Charlie's introduced you to our holographic pilot."

Imee nodded. "This is all too fantastic to take in. Shannon said we'd be in England within twenty minutes."

Uncle Merl nodded. "Scotland actually. The good news is that I've isolated the neurotoxin that those nasty buggers use. It's a derivative of tetrodoxin." He looked at us as if expecting we would know what that was. He sighed. "What do they teach in schools these days? Tetrodoxin's the venom of the genus *Hapalochlaena*, better known as the blue-ringed octopus."

Imee nodded. "I've heard of that. I thought that could kill you inside of minutes."

Uncle Merl nodded. "Fortunately, those beasties don't deliver a large dose. Even so, I've had to slow your friend's metabolism to delay the effect of the poison. AB's watching him."

"Do you have an antidote at your lab?" My uncle never seemed to get to the point.

"Of course. I've got antidotes for most of the known world toxins in my lab. That's why we're heading there." He looked at me as if I was an idiot. "Now I've got to get back to my patient."

As was his nature, he didn't wait for a response. Imee put her hands on her hips and stared at me. She didn't say a word, but started to tap her foot on the deck of the ship. From the look in her eye, I knew that I'd never win this staring contest. "What?"

"I think it's explanation time. Atlantis, yetis, a flying saucer . . . "

I started to pace and then looked over at Imee. "You're right. You deserve an explanation. Want a seat?"

At my thought, a chair rose up from the deck underneath Imee. She glanced back behind her in surprise, but then stepped forward. "I think I'd rather stand."

"Suit yourself." I sat in the captain's chair and swiveled to face Imee. "You know how we found the dead astronaut on the Moon. Well, that's just the beginning . . ." I told her about escaping from Trolga's men, going back to the Atlantean base on the Moon, how the Lemurians and Trolga chased me out, the rescue of Uncle Merl and Nim, our quick flight to Earth, the Lemurian attack in orbit, and meeting AB in the forest. I paused to catch my breath and think about whether to tell Imee about Galadriel and my true quest.

Imee didn't give me much of a choice. "I know that look, Charlie. Give it to me straight. If we're going to get Richard and Rhea back, I need to know everything."

"Look. Bottom line, if we don't find the scepter it could be the end of the world as we know it. That's why rescuing Rhea and Richard isn't enough. I need you to understand that." I held Imee's gaze.

"Even without telepathy, I've always had a pretty good bullshit detector. And although what you said sounds like the biggest pile of bull I've ever heard, I've seen too much."

*That's enough for now, Charlie.* Uncle Merl walked into the control room as Imee looked over at him. She started to ask him something, but he raised his hand. "Shannon, are we close to our destination?"

"Hovering at 75,000 feet, as you requested."

Imee and I looked at the viewscreen. We were so high that we could see all of Great Britain and part of Scandinavia.

"Any aircraft in visual range of us or the destination?"

"No."

"Good, please descend—and turn off the viewscreen."

The viewscreen blinked off.

I looked over at my uncle. "Why turn it off? I'd like to see. Shann—"

My uncle placed his hand on my shoulder. "Don't. We're descending too fast. We'd get sick if we watched."

Imee took a few steps. "Amazing. I don't feel a thing."

"That's a good thing. Charlie probably remembers what it felt like when the inertial dampeners started to malfunction."

"After the attack?"

My uncle nodded. "I'd planned to drop you off with Aku Brugal regardless, but I had to eject you in the life pod after the Lemurians attacked us."

"So the ship really was damaged. That wasn't all a stunt you pulled?"

My uncle gave me his best "I'm hurt" look and shook his head. "I wish it was. I did manage to regain control and get the ship to Scotland. With the help of the Lady and her database, I repaired the damage to the inertial guidance system and got to the Bahamas to meet you. But we are here, and I need to tend to young Mr. Gage." Without a second thought, Uncle Merl turned and left us in the control room.

Imee looked over at me, her hands on her hips again. The control room looked very spartan now with a console in the middle and no chairs or screen. "So, a flying saucer, telepathy, Bigfoot and Atlantis." She shook her head. "Hard to believe. What's next. Do we head down a rabbit hole into Wonderland?"

I shook my head. "I know, I know. Sometimes I wish that I'd just wake up in my bed in Seattle and that this would all be a dream. But it's not. More importantly, Trolga took Rhea . . . and Richard. We have to find them."

Imee nodded. "At least I know that part's true. God knows what Trolga wants them for. As to the scepter and the end of the world . . ." She shook her head.

"Hard to believe. I know. But, as you said, you've seen too much." I shuddered at the thought and quickly changed the subject. "How are your hands?"

Imee looked down. Her eyes widened. "They don't hurt and they're already healing! Your uncle must be a magician."

I chuckled, thinking about Uncle Merl as the man behind the myth of Merlin.

"What's so funny?" Imee's eyes seemed to bore into me.

"Everything you said." I scratched my head trying to think of a better comeback. I had nothing. "Shannon, turn on the view screen and show us where we are."

An image of darkness appeared in front of us. I was about to ask Shannon if she had night vision when lights illuminated a large empty room. Uncle Merl appeared in the edge of the image, pushing a hovering gurney in front of him. I could just make out Jamie's face lying on a pillow.

Uncle Merl must have read my thoughts. *I'm taking him to the lab to give him the anti-venom. Go to bed. It's late. I'll see you in the morning.*

"Spying on your uncle, are you!" AB had somehow appeared behind us undetected.

I practically jumped out of my skin. *How'd you do that?*

Before AB could answer, Imee said, "How can anything as big as you are—no offense—manage to sneak up on us like that?"

"Have you ever wondered why nobody has ever proved that Bigfoot exists? We're all about stealth." He took a couple of awkward steps, making a loud thud as each foot landed. He smiled, baring his canines, but his smile broke into a yawn.

Imee laughed, but then she yawned.

"Been a long day. How 'bout I show you to a couple of rooms so we can all get some shut eye. I expect we'll have a long day tomorrow." They walked down the ramp into the hangar.

I nodded, trying to suppress a yawn.

AB pushed a button on an elevator and took us up a couple of floors. He took me to a room first and let me in. "We'll meet in the kitchen in the AM."

I focused on the large bed in the middle of the room. "How will I find it?"

AB glanced back at Imee and then at me. "Just follow your noses." He closed the door.

I awoke with my clothes still on, lying on the bed. Must've been more tired than I thought. I hit the bathroom, used the toothbrush conveniently sitting in a cup by the sink, washed my face and then headed out into the hall. Sure enough, I could smell bacon cooking. The smell seemed stronger to the right, so I headed that way. A door opened into a spiral stone staircase. The smell seemed to be coming up the stairs. I headed down.

At the bottom of the stairs an old wooden door with wrought-iron bands stood open. I stepped through into a large stone kitchen with high vaulted ceilings. While the room fit in well with an old castle—stone floors, wooden beams across the ceiling and a huge stone fireplace with a big iron witch's pot suspended from an iron handle—everything else was modern.

AB had his head in a stainless steel refrigerator. A platter filled with scrambled eggs, sausage and bacon sat on the huge butcher's block that served as a table in the middle of the kitchen.

Imee had beaten me down and was seated at the table with a cup of coffee in her hands.

AB paused. "Ah, there it is." He pulled out a bottle of ketchup.

"What's that for?" I poured a glass of orange juice from the pitcher on the table and sat down.

"All civilized people have ketchup on their scrambled eggs." AB walked toward the table.

Imee shook her head.

I grabbed a plate and served myself before AB got to the table. I pointed my fork at Imee. "You'd better get some before AB sits down."

She nodded, grabbed a plate and served herself. "At least he didn't make haggis."

AB took a seat. "Tried it when a student here. Didn't like it." He pulled the platter in front of him and started eating.

"Aren't you going to save some for Uncle Merl?"

AB shook his head and swallowed a mass of eggs and sausage. "Your uncle's tied up tending to Jamie." After another bite, "You two hurry up. I thought you'd like a tour of the castle before we take off."

I looked over at Imee who was halfway through her eggs. "What do you mean? I thought we'd be here for days for Jamie to heal."

AB shook his head. "Your uncle administered the antidote last night. Jamie'll be good as new when he wakes up."

"But what about the lacerations on his feet?" Imee lifted her hands, flipping them over, examining them.

AB pointed with his knife covered in ketchup. "I think you just answered your own question."

"That's amazing. How did Dr. Ambrose do it?" Imee put her fork down.

He answered as he slathered ketchup onto the last of his eggs. "He's had a great deal of time and experience to work on formulas based on old herbal remedies . . ."

*Careful. You can't tell her how old Uncle Merl is.*

AB smirked at me. ". . . and he had a great deal of help from Atlantean medical texts."

Imee nodded. "If he patented his salve, he'd make a mint. In fact, by slowly bringing Atlantean technology to market he could become richer than Richard's father." Imee seemed deep in thought.

"Your thoughts bely your age, young lady." AB stuffed an entire sausage into the cavern he called his mouth.

Imee looked suspiciously at AB and then at me. Pointing at AB, she said, "Can he read my mind also?"

I was about to answer, but AB swallowed his sandwich and answered. "Of course, but that would be rude. Besides, it's painful to read the minds of you lesser *hominids*."

Imee looked back at me. "He's much better at it than me. I'm a neophyte."

"Wet behind those pointy ears, I'd say," AB joked between bites.

Imee didn't react and seemed withdrawn. I reached a tendril of thought out toward her, but something seemed to block me.

"Ok, if we're all done, how about the dollar tour?" AB didn't even wait for a response. We followed behind his loping stride. He walked through a dining room with a table that seated about twenty. A suit of armor sat between each window, and old portraits lined the opposite wall. I wanted to stop and look around, but AB kept up his typical pace.

"What about these suits of armor?" I yelled up to AB.

He waved his hand dismissively. "Seen one, seen them all. Come on."

Imee grabbed my arm. I stopped. She looked over at the portraits. They were all men in medieval outfits. I was more interested in the suits of armor.

"Look closely." She pointed at one. "That one there sure does look like you."

She was right. He looked even more like my maternal grandfather. "Hey, AB, these guys look a bit like me—and some of them have slightly pointed ears."

AB turned, tapping his foot. "They should, they're your ancestors."

I looked around again.

"It's your uncle's place, so these are your ancestors. What's the big deal?"

"But my family's been in America for several generations."

"And they, at least on your mother's side, were originally from Scotland." AB put his hands on his hips. "Look, we don't have a lot of time. I'm sure your uncle'll give you the pound-sterling tour next time, but this is the dollar tour."

We came to the entrance hall with a huge wrought-iron chandelier hanging down in the middle and a wide staircase leading up to the second floor. I thought AB was going to turn toward the double front door, but instead he started up the stairs. We followed. He stopped on the landing at the top and pointed out the leaded-glass window. It looked out on a courtyard. Small pebbles surrounded a grass island in the middle. I focused on the vintage British racing-green Aston Martin parked next to the grass island. It looked just like the one in the first Bond movie I'd ever seen.

"Well, what do you think?" AB looked at me.

"Awesome ride. Does it belong to my uncle?"

AB's shoulder's drooped. "I don't know. I wasn't talking about the car."

Imee nudged me. "I think he's talking about the sword in the stone."

"The what?" I looked back out the window. A pond sat in the middle of the grass island.

Imee pointed to the middle of the pond. A stone bridge lead to a small island in the middle. The island was basically a large rock. A sword jutted out from it.

I stared at it for a minute. My uncle was Merlin, after all. Maybe it was the Sword in the Stone.

"No, that's not the Excalibur that young King Arthur wielded. Some past student of mine gave it to me as a gift. It appeared one morning after he left. I haven't had the heart to move it—yet." Uncle Merl had come up behind us. AB looked hurt at Uncle Merl's comments.

"Come on, AB, don't be such a baby. It's one of my favorite features of the castle."

"Has anyone ever tried to pull the sword out of the stone?" Imee asked Uncle Merl.

"Of course. Many have tried, but few have succeeded." Uncle Merl gave me a wink. "Want to try?"

"Sure. But, before we do, how's Jamie?" Imee looked guiltily down at her feet.

"Much better." Uncle Merl pulled out a gold pocket watch. "He should be up and about soon."

"That's great news." Imee looked at her hands, which had almost healed. "Even the deep lacerations?"

"Well, they're not fully healed, but he'll be able to get around. I put a healing gel on them that will seal the wounds and enhance healing." He pointed to Imee's hands. "Similar to what I put on your hands, just stronger and more binding."

The ugly scrapes on Imee's hands had turned to a muted pink, and the cuts had sealed. She scratched her left palm and shook her head. "Doesn't even hurt any more, just itches. Why haven't you released your formula?"

Uncle Merl shook his head. "Young minds . . . Come on, I'd like to see if either of you are this generation's Arthur." He took off down the stairs with a brisk stride.

Imee looked over at me, and I shrugged and followed my uncle.

We got to a heavy wooden door with wrought-iron braces that lead out to the courtyard. Uncle Merl pushed it and walked out. "Come on, come on. Daylight's wasting."

His feet crunched as he walked across the pea gravel in the courtyard. Surprisingly, he made far more noise than AB. Uncle Merl walked down the steppingstones to the pond at the center. The stones, instead of going in a straight line to the pond, curled around in a spiral.

Uncle Merl looked back. "STAY on the steppingstones."

Given his tone, we did, but Imee looked over at me questioningly.

In answer, a deep voice behind us said, "Can't break the spell. Stay on the stones!"

*For real?* I directed my thought at AB.

Uncle Merl answered. *Don't be ridiculous. Grass is hard to grow in this climate.*

Imee kept on the stones in front of me, following Uncle Merl. "So, AB, what kind of spell are you talking about?"

"Pish posh, my dear. I thought you'd have learned to ignore his bad jokes by now. The spiral is soothing and gives my little island of grass a Zen feel to it. Can't you grok it?" Uncle Merl stopped as he reached the pond and the stone bridge to the small island and the sword in the stone.

"What?" I looked down at the grass. Grok?

Uncle Merl ignored me. "My dear, why don't you go first. See if this generation's Arthur will be a lady."

Imee stepped across the bridge and looked back. "Here goes nothing." She rubbed her hands together and grabbed the leather-wrapped hilt of the sword with her right hand. She pulled. It slid right out.

"I did it!" Imee looked gleefully like her old self. She looked at the sword. "It says Excalibur right here." She pointed along the blade.

Uncle Merl stepped up to her and extended his hand. She placed the sword in his hand. He flipped it over. "And made in China on the back. See?" He showed the writing to Imee.

"Too bad. I've always pictured myself as a superhero." Imee retreated back over the bridge.

Uncle Merl replaced the sword in the stone. "Next." He nodded to me.

I stepped across the bridge, gripped the sword with one hand and pulled like Imee had, expecting it to slide right out. "It seems to be stuck." I used both hands and pulled again, propping one foot against the stone to give me leverage. I grunted and groaned. It wouldn't budge.

Imee smiled. "I guess you're not Arthur, Charlemagne."

I pulled again, but shrugged. "How about letting the big ape take a shot? He should be able to yank the entire stone up if the sword doesn't come out."

AB flashed a snarl at me, took one stride across the bridge, and stood next to Uncle Merl. My uncle nodded to him. He looped his left pinky around the hilt and slid the sword right out. He lifted it over his head and let out a war cry so loud we all covered our ears.

"What the hell was that?" I'd never heard Uncle Merl use profanity.

"What, you don't like my imitation of William Wallace?" AB brandished the sword again.

Uncle Merl shook his head. "If William Wallace had yelled like that and was as big as you, he wouldn't have needed a sword. He would have scared the English right out of Scotland! Now, let's check on young Master Gage and see when he'll be ready to go." Uncle Merl turned to leave.

"Where?" Imee asked before I could.

AB handed me the phony Excalibur. *Stick it back in the stone, boy.* "Yes, Dr. Ambrose, where to?"

I slipped Excalibur back in the stone and then gave it a tug. It wouldn't budge. There had to be a trick to it. Given time, I'd figure it out.

"I'm fairly certain where Dr. Larsen took the scepter, Richard and Rhea." In his typical fashion, he started back across the spiral stones without waiting to see if we would follow. We did.

"Where's that, Uncle Merl?"

"From where they launched their attack on our spacecraft."

"Somewhere in the Himalayas?" I didn't know the exact location of the attack.

My uncle nodded as his feet began to crunch on the pea-gravel drive again. "There's always been a darkness in the area that Atlantean agents can't penetrate."

Imee's ears perked up. "And why do you think they traveled there?"

"Because I put a tracer on young Ms. Harte. It disappeared at the edge of the suspected Lemurian stronghold."

"You did what?" *Why would you do that?* I couldn't believe it.

"Just like Dr. Larsen put a trace on Jamie, I put one on Rhea, just in case she was taken." *Actually, put a trace on you as well, but no reason to broadcast that to Imee. She's more than she seems.*

"And are you reading our minds as well?" Imee crunched her way past me on the pebbles to stand next to Uncle Merl. She grabbed his arm.

Uncle Merl stopped and looked down at Imee's hand on his arm. She looked him in the eye and then let go.

"Why no, that would be quite rude. AB, care to elaborate?" Despite the pea gravel, AB had crept up behind Imee without her knowledge.

Imee turned, bumping into him. She took a step back. AB stepped in front of her, mere inches away. She pushed him, but he didn't budge. She stepped back again. He stepped forward again.

Imee looked at me. "What's he doing?"

I shook my head. I had no clue. *What're you doing?*

*Making a point.* AB gave Imee a massive grin filled with canines. "Makes you uncomfortable when I crowd your personal space, doesn't it?"

"Damn right." Imee stood, feet split apart, with her knees slightly bent. She looked like a snake ready to strike.

"So why would I—" he looked over at Uncle Merl "—*we* do something even more intrusive like read your thoughts without your permission?"

Uncle Merl smiled. "As I said, quite rude. It's just not done."

Imee took a breath, her stance relaxing. "I understand. It just makes me uncomfortable that all three of you could do it if you wanted."

Uncle Merl nodded. "Clearly. But Charlie can't read your mind."

She looked over at me. "But he did when we were pulling Jamie up out of the cave."

I nodded. "I could. Clearly. But she couldn't hear my answers."

Uncle Merl scratched his head. "Emergency exception. Younglings at courting ages typically can't communicate via telepathy because it could ruin procreation. It's instinctive. I guess, given the emergency, neither of you had any prurient thoughts coursing through your minds and, as a result, the block on inter-sex telepathy lifted." Uncle Merl nodded to me. "Go ahead, Charlie, try and read Ms. Castillo's thoughts."

Imee nodded. "Go ahead. I'm expecting it."

I shrugged, looked over at Imee and sent a tendril of thought toward her. It seemed to stop just short of her. I tried harder, willing the tendril to push forward, into Imee's head. I began to break out into a sweat. I pushed hard, breaking through whatever had blocked me. Rather than clear thought, I got a jumble of fleeting, meaningless images. I broke the link and took a deep breath.

I shook my head. "I can't do it now, even with your permission."

Uncle Merl nodded. "Hard to beat evolution. Something that I once said to an old student of mine. Name was Derwin I believe."

Imee looked shocked. I couldn't believe that my uncle would make a slip about his true age to anyone.

AB patted Uncle Merl on the back and laughed out loud. "Good one, Dr. Ambrose, but these two are way too young to remember *Bewitched.*"

Both of us looked blankly at AB. "Derwin. That's what Endora called her son-in-law, Darren."

It still didn't mean anything to us, but Uncle Merl let loose with a grin. When neither of us smiled back. He shook his head and mumbled something under his breath.

"Well, time to pack up and be on our way." He headed back into the castle.

# CHAPTER 39
## EXCALIBUR

Jamie sat eating a burger at the butcher's block in the kitchen when we got there.

Imee rushed over to him. "How're you doing?"

Jamie put down the burger. "Much better. Can't believe that I can already walk on my foot." He wore a boot on his injured foot. He stood and took a few steps around the kitchen, then sat back down. "I don't know what you did, Dr. Ambrose, but it's a miracle." He grabbed the burger and took another bite.

Uncle Merl nodded. "No miracle, just good old-fashioned science. Now, since you can walk, you should be good enough to rejoin us on our quest." Uncle Merl waved his hand in the air with an exaggerated flourish and a holographic screen materialized at the end of the table. A map of India and Nepal appeared in the hologram. Uncle Merl picked up a laser pointer. "The attack on us originated from the Uttarakhand state of India, somewhere in the Himalayas near Nepal." He pointed the laser at the area on the map. A rough circle encompassing a small corner of the map right on the boarder darkened.

AB snarled. "Yeti country."

Uncle Merl nodded. "Somewhere in that area is a Lemurian enclave. Now I happen to have an old friend that lives in the foothills of the Himalayas, not too far from there. He's expecting us."

"Are we taking the Atlantean saucer?" I asked.

"Yes, but we can't get too close to the shaded area. We'll land just outside the area and meet my friend."

"And what do we do once we get there? Do you have a plan for getting into the Lemurian enclave?" Imee grabbed a Coke out of the fridge and started pacing.

"I've got a few ideas, but want to talk with my friend about them. He's been watching them for quite some time." Uncle Merl was never one to show his cards.

"What if AB dyes his hair white and goes in as a Yeti?" The idea just popped into my head.

AB gave me a glare and bared his canines, but Uncle Merl chuckled disarmingly. "Not a bad idea at that, Charlie. AB would look great in white."

AB scowled. "What about the smell. I do NOT smell like a yeti."

"I'm sure we could fix that." I was glad that Uncle Merl said that rather than me.

AB pushed back from the table. "I've lost my appetite."

"Good, I thought you were going to eat me out of house and home, just like you did when you were a student. That's why I graduated you early. Couldn't afford to feed you."

Imee continued to pace. "Jokes aside, do you have a plan? I have access to resources."

Uncle Merl raised an eyebrow, while Jamie and I looked over at Imee. "So, Ms. Castillo, I've known for some time that there's more to you than meets the eye. Care to share?"

Imee gave Jamie and I a furtive look. "Forrestal Security hired me out of Cal Tech to work on the DeMarco security detail. Richard's profile indicated that he had an interest in passive exotic girls, especially oriental. I fit the bill, at least as to exotic. I was young enough to get away with being a high school senior, so they recruited me. As to passive, they provided me with tapes of Richard when he was in high school in New Jersey. I watched how he interacted with girls and learned what he liked in a girlfriend."

"You're damn good at acting like a ditz. You had Rhea fooled. And you were her best friend!" I shook my head.

"Look, I like Rhea and really do care for Richard, but I had—have—a job to do." Imee crossed her arms.

"And to think that I was pissed when you went for Richard instead of me." Jamie stepped closer to Imee. "At least now I know it wasn't me."

Imee smiled at Jamie. "I do like you . . . " She left a silent "but" hanging in the air.

"And Richard! I never knew he lived in such a fishbowl. No wonder he's an ass at times." I looked over at Imee. "So how can you help us recover Rhea, Richard and the scepter?"

"With Richard missing, I have the total resources of Forrestal Security to back me up. I can get a team of former special ops professionals to any location in the world with forty-eight hours' notice." Imee looked around the room.

Uncle Merl shook his head. "Not sure whether that'll help with what we're facing. By the way, have you said anything to your team about Atlantis or"—nodding his head toward me—"Charlie's quest?"

Imee shook her head. "Are you kidding? They'd think I was effing nuts." She looked around. "Look, I didn't believe any of it until Trolga rode into the cave on the back of that huge hammerhead. I thought the whole quest was a nice distraction and a bit of a fantasy." She glanced over at me quickly and then back at Uncle Merl.

"Do you mind if I verify what you're saying?" Uncle Merl locked his eyes onto Imee's.

She met his gaze. "You mean read my mind? Isn't that kind of like rape?"

Uncle Merl shook his head. "There's a difference. I'm asking."

Imee nodded. She glanced around the room. I gave her a half-hearted smile.

"Ok. Will I feel anything?" She turned her palms up.

Uncle Merl shook his head. "No, but it will be easier if you relax and think about what we're doing."

Imee nodded. I took a deep breath, closed my eyes and focused. I could see the auras of those around me. A bright blue light roughly the shape of a man stood where Uncle Merl was. A tendril of white shot out from the center of the blue light and hovered around the pale green light hovering where Imee stood. The tendril seemed to caress the pale green light, which brightened slightly. I didn't pick up any thoughts from either Uncle Merl or Imee.

*AB, do you hear anything?* I projected a thought at AB.

*SHHH!* An image of a finger in front of AB's snarling mouth appeared in my head.

I opened my eyes. Imee was staring straight at Uncle Merl. Jamie watched while munching on a burger. AB shook his head at me.

It didn't take long. "Thank you, young lady." Uncle Merl turned to us. "It appears that Ms. Castillo is telling the truth." He looked intently at her. "Feel OK?"

Imee shrugged her shoulders. "Fine. Like you said, I didn't feel a thing."

Uncle Merl nodded. "You have a very disciplined mind for one so young."

"Thank you. Now that you've read my mind, what about I bring in the cavalry?"

Uncle Merl shook his head. "That would be a mistake. Not only would the Lemurians tear them apart, but the world isn't ready to learn about either the Lemurians or the Atlanteans. For the time being I have to ask you to keep that element of our quest secret."

Imee nodded. "I guess that you know that I'll keep your secret . . . unless it endangers Richard's life."

Uncle Merl nodded. "Despite having hidden your true purpose from those around you, I sense that you are an ethical person."

"Thank you."

"But why keep everything secret?" I looked up at Uncle Merl. *Tell me telepathically if you don't want the others to know.*

*Duh.* The thought resonated from AB.

*Now, AB, he's a mere child.*

Uncle Merl shook his head. "It's been a secret since the beginning of mankind for several reasons. The most obvious is that mankind isn't ready for Atlantean technology. Think about your quest to stop DeMarco from using the Atlantean device that wiped out Lemuria. What do you think the nations of the world would do with that kind of power?" Uncle Merl paced back and forth. "I've watched mankind grow for over a thousand years . . . "

I glanced over at Imee, as did Uncle Merl. Imee's eyes widened. "By the way, young lady, my age is confidential as well. A strict secret."

"Merl Ambrose." She tapped her index finger on her temple. "Merlin." She looked expectantly at Uncle Merl.

He shook his head. "Merlin's a myth. But some of the myth of Merlin is based on fact. One day, perhaps, I'll tell you my tale."

"And the sword?" She glanced in the direction of the courtyard and the pond.

He shook his head again. "No, that's not Excalibur. Excalibur's actually the Scepter of Apollymi."

"What?" Imee and I spoke at the same time.

Uncle Merl nodded. "Yes, I started to tell you before, Charlie, but we were interrupted. The scepter is a ZPEG—zero-point energy generator. While not a sword, it can appear as the wielder wishes. In the past it took on the form of a sword since that is what medieval humans could understand. If the wielder had sufficient Atlantean genes, he or she could focus some of the zero-point energy in the ZPEG. As a sword, Excalibur was invincible. Nobody, not even a Lemurian, could stand before it.

"But that's a story for another day. As I was explaining, *Homo sapiens* are not ready for Atlantean technology like the weapon in Antarctica and the ZPEG. Charlie, you've seen what it can do, but Ms. Castillo hasn't." Uncle Merl turned toward Imee. "If you were telepathic, I could send you a mental image, but, since you're not, envision a massive chunk of Antarctica being ripped away from the Earth. The seas would rush in, mega tsunamis would scour the coastlines, and massive volcanos would belch death and destruction around the globe. Few humans would survive, and those that did would end up in the hands of the Lemurians, living as slaves—or worse. And that's just one piece of Atlantean technology. No. Humans are not ready for such power." Uncle Merl stared off into the distance. He turned back to Imee.

"Even if they were, think about what people would do if they knew that they'd been manipulated—some would say bred—since the beginning of their existence. They would rage against the puppet masters. Eventually they'd find the remnants of the Atlanteans. And while the Lady and her kin could destroy mankind, they would destroy themselves before doing that. The same cannot be said about the few remaining Lemurians. They're already trying to decimate mankind so they can thwart the Atlantean plan and dominate the remnants of civilization. That's why we must stop them.

"There's much of which you're not aware. Perhaps, after we rescue Rhea and Richard, the Lady Galadriel will allow you to visit so you can learn more, but for now..."

"Galadriel? Like *Lord of the Rings*?" Jamie perked up at the name. "Damn, I thought they were Vulcans." Jamie eyed my ears.

I shook my head. "No, that's the name I thought of when I met her. She liked it and said that would be her name for this 'Age.'"

Jamie smiled. "Not a Vulcan and not an Elf. I wish Rhea were here."

At the name, a picture of Rhea appeared in my thoughts. She seemed to be struggling alone in a dark place. Dozens of glowing blood-red tendrils bound her.

I cried out. "Rhea!"

"What?" Uncle Merl was the first to respond.

"I saw her. In a dark place. She was being lashed by blood-red tendrils."

"Imagination?" Imee turned to Uncle Merl.

He shook his head, but looked at AB. AB also shook his head. "I saw the flash in Charlie's mind. It's real."

"How? Where is she?" I turned from AB to Uncle Merl.

"You're the one that had the vision. Think. Can you pull yourself back from where you saw her?" AB said.

"Wait." Uncle Merl grabbed my arm. "Don't go back to that vision."

"Why?"

"It could be a trap."

"But Rhea."

"And Richard." Imee chimed in.

"Like I said, I'm fairly certain I know where they were taken." He looked over at Jamie, who'd walked over to the fridge. "If you're all ready to go . . ."

Uncle Merl also walked over to the fridge and opened it. "Damn, no Snickers." He pulled out a Milky Way.

Imee eyed it.

He grabbed another and flipped it to Imee. "Have one." He flipped one to me as well. "If we're going to the Himalayas, you should eat now."

AB started to growl, but Uncle Merl pulled out the whole box and threw it. AB caught it in one hand. "What, I'm not a pig. Three or four would have sufficed."

"Good. Now we can get underway."

# CHAPTER 40
## OVER THE KHYBER PASS

The trip on the Atlantean saucer was uneventful. Imee tried to press Uncle Merl on his plan, but with little success. He said he had to focus on flying to avoid aircraft and satellites. I worried about crossing over Russia, but Uncle Merl assured me that the Atlantean craft would be invisible to the Russians. As we crossed over the Caspian Sea, Uncle Merl slowed the ship and began to descend.

"What about the Americans in Afghanistan, or the Pakistanis?" Imee looked down as we rapidly approached white-capped mountains.

"Don't worry about it. I'm only concerned about the Lemurians picking us up. If we fly in low enough over Afghanistan and Pakistan, the mountains will shield us."

Jamie and I watched as we descended into the mountains.

Imee pointed. "That's the Hindu Kush range. The Afghans have used it for centuries. It looks like Dr. Ambrose is going to bring us in along the ancient Khyber Pass."

"Smart girl. Surprised you recognized it from the air." Uncle Merl kept his eyes on the holographically displayed instruments in front of him.

The craft slowed rapidly, and the scene below us moved along as if we were in a helicopter.

"Why so slow? Won't that let them see us?" Jamie pointed down at a caravan of trucks chugging through the Khyber Pass.

Uncle Merl looked over at me. "Why don't you answer, Charlie?"

Not sure whether Uncle Merl was too focused to answer or testing me, I thought for a minute. Imee smiled. She seemed to know the answer. Jamie crossed his arms and gave me the look he'd often given me in class when a teacher asked a tough question. "Well . . ." I looked at the hologram of the Khyber Pass road below us. "We're invisible to the naked eye and to radar, so they won't see us . . ." Then it came to me. "But if we travel too fast we'd make noise and potentially create wind. That might be noticed. After the Afghan wars, people are very leery of things flying over them."

"Correct, young man. You at least paid attention in some of your classes." Uncle Merl leaned back, put his hands together and popped his knuckles. "Even at this speed, we should be landing near Haldwani very soon."

I looked down at the road. We appeared to be skimming very close to the surface. "Why aren't you flying us. It looks like we're very close to the surface."

Uncle Merl nodded. "We are, but the auto pilot can easily handle that. I've programed her to keep us about fifty feet about the surface. That should keep us below any line of sight from the Lemurians."

As I watched the craft dip and lift rapidly with the terrain, I was very glad for the inertial dampeners. Just watching the rapid motion made me feel a bit queasy.

Imee surveyed the map in front of us. "Haldwani's about fifty miles from the edge of the dark area you showed us in Scotland."

Uncle Merl nodded. "Wish I could get closer and even land at my friend's temple, but the Lemurians are probably keeping an eye on it. We'll be taking ground transportation. In fact, go get your stuff together so we'll be ready when we land." He looked down at an old analogue watch he always wore. "Be back here in ten minutes."

We all took off. My compartment was not too far from the control room. As I approached, a door magically appeared in the wall and slid open. I looked over my shoulder at Jamie. A neon light showed him the location of his compartment. A door appeared and opened for him as well.

I knew that the ship would respond to my thoughts, but wasn't sure how Jamie and Imee would get the ship's attention. I thought *backpack*, and a drawer slid seamlessly out of the wall. I lifted my backpack out and opened it. My mother's journal sat on the top. I slid it to one side. I still had the peanut butter from the Moon. Not a bad idea to take it given where we were headed. I also had my perfect-game ball, a picture of me and my parents, and the Atlantean teaching device. I focused on it and it floated right out of the backpack. I didn't know whether I'd managed to levitate it or whether it did that on its own when activated. At my thought, a comfortable green shag rug appeared below me. I lowered myself down, sat, and closed my eyes. I focused on the teaching device. My mind seemed to meld with it. The entire ship came alive in my mind. I could practically feel its systems as if it were part of my body. I laughed as we floated up and down over the Indian landscape.

Uncle Merl was right; we were close to our landing area. I extended myself forward, in front of our path. A bright light glowed from a location to our northeast. Our destination. The light appeared too similar to Uncle Merl's aura to be anything else. As we approached, I noticed a null area beyond the light. The area wasn't exactly dark. Rather it was like a void in the middle of the landscape. My mind couldn't fathom what it was. I extended myself toward it when I felt a presence beside me.

*Don't!* AB said. His fur sparkled in radiant light.

I looked up at him. *Why?*

*Because they might detect your thoughts. Our only real hope is that they believe you died in the grotto in the Bahamas.*

I pulled back from the vision and returned to my body. Surprisingly, AB was not in my compartment. *AB?* With the help of the educator, I reached out a tendril of thought. AB stood behind my uncle in the control room.

*Come on back, Charlie. About time to land.*

I looked at the hologram in front of my uncle and AB. We were slowing rapidly. I picked the educator out of the air and laid it gently in my backpack. I then exited and headed for the control room. I was the last to get there.

We hovered over a riverbed. A road paralleled the river. "What're we doing?"

Imee answered without looking back at me. "Looking for a place to set down where the ship can be hidden."

The ship drifted slowly to the west over the road. "There." Imee pointed. It looked as if a fire had cleared several acres of trees just over a hill from the road.

"Good eyes." Uncle Merl shifted the ship in that direction. "We won't be visible from the road, and we'll still be close enough to pick up our ride." He angled the ship downward and it settled onto the ground.

"Ok." Uncle Merl stood up. "Ready to catch our ride?"

Everyone nodded.

"Did you contact them by telepathy?" Imee focused on Uncle Merl.

He chuckled. "Texted the old-fashioned way, young lady. Telepathy is not to be trifled with." Uncle Merl glance my way and then headed for the exit. We followed.

The ship had landed in the middle of the burned-out field. When we got to the edge of the trees, we looked back. The ship didn't so much as vanish as blend into the landscaping. A hill covered with dust and rocks sat where the ship had been moments before.

"The Atlanteans are better at camouflage than we are." AB whistled. We heard a crunch of leaves as Uncle Merl entered the woods. He signaled for us to follow. "Our ride will be picking us up in about twenty minutes. I'd like to get at least a mile further up the road if we can."

He set off at a solid clip for an old man. I guess all those years studying with the Druids had given him a knowledge of the forest that none of us would ever have, except perhaps AB. Despite her prior awkwardness, Imee moved with the grace of a gazelle, casually leaping branches and downed trees, while barely making a sound. Jamie and I had to keep our eyes down to avoid tripping. I stayed with Jamie, looking down at the boot on his foot, but he seemed to be moving well. My uncle paused for a minute and looked back, as if he'd just remembered Jamie's condition. Satisfied at our progress, he continued at a slightly slower pace.

I looked around and didn't see AB. *AB, where are you?* I attempted to whisper.

*Scouting. No telepathy unless absolutely necessary.* His thoughts cut off abruptly.

Made sense. AB could move quickly and quietly in the forest while remaining camouflaged.

One short hill remained before we'd make it to the road. Uncle Merl paused again. Imee was right next to him, with me and Jamie lagging a bit. Jamie breathed heavily.

"You ok?" I grabbed Jamie's arm.

He nodded. "Yep, just a bit winded. Still don't have my Earth legs back."

Uncle Merl turned to us and held up a finger in front of his lips. We could hear birds chirping. Leaves rustled to our left. I thought it was AB, but it turned out to be what looked like a huge chipmunk with a bushy tail and black-and-white stripes down its back. A shadow dropped out of the sky and picked up the creature in a pair of large talons. It kept going without hesitation.

AB appeared from behind a tree as the raptor swooped away with its prey. "Man, that was cool. Did you see that falcon pluck that squirrel up in a heartbeat?"

AB nodded at Uncle Merl. "All clear. Nobody near us and nobody approaching the road." He took off toward the road and we followed.

"So, was that a merlin falcon?" Imee asked.

Uncle Merl shook his head. "It was a falcon, but not the graceful merlin falcon. They don't live in this area. That looked like an Amur falcon."

Imee nodded.

We followed AB up a short hill and then back down again. The road appeared in front of us.

Uncle Merl paused. "There's a fairly clear path along this side of the road. Let's stay on it so we remain somewhat under cover. AB, lead the way."

AB shrugged his shoulders and took the lead.

After trudging through the woods, the path, covered in pine needles, seemed relatively easy. I wasn't sure of the local time, but it seemed to be getting darker. After about half an hour we reached the parking lot of a small gas station. A small bench with a plastic blue overhang sat to one side of the lot. Uncle Merl walked right to it and took a seat.

"Anyone else need a seat?" Uncle Merl focused on Jamie.

Jamie took a seat and sucked in a breath.

"How's your foot feeling?" Uncle Merl asked.

"It doesn't really hurt." Jamie reached down and touched the boot.

Uncle Merl nodded. "Good. Our ride'll be along momentarily."

Uncle Merl took a deep breath. The sun was settling behind the hills. "Ah, here we are."

An old turquoise lorry chugged into the parking lot. It backfired as it came to a stop in front of us. As it neared I noticed that some of the turquoise paint had flaked off its hood, revealing a mustard-yellow undercoat.

Before I could say "That's our ride." a young lady in blue jeans and a checkered lumberjack shirt jumped out of the driver's seat. She pulled off a dusty old fedora, shook her hair, and threw the hat onto the front seat of the truck. She walked over to Uncle Merl with a business-like stride and extended her hand.

"Dr. Ambrose, I presume."

Uncle Merl took her hand and shook it. "You have me at a disadvantage."

"Sorry. Name's Kyra Anand. I work with Saddhu Vidya Sidon at the monastery." She looked around at us. "Shall we go?" Her English had a distinct British flavor.

Uncle Merl nodded. Kyra walked to the back of the truck, opened the tailgate, pulled the flap of canvas to one side and pulled out a step stool.

"Ladies first." Uncle Merl let Imee climb in.

I looked over at Kyra. "How about I ride up front with Ms. Anand?"

Uncle Merl shook his head. "Better for all of us to get in the back of the truck where prying eyes can't see us."

Jamie and AB had already climbed in. Uncle Merl followed and I climbed in after him. Kyra put the step stool back in the truck, closed the tailgate and pulled the canvas over the back.

I looked around as my eyes adjusted to the drop in light. A hard bench ran the length of one side of the truck, but nobody was sitting on it. Instead, AB had grabbed a light-blue beanbag chair, thrown it against the front of the truck and sat down. The others followed suit. I stood frozen for a minute, looking at Uncle Merl descend slowly into a beanbag chair. I heard a grinding noise, and the lorry jarred forward, knocking me onto the bench seat. AB threw me a beanbag chair.

"These are much more comfortable."

I threw it on the floor and sat down. My body sank into the chair. Rather than jarring turns and bumps, the chair translated the motion into a gentle rocking. Given the darkness and the rocking, my eyes grew heavy.

# CHAPTER 41
## BRAHMAPARUSH

N ext thing I knew the canvas at the back of the truck flew open. I blinked at the full moon shining in through the opening.

AB tapped me on the foot. "Wake up, sleepyhead."

The others were out of the beanbag chairs and Imee had already gotten out. Uncle Merl was right behind her. AB stuck out his huge hand and yanked me out of the chair.

"Hey, you almost pulled my shoulder out of joint." I rubbed my shoulder mockingly.

"Sorry. I forget how frail you *Homo sapiens* are." AB jumped out of the truck, bumping his head on the metal frame for the canvas.

I jumped down, laughing.

"Watch yourself, young whelp." AB rubbed his head.

"Come on, you two. We've got a meeting with my old friend, Vidya." Uncle Merl turned to Kyra. "Ready?"

"Yes, sir. Please follow me." Gravel crunched under Kyra's boots as she walked through the courtyard. "And be silent. Many of the monks are in meditation."

I looked around as we walked. The walls of the structure were painted a muted pink. Two large wooden doors opened in front of us. Monks dressed in orange stood at either side of the door. They bowed as we walked through. Kyra led us up a hill through several gardens. I detected a savory smell in the air. I wanted to ask about it, but remembered Kyra's request. I looked over at AB. He clearly smelled it as well. He looked at me and rubbed his stomach.

We passed through several more gates and finally reached a lonely little stone cottage nestled in the middle of a garden. The moon shone above it. Kyra knocked gently on the door, opened it and motioned for us to enter. Uncle Merl entered first. We followed. The only source of light emanated from the fireplace, causing shadows to dance around the room as the flames flickered. The room contained little furniture. A bed roll sat in one corner, while a short round table with no chairs sat in the middle of the room. A tea cup and a bowl sat at each of six spots on the table.

A shriveled old man dressed in a saffron-colored robe sat in one corner of the room. Uncle Merl nodded to him, even though he had his eyes closed. Uncle Merl signaled us to sit at the table. He folded his legs in the lotus position and sat. I looked over at AB, but he didn't blink. He did the same, his knees barely fitting under the table. I sat and merely crossed my legs in front of me. Imee sat to my left and Jamie to my right. Kyra brought a pillow and laid it under the table for Jamie.

"Please, put your leg up on this. Dr. Ambrose apprised us of your recent injury."

Jamie nodded. "Th-th-thank you." He stuttered a bit.

He couldn't keep his eyes off Kyra. He'd always liked the exotic-looking girls on the Moon, Imee being one of them. She took no notice of his attention. Rather, she went over to the fireplace and pulled an iron kettle from the fire.

Without asking, she poured tea for everyone. I looked over at Saddhu Vidya Sidon, waiting to see if he would join us. His eyes stayed shut. He seemed oblivious to our presence.

Uncle Merl picked up the cup, sniffed at it deeply and took a sip. "Vidya, your ginger Darjeeling is excellent as usual. Are you going to join us for a cup?"

The saddhu did not answer.

AB and Imee both lifted their cups and drank as well. "Quite good. A spot of tea always helps my digestion," AB said with a perfect British accent.

I lifted my cup and sniffed at it. I'd never liked tea, but it actually smelled quite good, like ginger, orange and some herbal scent I couldn't place. I took a tentative sip. It did taste good and gave me a soothing feeling.

Kyra replaced the tea pot on the iron in the fire and pulled out a large caldron. She stirred the cauldron and I detected the smell of herbs, but no meats. She ladled some into a wooden serving bucket. I took another sip of tea. The saddhu remained motionless in one corner. Jamie and Imee seemed happy sipping their tea, as did my uncle. AB watched Kyra closely as she ladled the stew in the serving bucket. Just like AB: always hungry.

Kyra seemed to intuitively notice that as she served AB first. He also seemed to have a larger bowl. As usual, he didn't wait for everyone to be served but just dug in. Kyra efficiently filled everyone's bowls and then returned the bucket next to the fireplace.

Uncle Merl picked up his spoon, looked around the room and said, "Dig in. Vidya's stew is excellent."

I didn't know why everyone was so quiet, but they all started eating. I picked up my spoon and did as well. The stew tasted savory, with a slight hint of curry. I identified potatoes, carrots and onions, but I didn't see any meat in the stew.

I looked over at AB. No meat . . .

AB gave me a mental *Shhh*, nodding his head over at the saddhu.

Everyone stayed abnormally quiet. I began to feel quite relaxed and lighter, as if I were back on the Moon. I wanted to speak, but my lips seemed frozen. My eyes widened, but both Uncle Merl and AB gave me a reassuring look. I tried to relax, but when I looked over at Jamie and Imee, both of them were yawning. Jamie laid his head down on his arms and seemed to nod off. Imee seemed startled and tried to get up, but Kyra went over to her and supported her as she too collapsed on the table.

I thought about standing up, but I seemed almost weightless now. Light began to grow in the room. It seemed to be coming from the saddhu. Light seemed to be burning through his skin. Suddenly it burst through the red spot on his forehead. The skin on his forehead seemed to split and separate. It tore in both directions, up into his sparse grey hair, and down past his nose and chin to his neck.

A dim light that I somehow knew was Kyra walked over, pushed down on the skin, and it all peeled off and fell back. The light drifted out of the corner and took shape in front of me. A young man in his twenties appeared to hover before us in the lotus position

"Welcome, young Charlemagne. I am Vidya Sidon." The man lowered to the floor next to Uncle Merl.

I glanced over at Uncle Merl, who merely sipped his tea. "A pleasure to meet you, sir." I glanced over at my friends.

He shook his head as Kyra poured him a tea. "No worries. They're fine. They just succumbed to the tea."

I looked down at the tea and peered at him quizzically. "But . . ."

"Yes, yes, I forget how young you really are. You, your uncle and your large hairy friend . . ."

AB let out a brief snarl, but then smiled and signaled Kyra for more stew.

". . . did not fall asleep because the harmless agent in the tea merely affects humans and Lemurians. I serve it to all my guests because that devil, Rusha, has attempted to infiltrate this temple several times. While I have known your uncle for centuries, Rusha has gotten quite good at glamours. This tea would have put any Lemurian agent to sleep."

I thought about Trolga, picturing her with a beak like a griffon.

"I don't mean to be rude, but your thoughts leaked out. I believe that I have met the creature. Like most Lemurian constructs, a bastardization, this time of Garuda." The saddhu looked over at Uncle Merl. "He lacks training."

"Dear Vidya, I'd like nothing more than to leave him here with you for a decade or two, but, unfortunately, I cannot. While he only recently awakened to his heritage and is a mere teenager, the Lady placed a task at his feet that he must accomplish. Perhaps once that is over . . ."

My mouth dropped open at the thought of spending a decade in this temple with the saddhu.

The saddhu nodded. "I did not realize he was quite so young. His aura and his access to the aether belie his age."

Uncle Merl nodded. "Yes, he is genetically almost pure Atlantean. The Lemurians discovered this and accelerated their plans."

"So, you have to go to Rusha's lair?"

Uncle Merl nodded. "Without going into too many details, yes. Not only have they taken something that concerns the Lady, but they've also taken several of Charlie's friends."

The saddhu rubbed his chin and seemed to levitate off the floor. "Quite the quandary. Do your young friends and the most noble sasquatch understand what they are up against?"

AB smiled at the saddhu's words, but then seemed to have some doubts. "She is protected by—" AB spat into the fireplace "—yetis. They know that much."

The saddhu looked over at me. "So, you've met Rusha's minion, the one you call Trolga, and you've run across yetis, but you still want to proceed." His eyes bored into me.

I crossed my arms and met his stare. "Yes, sir. They've got Rhea and Richard, and they stole the Scepter of Apollymi from me. I've got to."

He continued to stare at me. "Do you mind if I read your thoughts?"

I nodded. A tendril of light seemed to drift from his belly toward me. It touched my belly button. While I could tell when AB and Uncle Merl entered my thoughts, I didn't even sense his presence.

The saddhu took in a deep breath and the tendril receded. He looked over at Uncle Merl. "Is this true that they've taken the key to Atlantean technology?"

Uncle Merl nodded. "I'm afraid so."

The saddhu nodded. "Young man, despite your promise to the Lady, you don't have to do this. And doing it for young love is not a reason to face Rusha."

I started to respond, but he stopped me.

"Let me tell you about Rusha before you commit to go any farther." He took another deep breath. "Rusha is a Lemurian. How she survived the cataclysm that destroyed both Lemuria and Atlantis, I do not know, but she has been here since the time of legend, before true historical records. When I was young my parents told me stories of the brahmaparush that lived in an ancient temple in the mountains. They would swarm out at night, violently attacking any poor victims they might run across. They would bite a victim's neck and suck all the blood out, then, once the body was drained of blood, they would crush the skulls and eat the brains. Finally, they would rip the intestines out of their victims and use them as necklaces as they danced around the desiccated corpses. The stories scared the hell out of me and my younger sister.

"Rusha was the worst of them; their queen. Her stronghold was rumored to be a week's travel to the east by oxcart. Travelers from the east told stories to the elders of our village of Rusha, and how villages had to pay tribute to her in the form of cattle and teenage children at least once a year or face her wrath. Most villages heeded. Once the children left, they never returned. But travelers told stories of deserted villages with streets littered with bones.

"I thought that perhaps Rusha and Kali were the same. I said as much to my father, but he explained that Kali was a goddess that lived in myths and legend, but that Rusha was real. I made the mistake of laughing, and he took up a switch and beat me with it.

"When I turned sixteen years old, I learned far more about Rusha than I wanted. A runner came from the largest town in the region. While my father sent me home, I snuck out and hid behind our chief's house to listen in. Rusha's minions had come to the town to demand that the entire region start providing tribute to Rusha. The town was many times larger than our village and held sway over a dozen villages our size. The chieftain had four beautiful teenage daughters. Rusha had demanded that two of them be surrendered by the next full moon or she would release her brahmaparush on the entire region.

"The messenger said that each village would be required to make a proportional sacrifice to Rusha, and that her minions would be by within a fortnight to collect the sacrifice from each village. That caused a stir among the village elders, including my father.

"Despite the rumor that there was no way to defeat a brahmaparusha, the messenger relayed that the chieftain had decided to fight. He'd pledged one of his daughters to a wealthy maharaja to the south, who promised both wealth and an alliance. What Rusha asked would ruin that alliance.

"My father did ask whether the maharaja would send troops to support us, but the messenger shook his head. The chieftain wanted to prove his worth to the maharaja. Plans were made for our men to join with those of the town and the other villages to assault Rusha's temple.

"I snuck home. When I awoke, my father had our family talwar lying on a table, using a whet stone to sharpen it. While it had a simple hilt and sheath, its blade was well known and had been passed down for generations. My father noticed me looking. I asked to join in and looked up at the parashu on the wall. He shook his head, explaining that, were he to fail, I would need to take care of my mother and sister. He did get the parashu down and threw it to me. I caught it, but the blade clanked against the floor. It was much heavier than I thought."

The saddhu paused briefly in his tale and looked up at the wall over the hearth. An old curved saber was mounted above it.

"That's the talwar?" I asked.

He nodded.

AB got up to take a closer look.

Uncle Merl grabbed his arm. "Let Vidya finish. Time is short." He looked over at the saddhu and raised an eyebrow.

The saddhu gave him a subtle nod.

"Yes, yes. I rarely get to tell this tale. Be patient. Now, I was about to join the battle, but my father talked me out of it.

"Less than a week passed, and the men of my village were practicing with their arms. It was late in the afternoon and they were set to leave the next day. A man flew into town on horseback. He jumped off, out of breath, and ran to the chieftain's house. My father ran over as well. He returned half an hour later, looking pale. My mother asked what had happened. He didn't mince words, despite me and my sister being in the room. Rusha and her minions had attacked the town. None survived. Rusha was making an example that she must be obeyed. She was rumored to be on the way to our village.

"My father instructed us to pack up and leave immediately. He would stay to defend the village. My mother shrieked and pleaded with him to go as well. The conversation was for naught. As they argued, a wailing sound came from the edge of the village. We rushed out the door.

"Dark shapes ran through the village. One grabbed my neighbor's child. It lifted her up and bit her neck, then dropped her to the ground and emitted a hideous shriek. My neighbor rushed him with a parashu raised over his head. The creature laughed, sidestepped the blow and grabbed my neighbor. My neighbor was the village blacksmith and a big man, but the creature lifted him by the neck with one hand. He sank his teeth into my neighbor's neck. His legs kicked violently. After a brief time, the legs stopped kicking, and the creature dropped the dead husk to the ground. The wind shifted, and the scent of blood filled the air, almost making me gag. We were petrified into silence.

The creature stepped on our neighbor's head, crushing it. A scream pierced the silence. I looked over at my sister. It had come from her.

"The creature saw us and smiled, blood dripping from its fang-like teeth. It loped toward us on all fours. My father stepped forward, unsheathing the talwar. I stepped up next to him, but he pushed me back. In no time, the creature was upon us. It leapt, ignoring the sword in my father's hand. With speed that was barely visible, my father sidestepped and struck. The creature tried to dodge, but my father's blade caught its arm, slicing it right off. The brahmaparusha howled, but rolled and got up. This time it approached warily. It feinted to the left and then lunged, knocking my father to the ground. My mother rushed forward, screaming. She pulled at the creature. Her screams released me from my paralysis. I jumped in, yanking the creature off my father.

"It was dead. My father's sword had killed it, but not before it had ripped my father's throat open. I took the sword from my father's hand and yanked it out of the corpse of the creature. It tingled in my hand. I looked around. Three of the creatures circled us warily. A burst of energy shot through me as I tightened my grip on the sword. It seemed to be glowing. I looked over at the creatures. A blood-red haze of light pulsed around them.

"The first charged me. My mother screamed. The sword danced in my hand. The creature, severed in two, lay at my feet. I had no clue what I'd done, but it felt natural. The other two creatures continued to circle me. I kept the blade between them and my mother and sister. I expected them to charge, but they backed away slowly. I thought that was the end, but a brilliant blood-red light appeared at the end of the road into the village. As it approached, I could see a creature within the glow. At a distance, it appeared like a human female. As it approached, I could see it was naked, with supple breasts and a fine downy pelt between its legs.

"She stopped about ten paces from me. I heard a voice in my head: *Let go of the sword and come to me.* She opened her arms as she approached, gesturing with her hands for me to accept her embrace.

"The sword inadvertently lowered in my hand. I couldn't help myself. I took one step forward, then another. She was beauty incarnate. I hungered for her. The tip of the sword dragged on the ground as I slowly moved forward.

"A scream erupted behind me, tearing me from the siren's trance. I looked back. A creature had grabbed my sister and was attempting to drag her away. My mother beat at it with her fists. I lifted the sword, ready to lunge at the creature. I didn't get the chance. The female siren moved faster than possible, grabbed the creature, and ripped its head off.

"She then threw my sister back at me. Now I could see her for herself. She looked more like a naked shrew than a woman, shriveled, with leathery skin and large growths all over her. She wore a necklace of skulls and a crown of interwoven finger bones. She opened her mouth, which was filled with dagger-like teeth.

"As she stood there, she eyed me warily, like a pit viper. The villagers began to stream out of their huts and houses. They walked as if in a trance, passing right by her. She struck like lightning, grabbing a friend of my sister's from the column, picking her up and biting her neck, then discarding her to the side of the road. My sister moved forward, but I grabbed her.

"The queen of the brahmaparusha laughed. I heard her in my head again: *I leave you with your mother and sister, but come after me and they will more than die.* She then turned and left. That was Rusha."

The saddhu lifted a cup of tea and took a sip.

I waited, anticipating a finish to his story, but, evidently, he was finished.

"But why'd she let you and your family live?"

"Because she's a coward," Uncle Merl answered. "Near immortality can do that."

I nodded. "So what happened after that, Saddhu?"

He didn't answer, merely nodded to Uncle Merl.

"I happened to be traveling in India at the time. When I heard the tale, I came to Vidya and took him, his mother and sister to safety, far away from Rusha and her minions. While she might not risk herself, she would risk her minions, trying to kill off Vidya and his line since they posed a risk to her."

"What risk?" I asked. Uncle Merl appeared disappointed.

AB came to my rescue. "The Saddhu Vidya Sidon is genetically very much like you. Atlantean genes dominate his human genes. As such, he could resist Rusha and her compulsions. Your uncle took him back to Scotland and trained him. In fact, he arrived just before my grandfather departed."

"Your grandfather?" I looked from AB to the saddhu.

The saddhu gave AB a subtle nod. "Yes, young cousin. I learned of the sasquatch race and their role as protectors of the Atlanteans many years ago from your uncle. I chose to return and keep Rusha in check to the best of my ability." His face darkened, and he looked over at Uncle Merl. "Her shadow is spreading. Others who have stayed hidden are starting to answer her call."

Uncle Merl nodded. I looked from one to the other. They both sat silently, seemingly lost in thought.

"So how old are you?" I asked.

The saddhu chuckled. "None have dared ask me that question. But it is time for me to fake my death again and be reincarnated in a young man's body." He pointed over at the husk in the corner. "Kyra, the great granddaughter of my sister, will help me." Kyra came forward and nodded to me. "Cousin."

"So, we're all related?" I looked over at Kyra and the saddhu. They had dark Indian skin and looked nothing like me.

The saddhu signaled Kyra. "It is time for the other tea." Kyra grabbed a pot and poured tea into each of our cups. "All humans are related, but we that are awake in this room all carry a dominant Atlantean gene. As such we are cousins."

I nodded and took a sip of the new tea. Energy flowed into me with the sip. I took another sip and looked over at Jamie and Imee. They had begun to stir.

"Yes, yes, it is time to tell you of my plan to get you into Rusha's stronghold." He paused. "That is, assuming you are still willing to go in there after my tale."

I nodded. "Of course. I have no choice."

Uncle Merl gave the saddhu a knowing "I told you so" nod.

I smiled. "What will my friends remember?"

"Nothing. They will awake refreshed, but will not remember having gone to sleep. As soon as they awaken, you will learn the plan."

# CHAPTER 42
## OUT OF THE FRYING PAN INTO THE FIRE

Our lorry bounced and bumped its way up the rocky road into the mountains. I never thought that I'd have fond memories of how much the Moon buggies had bounced on my field trip, but that was under one sixth Earth gravity. This was just as bad, but under full Earth gravity. Bone jarring. I wondered how AB, Imee and Jamie felt in back. At least they had sack chairs and didn't have to sit on the crates of food.

It had started getting cold as we climbed into the mountains and as the sun set. I was glad that the saddhu had gotten us hooded cloaks to wear. Not only would they serve to disguise us, but they were also quite warm.

I turned to Uncle Merl. "So, you think the plan will work?"

He kept his eye on the narrow mountain road. "We have a fighting chance. The element of surprise is on our side."

We crested a hill and the sun appeared behind us, illuminating the path ahead. The road switched back and forth up the mountain. Much of it remained in shadows. I could see a couple of other vehicles up ahead of us, but not many. Snow crowned the mountaintops ahead, but the road never got to the top. It must be leading to a pass further down.

Uncle Merl looked over at me. "Take a nap. When we get close, I'll wake you."

I was going to say I wasn't tired, but instead a yawn came out. I'd been up all night talking with Uncle Merl and the saddhu. I pulled my hood up and leaned against the window. The rocking of the lorry had me asleep before I knew it.

I awoke with a start as the lorry jerked to a halt. I looked around. We were back in shadows on the other side of the mountain. Snow carpeted the valley floor. Up ahead of us a small village was nestled between the road and a small creek. At the end of the valley, pushing up against the mountain, stood our destination—Rusha's temple. It was built right into the side of the mountain. Even at this distance you could tell it was ancient. Rounded towers rose out from the side of the mountain.

Uncle Merl opened the door and got out. I did as well. We walked to the rear of the lorry and flipped open the canvas cover. Imee and Jamie squinted at the morning light.

"Charlie?" Jamie asked.

"Who else?"

"Given what we've been through, I don't know. Darth Vader?"

Imee crawled out and Jamie followed.

Jamie stretched and looked around. "Hey, where's Chewbacca?"

I looked at Uncle Merl. He stared off at the village ahead.

"We changed the plans a bit while you were sleeping. AB got out and will join us later." Uncle Merl signaled us to walk around to the front of the truck.

He opened up the hood and pretended to look at the engine. "Now, the village is about five klicks in front of us, and the temple is another two klick beyond that, so we have a few minutes to review our plans before we go any farther.

"As planned, the oil line is cracked and leaking. We'll barely make it to the village. Of course, they won't be able to fix it so we'll have to spend the night. That bus that you see in front of us, turning into the village, is filled with pilgrims."

"Why would anyone come on a pilgrimage to see Rusha?" Jamie asked, and then looked over at Imee to see if she was going to elbow him.

"Now that's a good question." Imee looked up at Uncle Merl for an answer.

"We don't have time for a full answer, but some people are drawn to evil like moths to a flame. They've been around throughout history. To quote an old friend from many years ago: 'The mind is its own place, and in itself can make heaven of hell, a hell of heaven.'" He looked over at me expecting me to understand but shook his head. "Education has gone to pot these days. Too reliant on technology and no study of the classics. So you've never heard: 'Better to reign in Hell, than to serve in Heaven'?"

I looked at my iLet. No signal. I looked over at Imee and Jamie. They didn't have a signal either.

My uncle saw that and merely shook his head. "Well, assuming we survive, I may have to take a personal interest in your education.

"Now, those pilgrims are not nuts. They're not seeking death or servitude to a vampire like Rusha. Rather, they are some of the millions of poor and homeless that litter the streets of India's major cities. The evil worshipers are the ones that brought them here with promises of life in a mountain temple, breathing clean air and tending to the monks. Recruits come up monthly to satisfy Rusha and her minion's blood lust. Given the millions of poor and homeless, recruits are easy to find.

"Unfortunately, we can't focus on the plight of those poor people right now. We need to focus on Rhea, Richard and the Scepter of Apollymi. Now, do each of you have the pill that Vidya gave you?"

We all nodded. "Good. Take it before you go to bed tonight." Uncle Merl pulled some tape out of a pocket and put it on a leaky hose from the radiator. He handed the tape back to me. "Now, tape those knives that Vidya gave you to your legs. And do it carefully. You may be walking a long way."

I nodded, tore the tape and started taping the small blade to my leg just above the inside of my left ankle. I then handed the tape to Imee.

Uncle Merl stared at the village while we did that. He turned back to us. "Now that our reason for staying overnight is in place, back in the lorry. It's time to jump out of the frying pan and right into the fire."

# CHAPTER 43
## ZOMBIE ANTS

I slowly came out of a fog. My feet moved forward on their own. A line of young people stretched in front of me in single file. I tried to stop, but couldn't. My feet just kept moving, following the path. I tried to look around but my head wouldn't turn. I looked ahead. The first of the pilgrims had reached the entrance to the temple. Torches stood at the entrance. I couldn't look up but knew that the ornately carved stone above the door climbed upward into a spire.

I rotated my eyes downward. At least they were obeying my thoughts again. Thank goodness they hadn't changed my clothes. I was concerned that they might. I glanced to the side. My hood was up. That was good. It hid my face. Not that I expected anyone to be on the lookout for me.

I focused on my fingers, willing them to wiggle. It didn't work. I started to panic, but then took in several deep breaths. The saddhu had said that it would take some time for his drug to counteract the zombie drug that we'd ingested at dinner. But what if it didn't? Now that I was close enough I noticed that the guards at the gate were actually brahmapar . . . something. What the heck, Indian vampires. Their eyes glowed red, and they wore necklaces of bone. They seemed to be smiling. One grabbed a young woman out of the line, picked her up, bit her neck, sucking the poor thing's blood out, and then dropped the dead husk of a body to the ground. The zombie drug worked so well that the poor thing hadn't even struggled. I only hoped that she hadn't felt anything. I also thanked God that the zombie drug was still working enough to keep me from vomiting.

I heard a high-pitched squeal. The vampire cowered back against the wall. A huge yeti came out and pointed off into the distance. This must be one of those males that AB had described because it was at least ten feet tall. The vampire seemed to know it had done something wrong. It let out a wail and tried to push past the yeti, but the huge beast shoved it away. The vampire then started running toward the hills. It ran fast, faster than any man. It dodged back and forth, but to no avail. A shaft of light shot out of the temple, dropping the beast in its tracks. It must have violated some rule by taking the poor child. That gave me some cold comfort that we would all be safe—at least for a while.

My hands had balled into fists. I relaxed them, thankful that the zombie drug was wearing off. I only hoped that the yeti and the remaining vampire hadn't noticed, but they were looking at the smoking remains of the other vampire. I was almost to the gate. Hideous carvings of what I hoped were mythical creatures covered the arched gate and continued up the spire above it. As I walked through the gate, one of the carvings was clearly a vampire. I shuddered, thinking that perhaps all of the creatures were real somewhere.

I could now wiggle my toes. I tested myself, shortening one step. I had motor control back! More yetis and vampires dotted the courtyard beyond the gate. What a nightmare! I carefully followed in line behind the others. We walked across the courtyard and then down some stone steps through a door under the next building. It became dark, and I feared that I would misstep. Fortunately, the floor was smooth and the corridor straight. My eyes adjusted as a light appeared off in the distance. We walked down a stone corridor for a long time. I thought about counting steps, but it was too late for that. We'd already traveled for at least ten minutes. I started hearing weeping and yelling in front of me. We were coming up on a turn. That might give me a chance to look behind me. As we rounded the turn, I didn't see any guards of any type in front of me so I took a risk and swiveled my head to look behind me. A young man with a blank stare was right behind me. I searched for Imee and Jamie, hoping they hadn't had their clothes changed either. There, ten people back, was Imee. And Jamie was just two people behind her!

I swiveled my head back around, with a smile on my face. Good timing. I wiped the grin off my face as a yeti appeared twenty feet in front of me. Luck was with me again since its head had been turned away from me. In these close quarters it sure did smell. This one was probably a female because it was no larger than AB.

The wailing grew louder. As we rounded another corner, we started to pass closed and locked wooden doors on both sides of the corridor. We passed several corridors but kept moving straight ahead. I wondered how the zombies knew which way to go. The macabre conga line finally turned down a side corridor. I followed in my place. When they reached the end, people were turning into doors held open by a small man. As the room filled, the man would signal the next person to stop. He would then close the door and open the next cell, signaling for the next group to march in. I started to worry that Imee, Jamie and I would be in different cells, but when the line stopped with only one person in front of me, I was fairly confident that they would both make it to my cell.

I followed the person in front of me. They stopped at the wall in the back of the cell, turned and sat down. I did the same. The pilgrims filed in behind me. The cell wasn't that large and had started to fill up when Imee turned into the cell. Jamie came in and they shut the door behind him. He sat down as well. I waited until I didn't hear any more footsteps. Then I made my way to Imee and Jamie. They were both sitting, staring straight ahead.

I leaned down and whispered, "You guys ok?" Imee nodded. Jamie shook his head, and then nodded as well. I extended my hand to Imee, helping her up. We both then helped Jamie up. It seemed to be taking longer for him to get over the effects of the zombie drug.

"Let's get out of here before the rest of these poor people get over the effects of the drug." I glanced around the room. Everyone remained in a trance-like state.

Imee was up and over to the door. "It's locked." She looked through the window at the door across the corridor. It looked as if it had a simple latch mechanism. She tried to reach her hand through and grab the latch. "I can't reach it."

Jamie was just now getting back to himself. "So we're stuck?" His eyes widened.

"Not hardly," Imee said. She took her nanothread bracelet off, laid it on the ground and then pulled the knife out of the makeshift sheath she had created with the tape. She carefully worked the nanothread so it locked onto the knife.

"Why not just use the nanothread to cut through the bars?" I grabbed a bar and pulled on it. It seemed to be old metal. In fact, I might just be able to yank it out. I grabbed ahold and . . .

"Stop!" Imee stood up quickly.

"Why?"

"Because if we leave evidence of our escape, they'll start looking for us. We need to keep the element of surprise."

I nodded. Sometimes I surprised myself with my level of stupidity.

I guess Jamie noticed my look. "Don't take it too hard. I thought the same thing. Remember, Imee's a trained assassin." Jamie grinned at Imee.

Imee scowled and shook her head. She slid the knife through the bars and began rocking it back and forth.

"Assassin?" I looked over at Jamie, who was smiling.

"Well, she broke my heart." Jamie chuckled. At least his gallows humor was back.

We heard a click as the latch lifted. Imee pulled the door open. "Voilà." She bowed, signaling us to exit.

"Nice job, Lady Croft." Jamie looked up and down the corridor.

Imee ignored his comment. "Let's go." She didn't even wait for a reply. When she got to the end of our corridor, she held her hand up. We stopped. She looked both ways and then walked back down the corridor a few paces.

"Look," she whispered, "I've been trained for this sort of thing and you two haven't, so follow my lead. Watch for my hand signals. If I hold my hand up that means stop. My hand slicing in front of my throat means shut up—and quick. Now, let's put our hoods up. In case we're seen they may think that we're some of the servants that they must keep around."

"What about the yetis and the brahma— vampires?" Jamie asked. He reached down toward the knife at his ankle.

"I doubt that little knife will do much good, but our key to getting out alive is surprise. They won't expect anybody that doesn't belong here to be wandering around. The vampires aren't going to kill their servants."

"But the vampires and yetis are both telepathic. Won't they . . . "

Imee didn't let me finish. "Hopefully not. Every telepath I've met seems to avoid invading the thoughts of others. If they think we're servants, they'll ignore us. Just keep the hoods up, your heads bent down, and walk slowly."

"But what if—" Again, Imee didn't let me finish. "Let's not go there. If they take us we won't go down without a fight, and remember, your uncle's here somewhere. Now, let's stop wasting time and start looking for Richard and Rhea."

She walked to the edge of the corridor again and looked both ways. She turned left.

"Why left?" Jamie asked quietly.

Imee stopped and turned, her hands on her hips. "Because right is the way we came in. And keep quiet. If we alert any of the poor souls in the cells they may start making lots of noise. That'll bring guards and we don't want that to happen."

She walked down a dimly lit corridor. I looked around more than I had during the nightmarish zombie walk in. Cell doors spaced every fifty feet or so punctuated the corridor. While the original section of the corridor we'd entered was concrete, this section seemed to be dug out of rock. We must now be somewhere under the mountain.

Imee held up her hand as we came to an intersection. Our corridor continued forward, but the lights were even dimmer. Several low moans also seemed to be coming from somewhere down there. The cross-corridor seemed to have better lights. Nobody was coming from either direction. Imee turned left. After a few minutes our corridor ended with a large steel door with a metal mesh window. We crept up to it and Imee peeked through the window. She signaled for us to be quiet and put her hand on the handle. I held my breath. What if it were locked? We'd have to backtrack. The handle turned and Imee opened the door. She popped her head around the door and looked both ways. She signaled for us to follow.

This corridor appeared to be of concrete, not carved out of rock. The ceiling was also higher, with pipes running along it. It ran for over a hundred yards in both directions. Imee turned to the right. We followed. We passed several doors that looked normal rather than like cell doors. I heard voices behind one of the doors, but Imee continued on. We rounded the next corner and my heart caught in my chest. A yeti walked toward us, it's head just below the pipes. Imee kept going and I followed. I wanted to look back and check on Jamie, but didn't. As Imee had said, I kept my head low. Imee moved to one side and stopped as the yeti closed on us. It slowed as well. I held my breath, both from fear and to avoid the smell. It gave us a guttural grunt and then moved on.

After it turned a corner, Imee stopped and looked back. She smiled and wiped her hand against her head. She then turned and continued on. I started to wonder where she was going when a person dressed somewhat like us, wheeling a cart, turned a corner in front of us. The person unlocked a door and pushed the cart into the room.

Imee dashed forward and managed to get to the room before the door closed. Jamie and I looked at each other and then ran forward. The door had closed. I tried the handle. Locked. We heard a couple of grunts, and then the door opened. Imee signaled us to come in. When we entered, Imee had a young Indian girl tied to a chair. She looked terrified.

"Based on the content of the cart"—I looked over. Stacks of metal trays filled the cart— "I'd say that this young lady knows her way around here pretty well. A perfect person to question to figure out where they're keeping Rhea and Richard." Imee looked from us to her captive.

I nodded. "Yes, but she's Indian and none of us speak Hindi."

Imee smiled broadly and turned to her captive. She rattled something off in a foreign language. A look of surprise crossed the face of the captive. She replied. The exchange went back and forth for a few minutes. I scanned the room. It held a cot, a sink, a toilet and several straw baskets. One had a scant few items of clothes in it, while another had a couple of plates and forks.

"If you will all look away." Jamie was standing in front of the toilet. I glared at him. "What? I really have to go."

Imee looked up from her captive and smirked, but continued her questioning while Jamie did what he needed to.

"Does she know where Rhea and Richard are?" I asked when she had finished.

"She's seen Rhea and knows where they've been keeping her."

I smiled broadly. "But . . . "

Imee shook her head. "But she hasn't seen Richard." Imee paused and looked at us. "Look, you guys might not be all that disappointed in that, but protecting Richard's my job—and I really care for him." A tear formed at the corner of her eye, but she quickly brushed it away.

I walked up to her and gave her a hug. "Look, when we get Rhea she's certain to know what happened to Richard." I gently held her shoulders. "You ok? You know, you've been amazing so far."

"Thanks, Charlie. We'll save them both, won't we?"

I nodded. "About our friend here . . ." I glanced over at our captive. "Did she give you enough information to find Rhea?"

Imee nodded. "I think so. She's not far."

"Good. Do we take her with us?"

Imee shook her head. "No. Too much of a liability. She just finished her shift, so if we leave her here, she shouldn't be missed."

"Good."

Jamie started to untie our guest.

"What are you doing?" Imee went over and tightened the knots again.

"I thought we were leaving her."

"Yes, but we can't afford to have her blow the whistle on us."

"But she looks so meek." Jamie looked down at her.

"Wouldn't you if you were surrounded by these brahmaparusha and the yetis?" Imee tore a piece of cloth off our captive's robes. She said something in Hindi, and the woman meekly dipped her head. Imee then stuffed the gag into the woman's mouth and tied it behind her head.

"Ok." Imee went over to one of the baskets and pulled out clothes similar to what the woman was wearing. "She's about my size so I'm going to put her clothes on."

We nodded, but Imee waved her hand at us. "Turn around, please."

We did, but Jamie glanced over his shoulder and then back. He winked at me.

Imee grabbed the cart. "Now, I'll take the cart and you two walk about ten steps behind me. If we run across those demons or yetis again, just do like you did last time."

We both nodded. I opened the door for her and Imee pushed the cart out into the hall. Jamie and I followed.

This time, there was little hesitation in Imee's step. She went right, made it to the first intersection, turned right again and then left at the next. I lost track of the turns. I hoped that Imee remembered since we didn't have the internet or GPS. We passed a few people dressed like Imee, but they barely gave us a glance. Like us, as soon as they saw someone else, they began looking down at the ground in front of their feet.

Imee stopped in front of a door. She knocked gently.

"Just a minute."

My heart stopped. It was Rhea's voice.

She opened the door. Imee kept her head down. "Oh, somebody already took my tray." She turned without even looking at Imee or beyond her at us. Her head drooped, and she shuffled back in the door. Before it closed, Imee pushed forward.

Rhea turned. "What the . . . Imee!"

"Shhh." Imee ran up and hugged Rhea.

I grabbed the cart and pulled it into the room. Jamie followed and closed the door.

As soon as Imee released Rhea, I ran up and hugged her.

"Oh my God, Charlie!" She squeezed me tight. I hugged her back, not wanting to let go. We stopped when Jamie cleared his throat.

Rhea turned to Jamie. "And Jamie. Thank God. I thought you were all dead." She hugged Jamie and gave him a kiss on the cheek. "How the hell did you get here?" Rhea's eyes started tearing up, and then she totally broke down.

I took her in my arms. Her head dropped to my shoulder as she sobbed. I kissed the top of her head. "It's ok now. We're going to get out."

"We'll have time for tears later, Rhea, but for now I need you to pull it together." Imee sat down in a dark-red cushioned chair at a heavy inlaid wooden table.

Imee's comments were so out of character that Rhea stopped crying and looked over at her. Imee pointed to another chair.

Rhea sat down. I walked around behind her. "No time for details, but Imee's not who you thought she was." I looked around the room. It looked as if it were out of *One Thousand and One Nights*, with tapestries, heavy furniture, and paintings of Indian deities in gilded frames.

Rhea looked Imee in the eye. "You even look different. Confident."

Imee nodded. "No time right now, but to put your mind at ease, I'm highly trained. Richard's dad hired me to be his bodyguard."

Rhea's jaw dropped. "You've got to be kidding." She looked over at Jamie and then back at me.

I nodded. "Amazing, but true. She had us all fooled. We wouldn't have gotten in here without her."

"Now, Rhea, you mentioned Richard. Do you know where he is?" Imee watched her intently.

"They drugged us in the submarine. The next thing I knew, Richard and I were on a luxurious jet. Trolga apologized for the gas and said that her sub pilot was new and that he'd pushed the wrong button. Her excuse and apology seemed hollow, but Richard just held that scepter in his lap and went along with her answer as if nothing had happened. She offered us drinks and food and treated us like royalty. I asked about you three and whether she'd gotten you out of the cave, but Richard answered that of course you were out. Hadn't Trolga promised? Trolga smiled and nodded. They talked about Richard's father and his discovery in Antarctica. Richard was obsessed that the scepter would grant his father access to something that would make him the first trillionaire in the world. He ignored me and focused on the dribble Trolga fed him.

"I tuned them out and must have nodded off. I awoke when we were on final approach. We landed not too far from here. Trolga had a helicopter waiting for us. It flew us into the temple grounds." She paused for a minute. "I still can't believe this is real. It feels like a nightmare."

I squeezed her shoulder.

"Anyway, when we arrived, Trolga took us through the main temple entrance into a large banquet hall. Trolga seated us to the left and right of a gilded chair that could have been a throne. We didn't have long to wait before the Lady Rusha entered the hall. A hush grew over everyone there. The main doors opened and a beautiful woman in a royal-blue, pink and gold sari walked into the room. Everyone, including Trolga, stood and bowed. Richard did as well. She walked over to us, nodding at those in the room. Those not seated bowed and took several steps backward as she passed them. Richard attempted to pull the chair/throne out for her, but it was too heavy for him. Two large men came forward, pulled it out and Rusha sat down.

"She extended her hand, which Richard kissed as if she were the Queen of England. She laughed, thanked him and told him to sit. She had a huge star ruby in an ornate gold setting just below her neck. She noticed me staring and told me it had been in her family for a long time."

Imee looked a bit impatient.

"Anyway, to the point. She and Richard talked about Richard's father's expedition to Antarctica and his finding of a potential power source that could revolutionize the world. Despite what Trolga had said, she didn't want a reward for delivering the scepter to Richard's father or for delivering Richard to his father. Rather, she wanted Richard to negotiate a deal with his father so she could invest in his venture. Of course, Richard told her that his father didn't need her money and she laughed. After all, wasn't she contributing the scepter, and wasn't that worth far more than money?

"By the end of dinner, they'd cut a deal. Rusha would fly Richard down to Antarctica to deliver the scepter to Richard's father in exchange for 7.5% of the proceeds derived from the venture. After dinner she graciously left us and had two handsome men dressed like butlers deliver us to two opulent rooms. When I awoke the next morning, it was late. Richard had gone. He'd left me a note asking me to check on Imee, and that he'd call me once he got back from Antarctica."

"So Richard and the scepter aren't here." Imee looked down and then back up at Rhea. "We need to get out of here. Do you know the way to the entrance?"

"I think so. But there are guards at the entrance. They've allowed me to wander around but told me not to try and go outside."

"Hopefully we have some surprises in store for them. Now, do you have any nondescript clothes that you can put on?" Imee looked around what appeared to be a royal suite compared to the room that the food server had lived in. She went to a wardrobe and opened it. It held a number of Indian outfits, but none of them nondescript. The bikini that Rhea had been wearing in the Bahamas was also in there. Imee picked out the least opulent, a light-blue sari, and handed it to Rhea. Rhea went into the bathroom and slipped it on.

I held back a whistle when she walked out. The exotic look accentuated her beauty.

"Put your tongue back in your mouth, Charlie. Any clue where your uncle is?" Imee had her ear to the door.

I shook my head.

"Well, assuming we can get there, we'll meet in the village if not before. Let's head out." Imee opened the door and looked out.

Rhea leaned over to me. "Definitely not the old Imee."

I nodded.

Imee popped her head back in. "Ok, Rhea, you take the lead. I'll follow, head down, right behind you. Charlie and Jamie will walk together about ten paces back. Let's go."

Imee stepped out into the hall. Rhea followed, then Jamie and I. Rhea looked back once, but then moved forward along the corridor. She didn't head back the way we came, but went into a more crowded section of the complex. We passed several people who dropped their heads and stood to one side as Rhea passed. The corridor ended in a brightly lit courtyard. I squinted as we entered. We must have passed the entire night in our escape and search for Rhea.

Two huge bronze double doors stood open at the end of the courtyard. I could see the valley beyond. I took a deep breath and followed behind Rhea and Imee. I remembered the Indian vampires and the yetis that had stood guard when we'd come in. I saw no evidence of them. I gave Jamie a glance. He crossed his fingers.

We made our way across the courtyard at as normal a pace as we could manage. We had almost reached the gate when two huge yetis turned, holding massive axes in their hands. A handful of smaller yetis and brahmaparushi stood behind them. Rhea paused. Imee walked up to her and whispered something in her ear. She then stepped forward and said something to the yetis in Hindi. They stood, frozen. Imee started to walk toward them. It looked as if she was going to try to make a dash through the entrance.

She leapt forward, but stopped short as Trolga stepped out between the two yetis, leveling a gun at her.

"Miss me?" She smiled and nodded to one side. Four smaller yetis walked between the two titans at the entrance and grabbed our shoulders.

# CHAPTER 44
## GLOATING

Stygian darkness pervaded. Slowly a blood-red tendril threaded its way through the darkness. The blood-red tendril did nothing to illuminate its surroundings. No light seeped out from it. It was merely there, in the darkness. It moved with a purpose, seeming to avoid invisible obstacles in its path. As it stretched forward it seemed to sense something. It began to whip back and forth. It came to rest on a hard, smooth surface. The tendril expanded and planted itself against the surface as if it had bitten into it. Small threads of blood-red began to stretch across the surface. Other tendrils rapidly snaked in behind the first, wrapping themselves around it, making it thicker and thicker. The tendrils spread rapidly across the smooth surface. Cracks began to form in the surface like cracks in the ice of a pond when something heavy starts to cross.

One tendril began to wiggle through a crack. It found purchase, and others joined it, pushing against the smooth surface. The lead tendril finally pushed through like the proboscis of a mosquito pushing through a layer of skin. The darkness, while pervasive, was not total. Off in the distance twelve glowing cylinders of blue light illuminated its way. One was markedly brighter than the others. It sat off to one side. The tendril headed straight for the brightest cylinder. As it approached, a pale form grew within the blue glow. The tendril stopped in front of the blue glow. Inside, a hairless shriveled form tucked into the fetal position seemed asleep. The tendril began to expand and took the form of a beautiful woman with shoulder-length blond hair, large breasts and long legs, wearing a shear white gown. The only remnant of the blood-red tendril was in her cat-like eyes. They glowed like hot coals in the dark. The woman took a finger and tapped against the edge of the blue glow.

The eyes of the desiccated form popped open. They seemed lost momentarily, but then they focused on the woman. The blue glow became opaque, and then slowly cleared. In the middle of a clear blue light hovered a tall woman dressed in a white gown. A golden helmet covered her blond locks. She held a spear in her right arm with a shield tucked behind her. Her almond-shaped turquoise eyes bored into her visitor.

"Rusha, how dare you! Be gone." She extended her spear in the direction from which the red tendril had come.

Rusha laughed. "Come now, Athena, or should I call you Galadriel?"

Galadriel's eyes narrowed. She thrust her spear through Rusha, whose form evaporated, but then reformed.

Rusha laughed again. "That tickles." She paused. "Isn't that what you said to young Charlemagne when he extended his arm through your form?"

Galadriel pulled her spear back and pointed to her side. "You will leave or you will suffer the consequences." In the distance an owl hooted. Several more hooted from the opposite direction.

"Now, now, I'm only here for a social call. You could be more hospitable." Rusha waited for a response. When none was forthcoming, she continued. "Nonetheless, as you have surmised, I now have your life's work in my grasp." An image of Charlie, Rhea, Imee and Jamie, flanked by two large yetis, appeared next to Rusha. Glowing chains led from their hands to Trolga.

"Even now, my loyal servants await my arrival. Your work of millennia will now become nothing more than a cow to be milked by me." Rusha glanced around. The hooting of the owls had stopped, but she could now hear fluttering wings. "Your precious scepter has been returned to Atlantis, and the fate suffered by Lemuria will soon be the fate of what's left of Atlantis and the 'humans' you created in your image. It's over. Rather than destroy you, I'll watch you as your dreams crash around you."

Galadriel thrust her spear forward, aiming at Rusha's chest. This time when Rusha's form evaporated it reverted to the blood-red tendril which rapidly withdrew from Galadriel's presence. Owls swooped over Galadriel and pursued the tendril, but it escaped back through the crack in the dome before they got to it.

Galadriel shook her head and looked at the image of Charlie that seemed to linger next to her despite Rusha's rapid departure. "I hope Nimue's right to have confidence in me and in you, Charlie." The image of a goddess departed, replaced by the shriveled body in the middle of the blue mist. Its turquoise eyes slowly closed as its head drooped.

# CHAPTER 45
## RUSHA'S TALE

We marched through much of the temple to the very back, where we reached a blank wall. Trolga nodded, and one of the yetis extended its hand along the wall. The wall disappeared, and a large room appeared in front of us. We walked in. I looked back as the wall reappeared. That got me a shove in the back by one of the yetis.

The room had high ceilings with diffused light. Like the Atlantean base on the Moon, I couldn't tell where the light was coming from. Equipment was scattered about the room on metal tables. Along one wall stood a row of life-sized glass tubes filled with a dark-green viscous liquid. They weren't empty. I looked closer. Bodies of human and inhuman creatures in various stages of dissection floated in the tubes.

We didn't have long to wait. Our yeti guards kicked us behind the knees, dropping us to the ground, and then knelt behind us, heads bowed. The beautiful woman that Rhea had described floated into the room on a hovering throne. It slowly descended in front of us. She radiated beauty, drawing me in like a moth to a flame. I recalled the saddhu's story about Rusha and how, like a siren, she had drawn him toward her. I focused, trying to break her siren's call. Jamie tried to move forward, but his guard stopped him.

Rusha got up from her throne and walked in front of us, staying well out of arms reach. She looked us over and then focused on me. "Well, young Atlantean, I'm glad you survived the traps that my underlings set for you. I have wanted to meet you."

I kept my eyes down. She nodded to one of the yetis. He grabbed my hair and yanked my head back. I'm glad he did. While she appeared more beautiful than a Victoria's Secret model, her blood-red eyes were filled with venom. Their evil broke her spell over me.

"I understand that you care for my dear distant daughter, Rhea." She glanced over at Rhea, who held her head up high.

"I'm not your daughter." I felt strength behind Rhea's statement—firm with no hesitation.

Rusha merely laughed. "Oh, but you are. Just as young Charlemagne is a son of Atlantis." She walked back and forth in front of us.

"Let me tell you a tale." Rusha sat back down on her throne. "Ages ago, in what you would call the Paleolithic, in this very location, a young Lemurian woman was working with a team of top geneticists. The Atlanteans had refused to give us the secret of their extreme longevity..."

I started to interrupt, but received another kick from the yeti behind me.

Rusha gave me a glare and then continued. "So our government set up this facility, well away from the prying eyes of any Atlantean spies. We were given fifty captive Atlanteans to work with. First we questioned them, but they weren't scientists and had no clue why they lived more than ten thousand years. It was the norm for them. We Lemurians had managed to stretch our lives to around five hundred years, but that was a drop in the bucket.

"The Atlanteans 'shared' their nanotechnology with us, but no matter what our scientists did, the nanites failed within a decade. They worked great at first, making the trial subjects look and feel young, but when they failed the subjects aged rapidly. We were convinced that the Atlanteans had done something to the nanites, but they denied it. Their scientists claimed to be as perplexed as we were.

"We had learned of the Atlanteans' discovery of a way to enter suspended animation indefinitely. They shared that with us and offered us several seats on their planned interstellar journey to visit the nearest extrasolar habitable planet that they had found orbiting the star you call Proxima Centauri. While some on our Supreme Council wanted to continue to work with the Atlanteans and go to the stars with them, many believed the Atlanteans were withholding the secret of eternal life from us.

"I discovered a gene in the mitochondria in Atlantean blood that enabled it to continually regenerate. I had synthesized it and was about to start testing when the end came. The Lemurian army arrested the Supreme Council and nuked the Atlantean capital. While the Atlanteans had a huge technological edge over us, they were wimps. Our military was sure that they would cower and surrender.

"News reports from Lemuria indicated that the Atlantean government that had survived was willing to give us everything rather than face mutual destruction. That's when they launched their insidious attack on Lemuria. They had developed a superweapon that temporarily negated the effects of gravity. They used it against our home island, sending it careening into space and killing a huge segment of our population."

I started to say something again but felt a searing pain in my head. *I can read your thoughts, young Atlantean. DO NOT interrupt me. The rotting remains that call themselves Atlanteans have lied to you. NOW, listen to the truth or I might just need a snack.* She sent me a visual of Jamie's neck and her teeth sinking into it. I shuddered and dropped my head.

"What those cowards didn't anticipate were the earthquakes and tsunamis caused by ripping Lemuria from the bosom of the Earth. The effects rippled across the globe, destroying the remnants of Lemurian civilization and causing a global shift that buried Atlantis under miles of snow and ice.

"We at this research facility were some of the few survivors from Lemuria. We were far from the coasts devastated by the tsunamis, and we had provisions to survive a protracted nuclear war. As the ash clouds approached, we sealed ourselves in this facility below the mountains. Many of my colleagues suffered abject depression as we lost touch with one base after another. I focused on my breakthrough, testing it on lab animals. All of the tests seemed perfect. From hamsters to monkeys, the DNA therapy caused age reversal in all of them. After we'd been underground for over five years and the hamsters were still alive, I decided to try out the therapy. I was too young for it to make a difference, so I selected Dhruv, the senior member of our team, as my guinea pig. At just over three hundred years old he was starting to show his age. The time underground and away from top healthcare had taken its toll on him.

"I slipped the gene therapy in his breakfast over a one-week period. By the second week after the treatment, he looked one hundred years younger and had a skip in his step. During the third week, he came to my office. I assumed he was there to confront me. He'd never liked me since I was the only member of the team capable of challenging him intellectually. Instead, he came on to me. Shocked, and turned on, I relented. After lying in his arms, I admitted what I'd done. He said he'd guessed and was grateful."

Rusha's eyes glowed with fire as she spoke of her ancient lover. She stopped to take a drink from a golden chalice that one of her minions brought to her. A dark red droplet clung to her lips. She licked it off.

"After my success, I tried the therapy on the other members of my team. The aging process reversed in all of them. As the young-est, I was the last to try the therapy. Given my age, I didn't feel any difference. The only question was would the therapy keep us alive as long as Atlanteans.

"By our twenty-seventh year underground, the computers told us that it was safe to go back outside. Despite our high-tech recy-cling technology, we were desperate to get out. Conditions remained very cold due to the extended winters caused by the volcanic ash from the massive eruptions that followed the destruction of Le-muria. We had to melt our way through tons of ice and snow. Once we got out, we cleared the area around our suborbital aircraft and took off to see what had happened to our world. We stopped first at Lemuria. Nothing but ocean remained where the thriving island of Lemuria had once stood. The gravitonic forces unleashed by the Atlanteans had dug deep into the Earth. We measured a water depth of over thirty thousand feet where our capital had once sat. Over a thousand miles of rolling hills, pristine mountains and white sandy beaches were totally gone, replaced by the deep waters of the Pacific Ocean.

"We'd known something horrible had happened, but hadn't known the extent of our loss when our communications net had collapsed. Now we knew. Anger surged through us. We flew directly to Atlantis. When we got there, we knew that at least the Atlanteans had suffered a similar fate. We'd known that the Atlantean capital city had been nuked, but all of the coastal cities showed total dev-astation beneath the ice. It didn't take long for us to figure out that tsunamis had scoured the coastlines of the Pacific Ocean.

"The balance of Atlantis not destroyed by the tsunamis had been buried under untold tons of ice and snow. The device used by the Atlanteans to destroy Lemuria had caused a polar shift. The south pole now sat in the middle of Atlantis.

"We looked for other survivors, but found no Atlantean survivors and only a handful of Lemurians. The tidal waves had wiped out all coastal communities, and the decade-long winter following the destruction of Lemuria destroyed most of the inland communities that had survived. We did keep in radio touch with several other small Lemuria bases, but none of them were as well equipped as ours.

"The years after the end of the war were a nightmare. We stayed in this base, expanding it, adding hydroponics and sending out hunting parties to locate meat to supplement our diets. We kept in touch with the other Lemurians, but kept my secret of longevity to ourselves. Despite our small numbers, given our knowledge of genetic engineering we believed that we would repopulate the world with Lemurians. While Atlantis may have died under the waves and ice, Lemuria would rise again through us.

"After several decades we emerged from the base to begin exploring the globe. Even after decades, the winters remained harsher than they had been prior to the war. We quickly over-hunted the area around our base. We did locate a small tribe of giant *hominids* that had managed to hang on despite the long winters we'd suffered through. We captured several and slowly began to manipulate their genetic codes, making them stronger and smarter. They had rudimentary telepathic skills which we enhanced so we could communicate with them. They became our faithful servants, the yetis."

Rusha gave a slight nod to the yeti guards who genuflected deeply in response.

"Once the weather had returned to normal, we emerged from the base to return to the surface and implement our plan to repopulate the planet. All of us paired off with the best genetic mates within the group. We knew that, given our small numbers, we would have to mate with almost all of the members of the opposite sex to create a sufficiently diverse genetic base for us to survive. I was one of the first of our group to get pregnant. The pregnancy seemed fine until early in my second trimester. I went into early labor. My child didn't make it."

Rusha paused momentarily from her tale. I looked around the room. Despite our situation, everyone seemed to be focused on Rusha's tale. I gave Rhea a slight smile and she smiled back.

"Shortly after my miscarriage, the other women began to miscarry. At first, we thought nothing of it. While not as low as the Atlanteans, our birthrates had always been low. We thought that perhaps there was an environmental cause due to having been sequestered in our underground base for so long. We ran tests. I discovered that the manipulation of our mitochondria that constantly renewed our cells and kept us from aging had an unknown side effect. It resulted in our bodies attacking any cells that were not our own. The foreign DNA in our children triggered an attack once it reached a certain stage of development.

"Needless to say, we were devastated. Despite our resources and genetic knowledge, we couldn't change the result. While we could live exceedingly long lives, we would not have children of our own. We decided to seek out the other Lemurians and keep track of them. Since they lived in smaller pockets than we did, we would go dark on them, but follow their progress. Once their technology dipped, as it invariably would, we would take control of their populations and start an aggressive breeding program. While our lines would stop, Lemurians would continue with us ruling them.

"Just over a thousand years later, with several generations of our breeding program moving forward, we learned of another side effect to my mitochondria longevity treatment. We had begun to age again. Dhruv was the first as his grey hair returned. It started gradually. Then it accelerated. Wrinkles, grey hair and aching muscles came back with a vengeance. Something was wrong. I took blood samples from all of us and saw the changes in our blood. Somehow our blood wasn't regenerating like it should.

"After years of work without a cure, several of the older members of the group were bedridden. Even I, the youngest, felt the ill effects of aging. I came upon the cure when I started experimenting on our Atlantean captives. Even without my longevity enhancements, they had aged very little. I started taking blood samples from them. Their blood did not degenerate like ours. I happened to spill a vile of Atlantean blood into a petri dish with my blood in it. I was about to throw the contaminated sample out when I stopped and looked through a microscope. My blood cells were attacking the Atlantean cells. Once the process was finished, my blood cells looked young again. I compared them to a new sample I took from myself. Sure enough, the cells that had devoured the Atlantean cells had regenerated.

"Dhruv faded the fastest, so, again without telling him, I transfused a pint of Atlantean blood into him. Within days his aging had reversed. I took the next dose and then treated the rest of my compatriots. Atlantean blood somehow reinvigorated our blood. We soon learned that every ten years or so we would need a new transfusion of Atlantean blood. Since it's hard to keep secrets from telepaths, they knew what we were doing. Many refused to eat and we had to force-feed them. Some lost the will to live. Despite everything we did, they withered and died.

"Now that we knew we needed their blood, we did everything we could to keep them alive. We periodically took blood from them and stored it, but it lost its vitality over time. Fresh blood seemed to work much better for us. Several thousand years after the War, we were down to our last Atlantean, a female. She should have remained young but looked ancient. We rotated taking blood to retain our vitality, and my turn was up. I was aging rapidly, with my skin wrinkling and hair turning grey. I went in to get a blood sample and found that somehow she'd slit her wrists. She was barely alive, lying in a huge pool of blood. Blood that I desperately needed. I had nothing to collect her blood with, so I grabbed her wrist and started sucking the blood directly from her wrist. The blood gave me a surprising immediate boost and seemed to work faster than a transfusion did. I stopped just before she died, ran outside and pushed the alarm bell.

"We had an emergency meeting after her death. We figured that at best we had ten to fifteen years of life left each. Having death back on the horizon after having banished it created a panic. We started experimenting on local monkeys, and even on our servants, *Gigantopithecus*, the precursors of the yetis, but the effect of their blood was minimal, buying us months instead of years. While any mammal's blood would work, the best blood came from Atlanteans. We started culling the stock of Lemurians whose technology had declined, but they were located far away and remained in small numbers. While

Lemurian blood worked longer than most, we were loath to take from our own species. At least that's what I thought. One night I woke up to a pain in my arm. I tried to move, but I couldn't. A shadow moved around my room. I looked down. An IV pierced my arm, my blood seeping into a bag next to me.

"'What the hell do you think you're doing?' I said. I struggled at my restraints, but to no avail.

"The man came out of the shadows. 'We drew straws. You lost.' He grabbed the IV bag and squeezed it. 'We'll put you on a blood-producing drug. You should be able to supply the rest of us for years.'

"'So, you've decided to turn me into a cow, then?' I spit at the man, nailing him in the face.

"He pulled out a cloth and wiped it off. 'You were always a cow. Now we get to milk you.' He walked out of the room.

"I screamed telepathically, not believing that the rest of the survivors had agreed with him. When there was no response, I assumed they'd buffered the room, like we had all of the rooms for the Atlanteans. I looked around. I had a knife in my drawer on the other side of the room, but I couldn't reach it. The restraints were too tight. After struggling in futility, I lay back and began to think. While both Atlanteans and Lemurians were telepathic, some Atlanteans also had limited telekinetic abilities. Perhaps by taking their blood I had developed them as well. I focused on the drawer first, picturing it in my head. I willed it open. Nothing happened. I took several deep breaths and relaxed as much as I could, focusing on the drawer. I envisioned it opening. I then pictured the knife sitting there. I visualized the knife floating up out of the drawer and then slowly drifting across the room.

"I heard footsteps. I kept my eyes closed and focused on the knife. I visualized it hovering over my right hand and slowly lowering down. It could have been my imagination, but I felt something drop to the bed as the door opened. I wiggled my fingers around and, sure enough, the knife was there! My captor walked in and saw the drawer open. He looked over at me and then back at the drawer. He walked over, looked in it and closed it.

"'What, my blood's not enough, now you want my panties as well? Go ahead, take them!' I spoke with as much derision as I could muster.

"He checked the first bag hanging next to me. It was almost full of my blood. 'By the time we pull the next bag from you, you'll lose your sarcasm.'

"'Don't count on that.' I spat at him again but missed.

"He smiled and looked around. 'Thought I had more bags in here. Guess I'll need to get another. Be right back. Don't go anywhere.' He winked at me.

"As soon as he closed the door, I started working the knife on my restraints. I got my right hand free and then reached over and loosened my left so I could easily slip it out. I then loosened both leg restraints so I could slip my feet out easily. I'd have to make my move before giving up another pint of blood. I'd be too weak to do anything. I already felt lightheaded. I heard footsteps and he came in again. He placed several bags on the tray next to the bed.

"'I'm a bit thirsty.' I licked my lips. 'If you want my blood, I'll need fluids.'

"He nodded. 'I'll get you some water, but if you try to spit on me again, I'll knock your teeth out.'

"I nodded. 'Promise.'

"He went to the sink, poured a glass of water and brought it to me. With one hand he lifted my head up and with the other lifted the glass to my lips. I started to drink, but, as swiftly as I could, I lifted the knife and stabbed him in the neck. He tried to pull away, but not before I pulled the blade across his neck. Arterial blood spurted into my face and down my chest. I dropped the knife and grabbed his head between both hands, pulling his now smiling neck down to my lips. I drank deeply, letting the spurts of warm arterial blood shoot down my throat.

"Immediately energy surged within me. I kept drinking and drinking until I'd drained him dry. I then pushed his corpse off me onto the floor. I pulled the IV out of my arm and looked down at the blood seeping out. As I looked at it, the blood clotted and stopped flowing. I looked in the mirror at my hair, face and torso covered in blood. I didn't have much time. I ran to my lab, grabbed my override card and a gas mask, and hit the biohazard lockdown button. A siren sounded and all of the doors to the entire lab locked down. I used my override access to search the entire facility and found half a dozen others chained to their beds with IVs hooked into them. I programed the computer to release knockout gas throughout the facility. I then quickly made my way through the facility, tying up all free members of the team."

# CHAPTER 46
## BULL AND COW

Rusha's eyes glowed as she told the tale, particularly when she spoke of sucking the blood out of her former compatriot. I looked around the room. All eyes were focused on Rusha. Perhaps like a cobra, she somehow hypnotized them. Even the yetis seemed to be staring at her. Rhea had a blank look on her face, staring straight ahead. I wanted to leak out a tendril of thought, but didn't dare, remembering Rusha's threat.

Rusha was staring at me.

"So, young Charlemagne, bored with my story?"

I shook my head. "No."

"Well, there'll be plenty of time for me to finish the tale later. If you hadn't guessed it, you will now be my cow. You are young, strong and Atlantean. You will last thousands of years, so there will be plenty of time for you to hear the full tale. Now, I'm getting thirsty, and I'm looking forward to introducing lovely Rhea to the pleasures of eternal life and feasting on blood."

"Nooo!" I yelled.

"Oh, don't worry. I'm going to breed her to you to continue my genetic experiments. A Lemurian/Atlantean hybrid might have some very useful traits."

I looked over at Rhea, who remained in a trance-like state.

Rusha laughed. "I have long forgotten the obsession of youth with sexual intercourse. No, young Atlantean, you will not have that pleasure. Instead you will be both bull and cow. Let me assure you, you will garner no pleasure whatsoever when we remove your semen from you."

A picture of a large needle approaching a bull's testicles filled my head. I cringed. Clearly Rusha could read even the most fleeting of my thoughts. My thoughts reached out toward Galadriel. *We've been captured by Rusha, what . . .*

*STOP!* Rusha's telepathic command hurt. It was so loud I cringed. *You think I'm an idiot. All thoughts are blocked from leaving this complex. But I'm tempted to let you reach out to that shell. She's dead, they all are, but they just don't know it.*

"Now, I grow weary of this. I think it's time for a pick-me-up." Rusha pointed at Jamie and signaled a yeti to bring him forward.

The yeti pushed Jamie forward. He stumbled. The yeti yanked him up.

"NO!" I yelled, but couldn't move.

Rusha laughed. At that moment, Trolga raised her weapon and shot the yeti pushing Jamie forward. It dropped to the floor. A small brown spot appeared over its heart and the smell of burnt fur filled the air.

"That will be quite enough," Trolga said, leveling her weapon at Rusha. Trolga's body began to shimmer. Uncle Merl appeared. He glanced at me and gave me a wink. "Fascinating tale, but we'll be leaving you now." Uncle Merl signaled for us to move behind him. I tried, but the yeti maintained its grip on my arms. I glanced around. None of the yetis had released any of us. In fact, several more had appeared behind us.

"I'm not kidding, Rusha, let us go or I will shoot." Uncle Merl took a step closer to Rusha.

Rusha merely laughed. "Go ahead."

Uncle Merl did not hesitate. He pulled the trigger. The beam from the gun seemed to shimmer right in front of Rusha. As Uncle Merl held the trigger down, I noticed more shimmering to my side. The yeti holding Rhea began to morph. As it did, it pulled a weapon out.

"Uncle Merl . . ." My warning came too late. The yeti shot Uncle Merl. He dropped to the ground and began to convulse.

A laugh erupted from Rusha. The yeti holding Rhea had morphed into Trolga. She stepped forward and looked down at Uncle Merl. While his eyes looked as if they would burn a hole in Trolga, he continued to convulse. "Sauce for the goose, Dr. Ambrose, is sauce for the gander." Trolga laughed again. "You'll wish that I'd killed you, but Mistress Rusha has other plans for you. Like the wireless taser that DeMarco Industries makes?"

Rusha smiled broadly, showing her shark-like teeth. "Yes, like your young nephew, I will enjoy milking and feasting on your blood for years to come. Given your genes, you may survive for another thousand years. Between you and your nephew, there will be plenty of Atlantean blood to sustain me for millennia." She nodded to the new yeti that had grabbed Jamie. It pushed him forward as another kicked the gun away from Uncle Merl and picked him up.

"For now, this poor specimen of a human will have to do." She signaled with her crooked finger as the yeti brought Jamie closer to her. His eyes widened, but his body remained frozen. The yeti thrust Jamie into Rusha's arms. She grabbed his throat with one hand and lifted him up, inspecting him. She leaned in and pressed her lips against Jamie's throat. His eyes widened even more.

I struggled to move my arms and legs, but they stayed firmly cemented in place. "Stop!" I screamed.

Rusha pulled her lips away from Jamie. Small drips of blood trickled down his neck. Rusha shook her head. "Must I gag you?"

I tried to give her a sarcastic answer, but nothing came out. Somehow she was controlling me. I could still move my head, but that was all I could do. Even my yeti guard had released my arms.

"When will you learn that you are helpless?" She licked her lips. "Not bad. Youth does have a subtle flavor, and this is my first taste of one who's been to the Moon." Jamie's pupils swelled as sweat dripped down his face. Rusha raised her lips to Jamie's neck again. I stared in horror as Rusha appeared to be giving Jamie a hickey. She pulled away again, smacking her lips.

She looked over at Rhea. "Now, daughter, it's time for your initiation."

Rhea's yeti guard released her. After a pause, she took a step forward. It looked as if she were fighting it, but each step came a little quicker. She was losing her battle.

This couldn't be happening. I struggled but couldn't move. Imee looked like a statue, and Uncle Merl remained convulsing on the floor. Rhea had almost reached Rusha. I couldn't watch. I closed my eyes. Something glowed brightly at my feet. It began to levitate off the floor. I focused on it. It floated up toward my hand. I squeezed it. I could feel the seams. It felt like my no-hitter baseball. I rotated it in my fingers, gripping it with my two-seam fastball grip. I prayed that the ball was really in my hand. I opened my eyes. Rhea was leaning her lips toward Jamie's throat.

"No!" I screamed. Not even looking, I wound up and hurled the ball at Rusha. She looked shocked as it approached. She raised her hands up, but the pitch was perfect. It went right between her arms, smashing into her huge star ruby necklace.

The necklace shattered as a high-pitch scream erupted from her throat. Her throne lifted off the floor and darted away from us. Her scream faded and then cut off as a huge wall dropped in front of her receding throne.

Nobody in the room moved. I suddenly felt very weak. Rhea caught Jamie under the arms as he collapsed. Two yeti guards charged her, but my yeti guard intercepted one, flipping it to the ground, pinning it. I grabbed a table, steadying myself as Trolga turned toward me, the taser in her hand. A smile began to form on her face, but Uncle Merl moved like a blur. He grabbed the taser from her hand and fired it at Trolga before she could react. She dropped to the ground, convulsing. My yeti guard and Rhea's circled each other. They dove for each other and began wrestling on the ground. Imee's guard released her to help the other yeti, but Imee somehow managed to grab its arm, flipping it over her shoulder. She then kicked it in the head, making it go limp.

We all got out of the way as the two yetis fought. They looked alike, and I lost track of which was which. One got on top of the other and seemed to be getting the upper hand when the other used its legs, flipping its opponent over its head. Uncle Merl didn't hesitate. He tazed one, ending the fight. Only one yeti remained standing.

"How'd you know which one to taze?" I looked at Uncle Merl for an answer.

The yeti shook its head and grinned. It looked over at Uncle Merl. *Can't I just parboil 'im and eat 'im?* The yeti extended a hand to help me up.

"AB!" I gave him a big hug. He hugged me back and rubbed my head. "Hell'uv a disguise. You even smell like one of them." I pushed away from AB.

He laughed. "I really do need a bath. Yetis stink."

Uncle Merl zapped Trolga and the two yetis again with the taser. "Enough old home week. We need to get out of here while Rusha's minions are in disarray. Let's go."

I took a step toward the entrance, but stumbled.

Uncle Merl pulled two lozenges out of his pouch, took one, and handed one to me. "Here, suck on this." He went over to Rhea and Jamie. Both of them looked quite dazed.

I started sucking on the lozenge. It gave me an immediate burst of energy. "Wish you'd given me this during exams. What's in it?"

"Coca leaf extract, among other things."

Imee held Jamie up while Rhea remained frozen in place. Uncle Merl walked up to them and stuck a lozenge in their mouths. Rhea snapped back fairly quickly, but Jamie remained pasty and pale. His neck looked like a lamprey had been attached to it. Uncle Merl pulled a bandage out of his bag and slapped it on Jamie's neck. Jamie gave him a weak nod.

"Can I have one of those lozenges?" Imee walked over to Uncle Merl.

"Why? You seem fine." Uncle Merl put an arm around Jamie to help him walk.

"Because I could use an edge if we run across any resistance."

Uncle Merl nodded and handed her a lozenge from his bag. "Now, let's get the hell out of here."

"Why not kill them first?" Imee looked down at Trolga and the surviving yetis.

Uncle Merl shook his head. "Killing is the last resort."

I looked at Trolga lying on the ground and shook my head. She'd tried to kill us several times, kidnapped us and delivered us to Rusha. I'd never understand my uncle.

"Then we've got to at least secure them." Imee looked around the room, but saw nothing she could use to tie them up with.

Uncle Merl reached into his bag and then walked to Trolga and the yetis, forcing something into their mouths. "They'll be out for at least twenty-four hours. Now, if you're satisfied, let's go."

We headed back for the entrance where we'd been captured. AB, still looking like a female yeti, led the way. I walked next to Rhea, saying nothing but keeping an eye on her. Uncle Merl helped Jamie, walking behind us, and Imee brought up the rear.

While I'd felt hollow after throwing my 'baseball' at Rusha, I now felt energized. I looked around at the corridor. It had an antiseptic feel and didn't seem ancient. Perhaps this wasn't part of the original Lemurian lab. We came to the wall at the end of the corridor that separated this hidden section of the temple from its main hall. Trolga had managed to open the door with her palm. I wasn't sure how we'd get out until AB put his hand on the scanner and the door opened.

He signaled for us to head to the huge bronze doors. Several people dashed across the main hall, but none paid us any attention.

I thought about all of the poor souls that had been marched in with us. *What about all of their prisoners? We can't just leave them.*

Uncle Merl hesitated, but then continued forward. *Our mission's too important, and the odds of us releasing them too slim. Look to your left.*

I did and was horrified. A handful of prisoners cowered in the center of an open room, a fire pit in the center. A brahmaparush rushed in, grabbed one and then bit its neck. Another one dashed in and then another.

*The priests are satiating the brahamparush to keep them in control since Rusha's influence disappeared. We've got to get out while they're preoccupied.*

AB didn't wait. He pushed one of the bronze doors. He glanced around, and, as he did, a large arm grabbed him and threw him down the steps like a rag doll. The huge male yeti then stepped in front of us, opened its mouth and let out a deep-throated scream. He stepped toward us as Imee stepped in front of us. The huge yeti paused, not quite sure what to make of the diminutive human that dared to challenge him. While he was distracted, Uncle Merl squeezed the trigger on the taser. Nothing happened. The charge must have been depleted. The yeti seemed to laugh and then stepped toward Imee, attempting to grab her. She slid under his grasp and between his legs, kicking hard at his ankle as she did.

The yeti gave out a howl and then turned to face her again. She danced around, jabbing at him with a knife, cutting his legs and arms, but the yeti couldn't grab her. She danced down the steps to the right as the yeti lunged after her. It moved far faster than I'd have thought, but Imee continued to stay out of its grasp. I could tell that Imee was tiring. Uncle Merl ushered us behind the yeti and out of the temple as Imee distracted it. He held his finger to his lips, signaling us to be quiet.

He started down the steps.

*What about Imee?*

*She knows what she's doing. Keep moving!*

We made it down the steps and started to hustle down the dirt road. I looked back. The giant swept an arm at Imee. While she cut him, she couldn't dodge the blow entirely. She shot through the air about twenty feet. She lay there looking dazed. As she slowly rose up, the yeti closed on her.

I started to yell, but then AB stepped in front of Imee, letting loose a deep-throated howl of his own that seemed to echo down the valley. As the yeti approached and thrust his arm at AB, AB grabbed the arm, twisted his body and flipped the yeti over his shoulder in a classic judo move. Before the yeti could move, AB had its arms behind its back, twisting them. I heard something crack, and the arms went limp. The yeti howled, but this time in pain. AB rolled it over and stuck his foot on its neck. The yeti let out a light grunt. AB lifted his foot and turned his back on the huge yeti. It managed to stand, but instead of attacking AB, it took off toward the mountains.

AB helped Imee up and walked toward us. As they approached, a truck zipped around the corner and screeched to a halt in front of us. The driver door popped opened and Kyra jumped out.

"Get in—quick." She looked back over her shoulder.

I looked back. A dozen or so yetis were making their way toward us. We didn't need any encouragement.

# CHAPTER 47
## FIGHT OR FLIGHT

The truck jostled and bumped its way along the road. Thank goodness for the beanbag chairs. The rapid turns would have slung us back and forth without them. As it was, I was glad that I didn't get seasick. Jamie looked a bit green, but that could have been from Rusha feeding on him.

I looked over at Rhea. She stared at Jamie. I scooted my beanbag chair closer to her. "How do you feel?" I whispered.

She glared at me. "How do you think?"

"I'm sorry. I wish I could have stopped Trolga from taking you."

"No, that's not it. It's . . ."

"What?"

"It's like I wanted to do it. Part of me still thinks about it."

"You mean?" I looked over at Jamie.

Rhea nodded, tears in her eyes.

"But that was Rusha in your head. She made you."

"Yes, but why is there a lingering thirst in the back of my mind. Maybe I'm one of them?" She put her head in her hands and started to sob.

I slid into her beanbag chair and put my arm around her. "It's Rusha. She's ancient and a very powerful telepath. It's not you. I know you. You'd never want that."

Rhea lifted her head. "You really think that?"

"I don't think that, I know that. I felt her in my head. She made herself look like Aphrodite in my mind. She wanted you to go down that path, implanted those thoughts in your head."

Rhea looked over at Jamie, shuddered, and then leaned her head against my shoulder. "I hope you're right."

355

I stroked her hair and then lay back next to her. When the truck jarred to a stop, a huge shadow loomed over us. AB extended his hand. *You guys are sooo cute together.*

Rhea took his hand and got up out of the beanbag chair. I glared at AB and took his hand. *Quite a feminine hand you've got there. No wonder you easily passed as a yeti female.*

AB yanked me up, almost pulling my shoulder out of joint. *Watch it or you'll be a female bonobo next Halloween.*

I didn't know what a bonobo was, but I knew it was something that would make me look like an idiot. I jumped down from the truck to join the others. The place seemed familiar. Rhea and Imee looked up the hill into the trees. A light dusting of snow covered their tops.

I walked to the side of the road. Uncle Merl was talking with Kyra. He finished and walked back to us.

"AB, how fast are yetis?"

AB scratched his head. "They can jog about twenty miles per hour, but they're telepathic. If there are any in this area, they may already be looking for us."

Uncle Merl nodded. "We've got to get to the ship, ASAP. Besides the yetis, I don't want Rusha to recover enough to target us with her plasma cannon."

"I thought she was hurt bad," I said.

"You did hurt her worse than she's been hurt in centuries, but she's very resilient and vindictive. She'll get after us as soon as possible, and she'll know where we're going. AB, you take the lead and we'll follow you to the ship."

AB didn't hesitate. With two huge strides he entered the tree line.

Uncle Merl started into the trees.

"Wait, what about Jamie?" Rhea looked back at the truck as it started up.

"He's going with Kyra to stay with Vidya."

"Why?" I asked, glancing over at Rhea.

"I'd think that was obvious. Rusha drained him of a significant amount of blood. Given what he's been through, he needs time to recover. Vidya can heal him both physically and mentally."

"But what about Rusha coming after him and Saddhu Sidon?" Imee looked anxiously at Uncle Merl.

"Vidya has his defenses. They'll be fine, but we won't if we hang around here much longer flapping our lips." With that Uncle Merl strode into the forest. Imee and Rhea followed close on his heels. I looked up the road at the cloud of dust as Kyra and Jamie headed back to the monastery. The truck lurched as a huge boulder rolled in front of it. My jaw dropped as a huge male yeti stepped from the tree line. Several more stood in the shadows of the trees.

I hustled into the wood. *Uncle Merl, yetis just attacked Kyra and Jamie. We've got to go back to help them.* I expected Uncle Merl to turn around, but he kept striding into the woods, even picking up his pace.

*Did they see you?*

*I don't think so, but what about . . .*

*Kyra knows what she's doing. Hurry and keep as quiet as possible.*

Uncle Merl moved far faster than I thought he could. I was out of breath by the time I caught up with them. As I did, AB popped up in front of us with his fingers to his lips. He pointed to our left. A yeti was walking toward the field where the spaceship was hidden. AB signaled us to parallel the field before turning toward it, and then took off in the direction of the yeti.

Before we got far we heard the banshee-like howl of a yeti. I looked back, almost stumbling, and then turned and followed the others. As we walked toward the ship, Uncle Merl signaled it to open its door. As we waited for the door to slide open a yeti appeared at the edge of the clearing.

Imee moved in front of us. "Get aboard. I'll slow it down. If I don't make it, give Richard a hug for me." She started running toward the creature.

*It's me, AB. Stop Imee. Yetis are close behind.*

I yelled. "Imee, it's AB. Come back." She stopped, looked at the hulking beast heading toward her, and then started back toward the open door of the ship.

*I'll be glad when you get rid of your disguise.* I waited at the top of the ramp for AB.

*You're telling me.* AB trotted toward us.

I saw movement in the clearing behind him. Two large yetis followed behind AB, but something small, moving fast, was catching up to him. It would reach AB well before he made it to the ship. It was a brahmaparush, running like a cheetah.

*AB, hurry.*

AB started running faster than I'd ever seen him move, quicker than any human sprinter. But that wasn't fast enough. The brahmaparush would still reach him before he got to the ship.

*If I don't make it . . .*

*You'll make it. Keep coming.* I tried hard to hide my thoughts, but he wasn't going to make it. I didn't know how strong the brahmaparush was, but the yetis were now closing on him too. I doubted that he'd be able to take the brahmaparush before the yetis got to him, and he'd never be able to defeat them all. Before the brahmaparush reached him, AB turned to face it. It leapt from over twenty feet away, crashing into him. AB threw it to the ground and took off toward us. The brahmaparush tried to stand but dropped back to the ground. I looked over my shoulder. Imee stood there with a laser rifle, smiling.

I looked back at AB. He had a lead on the yetis, but they seemed to be closing on him. I yelled for AB to hurry. He had a hundred yards left, but they were only fifty yards behind him. Imee grabbed my arm and pulled me inside the door.

"Shoot them?" I looked at the gun in Imee's hand.

She shook her head. "Out of power. We've got to take off the instant AB gets on board. Use your telepathy to let your uncle know when to go."

I nodded. *Uncle Merl?*

*I'm ready. Let me know when . . .*

AB dove through the door, sliding into the wall on the other side.

*NOW!* I glanced around the corner. The yetis were at the foot of the ramp. *NOW!* The door closed. As always, I couldn't tell whether we'd taken off or not. I hit my head with my hand. *Shannon, have we lifted off?*

*Yes. Welcome aboard.*

AB sat against the wall, sucking in breath. He nodded toward Imee. "Nice shot."

Imee nodded back. "Thanks. Lasers really make it too easy. Just wish they'd hold a charge."

I extended my hand, but AB waved me off. "Just needed a sec." He took a deep breath and then stood up. "Guess I'm finally starting to feel my age." He looked from me to Imee. When neither of us reacted, he slapped me on the back. "That's a joke. You try running flat out for over a mile and then fighting a vampire and see how you feel." He headed off for the control room. As if to make a point he took huge strides. We took off after him. The door to the control room silently slid open. We hustled in.

Uncle Merl sat in a control chair right out of the latest Star Trek movie. He seemed very focused on something and merely pointed with his hand for us to sit. Rhea was sitting next to him. She smiled as we entered. Three chairs rose from the floor next to him. AB plopped down in a massive recliner next to Rhea. A large glass filled with a frothing beverage rose from the floor next to his chair. He grabbed it and took a large swig, sat back and picked up his feet. A footrest popped up under them.

I sat on the other side of my uncle in a more normal chair on a swivel. Imee sat next to me in a similar chair. I leaned over toward Imee. "If we only had some popcorn . . ."

"That's one hell of an idea." The smell of popcorn filled the air and a bowl rose up from the floor next to AB. He stuffed a handful into his mouth.

Imee looked over at the popcorn.

"Want some?" I asked.

Imee nodded. "And I'd love an orange soda to go along with it. But where does it come from?"

I shook my head. "Not sure. Atlantean technology." I pictured Shannon and then asked for the popcorn and orange sodas telepathically. They slowly rose next to me and Imee.

She smiled, gabbed a couple of pieces of popcorn and popped them in her mouth. She then took a sip of orange soda. "Mmmmm, good."

Rhea looked over. "What about me?"

I smiled. *Shannon, popcorn for Rhea please.* It appeared in front of her. I looked up at the screen in front of Uncle Merl. A blue blur slid below us.

"Are we over the ocean?"

Uncle Merl took a deep breath and swiveled his chair to face me. "We just passed the point where the Lemurians could track us with their plasma cannon."

He looked over at AB. After a brief pause, AB handed him his bowl of popcorn. Uncle Merl popped a few pieces in his mouth.

"So where are we?" Imee asked.

Uncle Merl nodded and swallowed the popcorn. "The southern Indian Ocean. We should be approaching the coast of Antarctica shortly. We'll stay low until we get over the Amery Ice Shelf and then head up a thousand miles or so to give our sensors a chance to locate the DeMarco compound. Once we do, we'll take a look at the topography in the region and figure out the best way to approach the compound." He took another handful of popcorn and handed the bowl back to AB.

"Why not just contact Richard and go in the front door?"

Uncle Merl looked over at Imee. "I know that you care for Richard very much, but keep in mind he's been in the hands of Trolga and Rusha for days. They're both powerful telepaths and could have implanted who knows what in Richard's mind."

Imee scowled, but then nodded. "You're right. A bit unprofessional of me. We've got to assume that we'll be unwelcome guests. Richard's father might even turn us back over to Rusha."

Rhea shuddered, dropping the bowl of popcorn on the floor. I had no doubt that whatever Rusha had planned for us before would be far worse now.

A thin line of white appeared in front of us. It rapidly grew as we approached at north of Mach 3. It looked as if there was a cliff in front of us, but Uncle Merl smiled. The ship rose as we closed on the coast. A blur of white rather than blue now passed underneath us. A thin ribbon appeared in front of us.

"What's that?" I pointed at the ribbon.

Uncle Merl shook his head. "As a descendant of Atlantis you should at least know the geography of your ancestral home."

*Shannon, what's that ribbon in front of us?*

*The Transantarctic Mountains.*

"Give me a minute." I pretended to think. "That's the Transantarctic range."

Uncle Merl shook his head again. "I can't wait until this quest is over so I can give you a proper education. I heard your thoughts leak out. Not only do you need a basic geography lesson, you need basic telepathy lessons as well."

Imee laughed. I scowled at her. The thought of years of getting taught by Uncle Merl or the saddhu gave me almost as much of a shudder as being captured by Rusha.

We started to slow and then stopped. The mountain range remained in front of us.

"Why'd we stop?" Rhea asked.

Uncle Merl smirked. "Where are we? And no asking Shannon."

I looked at the screen. "Shannon, please pan 360 degrees at a speed that we can observe."

The screen did start to pan. The ribbon from the mountain range was in front of us, but there was nothing but white behind us. We must not have been high enough to see the ocean from where we were.

I shook my head and looked over at Imee. She was grinning like the cat that ate the canary. "Do you know?"

"I think so." She looked over at Uncle Merl.

Uncle Merl nodded.

"Well, given the mountains in front and the vast expanse of white behind us, and given your uncle's penchant for teaching you lessons, I would have to say that we are hovering over the South Pole." She looked over at Uncle Merl.

He nodded. "Very good, young lady. Now, enough of that brief lesson. Time to find out where we need to go."

I looked at the view screen. The sky rapidly darkened as the curve of the Earth appeared. We left the atmosphere, and thousands of stars appeared against the coal-black background of space. I looked down, able to see the whole of Antarctica below us.

"How long will it take Shannon to find Mr. DeMarco's base?"

"Already found it. Despite his state-of-the-art communication system, he couldn't hide it from Atlantean technology." A map of Antarctica without ice appeared in the view screen. A green dot flashed to our left.

"I know that everything is north, so what direction is that?" Uncle Merl ignored my question. The map shrank, and another identical map appeared next to it. Dozens of red dots spread across the map like zits on my old friend Eric's face.

"Shannon, slowly overlay the two maps and zoom in on the Ellsworth Mountains." The images merged and zoomed in. As they did, many of the red dots dropped off the margin. Finally, there were only two dots left, the green one and a red one. They merged.

"Fairly high up and not too far from Mount Vinson. That's probably why the Atlantean base remained intact after the war." Uncle

Merl focused on the map. "Shannon, zoom in again and overlay any known entrances to the Atlantean base."

Several dots appeared along the slope of a bare mountain.

"Now overlay present day ice at the locations."

White now blanketed the image. All of the locations but one appeared to be buried under ice.

"Zoom in on that one location." Uncle Merl pointed to the lone spot. A landing strip cut into the ice appeared, and several small hangars came into focus. A vehicle came out of the mouth of the cave and drove toward one of the hangars, while another drove from the hangars toward the cave.

Imee walked forward and studied the image. "Looks like they cut through several hundred feet of ice to gain entrance to the cave and then expanded the opening to handle large vehicles." She looked closely at the image. "How detailed is this?"

Uncle Merl paused. "Resolution is down to about an inch."

Imee raised her eyebrows and nodded. "Doesn't look like any fencing. They probably have electronic surveillance out for several miles. I wouldn't doubt that Mr. DeMarco has a dedicated web of nanosatellites covering this entire area to detect any aircraft or vehicles approaching." She looked up. "Do you think they spotted us?"

Uncle Merl shook his head. "The only systems on Earth that I know of that could detect this ship are in the Lemurian base. There's no way that Rusha would share those with DeMarco."

"Good. Think we can land inside their outer perimeter?"

Uncle Merl nodded. "There's a small snow mound"—he pointed at the feature—"near the outer boundary that looks big enough to hide the ship until we get out. Once we exit, the ship will use active camouflage like it did in India. Any ideas on how to get in? After all, your company is probably the one that DeMarco hired to set up the security system."

Imee smiled. "Yes, you're probably right. That does give us a leg up. Once in the outer perimeter we should be able to approach the hangars if we have good warm camouflage."

Uncle Merl nodded. "We do. Thought about that and already put the specs in the ship's computer. The items are ready for us and will fit since the ship measured each of you as you came on board." Uncle Merl glanced at AB who was getting up. "Where are you going?"

"To wash out of the Yeti costume." AB's fur rippled in a shudder. "Don't know how you guys can bear to sit here with me. The stink is awful." AB strode for the door.

"Hold on."

AB stopped. "NO! You don't mean . . ."

"Sorry, but the white fur is perfect cover in this environment. Besides, there's a chance that Rusha sent a few yetis down here to keep an eye on DeMarco and his team."

AB shuddered again. "What I do for the cause." He shook his head. "But I'm not a yeti, so I may freeze in forty below temperatures. I'll need something to wear, and, if that's the case, why the yeti camo?"

Uncle Merl smiled. "Good try, but once underground, you'll need to strip off the suit. Best if you still look the part of a yeti. We may have to be your prisoners again."

AB muttered, "You better hope not." He plopped back in the chair.

Uncle Merl ignored him. "So, what do you suggest?"

"Can the ship jam Mr. Demarco's communications links and make it look like it's some kind of natural glitch?"

Uncle Merl nodded. "Of course. It can even create false auroras if need be. Why?"

"My credentials will get us in the second tier so long as they can't check with the home office."

"But what about us?" I chimed in.

"The company knew that I was traveling with all of you. You may not have free reign in the facility, but we can deal with that once we get inside."

"At least we know where the scepter is, and we've got a map of the old facility. We should be able to find a way to . . ." Uncle Merl coughed ". . . get to it."

"How do we know where the scepter is?" Rhea asked.

"A ZPEG gives off a distinctive energy signature. The ship has it . . ." Uncle Merl cleared his throat as the image on the screen created a 3D image of the complex and slowly zoomed in. "Here, on the penultimate level." A green light flashed in a spot in a large room near the bottom of the complex.

"Good." Imee nodded decisively. "When do we go?"

Uncle Merl stood up. "Now's a good time." A table lifted next to him with five mugs filled with a steaming beverage. Uncle Merl lifted one. "Drink up. It will insulate you somewhat from the cold and will give you energy for at least twenty-four hours." Uncle Merl lifted his mug and drank it. "Now, I'm off to suit up. I suggest you all do as well. Shannon will lead each of you to your quarters to change."

# CHAPTER 48
## NIMUE

I had expected a big white parka with a fur-lined hood. Instead the suit was thin, almost like the suits that Olympic ice skaters wear, with a hood that totally covered my face, and built in gloves that could be unsealed and pulled off. I didn't see how it would be warm enough, but knew better than to question Uncle Merl. I left the hood down around my neck and the gloves off. I thought about taking my backpack. The problem was, it wasn't white and would stick out like a sore thumb. I left it and walked out.

Shannon hovered outside my room, waiting for me. *If you will follow me.* She started off down the corridor.

*Where are the others?*

Like the hologram she was, she didn't pause. *Waiting for you at the door.*

*So, we've already landed?*

*Yes.*

We came around the bend and the others were waiting.

"Ah, there you are." Uncle Merl turned to the others. "A quick word about the suits. They're designed from the Atlantean fabric used as liners to their space suits. They'll be plenty warm enough." Uncle Merl gave me a sidelong glance as if reading my mind.

I wasn't paying attention, but rather was looking at Rhea in her skintight suit. It didn't leave much to the imagination.

*Pay attention!* AB admonished.

Uncle Merl scowled at me. "So, Charlie, once inside, how do you change the look of the suit?"

I shrugged. I'd been looking at Rhea. She smiled at me as I glanced at her again.

He shook his head. "You won't have to. The suits have adaptive camouflage. They will change once we enter the cave environment." His suit changed and appeared like his typical attire of a pair of blue jeans and a wrinkled button-down shirt. "But, for those of you that are telepathic"—he stared at me—"you can make them look like just about anything." His suit now changed into a military uniform.

Rhea laughed.

AB had changed his suit into a blue robe with a pointed blue wizard's hat.

Uncle Merl turned and smiled. "Touché. Now, shall we get on with it." He lifted his facemask and slipped on the gloves. "By the way, when the masks are up, you will have a com link to the rest of us. Now, masks and gloves on."

I walked over to help Rhea get her mask on, but she had it on by the time I got there. The door started to open.

A blast of super cold air hit me. I turned my back to it and quickly pulled up the hood and slipped on the gloves. I felt like Spiderman with my head and face completely covered, but the suit stopped the chill and I could see out comfortably. In fact, the suit even had a heads-up display that showed me who was in each suit. We walked away from the ship and around a small mound.

"Something's wrong." AB stopped. His head swiveled back and forth. "There!" He pointed.

I squinted. A rooster-tail of snow headed straight toward us. I wondered if the suit had enhanced visual capabilities. I thought about it, but my vision didn't zoom. Oh well, couldn't have everything.

"And there." AB pointed in another direction. Another rooster tail was shooting up out of the snow.

I heard Imee's voice over the com link. "Dr. Ambrose, can you get the ship to jam communications now, before whoever or whatever is coming toward us reports something?"

"Done."

"One more. They've got us surrounded." AB pointed behind us, in line with the ship. I looked back. The ship already looked like just another mound of snow.

We pulled together.

"They must have seen us exit the ship or seen snow kick up at landing," said Imee. "Dr. Ambrose, let me take the lead. My ploy with credentials might work now."

Uncle Merl nodded. "As van Moltke said, 'No plan survives first contact with the enemy.' So much for our plan."

"What?" I looked over at Uncle Merl.

"Never mind. Our guests are about to arrive. AB, you've got the best eyes. They're moving way too fast to be men on foot. What are they?"

AB looked from one to the other. "They're huge, bigger than male yetis, and they're bipedal." He looked over at Uncle Merl. "Frost giants?"

Uncle Merl shook his head. "Not here. Besides, Thor killed them all years ago."

"What? Thor?" Rhea asked.

I shuddered, thinking about that giant hammerhead. I knew that wasn't the Thor he was talking about, but the memory came back.

"Never mind. Irrelevant. Ask me later."

As they approached, the visitors slowed to a normal pace. They were huge, at least fifteen feet tall, and covered in white camouflage. They had what looked like large snowmobile helmets on their heads, and each carried a large weapon that looked like a powerful laser.

They stopped. An amplified voice boomed at us. "You are trespassing. You will come with us."

"Who are you and what do you mean, trespassing? This is Antarctica. It doesn't belong to anybody." Uncle Merl sounded incensed.

A shot from a laser was their answer. "Come with us. We're authorized to use deadly force. No more questions!" Two of the giants stayed behind us, while the third took the lead. "Follow in single file," a booming voice from behind us said.

The giant took steps like a person, but it was clearly mechanical. I couldn't tell whether it was a robot or whether someone was inside the device. At least it walked slowly enough for us to keep up with it. I wondered if AB's camouflage was holding up to the giants' electronic sensors. They hadn't paid AB any more attention than they'd paid the rest of us, so either they didn't care or his camouflage was working.

We were about a mile and a half from the hangars, which were behind a series of mounds. I caught up with Rhea and grabbed her hand, but that elicited a laser shot to my left.

"Single file," boomed the voice from behind us. I gave Rhea's hand a final squeeze, dropped it and slid back behind her. *What do you think we should do, Uncle Merl?* I watched Uncle Merl's figure striding silently through the snow in front of me.

*Let's hope that Imee's credentials hold up.*

*That's it?*

Uncle Merl gave me a mental shrug.

We closed on the last mound before the runway. The three giants came to a sudden stop. We stopped as well. The automatons didn't move as I stepped back, grabbed Rhea's hand and gave it a squeeze. I was about to move in front of the first guard when I picked up a mental gasp from Uncle Merl.

I glanced over at him. *What?*

He peered up to the left and didn't answer me.

*AB did. Nimue.*

I noted fear in AB's thoughts as well.

*Nim's back in Scotland.* I glanced over at AB.

His head was tilted up and to the left as well. *Not the cat. The person she's named after. Nimue.* AB gave a mental shudder.

A round object drifted rapidly toward us. It was hard to see at first since I could see right through it. It appeared to be a giant bubble.

"What is it?" Rhea asked me.

"Some kind of aircraft." It closed rapidly and began to descend. Uncle Merl continued to stare up at the craft. "Uncle Merl?"

He didn't answer. I glanced over at AB. "What's up with Uncle Merl?"

"Nimue," was his only answer.

Imee walked up to me, glancing from the stationary automaton guards to the approaching craft. "Who's Nimue? Is she worse than Rusha?"

AB answered, "Better and worse. My race owes her a great deal, but she is—inscrutable."

"What's that supposed to mean?" I shivered, but not from the cold. "Is she Lemurian?"

"No. She's more than Atlantean. She's also the Druid that re-cruited your uncle."

I walked over to Uncle Merl and grabbed his shoulder. "You ok?" He stood rigid as a statue. I glanced at his eyes staring up at the de-scending ship carrying Nimue. I waved my hand in front of his face, but got no reaction.

I walked over to AB. "So, what do we do?"

He gave me a forlorn look. "We wait—and not for long." He point-ed as Nimue's craft descended. It appeared to double in size as it set-tled into the snow. The ship looked like a huge iridescent snow globe sitting there. I could see a woman seemingly hovering in the middle of the ship. She focused her eyes on me, and I felt the onslaught of a mental assault. Images flashed before my eyes: my parents, Uncle Merl, Trolga, Rhea, Thor, Rusha and many others. Suddenly the pressure lifted. I staggered. Rhea and Imee grabbed my arms.

"You all right?"

I nodded. "I'm good."

The sphere was now opaque. A slit appeared down the middle and a stunning woman floated out and settled in front of us. All I could think of was that she was Aphrodite and Helen of Troy rolled into one. Red and violet flowers adorned her snow-white hair. She wore a sleeveless gossamer sky-blue gown, but didn't shiver in the bone-chilling cold. She glanced around, holding her gaze on each of us briefly. As her eyes passed over AB, he gave her a deep bow. When she reached Uncle Merl, he began to move again.

"Nimue, what's the meaning of this? You know..."

Nimue put her finger to her lips, silencing Uncle Merl. She smiled. "Why Merlin, it's been what, 250 years, and that's how you greet an old friend? The least you could do is introduce me to your traveling companions."

Uncle Merl scowled. "You know who they are and why we're here." He glanced over at me, and I felt a weight descend onto my shoulders again. "Why are you interfering?"

She laughed. "Just as you used to be, impetuous and impatient. Before giving me the third degree, join me on my ship so we can go someplace warmer."

Uncle Merl mumbled something under his breath and glanced at us. "Let's move. It's damn cold . . ." *and we have no choice.*

369

That last bit seemed to leak from Uncle Merl's mind. He headed for the opening of the ship, followed by AB and Rhea.

Imee stopped next to Nimue. "Thank you for your hospitality, Ms...."

Nimue laughed. "You may call me Nimue."

"Ms. Nimue. But, as Dr. Ambrose said, we have a mission in front of us."

Nimue shook her head. "Do not worry, young human. And yes, I have wiped this from the memories of the men in their automatons and have wiped their computers as well. They will have no memory of you or of this."

Imee's mouth opened, then closed. She entered the craft.

I paused and looked back at Nimue.

*Young son of Atlantis, fear not. I mean you no harm.* She smiled and extended her arm toward the door.

Uncle Merl and AB had said that it was impossible to lie telepathically, but I wasn't so sure. I entered the ship.

Nimue's feet settled on the floor, which was now opaque and a metallic color. She guided us to a room that looked like Richard's suite at the Seattle stadium. Several plush sofas and chairs sat in the room with a bar against one wall.

"Have a seat and help yourselves to refreshments. We'll be landing at my abode in just a few minutes." Nimue exited the room. The door closed behind her.

I walked toward the door.

"Don't bother, Charlie, it's locked." Uncle Merl grabbed a ginger beer from the counter. "Help yourselves. As that she-witch said, we'll be in her lair very soon." He sat down in one of the chairs. "Sit. Nimue's always been a good host."

Rhea had pulled her hood off and sat down. She smiled at me. "At least it's warm in here."

"Too warm if you want my opinion." AB grabbed a Coke and a bag of chips that he found sitting on the bar. He popped it open. "You all should eat. Cold saps calories. We might end up outside, and I doubt that Nimue will provide us with lembas."

I took heed and grabbed a Coke and a bag of chips myself. "Anybody else?" I glanced at Rhea. She nodded. Imee shook her head and walked around, examining the room. I grabbed another Coke and a bag of chips, took them to Rhea and sat down next to her.

"Thanks." She took a sip and leaned forward. "So, Dr. Ambrose, who's this Nimue and what do you think she wants?"

"Do you know the story of King Arthur and the Knights of the Round Table?"

Rhea nodded.

Uncle Merl shook his head. "In legend, Nimue is the Lady of the Lake. She gave Excalibur to Arthur and enchanted Merlin, trapping him in her cave." He gazed off into the distance, then shook his head. "Nimue is genetically Atlantean, but well beyond the originals. The Atlantean computers projected out where they would evolve over time. One Atlantean—we called him Kronos—took it upon himself to improve on their race rather than just recreate it. Nimue's the result. Her longevity, intelligence, and extrasensory capabilities are well beyond those of any other living thing. Rusha and the Lemurians found out about Kronos's research and attacked him about seventy thousand years ago. The result was the Toba eruption near Sumatra that almost destroyed *Homo sapiens*. It did destroy the super Atlanteans that Kronos had created, all but Nimue. She was quite young at the time, and Kronos had sent her to be educated by Galadriel."

Merlin looked up and paused. "We're landing." He started to pace. "Nimue was the Druid that took me from my family and educated me. She's telepathic and, through her ability to access zero-point energy, has telekinetic abilities as well. She is the most powerful being on the planet."

The door slid open and Nimue entered. "Entertaining the younglings, Merlin." She glanced over at us and smiled. "Please, follow me." She didn't wait for us to comply. Uncle Merl followed behind her. The rest of us took his lead.

We exited the craft and entered a large chamber. It remained dark, the only light coming from a large crystal in Nimue's hand.

She turned, her face illuminated by the light from the crystal. Her white hair draped down over her shoulders, and her emerald eyes shone. She brushed her hair back on one side, revealing one of her elf-like ears. She extended her arms. "Welcome to my abode."

Bright rainbows flashed across the chamber as light sprang forth from the walls behind Nimue. All of us shielded our eyes. The flashing subsided rapidly as Nimue lowered her arms. We were in a large cavern with huge crystals protruding from one side. Her ship sat behind us. I looked up, but didn't see an opening in the ceiling where it could have entered. Across from the huge crystals was a seating area with two sofas, two chairs and a coffee table that would look at home in just about any house in America. It looked totally incongruous in the cave. A large holographic screen floated in front of the seating area. It showed a replay of our landing just beyond Mr. DeMarco's airstrip.

I looked over at Uncle Merl. His shoulders slumped.

He ambled over to the sitting area and plopped down in one of the chairs. "So, Nimue, what do you have in store for us?"

Nimue seemed to glide across the floor until she stopped in front of Uncle Merl. "Funny you should ask, Merlin, but you are well overdue for your regeneration treatment."

"I thought I told you last time that I was done with that." Uncle Merl leaned forward slightly.

Nimue laughed. "You forget that we both read minds. What you said and what you thought deep down were two very different things. Besides, look at yourself. You've aged tremendously since I last saw you."

"Yes, but that was several hundred years ago. I should have aged." He sat back into the chair. It seemed to mold to his frame.

Nimue shook her head. "Your life span is so short. You need to be more careful. The radiation your tissue absorbed running away from the leaking reactor damaged you. You'd be dead in six months, a year at most, if I hadn't picked you up."

Uncle Merl shook his head. "Ridiculous. I just helped these younglings escape from Rusha's clutches. They could barely keep up with me."

I nodded. "He did keep a fast pace."

Nimue stared at me. "Think, Charlemagne. Does he look older now than when you first went to the Moon?"

His white hair had thinned and he did seem to have more wrinkles. I nodded. "Now that you mention it, he does—a bit."

Uncle Merl scowled at me. "Well, if that's it, pleasant visit, Nimue, but we've got pressing business to deal with." Uncle Merl tried to get up but couldn't. The chair began to envelop him. "What are you doing!" He glared at Nimue.

"Now Merlin, I knew that you'd argue with me, so I took matters into my own hands." As Nimue spoke the chair grew up over Uncle Merl's head.

I heard a faint *Nim . . .* but Uncle Merl's eyes closed and the chair encased him as if in a cocoon. It then slowly sank into the floor.

I stood. "What have you done to him?" I felt breath on my shoulder. AB. I gave him a brief mental thanks.

Nimue glided over the floor and poured herself some bright orange drink. She took a sip. *He's healing. If I'd waited, he would have died.*

*Can she lie telepathically?* I directed my thought at AB.

*I don't think—*

*Of course I can. You have much training to do. Merlin will have to direct that upon his return. Until then, finish your human education. AB, you are to be his guardian until Merlin's return. Do you accept?*

AB squeezed my shoulder and bowed his head. *Of course, Lady Nimue.*

I could picture AB's grin.

*Now, Dr. Merl Ambrose is ninety-four years old according to his records so it's high time for him to officially die. You'll find his will in Scotland. He leaves everything to Charlie.*

*What, he's dead?* I looked over at where Uncle Merl had descended below the floor in the chair/cocoon.

*No, of course not, but at the end of each normal human life span he needs to die. He already has his new identity ready to go. When he has fully recuperated, he will return under a different name, looking younger. He will contact you at that point, Charlie.*

*When?*

Nimue laughed. *In good time, in good time. Now, you have something important to do.* Nimue looked around the room at Imee and at Rhea. "You have to go now, but, before you do, accept a gift from me." A tray slid out from the wall behind us. Light flickered above it. Nimue glided over to the edge of the tray and extended a hand. "Each of you may select one crystal."

I looked down at the tray. Crystals and raw jewels of every shape and color filled it. I looked over at Rhea and Imee. Their eyes had widened. A king's ransom of jewelry sat in front of us.

Rhea picked up a crystal the size of an egg. "Diamond?" She looked at Nimue with wide eyes.

Nimue nodded. "Yes, but you can only select one crystal." She took the diamond from Rhea's hand and dropped it into a hole that appeared next to her in the floor. "Do not touch, just move your hands above the crystals. When you are ready, pick up the crystal you want. Once you touch a stone, that will be your selection."

Imee looked over the stones. Her hand hovered over the blood-red stones in the tray. She selected one and picked it up. She looked at it, looked over at Nimue, and slipped it in her pocket.

"A wise selection." Nimue stood silently as Rhea moved her hand over the tray. Her hand hovered over the green crystals. She started to reach for one of the largest green gems—I assumed they were emeralds—but pulled back. She shifted her hand and picked up a stone with a color that shifted between blue and purple.

Nimue nodded. "Interesting selection, daughter of Lemuria."

Rhea looked over at Nimue at the mention of Lemuria, but then pocketed the stone.

I stepped forward, but AB brushed past me. He didn't hesitate. He picked up a smoky stone the size of an ostrich egg.

Nimue nodded again. "The stone that represents your tribe."

"Thank you for the gift, milady." AB gave Nimue a bow as he slipped his gift into a pocket.

My turn. I scanned the contents of the tray. Light flashed off the crystals and gems. I recognized a star ruby like the one that Rusha had used to direct her power. As my hand passed over it, I felt nauseous and quickly moved my hand away. I glanced at the diamonds, emeralds and rubies, but something kept me away from them. My hand slid almost of its own accord toward the large hexagonal crystals in one corner of the tray. They looked like simple quartz, ranging in color from clear to brownish. My hand reached forward as if on its own and grabbed a clear hexagonal crystal about the size of a baseball. I could hear Jamie in my head sounding like Scotty from *Star Trek*. "Dilithium—now we can make warp speed, Captain." I smiled.

Nimue placed her hand on my shoulder, sending a shiver down my spine. "Good choice, son of Atlantis. Now you must all leave. Follow the passage." She extended her hand to our left. We glanced over as lights appeared in a tunnel that I hadn't noticed. When I looked back, Nimue was gone.

# CHAPTER 49
## INFILTRATION

I headed into the tunnel. The girls followed. I touched the wall. It felt perfectly smooth, as if carved by a giant laser. As we proceeded down the tunnel, it brightened in front of us. I glanced back. Darkness seemed to creep toward us. Nimue's cave was gone. The girls edged closer to me. AB towered along behind them.

The tunnel came to a bend. As we turned left around the corner, we entered a long cave. The walls were no longer smooth, with rock jutting out from the sides. I stopped and looked back. The tunnel we'd walked through was gone. I touched the wall where the tunnel had been. It felt solid.

I glanced over at AB.

He shrugged. "Probably a force field that looks like a natural wall."

Imee walked up and felt the wall as well. She shook her head. "I'll never get used to this. It's so surreal." She pulled the ruby she'd picked out of her pocket and looked at it. It glinted in the light. The light within it seemed to dim. I glanced around. I could see the girls' breath and felt a chill on my face.

"It's getting colder." Rhea pulled up her hood.

AB added, "And the lights are dimming. It appears that Nimue is prodding us forward."

"AB's right. We need to move forward."

Rhea glanced at me and Imee, and then headed forward. I followed right behind. We walked along the cave as it narrowed and widened. After roughly five minutes we came to a fork. We stopped.

"Now where?" Imee glanced down both tunnels.

I shook my head. The lights in the tunnel began to dim. "Anybody have a flashlight?"

Rhea and Imee shook their heads. AB shook his head as well, but pulled out a lighter. "This may give us a little light. I'm guessing that none of you selected the Light of Elendil?"

I smiled. "I wish, but then Shelob might be around the next corner."

That got a smile out of AB. He pulled out the lighter.

"Wait!" Imee grabbed his hand.

"What?" AB looked at her as the cave continued to darken.

Imee pointed down the tunnel to the right. As the light in the tunnel dimmed, we could see a glow coming from the end of the tunnel. "If we hurry, we might make it to that light source before it's too dark to see where we're going." She didn't wait and headed down the tunnel with her head down, carefully looking where she stepped.

We followed. Our eyes acclimated enough to the dim light so we could just see our feet. The tunnel turned sharply to the left. The light was coming from there. I glanced back. AB did as well.

"Stygian darkness. Nimue's covering her tracks." AB shrugged when we didn't react to his comment. We walked a few steps forward. I glanced back to see if the cave was still there. It was. No disappearing act this time.

The new tunnel seemed artificial, with smooth walls again. Since we had no clue where Nimue's cave was we could be anywhere, but I suspected we were now in the old Atlantean lab under the Antarctic Mountains. The tunnel ended in a brightly lit corridor. We stopped. I started to say something, but Imee stuck her finger to her lips. We listened. We could hear voices. They were getting louder. We stepped back into the shadows.

Imee whispered, "We need to grab somebody to question them."

"What if they get away?" Rhea fidgeted and glanced my way.

I slammed my palm against my forehead. "We've got a map of the facility. I had Shannon download it into my iLet." I tapped my wrist, and a three-dimensional hologram of the facility appeared above my wrist. A red dot appeared at the center of the map with a blue dot, us, at the periphery.

Imee put her hand over my wrist. The image disappeared. She then put her finger to her lips again with her other hand. When the talking had stopped, the sound of footsteps approached. I shut my iLet down and we carefully backed further into the tunnel—all of us but AB, that is.

*AB, they'll see you!*

I heard a chuckle in my head. *How quickly you forget.*

He stood still at the entrance to the tunnel. As the men approached, he seemed to fade out. I could barely make him out. Two men in white lab coats walked by. He stepped out behind them. The steps got softer as the men made their way down the hall. I stepped forward, but the men and AB had turned a corner.

"Where'd AB go?" Imee asked quietly.

I shook my head. "I'm sure he had a reason."

"So what do we do?" Rhea asked.

I flipped on the iLet and the map. "Let's see if we can find a way to the lab."

Rhea nodded, but Imee said, "You two study the map and I'll keep watch."

Rhea and I retreated back up the tunnel. I queried my iLet to run through various routes. We watched them, zoomed in on various sections, and tried to figure out which route would be best. I tried accessing Shannon to see if the ship's sensors could help, but we must have been too deep under the mountain. She didn't respond.

Next thing I felt a tap on my shoulder. I should have reacted, but I sensed AB just before he tapped me.

*You're getting better.*

*Thanks. Glad you didn't do that to Imee or Rhea. They might've screamed.*

*I'm not an idiot.*

I tapped Rhea on the arm and pointed at AB. He smiled. Rhea's eyes widened. "Can't get used to him creeping up like that."

AB gave her a bow. Imee walked up behind him. "How the hell did you get past me?"

AB bared his canines in a smile. "Evolution. We would not have survived the onslaught from your species had the Atlanteans not engineered camouflage into our genetic makeup. It works somewhat along the lines of telepathy, letting me involuntarily trick your mind into not seeing me. I have to actively think about letting you see me, or I would fade away."

As he said that, he started to fade out. I could see him, but Rhea's and Imee's jaws dropped. AB had never given them such a demonstration before.

"Why'd you follow those guys?" Imee seemed peeved and tense.

AB held up a badge. "Thought we might need this to get through some of the doors."

Imee's shoulders relaxed. "Good thinking." She looked over at us. "Find a route?"

Both of us nodded and started to talk at the same time. I tipped my head toward Rhea. "Ladies first."

Rhea smiled. "The lab's two levels below in the heart of the complex. We're right at the edge of the map. The tunnel must've been part of a large cave system that the Atlanteans exploited when they built the facility." Rhea pointed at my wrist and I flipped on the hologram.

She pointed at the flashing dots. Several lines ran from the red dot where we were to the blue dot. "Given the age of this facility, we don't know if any sections have collapsed or any routes are blocked. We know that DeMarco would have dug his way into the lab even if it were blocked, so, once we get close, we should be good to go. In the interim, we thought we'd move as close as we can to the center of the lab since the corridors around the periphery are more likely to have collapsed."

Imee started tapping her foot on the ground. "The point?"

I hadn't heard Imee get irritated with Rhea before, but then her persona as an innocent friend no longer existed.

To Rhea's credit, she stood her ground. "We need to know the route and the alternatives. The plan is to go in the direction that the two men came from into the heart of the facility. We will then follow this line." All but one of the lines on the hologram disappeared. "The key's getting down to the level of the lab."

Imee nodded. "Sorry, Rhea. A bit stressed and tired. Forgive me?"

Rhea nodded. "Me too. We're all tired."

"Let's go." I started to step out into the hall, but Imee grabbed my arm.

"AB goes first. His camouflage may come in useful. We will follow at a discrete distance. I'll take the rear. AB, raise your arm with a fist like this"—Imee lifted her right arm up with her hand in a fist—"if you need us to stop. Point forward when it's okay to move forward, and point back at us if someone's coming and we need to find cover. Ok?" Imee looked each of us in the eye. "Good. Let's go."

AB kept up a solid pace moving forward. He paused at the first corridor, holding his arm up with a fist. I took a deep breath.

*Everything ok?*

*Somebody down the hall. Wait. They just changed directions. They're heading to the control center.*

I pushed my mind forward and, sure enough, I could hear the thoughts of the man and the woman down the hall. They'd just received a call about the test being moved up and were hustling to the control center.

*We'd better hurry.* I thought to AB.

He signaled us forward. When we reached him, he explained the new plan to the others. He would keep a thread of thought tied to the two in front of us and follow them down to the control center.

AB rubbed his temples.

*You good?*

He nodded. *Yep, just painful to read ordinary* Homo sapiens. He stepped out into the hall and walked in the direction the two people had taken. We followed close behind. After several twists and turns, AB stopped us at a doorway. We waited a minute and then he opened the door.

"Hurry. Down two flights. Wait there." He held the door for us and we headed down, two steps at a time. When I got to the landing, I looked back. AB was squeezing the door handle. He grunted, and I heard metal groan. He waited momentarily and I heard someone try the door. It wouldn't open.

AB looked down at me and signaled me to keep going with a wave of his hand. I made it to the door below with AB right behind me.

"Ok. We're close. It's about a hundred meters down the corridor to the right. There's a jumble of people in the room." To me: *I can't read them. Can you?*

I extended my mind, but all I could detect was a jumble. I shook my head.

AB glanced over at me and Imee. "What do we do when we get to the control room?"

I hadn't really thought about that. Mr. DeMarco would certainly have some security, so I doubted that we'd be able to take the ZPEG back by force. "I guess we'll just have to persuade them to stop the test. If not, we'll have to improvise."

Imee looked at me skeptically and shook her head. "If Dr. Ambrose was right, failure is not an option."

I nodded. "We got in and out of Rusha's lair without anything better. If we can beat her, we can certainly beat mere *Homo sapiens*." I smiled at AB.

AB nodded. *Do not underestimate* Homo sapiens, *Charlie. They're extremely dangerous.*

I waited for the punch line. Nothing. I gave him a quizzical look. He shrugged.

"Ready? Let's go." AB opened the door.

I wished Uncle Merl was with us. Nimue knew the stakes and had sent us in this direction, but Uncle Merl had been fearful of her. She certainly had her own agenda. I only hoped it dovetailed with stopping Rusha's plan. Rhea smiled reassuringly.

We walked down the corridor to a large two-panel door. The door slid open as we stepped up to it.

# CHAPTER 50
## KING ARTHUR DEMARCO

A large chamber lay before us, but my eyes focused on Richard and his father standing near the middle of the chamber. Mr. DeMarco held up the Scepter of Apollymi and waved us in with it.

"Welcome, welcome. Please come in. You're just in time."

They stood near an elaborate chair raised up on a platform. It looked a great deal like the control chair in the Atlantean spaceship. Wires lead from the platform to a series of metal tables. Men and women in white lab coats huddled over laptops on the table.

I sensed something behind us. I glanced back. Two "frost giants" like the ones that had confronted us outside blocked the exit. Their facemasks were open, and I could see the men inside. The doors closed behind us.

"Tell your friend . . ." Mr. DeMarco looked over at Richard.

"AB."

"AB, that he doesn't need his deceptive camouflage here." Mr. DeMarco crossed his arms.

AB scanned the room and looked back at the frost giants behind him. "I'd comply, Mr. DeMarco, but there are many eyes in this room."

DeMarco waved his hand dismissively. "I trust these men and the scientists in this room implicitly. They've gone through the most rigorous background checks possible, have signed non-disclosure agreements, and are *very* well paid for their work and for their discretion."

DeMarco stared at AB. AB must have dropped his disguise because Mr. DeMarco's eyebrow rose slightly. He glanced over at Richard. "You weren't kidding."

Richard shook his head. "No, sir."

DeMarco walked over to AB and then around him. "Quite impressive, but I'd really like to understand this camouflage thing. I can see hundreds of military uses."

AB bared his large canines and let out a growl. The frost giants took a step forward, but DeMarco laughed and waved them back.

"Now, now, no false bravado here. My guards have orders to tranquilize any of you that make a false move." One of the white-coated scientists came over and whispered something to Mr. DeMarco. He nodded.

"We're just about ready for our first demonstration." DeMarco walked over to a table and sat down, placing the scepter in front of him. "Please sit. Want some tea?"

A man in a white jacket seemingly appeared out of nowhere with a tray set for tea.

To my surprise, AB took a seat at the end of the table. "Smells like dragon pearl jasmine. I'd love a cup." He embellished his statement with a British accent.

DeMarco laughed. "Richard told me you had quite a sense of humor." Another young lady in a black and white maid's outfit, looking totally out of place, walked in with a tray of sandwiches. DeMarco took one and then signaled her to offer sandwiches to the rest of us.

AB grabbed several. "So, Mr. DeMarco, you obviously know about Atlantis and this old base. What are you planning on doing here?"

DeMarco smiled. "Blunt. I like that. Let me give you some background.

"My interest in historical anachronisms goes way back to a cruise my grandparents took me on to Easter Island the summer after my father died. The moai statues seemed otherworldly. I started studying history and wanted to specialize in anachronisms like the moai, the Piri Reis map, Stonehenge and the legends of Atlantis. I studied hard and was heading to Harvard with a full ride when the crash of thirty-three occurred. My grandfather's business cratered. He lost everything. He couldn't face the shame. I found him in his den, dead in his favorite chair. In his suicide note, he asked me to forgive him and asked that I take care of my grandmother with the insurance proceeds.

"That's when I changed my path. I set my grandmother up in the best assisted-living home that I could afford with the life insurance proceeds and then went to Harvard. I vowed to make so much money that I'd never be in his position. Instead of studying history, I focused on business, taking a smattering of tech and psych courses. I worked my ass off, but took the time to make friends with the top nerds at Harvard and frequented the nerd bar for Harvard and MIT students. While brilliant, they had no business sense. I did. NanoNano and Qbits became the top tech startups since Facebook. The rest is history.

"Once I made my first billion, I started funding research into anachronisms. As my wealth grew, so did my funding. I endowed many edgy researchers. After reading an article on Atlantis written by Leslie Thomas I started funding her research.

DeMarco pointed at me. "I believe I funded a few of your trips to the Bahamas so your parents could research the Bimini road and lost Atlantis. Their discoveries led me here, to this old Atlantean lab, and your guidance lead Richard to this." He tapped the Scepter of Apollymi in his left hand.

I ignored the fact that Richard and Trolga had taken the scepter from me. "You knew my parents?" I asked as DeMarco paused for a sip of tea.

"Of course not. Never met them. Just gave them money to pursue Atlantis. Money well spent. Now, where was I?"

I interrupted his story again. "Did they come here?"

DeMarco frowned. "Young man . . . ."

"Dad" Richard interrupted Mr. DeMarco.

DeMarco glared at his son.

Richard looked sheepishly over at me. "Charlie's parents disappeared. That's why he moved to the Moon."

DeMarco looked over at me. "Sorry to hear that. Maybe after this is all over, I can help you find them. Now, as to the discovery. I had thought that mining helium-3 on the Moon would result in the next energy boom and propel me into becoming the first trillionaire on the planet. Unfortunately, helium-3 mining's very expensive. Don't get me wrong. Dahak Mining would have eventually made its new owners billions more than they paid me for it, but that was before today. Once we harness zero-point energy, every other source of energy will become obsolete."

DeMarco walked over to the control chair. He put his hand on it, resting the scepter on the arm of the chair.

I gasped as I noticed the slot in the side of the chair. It looked made for the Scepter of Apollymi to slip right into it.

DeMarco heard my gasp and smiled. "Yes, the scepter that Richard brought me does appear to be the key to the puzzle of this control chair." He stepped up on the platform and sat down in the chair. "Not altogether comfortable, but from what my scientists tell me, it could be the key to harnessing zero-point energy—which is why you're all here.

"My son—" Mr. DeMarco pointed the scepter at Richard, "—tells me that you—" he pointed the scepter at me. Energy surged toward me, "—Mr. Thomas, want to stop me from activating the ancient Atlantean devices, and you sabotaged my operations on the Moon."

I stepped back as the energy pulse from the scepter washed over me.

Mr. DeMarco laughed. "No need to fear reprisal, Mr. Thomas. I sold most of my interest in Dahak Mining before that little setback on the Moon. Besides, you didn't scram the reactor. My partner in this venture took care of that little detail. She told me about zero-point energy, rendering helium-3 mining moot."

The air next to the chair started to shimmer. A form slowly took shape. Rhea gasped as the image cleared.

"Trolga." I groaned.

She laughed. "Yes, Mr. Thomas, I set you up on the day you landed on the Moon. We knew about the Atlantean base and needed you with your Atlantean DNA to get in. I lost several pawns when the base's automated systems self-destructed, but you did lead us to the scepter."

I couldn't believe my ears. "You knew about my uncle, and knew that he'd take me to Galadriel?"

Trolga laughed. "Of course. We had the knowledge, and Arthur had the money. All we needed was the key." Trolga looked over at DeMarco holding the scepter. "Now that we have it, I'll become the wealthiest woman in the world!" She glanced over at DeMarco and smiled.

DeMarco nodded. "Yes, Olga. You have been a valuable ally for the past few years. Your work will be amply rewarded."

I looked over at Richard. Even he seemed surprised.

"She assured me that you could help find the Scepter of Ap . . ." DeMarco glanced over at Trolga's hologram.

"Apollymi."

"So she scrammed the reactor to get you off the Moon and in search of the scepter. She tells me it has quite the history. It could be the fact behind the legend of Excalibur." DeMarco looked over at Trolga.

I shook my head. "So you think you're King Arthur, then, sitting on that throne?"

DeMarco burst out laughing. He looked down at Richard. "He's got balls. You could learn something from him."

Richard nodded, and then turned and gave me an "if looks could kill" glare.

"I have no need for titles. I am already the wealthiest man in history. Croesus would be a mere beggar at my feet. I can buy and sell kings and queens."

I started to understand where Richard got his arrogance, but Mr. DeMarco was far worse. He had a glint in his eye that reminded me of Rusha.

I stepped forward. "Look, Mr. DeMarco, Trol— Dr. Larsen's lying. If you start up the Atlantean machine with the scepter, it will not activate a zero-point energy generator. It will activate an Atlantean antigravity device that will wipe out this base and most of Antarctica, plunging the world into a prolonged winter that will kill off most of mankind!"

Silence had settled into the chamber. Even the scientists working on the laptops had turned to stare at me.

DeMarco looked around and then burst out laughing again. "I should keep this kid around. I haven't laughed this much in years." He glanced over at Trolga, who was also laughing, looking right at me. Her glare was worse now than it had been that first time she'd attacked me on the Moon.

DeMarco glanced over as one of the scientists approached him. He stepped up on the dais and whispered in DeMarco's ear. He nodded.

"It would seem that we're ready to run the first test. As for your fears, young man, why would I listen to an unfounded story from a teenager rather than the advice of my top scientists?" He shook his head. "No, zero-point energy will revolutionize the world, bringing about a golden age for mankind."

He lifted the scepter.

"Did she promise you eternal life?" I stepped toward the dais.

DeMarco glared at me. "You're quite well informed. I hear that uncle of yours is quite smart. Where is he?" DeMarco looked at us. He turned to Trolga. She shook her head. "No matter. One old man, however smart, can't change things."

"Yes, but one young woman can." Imee had stepped forward, a gun in her hand. The guards in the frost-giant suits raised their weapons, but Imee yelled back. "Lower your weapons or I'll shoot. He knows how well trained I am." Imee nodded her head at DeMarco. "I'm a crack shot. I will not miss." They lowered their weapons.

DeMarco glared at Imee. "Well, Ms. Castillo, your true colors come out. I should have hired the other candidate to babysit my son."

He glanced over at Richard.

Richard's face reddened. He stepped toward Imee. "Imee, what the hell're you doing?"

"Stop, Richard. Another step and I'll shoot your father."

"Is this some kind of joke?" Richard hesitated. Imee looked deadly serious.

"No joke, Richard. I hired Ms. Castillo's firm to keep an eye out for you. They instructed her to get close to you and take care of you. I gather from the reports that she really threw herself into her work." DeMarco chuckled, but then got serious as he faced Imee. "You'll not stop me, Ms. Castillo." DeMarco signaled the guards. They raised their weapons and fired.

Imee got off two shots before the tranquilizer darts reached her.

"Imee, no!" Richard dove toward Imee, but too late to stop her shots. He tackled her already limp body.

Mr. DeMarco hadn't moved. He had a smug look on his face. Too smug. I remembered the Atlantean force fields. DeMarco laughed as one guard lifted Imee's inert form.

"You have balls too." He glanced at Richard. "What should I do with her?"

Richard stood there, glaring as they dragged Imee off. I couldn't imagine what Richard was thinking. He looked up at the piercing eyes of his father. "I don't care. She tried to kill you."

DeMarco waved dismissively at the guards. "Take her to a holding cell.

"Now, how about you, Mr. Sasquatch? Care to try anything? You're big and strong. It'd be interesting to see how you performed against my exoskeletons."

AB straightened up. He watched as one of the guards easily carried an inert Imee from the room. "Mr. DeMarco, despite what you might think, we sasquatch are passive by nature. We've observed you humans for a very long time. Your race has many redeeming qualities, but also many self-destructive ones. You have always had very short life spans, and that has troubled your kind for years. You always search for the fountain of youth. What will your billions or trillions accomplish when you are dust? You may be richer than Croesus, Crassus, Augustus Caesar, Akbar I, Rockefeller, Gates or a host of others, but they're all now dust. Gathering wealth of staggering levels is a futile attempt at immortality."

DeMarco yawned. He glanced over at Trolga. "What did you say the life expectancy of a sasquatch is?"

Trolga smiled widely. "About five hundred years." She licked her lips. "I think we could learn a great deal about longevity from studying him and his kind. Our research facility in India may be the best place for him."

DeMarco nodded. "Good idea. My geneticists tell me that the drugs and protocols you've developed will extend my life to at least 150. Five hundred plus sounds even better. Take him to a holding cell."

Another guard in the frost-giant exoskeleton came up behind AB. I expected AB to resist or do something, but he merely began to walk in front of the guard. *Physical assault is not going to work. Keep trying to persuade DeMarco to stop the test. If that fails, follow your instincts. They are your best weapons.*

The guard escorted AB from the chamber.

I looked up at DeMarco, and then the hologram of Trolga. He looked smug, while she appeared gleeful. I glanced over at Rhea, standing just to my left. She seemed in a daze, staring off at Trolga.

I focused on Trolga. "If you do anything to her I'll . . ."

DeMarco interrupted. "Young man, I thought that your parents would have taught you better manners. I had planned on you and young Miss Harte witnessing the successful tapping of zero-point energy, but I'd be more than happy to let you join your hairy companion."

"Sir," I started, "you've got to believe me." I looked over at Richard. "You can't trust them. Dr. Larsen is a Lemurian, the arch-enemy of the Atlantean civilization. They want nothing more than to destroy the last vestiges of Atlantis. You are playing into their hands."

DeMarco looked over at Trolga. "Right again. She told me you'd say that. She's already told me about her Lemurian lineage and their focus on genetic research and longevity. With the new funding that I can provide, we'll pass the inflection point where medical technology will outrace death. Of course, we can't release that to the world at large. Even with infinite and cheap energy, the masses would waste such a gift. True longevity will be kept to a limited few."

I shook my head. "They're planning on killing billions when you activate the chair."

"Don't be ridiculous. Olga and her Lemurian team will profit right alongside me. They have no interest in destroying what we've created." DeMarco looked over at Trolga.

"He's got quite the imagination, one of the most creative students I've ever had the displeasure to teach. Don't be ridiculous, Charlie. I've already taken Arthur's most intensive background check and lie detector tests. He knows that I am absolutely loyal to him."

"Then why aren't you here, to witness the test?" I asked.

Trolga laughed. "I'm in India at our genetic research center, of course."

DeMarco smiled. "Olga's loyal to me and, more importantly, needs my resources. Now . . ." DeMarco glanced over at the nearest table filled with laptops. He got a thumbs up from a grey-haired scientist in a lab coat. "We're ready."

Mr. DeMarco started to put the scepter in the slot in the control chair. "Don't!" I stepped forward, but an arm grabbed me from behind.

DeMarco slipped the scepter in the slot and pushed it forward. At first nothing happened. Then the lights in the chamber dimmed, and then brightened.

"Project the results in front of me." DeMarco addressed one of the scientists.

An analogue speedometer appeared in front of us. A dark green arrow pointed at 12:00. It slowly began to move to the right.

DeMarco looked over at me. "Each mark represents a gigawatt of power." The needle continued to move around the circle, passing ten gigawatts.

DeMarco watched the screen as it reached and held at twenty-five gigawatts and smiled broadly. "That's more energy than any power plant in the world. And we've barely scratched the surface." DeMarco put a finger to his ear. "Looks like we're about done with the test. Our batteries are fully charged." He slowly pulled back on the scepter. Nothing happened. The meter continued to hold at twenty-five gigawatts.

He looked over at the lead scientist. "What's going on?"

The man nervously glanced over at DeMarco and then back at his screen.

"Well?"

"I don't know, sir. The flow of energy from the ZPEG isn't stopping."

DeMarco's face reddened. "Shut it down then."

The man hit a few keys on his computer. Instead of the power level dropping, the meter started creeping up over the thirty gigawatt mark.

"Our batteries are fully charged. Shut this thing down—NOW!"

The scientists looked nervously back and forth. One walked over to the control chair. As he did, I glanced around. Trolga's hologram sported a huge smile.

I glanced over at Rhea. She'd noticed as well. "What's going on?"

"I don't know, but if Trolga's smiling, it's not good." I glanced around. The guard seemed distracted.

Rhea squeezed my hand.

Trolga was staring right at me. I waited for a mental impact, but nothing happened. DeMarco's scientist looked pale. The meter reading now stood at just before midnight. It looked like over fifty megawatts was flowing through the system.

"Where's the power going?"

The scientist glanced nervously at his colleagues. "We don't know, sir, but it appears that several dormant pieces of equipment in this facility are turning on. The power must be flowing into them."

DeMarco glanced around the room. His scientists scurried around like chickens in a coop. His face reddened. He looked at me, giving me the evil eye. "Richard."

"Yes, sir." Richard pulled his gaze from the meter that now had its needle maxed out.

"Is Mr. Thomas capable of sabotaging this demonstration?"

Richard glanced over at me. He shook his head. "No, sir. No way. He's not smart enough."

I nodded. "I didn't do it. I suggest that you look at your partner over there." I pointed at Trolga with her canary-eating grin.

DeMarco faced Trolga's image. She started to laugh.

"What are you laughing at, Olga! If this is your doing, I'll get you and everyone that you care for." DeMarco glared at her. He tapped his ear and his eyes widened. "Why is our communication down?"

Nobody responded, but Trolga began to laugh out loud.

"Your threats are meaningless, Arthur. You can't touch me. In fact, soon enough, everything that young Mr. Thomas said will come to pass and you'll all be dead."

"What the hell do you mean?" He then turned to his scientists. "Shut the systems down and contact my security team." He looked over at the remaining guard in the exoskeleton. "Do you have contact with your home office?"

The man shook his head. "No, sir. All my remote systems are off-line."

DeMarco stood on the dais and glared at Trolga. "My resources are nearly infinite. There's nowhere you can hide."

"I won't have to. Once the Atlantean antigravity weapon charges . . ." She glanced over at something outside of the scope of her hologram. "In just a few minutes, you'll all be dead—blasted into space like Lemuria millennia ago."

DeMarco glanced at his scientists. They scurried around helplessly.

I glanced at Trolga, and then at the control chair. The stone inside the scepter pulsed with light. "It's the scepter. Remove the scepter. It's the key to the ZPEG."

DeMarco glanced at me. A surprised look briefly crossed his face, but then he grabbed the scepter and yanked at it, trying to remove it from the control chair. It wouldn't budge.

Trolga laughed. "So, Arthur, you can't pull the sword out of the stone—and yes, the scepter is Excalibur. A fitting end, wouldn't you say."

I glanced at the scepter and moved toward it. "Go ahead, Mr. Thomas, but you're too late." As she spoke the crystal within the scepter began to brighten. Trolga laughed as her image faded and the hologram winked out.

DeMarco climbed out of the chair, backing away from it. The light within the crystal started to pulse rapidly. We all backed away from it. It shattered, shards of crystal flying around the room. All of us dove to the ground. One piece must have grazed Mr. DeMarco, because when he stood, blood dripped from a gash on his cheek. He glanced over at the chief scientist. "You, stay here and get this thing shut down." The scientist cowered. "And you"—he addressed the guard—"make sure they stay at their posts and get this shut down."

The guard came to attention and the scientists eyed him warily.

"Richard, let's go." He headed toward the exit at a fast clip. Richard glanced over at us and then followed.

I looked over at the chair and the scepter. The scepter remained in its slot in the chair, but only a blackened shard of crystal remained within it. "What do we do now?"

Rhea shook her head. "No clue."

AB had said that I should trust my instincts, and my instinct was the scepter. I approached the dais and the scepter, grabbed it and shifted it back and forth. It moved, but nothing happened. Indirect lights from the walls and roof had kicked on. The Atlantean facility did seem to be back in business. I yanked the blackened shard from the scepter and threw it on the floor.

"We can't leave. We'd never find Imee and AB and get to the Atlantean ship in time. Even if we did, if the gravitonic weapon goes off, it will end civilization as we know it. I don't want to live in a world where Rusha and Trolga reign supreme over the remnants of mankind."

"What about the Atlantean that you met, Galadriel. Can you contact her?" Rhea looked hopeful.

I focused my thoughts on Galadriel, but nothing happened. I screamed her name as loudly as I could telepathically, but no response.

I shook my head. "No luck. If Trolga's got her claws into this project, I'm guessing she built in a dampener."

My instinct was telling me to sit in the chair. I did. I instantly felt a tingling throughout my body. I focused. If the Atlantean ship had a holographic controller, this base surely must as well. I thought, *Computer, what's your status?*

The response was quick. *Operational, but only limited access to systems.*

*What is the status of the zero-point energy generator?*

*Nominal.*

*Where's the power going?*

Rhea nudged me. "What's going on?"

I looked down at her. "I'm talking with the computer. It responds to me when I'm in the chair."

*The $#U$)#W\*W)@$$)(@\* device is operational and storing power.*

*What is that device? What does it do?*

*It is programmed to disrupt the flow of gravity over a certain area or object, thereby creating a repulsive force to push the target away from the gravity field currently constraining the area.*

Sounded like the gravitonic weapon. *What's its target?*

*The entire western side of Atlantis.*

"Shit." I looked down at Rhea.

"What?"

"The gravitonic weapon's activated and targeted on half of Antarctica."

"Turn it off!" Rhea looked hopeful.

"I'm trying." I switched to telepathy with the computer. *Switch off the gravitonic device.*

*Unable to comply.*

*Why?*

*It has built up too much energy.*

*When will it activate?*

*In five minutes.* A display clock appeared before me.

I looked over at Rhea.

"What's wrong?"

"I can't shut it off. It's built up too much energy."

"You can do it, Charlie, I know you can."

Scientists scrambled around the room, but they looked as lost as I felt. One darted for an exit. The guard turned and shot him before he'd gotten ten feet. He dropped to the ground.

I didn't have time to worry about the guard. *Is there any way to stop the device from activating?*

*It can only be shut off using the $%U40.*

*What's that?*

*The $%U40.*

*How much time's left? Display a countdown clock.*

Numbers appeared holographically in front of me. Rhea gasped as they appeared next to her—two minutes and counting. She looked up at me, desperation in her eyes.

Nothing. No ideas. My hand came to rest on the scepter. Now that the crystal was gone I felt no energy pulsing within it. I shifted it back and forth and nothing happened. I pulled on it and, unlike for DeMarco, it came free easily in my hand. I stuck it back in the chair and gave a mental command for the $%U40 to stop the gravitonic device, but the clock continued to count down.

I closed my eyes. Images of my mother and father passed before my eyes. I pictured Rhea, AB and Uncle Merl. How could I fail them all? My head drooped. I felt something warm in my pocket. I looked down. Something in there was glowing. I reached in and pulled out Nimue's gift. I glanced at the scepter, and then at the crystal. It couldn't be. I pulled out the scepter and started to slide the crystal into the spot where the old crystal had been. When I got it within a couple of inches of the scepter, the crystal shot out of my hand as if pulled by a magnet, settling in the cradle at the top of the scepter. It began to pulse.

I slipped the scepter back into the slot in the chair. I was about to slide it forward when one of the women in a lab coat pulled out a weapon and pointed it at me. I cringed, thinking I'd failed, closed my eyes, pushed the scepter forward, and focused on the thought: *Graviton shut down.* I heard a shot, gave a brief prayer, and waited to feel a bullet tear through me. It didn't. I opened my eyes.

"You did it. The clock stopped!" Rhea leaped up onto the dais and gave me a hug. I smiled and hugged her back. She pulled away, put her hands on either side of my face, looked into my eyes, leaned forward and gave me a long, hard kiss.

She pulled away. "Charlie, you're amazing!"

I smiled, speechless.

She gave me another quick kiss and then stepped back off the dais.

I looked over at the woman in the lab coat. The guard in the exoskeleton bent down over her. He stood, shook his head. He looked over at all of the scientists who had stopped their work, staring at the two bodies.

A loud voice trumpeted from the suit. "All scientists evacuate this room and go to your quarters." One scientist stepped toward the guard, but he raised his weapon. The scientists scrambled to get their laptops and took off out of several doors.

Once the room had emptied, the guard walked up to us. He bent to one knee. The exoskeleton opened and he stepped out. He appeared to be in his twenties and stood just a little taller than me. He was wearing army fatigues.

"Why'd you save me?"

The man smiled. "Turnabout's fair play. You just saved all of us."

I nodded and stepped off the dais. "Charlie Thomas." I extended my hand.

He took it, grasping it firmly. "Bob Reid. Good to meet you. And . . ." He turned to Rhea.

"Rhea Harte. Nice to meet you too." She smiled, looking into the man's ice blue eyes. Her eyes then scanned down at the blood seeping from under the woman in the white lab coat.

Bob shook his head. "Too bad, but we had a file on that scientist. She was part of the team sent by Dr. Larsen." He looked around. "My boss wanted me to watch out for all of them. Something about her bothered him."

I nodded. "Your boss must be a good judge of character."

Rhea squinted at Bob. "Bob, did you know Imee at Forrestal Security?"

Bob chuckled. "Good guess. We trained together. So, what you said about a gravitonic device destroying the world was true?"

I nodded. "I think so." I glanced over at Rhea. She hadn't taken her eyes off Bob. "We've got to get out of here before DeMarco or

Trolga—Dr. Larsen—figures out the graviton didn't go off. Can you go free Imee and my friend AB?" Rhea glanced from Bob to me.

Bob Reid thought for a minute and then nodded. "I can get close enough to the guards in the lockout rooms to free Imee and then get her help to free your friend. Is he really a Bigfoot?" Bob raised his eyebrows.

I nodded. "Yes, but he's a great guy. Just make sure he knows you're on our side."

"Point taken." He reached into his pocket and then flipped a small device to me. "Radio with a scrambler. Just go to channel 11. If something comes up, let me know. Otherwise, I'll let you know when I free Imee."

I handed the radio to Rhea. "Good. Once you free Imee and AB, come back and we'll follow you out."

He nodded. "To where? We're in the middle of Antarctica."

Rhea smiled at Bob. "We have a ride and room for you."

Bob nodded. "I'll contact you when they're free. Should take about ten minutes." He climbed into the exoskeleton and took off. I took a deep breath and looked over at Rhea.

She laughed, leaned over and gave me a kiss. "Jealous? He's really good looking. Those blue eyes . . ."

My face reddened.

"Don't worry, Charlie, I was just thinking about Imee. He's not my type—you are."

I smiled weakly.

"We don't have a lot of time. Got any ideas?" Rhea looked hopeful.

"Since I have the Atlantean genes, the chair responded to me. I'll sit back down and see what I can find out. Since I can focus better with my eyes closed, tap my arm if someone comes in or if Bob radios us."

Rhea nodded.

I climbed back into the chair and grasped the top of the scepter. I could feel power surging through it. It seemed to connect me to strands of glowing fibers running throughout the complex. I could barely make out the strands as I looked around. I closed my eyes and the strands brightened considerably. Most of them ran from the control chair on the dais but some seemed independent. They reminded me of a video of the nervous system in the body that I'd seen in science class with bright flashes flowing along the various lines.

I focused on the main computer, and an image of a brightly glowing object several floors below me came into view. Threads came and went from it all over the facility.

*Computer, can you disable the gravitonic device?*

*I don't understand what you are asking.*

*Can you destroy the gravitonic device?*

*You are not authorized for that command.*

Somebody must have turned the device on. It wouldn't have just started itself. Clearly one of Trolga's people had managed to access it so it would start syphoning off power once DeMarco turned power on.

*Computer, is there a video record of activity within the base?* I wasn't sure when DeMarco had first accessed the base, but if my parents had led him here it must have been roughly around the time that they disappeared. The last message that I'd gotten from them was that they were in southern Chile. That's about as close to Antarctica as you can get. They must have come here, notified DeMarco of their discovery and then disappeared.

*Visual records are available.*

*Please run the video of the first activity in the last couple of years.*

A beam of light began to illuminate a long corridor. I couldn't see much other than the beam of light. I felt a tap on my arm and opened my eyes.

"Charlie, did you turn this display on?" Rhea pointed to a hologram in front of the chair.

"Yes." I hadn't realized that the computer was displaying a hologram as well as a mental image. I spoke out loud. "Computer, please brighten the image."

*Of course.* The image brightened. We could make out two people walking into a large cavern. I caught my breath as my heart began to pound. My parents!

A chill ran up my spine as I watched them make their way into the chamber I was currently sitting in. As they did, lights from the wall slowly started to come on. My parent's Atlantean genes must have triggered the lights as mine had at the Lunar base. They approached the control chair. My mother's hand had rested where mine was now. I let out a sob.

Rhea looked up. "Your parents?"

I nodded. Tears trickled down my cheeks. Rhea stood on the dais and gave me a hug.

"I'm so sorry, Charlie." She brushed back my hair. "At least you know they were here. Maybe the computer can track them to when they leave."

I straightened up in the chair, suppressed a sniffle, and tried to put my emotions behind me. I smiled at Rhea. "Good idea. Computer, track the video feed to two minutes before the two individuals shown exit this complex."

The video skipped forward to my parents opening a door. They stepped into a stark room and looked around. My mother was taking videos with her phone. I chuckled to myself when I thought back about trying to talk her into getting a new one instead of the dinosaur that she used. She'd told me that it worked and she knew how to use it, so why get a new one?

Their eyes settled on something that looked like a large hourglass lying on its side. It was hollow and had no end on either side. It was about ten feet long, and the opening seemed slightly higher than my mother, maybe just under six feet. The device seemed to shimmer and wiggle like an iridescent soap bubble. They walked around the object, peering into each side. They must have heard a sound. Both looked back at the door. My father went to the door and glanced down the corridor. He came back in, grabbed my mother's arm and pointed down the corridor.

"Computer, freeze the picture and zoom out so we can see down the corridor."

"What is it?" Rhea asked.

"I don't know, but I know that look."

The picture zoomed out. A shape turned the corner and started down the hall. It loped rapidly on all fours. Dread seeped through me.

Rhea gasped. "It's a brahma . . . something. Like Rusha."

I nodded, horrified. We both recognized the person walking behind it. Trolga. I focused back on my parents. They looked around the room, but there was no other exit. If Trolga had killed them I swore that I'd get her. My mother touched the shape and the shimmering increased rapidly. They walked around the device and hid behind it as the vampire and Trolga entered the room. My father peered into the device. He tapped my mother's shoulder. She shook her head. He popped his head up over the device. Trolga spotted him. The vampire leaped for them. My father pushed my mother through the device, hunched down and followed right behind her. The vampire charged around the device and charged into it.

Rhea gasped again. The vampire shot through the other side, but my parents didn't! Trolga and the vampire walked around the device, looking through it. She touched the device, but it no longer shimmered. She pointed to the entrance and the vampire ran through again. Nothing happened. Trolga shrugged her shoulders, and she and the vampire left the room.

"Computer, where's that room? Show me a map to it!" I leaned forward.

The computer did not show a map.

"Computer, show the map!"

The computer finally responded. *You have an incoming priority message. It overrides all other requests.*

The image of Galadriel appeared in my head. *Charlie, you've got to leave. The Lemurians are heading to the base.*

*But my parents—*

*I know. Come back here. I'll tell you what happened.*

*You knew? You knew when you met me?*

Galadriel tilted her head to one side. *Charlie, its complicated. Please come . . .*

The image broke off as a siren sounded. Another countdown clock appeared.

"Shit."

"What?" Rhea looked at the countdown clock. "Is the graviton back on?"

I shook my head. "I don't think so, but I'll find out."

Rhea's radio went off. I nodded to her as she answered it.

*Computer, why's the alarm on?*

*Sensors detect a major Lemurian encroachment. The self-destruct has been activated.*

*Deactivate, NOW!* I mentally shouted at the computer.

*You are not authorized for that action. You have eighteen minutes and thirty-eight seconds to evacuate.*

*Deactivate!*

*Not possible.*

I looked over at Rhea. As I did, she glanced toward the door. Bob Reid in his exoskeleton entered with AB and Imee right behind him.

"What's the countdown clock?" Imee looked at the hologram which had gotten down to eighteen minutes.

I pulled the scepter out of the slot in the chair and jumped off the dais. "That's a self-destruct countdown. Lemurians are on the way."

"Lemurians?" The voice boomed from the exoskeleton.

I looked up at Bob Reid, AB and Imee. "No time. You've got to lead us out of here."

Bob responded. "Follow me."

He trotted off and we followed him.

I glanced back at AB. *Did you know about my parents?*

*Know what?*

*That they'd been here?*

*No.* He paused. *Really?*

I thought for a minute.

*Nimue said she could lie telepathically, but you said you can't. Which is true?*

*Both. Nimue is ancient. She's capable of far more than me or even your uncle. She could lie to you. I can't.*

I followed behind Bob, Imee and Rhea, thinking, not paying attention to where we were going. If Galadriel knew about my parents, was she really any better than Trolga. Did Uncle Merl know? He seemed to know everything. Had Nimue and he plotted for him to conveniently disappear, or was she telling the truth when she said he needed to regenerate? My head swam. All I knew was that my parents had been here and I needed to find out where they'd gone.

*Computer, what is the device in the video you showed us?* No response. *Computer, answer me.*

Still no response. Either I had to be in the control chair to communicate with the computer, or Galadriel had somehow shut down my connection to it. I almost bumped into Rhea. Bob had stopped and held up his hand. We had entered a large cavern filled with vehicles. People were scrambling all over the place. He pointed to a large vehicle on tracks. "Follow me to that vehicle. Imee can drive it."

She nodded.

"Get in—quickly." He paused. "We've got just over six minutes."

He didn't wait and walked out toward the vehicle. We followed. Nobody seemed to take note of us in all the confusion. We made it to the vehicle without incident. Imee jumped in first, got in the driver's seat and cranked up the engine. We weren't even sitting down before she hit the gas, heading out.

"Where's Bob?" Rhea looked around.

Imee answered. "He can keep up with us in the exoskeleton. Quicker for him to do that than to wait for him to get out and get in the vehicle."

Imee pulled outside the cavern and headed down a road toward the landing field.

I looked down at my iLet. "We'll never make it to the ship before the self-destruct goes off."

Imee nodded. "Going as fast as I can. Let's hope that the self-destruct isn't a nuke or something else massive." The vehicle continued to lurch forward. An aircraft took off as we drove past the runway. Another waited on the end of the strip. As the first one turned right, the second took off as well. Other vehicles streamed out of the entrance to the cavern like a swarm of ants. I wondered if the scientists that DeMarco had brought would get out. They might be my best chance to find out about my parents.

I glanced back down at my watch. Only seconds remained. I glanced over at Rhea. She stuck her hand out. I grabbed it. We felt a rumble beneath our feet. The vehicle shook. I looked back. A plume of snow and rock rose up over the mountain behind us. A huge mound of snow and rock shot down the side of the mountain, covering the entrance to the cavern.

Rocks started landing around us. Imee yelled, "Cross your fingers. We're close."

Boulders started landing on the runway behind us, like lava bombs shooting out of a volcano. One landed just to our right, causing Imee to swerve to the left. She straightened the vehicle, but then she looked in the sideview mirror again. I looked back. A huge split in the ice shot toward us, weaving back and forth. Imee glanced in the side mirror again and swerved hard to the left. The crack shot past us to our right.

I let out a sigh of relief. But then the crack shot back to the left, straight in front of us. Imee hit the brakes. We came to a stop just before the chasm. It looked like it was about ten feet across. There was no way we or the vehicle could jump over it.

The radio kicked on. We heard Bob's voice. "I've just received orders to stop you. There's a team coming up behind us. We need to get out of here ASAP."

I glanced back. Sure enough, several rooster tails of snow were rapidly gaining on us. "What do we do? AB, could you throw us over the crack."

He looked at it and then shook his head. "Doubt it."

"Maybe Bob could with that exoskeleton?" Rhea looked at Bob standing next to the vehicle.

"Imee?"

"Shhh." She signaled us to be quiet while she held one hand to her ear.

She started to back the vehicle up. Bob walked up to the edge of the crack and slowly fell forward. I thought he would tumble in, but his hands just reached over the side.

"We're going to use the exoskeleton as a bridge."

"Will it hold?"

Imee revved the engine. "What choice do we have?" She released the break and the vehicle shot forward. It rolled over the legs of the exoskeleton and then up the body. I looked down. The ice had split down a long way. I didn't see the bottom. I looked forward. The ice was splitting at Bob's fingertips. The vehicle kept going forward. As the front tracks hit the ice in front of Bob's fingers, the rear of the vehicle dipped slightly downward. I looked back. The feet of the exoskeleton were slipping down the other side of the crack. Imee punched the accelerator. The vehicle lurched forward as Bob's feet slid down into the crack. Ice dust obscured my view, but I didn't see Bob's exoskeleton bridge behind us. He must have fallen in.

Imee kept looking in the mirror.

Rhea asked, "Is Bob dead?"

We were coming up on the mound where our ship was hidden.

Imee didn't answer. She turned around the mound and then stopped the vehicle. She got out of her chair and opened the door.

"Charlie, the ship?"

I'd forgotten. I grabbed the Scepter, feeling the crystal pulsing within it, and thought, *Shannon, open the door.*

The snow next to us shook, and a door appeared in what looked like a snow bank. We got out and ran to the ship.

I took off toward the control room. *Shannon, close the door and take off.*

*Cannot comply. There is an animate object in the door.*

WTF, I thought to myself and turned back. Rhea and AB weren't far behind me, but I didn't see Imee. I passed Rhea and AB, running back toward the door.

Imee stood there looking out.

I grabbed her arm, but she shook my hand off. "Imee, we've got to go."

She shook her head. "We need to give Bob a chance."

"But he fell down the chasm."

Imee kept looking out through bloodshot eyes. "Those suits are amazing. He could have made it."

"Either Trolga or DeMarco are after us, maybe both. We can't stay."

I grasped Imee's arm. She glanced out, put her finger to her ear and mumbled something. She pulled her finger away and nodded. She slowly turned away from the door.

I looked out and then moved inside the ship. *Shannon, close the door.*

The door slid shut. I started to follow Imee, when we heard a tapping on the side of the ship.

"What's that?" I imagined Trolga's team outside the door.

"Shhh!" Imee listened closely. She smiled. "It's Bob, tapping Morse code!"

*Shannon, open the door.* Imee and I stood by the entrance as it opened.

An exoskeleton stood there, the visor open with Bob smiling. He got on all fours and crawled through the door in the exoskeleton. Once he got in, he opened it up and crawled out.

Imee ran and jumped into his arms. She hugged him and kissed him.

Man, Bob wasn't kidding when he said he'd known Imee. *Shannon, close the door and take off to a safe spot.*

Imee let go of Bob and turned toward me, tears in her eyes. "Thanks, Charlie."

"Not necessary. You've both saved me enough times."

Bob looked around. "Hell of a vehicle you've got here, kid."

I nodded. "Long story. Let's head to the control room."

# CHAPTER 51
## CASTLE

When we got to the control room, AB was sitting in the control chair with Rhea standing behind him. AB stood. "The com's yours, Captain."

I walked over to AB, knowing his joke. "Thank you, Number One."

*Shannon, where are we?*

*One hundred thousand feet above where we were.*

I looked around the room. AB had a table loaded with food in front of him. Rhea was looking over at Imee and Bob, but then walked over to me. She kissed my cheek. "Thank you for saving my life—again."

I shook my head. "We all saved each other."

Bob chuckled. "Modest, isn't he?" He looked down at Imee and gave her a squeeze. Imee nodded.

"So, what now, Captain?" AB said through a mouthful of peanut butter and jelly.

I slid into the control chair and put the scepter down next to me. As I let it go, exhaustion washed over me. "I don't know. Any ideas?"

"We definitely need a break." Rhea looked over at AB. "Where's the safest place we can go to rest?"

AB swallowed and took a sip of steaming hot tea. He glanced over at Imee and Bob. "My home, but not sure if we can go there. I'll have to check."

"No!" I shouted.

AB looked at me quizzically, then read my thoughts. *No, she wouldn't set you up.*

I shook my head. *But she knew about my parents and didn't tell me. I won't go back there.*

*I think you're wrong, but I can see that you've made up your mind.*

I nodded. "I guess the safest place we can go is my uncle's place in Scotland."

"It's yours now per your uncle's will." AB opened up a bag of chips.

"His uncle's dead?" Bob asked Imee.

She shook her head. "Long story, and I've got to check with my partners whether we can read you in." She glanced over at us.

I was too tired to make that kind of decision. Bob seemed like a good guy, but with all I'd gone through, I couldn't trust him. "Let's go to my uncle's." I glanced over at Rhea. Her shoulders slumped as well. She looked exhausted. She hadn't had time to rest since we'd been on Richard's boat in the Bahamas. While that was only a couple of days ago, it seemed like months.

AB nodded. "Good choice. Chip off the old block." AB projected an image of Uncle Merl into my head, but his choice of words made me think back to my parents. I may have saved the world, but it didn't feel like it. What I did feel was the loss of my parents. I'd traced them to the Atlantean lab, but they'd disappeared there. I vowed to figure out what had happened to them if it was the last thing I did.

THE END

# ACKNOWLEDGMENTS

To my readers, I hope you have enjoyed reading *Legacy of Atlantis* as much as I enjoyed writing it.

To all of those who helped me through the process of plotting, writing, rewriting, and editing *Legacy*, thank you. To the team at Gramarye, you are awesome. To Lou Aronica, you are an exceptional editor and your comments and suggestions proved invaluable. Thanks to Tom Stoughton for introducing me to John Adcox, the visionary behind Gramarye. John, thanks for bringing life to Gramarye. I've enjoyed reading your books and appreciate our time together discussing baseball and writing. To Heath Foley, I really appreciate your great illustrations. To my early readers, Craig, Brer, and several of my siblings, thanks for your encouragement. To my wife, Laura, and my three children, thanks for being captive audiences to my plot musings. I couldn't have finished *Legacy* without your support and encouragement.

As to locations in the book, I have snorkeled around the Three Sisters off Bimini. The tunnel under one of the sisters is real. Fortunately, while I have seen a few nurse sharks in the tunnel, I have never run across the Harbor Master. The legend of the Harbor Master, a giant hammerhead that allegedly roams the waters around Bimini, is what gave me the inspiration for Thor. The Bimini Road is real and remains a mystery to this day. As to AB and your sasquatch relatives, I've never seen you on any of my hikes. That camouflage must really work!

# ABOUT THE AUTHOR

A lawyer and entrepreneur, John Topping and his wife, Laura, are residents of Atlanta, Georgia. They have three adult children. An avid reader, John dabbled with writing while in high school at The Lawrenceville School and at the University of Virginia. He published an article on The Strategic Defense Initiative while at the University of Georgia School of Law. He began writing in his free time in the 1990s. Longstreet Press published his first novel, *Runaway*, a technothriller about global warming, in 2001.

John enjoys golf, fishing, tennis, and kayaking. He is a member of Northside United Methodist Church, Broadleaf Writers Association, and the Bonefish Tarpon Trust. One of nine children, John grew up with an appreciation of family and an avid interest in sports. John's father, the late Dan Topping, owned the New York Yankees for 22 years, winning 15 pennants and 10 World Series. His stepfather, the late Rankin Smith, owned the Atlanta Falcons.

For more information please visit www.johntoppingbooks.com.